I0730236

THE GIANT AND THE WITCH

Also by Rohan Davies

The Saga of the Witch

The Demon and the Witch
The Giant and the Witch

THE GIANT AND THE WITCH

BOOK TWO OF THE SAGA OF THE WITCH

ROHAN DAVIES

Copyright © 2025 Rohan Davies. All rights reserved.

Rohan Davies has asserted his moral right to be identified as the author of this work in accordance with the Copyright, Designs and Patents Act 1988.

The characters and events portrayed in this book are fictitious. Any similarity to real persons, living or dead, is coincidental and not intended by the author.

All rights reserved. No part of this book may be reproduced, or stored in a retrieval system, or transmitted in any form or by any means, electronic, mechanical, photocopying, recording, or otherwise, without express written permission of the publisher.

A CIP catalogue record for this book is available from the British Library.

ISBN: 978-1-7385416-2-1
Cover design by: Rohan Davies
Published by: Witchlore Publishing

www.rohandaviesbooks.com

TO DEVON

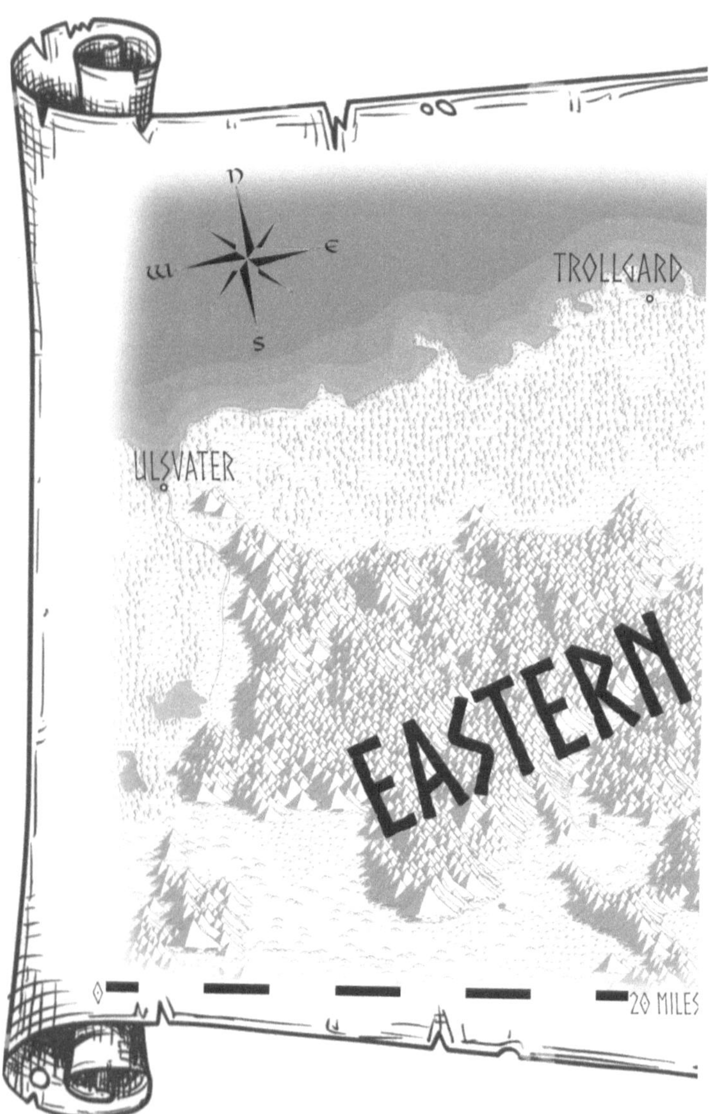

N
W
E
S
TROLLGARD
ULSVATER
EASTERN
20 MILES

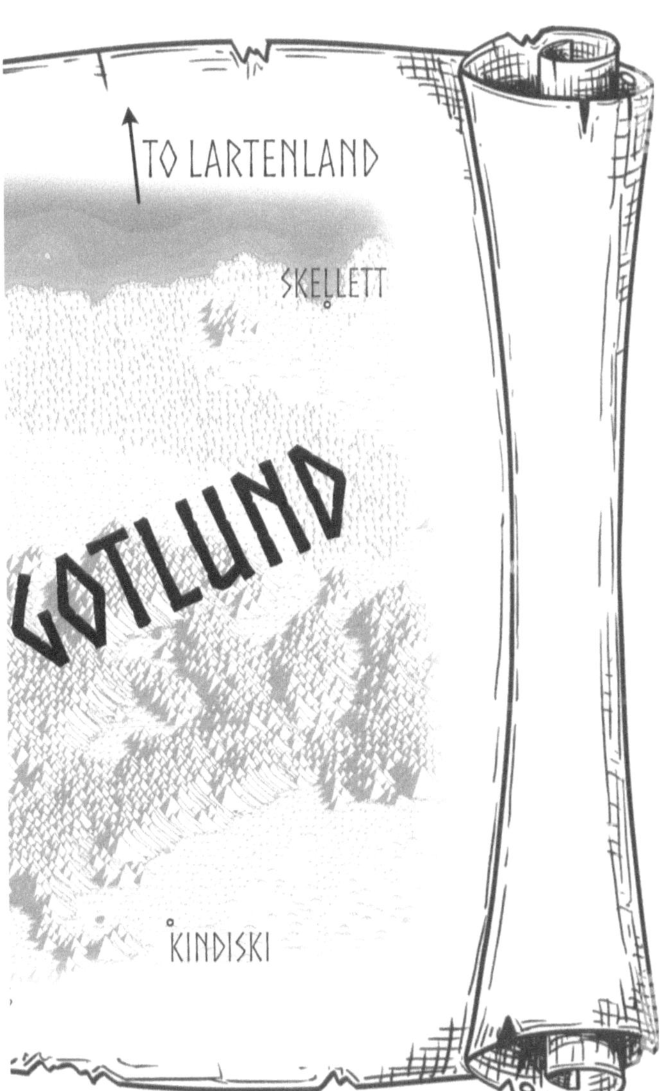

TO LARTENLAND
SKELLETT
GOTLUND
KINDISKI

ROUTE THROUGH SVARTALFHEIM

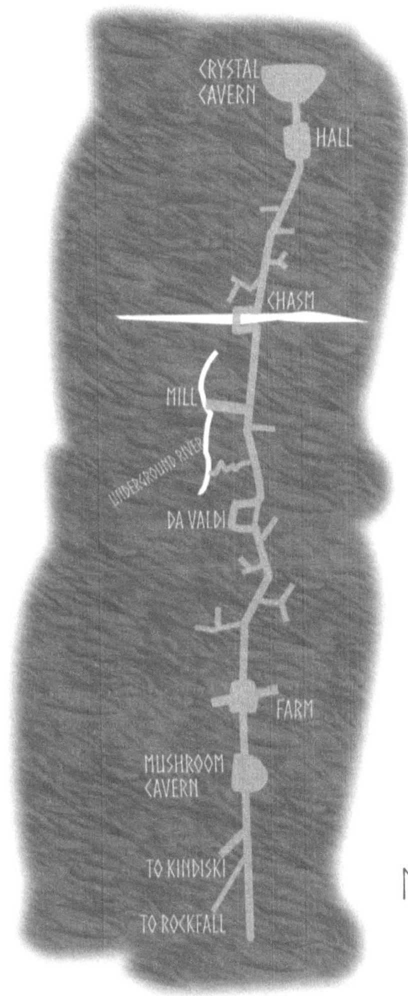

CHAPTERS

-1-

LAW AND CHAOS

Anike felt the demon lash out against the image of cold stone in her mind. It wanted to escape, to take control of her body again. Forces that she perceived as fire and lightning tore at her mental defences.

Shivering slightly in the late autumn air, still cold and crisp even though the pale sun was nearing its zenith, she drew her cloak around her and set down her basket so she could focus on the demon.

The prison in her mind had a stout door which she could open if she needed to draw on the demon's power, and the assault was concentrated on this. Anike deliberately reinforced the image of the rune of earth that held it closed.

She brushed her hands on her trousers. In truth, the demon had stood little chance of escape. It had been nearly two years since she had last lost control of it, and she had refined the prison over that time. It did not stop her from being aware of some of the demon's desires or perceptions but she had become used to identifying and ignoring any thoughts or urges it managed to slip into her mind.

She was more concerned about why it had attempted a struggle it knew was futile. It had been unusually active that morning, particularly since she had come to this part of the wood. Few large animals had their homes here, so most hunters went further afield and did not interrupt her gathering herbs for elixirs. Away from the town, with a sense of structure it abhorred, the demon was normally quiet, and sometimes she could almost forget about it. Its efforts this day suggested that there was something unnatural around.

The sound of metal on metal echoed down from further up the mountain slopes, and it was followed by a cry of pain.

Someone was under attack.

Retrieving her herb basket, she headed up the forested slope towards the sounds, hoping that she could find a way to intervene and prevent further bloodshed. If that failed, she could at least tend the wounds of any survivors.

She crested a rise and looked down into a slightly wooded depression some fifty paces across. Near its centre, just at the base of the opposite slope, an unkempt old man was scrambling on hands and knees, casting terrified glances over his shoulder. He had long dirty hair and beard, both brown but shot through with grey, and one leg of his mud-stained trousers was soaked with fresh blood. Anike was sure she had never set eyes on him before and she had thought she knew by sight all of Kindiski's population of six hundred after living among them for over a year.

The focus of his terrified attention was just behind him, another stranger to her but as different from the old man as ice was from fire. Dressed in black leather armour, he was powerfully built, carried a double-handed sword fully five feet long and walked with the assurance of a warrior. His short beard was jet black and neatly trimmed. Younger than the man he pursued, Anike put his age at twice her own twenty-one years.

As she saw him, she felt a surge of pure hatred from the demon and it renewed its bid for control. At the same time, the warrior raised his head, as if hearing an unexpected sound.

The demon's loathing for the black-clad man was far beyond its usual inclination for death and destruction. While she had no trust at all in the demon's motivation, it marked the warrior as unusual.

The older man tried to get to his feet, but his wounded leg collapsed beneath him. Rolling onto his back, he raised a knife and held it before him with a trembling hand. The warrior looked down on him, stepped forward and raised his sword.

"Leave him!" Anike shouted, for once the demon's antipathy for the black-clad man allied with her own instinct to protect.

Neither gave any sign that they had heard her. For an instant, the old man's expression changed from fear to a mask of pure hatred, but then the sword swept down. Anike fully expected to see blood spurt and a head roll, but instead he slumped to the ground and the knife fell from limp fingers. The warrior had struck with the flat of his blade.

Only then did the black-clad man turn his head to look at her. Even from thirty paces, Anike read determination in his features. His eyes narrowed slightly, then he glanced at the prone figure at his feet before advancing towards her up the wooded rise.

Aside from the sword, he only carried a knife – no bow or war dart – so Anike was confident that she could escape. But to flee now would leave the old man to die, and she wanted to find out what she could about these strangers. Even unarmed except for her dagger and unprepared for battle, she was not helpless.

She shook out her cloak and let folds in her sleeves fall open so that she could see the pattern of runes that she had dyed into them. Having been driven from her former home, she normally hid the rune patterns that could channel the demon's power. She could probably outrun the man but to defeat him she would have to use witchcraft.

The warrior covered half the distance between them, glanced behind him as if checking his position and took two more deliberate steps towards her, then his expression morphed from grim determination to undisguised hatred. An instant later she felt or saw, though neither word properly described her perception, a complex pattern of runes forming, linking her to him. She recognised the runes for ice and harm, but before she could fully interpret the pattern the warrior spoke *"Ranak"*, the rune for ice, in a cold, dead voice.

Frost formed about Anike, unnatural cold tearing at her body and lungs. Agony and astonishment flowed through her in equal measure, but the reason for the antagonism her demon had directed towards the warrior was now clear. Frost was a rune used by law witches, and her own demon was born of chaos.

Anike could only hold very simple rune patterns in her mind and to cast a spell of any great power or complexity, she needed to have it written down. The spell the black-clad witch had used was much more complex than she could have worked without it being laid out in front of her.

Her own face now grim, she pulled herself together and read the rune pattern dyed into her left sleeve, echoing it in her mind and using it to direct the demon's power at the warrior before her as she spoke, "*Eneki.*" The form rune for lightning was at the core of the pattern, and she named it aloud to activate the spell.

At almost the same instant the warrior said "*Unda,*" and Anike felt a water rune thrust into the pattern she held in her mind, disrupting the flow of energy. Her spell broke apart, her demon's power dissipating as the rune structure shattered. For a brief moment, tiny sparks intertwined with twists of mist crackled about her as the residual energy of her spell manifested. She automatically shut the demon away in its prison before it could take control, despite the surprise washing through her. Never having matched her witchcraft against another witch, she had not imagined that a spell could be countered.

The man advanced towards her, sword at the ready and cold hatred in his eyes. Trying to conjure lightning had exhausted her well of power and Anike knew she needed a few moments to draw in enough energy from the world around her to cast another spell. It was likely that the warrior would also require that time but that did not prevent him from using his sword.

She pulled back, thinking about the man's change in expression. The rigid control he had shown when attacking the old man was sharply in contrast to how he looked at her.

Shards of fear started to grow in her mind, but she suppressed them. Her demon was trying to take advantage of her anxiety in its battle for control and it was unusually desperate to overcome her will, seemingly driven by a hatred of the black-clad witch.

If he was under similar pressure from his own demon, perhaps he had already lost control. Retreating, Anike realised that she could now be facing a demon rather than a man. A demon would not need to read rune patterns to cast spells as it thought in runes and could direct the power at will. As a man, the warrior had shown a controlled demeanour but the law demon would want nothing more than to kill her, mirroring her own demon's desire. If the warrior had lost control when she had not, it might mean his will was weaker than hers, or that his demon was stronger.

In a few seconds, she had learned that her understanding of witchcraft was still incomplete, and she needed to put a little space between her and the warrior while she tried to comprehend what had happened. Lifting her cloak, she read the pattern she had dyed into the right side. *"Prana,"* she said, naming the rune of movement at the core of the design and casting her spell of flight. She rose into the air, out of reach of the sword. A law demon could have no power over movement and would not be able to follow.

She briefly considered flying away but that would mean leaving the old man to his fate. The witch had knocked the man out while his demon would have killed him so the man must have been in control at the time, but the witch clearly did not wish the old man well.

Another pattern of runes formed around her, and she felt the structure of a different spell including stasis and negation – an attempt to dispel her flight effect. In the instant of recognition, she realised that she too should be able to counter spells as they were cast. She visualised the rune of movement, the form directly opposed to stasis, and inserted it into the pattern forming about her. *"Prana,"* she said to activate it and released her demon's power just as the witch below said *"Ert,"* the name of the stasis rune.

She sensed the power flow from both demons, and the pattern round her seemed to sound a discordant note, then break apart. The stasis spell surrounded her with a faint distortion in the air like the ghostly image of a crystal, then it evaporated into a haze.

Her counter had blocked the spell, but Anike was aware of how close she had been to reacting too late. The middle of a battle was far from the best time to learn new techniques. Not wishing to fall should she fail to counter another attempt to bring her down, she descended to the ground well out of sword reach.

It would be vastly more difficult for the witch to dispel an effect at a distance than to counter a spell being cast on him as there was no connection through which to feel the rune pattern. It had to be a demon – it would have taken her hours to work out a counter to an unfamiliar spell and she could not imagine that any human was capable of devising coherent rune patterns so rapidly.

Holding herself ready to run or to counter, she watched the warrior. A demon's mastery of witchcraft made it extremely dangerous, but their desires were direct and elemental, and this one was evidently intent on killing her. She could use that single-mindedness and what she hoped was better knowledge of the terrain against it, but first she needed to recover. Keeping her gaze on the black-clad man, she put her hand in her bag and pulled out a small earthenware flask.

The witch regarded her with undisguised loathing and raised his arm. "*Kappa*," he named the earth rune aloud, and a short stone spear appeared in his hand, which he threw at her. She dodged, and the razor-tipped weapon flew past her before vanishing. There was no sense of a rune pattern touching her this time and Anike guessed that the spell had only created the spear, not guided it.

Not taking her eyes off the witch, she retreated while drinking the potion, letting it undo the harm inflicted by the spell of frost. She was trying to decide where to lead the witch so that they would be well away from the fallen old man and she would have the advantage, when she was interrupted by a voice from the trees behind her. She did not need to turn to know that it was Gunnar, the thirteen-year-old son of the arl.

"Anike!" the boy called. "I was hoping to find you here. You promised to show me some herbs. I thought..."

He came to a halt when he reached her side and saw the witch advancing up the slope. His hand went to his sword and he stepped in front of her.

Gunnar was as tall as Anike but with the thin build of a boy yet to reach maturity. As the arl's heir, he had been schooled in weapons from an early age, but Anike doubted he was anything like a match for the man he was about to challenge, even without witchcraft. Warriors did not live to any great age if they were not competent, and the man moved as if battle was his profession.

"No, Gunnar! He will kill you," she said to him urgently. "Go for help."

"I won't leave you, Anike," he said urgently. "Stay behind me." He drew his blade.

Fear rose within her, a sharp chilling sensation that the boy was about to get himself killed in an attempt to demonstrate his bravery to her. Gunnar had been entranced since he had first seen her, taking every opportunity to try to impress. Aside from the danger that the boy was putting himself in, she would much rather have avoided using witchcraft in front of him. Desperate to get Gunnar away, Anike sought something else to say.

Gunnar brandished his sword. "Stand down, stranger! I am Gunnar Reksson, heir to the arl!"

The cold eyes flicked to him, and lips curled in contempt. "*Ert*," came the demon's voice, and Gunnar gasped in shock. Anike recognised the effect as long ago it had been directed against her by the first witch she had ever seen. The form of stasis could be used to interrupt the beat of the heart or drain life away. Gunnar staggered but then drew himself upright as he tried to throw off the effects of the attack. "Witchcraft!" he gasped and charged.

"No!" Anike shouted, but she realised it was futile as the word left her mouth. Now she would have to reveal her power to Gunnar or let him die. She shook out her sleeve with the lightning spell on it, hoping that she could find a way to get it past the demon's counterspell before it killed the boy.

To her surprise, the man's brow furrowed in an expression of concentration. He lifted his greatsword to meet the attack and shifted his stance before executing a skillful beat that had Gunnar off balance.

Anike knew that her own demon was unconcerned about her health short of death or crippling injury, so she had expected the man in black to strike hard at Gunnar to kill him quickly, even if it had meant he received a wound in exchange. Instead, he had defended himself, deflecting the assault and setting himself up to strike – a longer and safer route to victory. If he had only faced Gunnar it would have worked, but his focus on the swordplay gave her an opening.

"*Eneki*," she said aloud, naming the form for lightning again as she read the rune pattern. With the witch's attention on Gunnar, he could not stop her and a bolt of lightning struck down from the sky onto the black-clad warrior's head. Electricity crackled around him and he staggered forward, crying out in shock, and the fluid swordplay that was about to deliver a lethal blow was interrupted. The hilt of his sword caught Gunnar's head, and the boy went down, stunned but alive.

The warrior straightened again. Smoke was coming from his armour and he was moving stiffly from shock and pain, but was still very much alive. He turned back to Anike. "I don't need you or the boy," he said, raising his sword and advancing.

Anike breathed a little more easily now he had moved away from his fallen victims, but she had no illusions she could beat this man physically.

Now he was closer, she could see runes engraved on the blade. It was not unusual for warriors to inscribe runes on their weapons, but they were usually little more than decoration. She had to assume that this man could cast spells with them in the same way that she used patterns on her clothes.

She back-pedalled, seeking to draw him away from Gunnar. His words suggested that the old man was his main objective, but she did not want to hand anyone over to him. He and Gunnar might be alive now, but she was loath to leave either to his uncertain mercy.

The words were spoken in Norse, showing that it was the man in control rather than the demon, and he ought to be as limited as she was in reacting to witchcraft. Even if he could counter her offensive spells, he would not be able to disrupt the effects that she invoked. Her flight spell still persisted, so she willed herself into the air and rose to a sturdy branch well out of sword reach. The warrior regarded her in an appraising manner and then cast a glance at his fallen opponents. He started back towards the old man while keeping his eyes fixed on Anike.

Feeling relatively safe, Anike read the lightning spell again. "*Eneki*," she called, triggering it, but this time the warrior spoke as well. "*Unda*," he said, invoking the opposite rune of water and her spell collapsed.

On reaching the old man, his face tensed in concentration for a moment then he read the runes on his sword. "*Barak*," he said, naming the rune for strength. Anike felt nothing and saw no visible effect, so whatever the spell was intended to do, it was probably directed inwards. The warrior bent and easily lifted the old man onto his left shoulder then started up the hill, head turned to keep an eye on Anike as he did so. His sword was still held firmly in his right hand.

She looked at Gunnar, who was breathing and moaning a little as he drifted in and out of consciousness. His injury did not look serious or urgent to her practised eye, well within the scope of her salves and potions, so she returned her attention to the departing warrior. While it seemed he could counter witchcraft cast directly at him, there were other things she could do.

Reading the pattern on her other sleeve, she cast an animation spell on her knife and launched herself into the air to pursue the witch in black. He sensed her approach and turned to face her, the old man still over his shoulder. As she closed to throwing distance, she hurled her knife at him. He deflected it with his blade but as it rebounded away to his right, beyond his line of sight, she used the spell to pick it up and drove it into the back of his knee where his armour was weakest. He cried out in pain and dropped the old man while she pulled her knife free with the spell. She set it dancing about his head, probing for an opening. The warrior wielded the great blade as if it weighed little more than a table knife, and she could only assume that his strength had been enhanced by his witchcraft. He met each of her thrusts, then struck the dagger away with a sharp blow. Before she could bring it back to attack him again, he looked down with a calculating expression and then cold-bloodedly ran his sword through the thigh of the man on the ground. It was not a wound that would kill quickly, but it would lead to death by blood loss if it were not bound promptly. The warrior regarded his handiwork for a moment then nodded, satisfied, and limped up the hill away from Anike.

Unable to give chase without letting the old man die, she watched the witch disappear between the trees then landed next to the bleeding man to assess his injuries. They looked to be more serious than those Gunnar had suffered, so she found a salve in her bag and applied it to the leg wound that the warrior had inflicted in such a calculating manner.

After that, she only had a little of the elixir left. Neither of the old man's other wounds were life-threatening. The puncture he was suffering from when she first saw him looked as if it had been made by a war dart or a conjured stone spear, but both it and the blow to the head could wait for treatment. There was only enough salve to treat one more injury and Gunnar had suffered too.

While she knew nothing of the man before her, she felt a strong instinctive empathy with him despite his ragged appearance, but realised that the sensation was coming from her demon. She wondered if the unkempt man was another witch, with a demon tied to chaos like her own. If so, he might be extremely violent when he awoke. It was better to revive Gunnar and have him help get the man back to her home where she could treat him properly.

Her own demon, which had been straining against its bonds throughout the battle, had quieted a little. She took that as a sign that the law witch had indeed retreated for the moment and was not hiding nearby.

Anike guessed that his purpose had not been to kill this old man but to capture him, and his last actions suggested a tactical withdrawal rather than real flight. He must have wanted a chaos witch alive for some reason, though she could not begin to fathom what that purpose could be.

There had been a Larten accent in the few words he had spoken. Lartenland was only a day's sailing north of Gotlund, but the two islands were not on friendly terms. She had to wonder what a lone Lartenlander was doing so far south, separated from the coast by at least thirty miles and a mountain range.

She went back to Gunnar and examined him. He had acted bravely but with the foolhardiness of youth. Alone, he had stood no chance against a seasoned warrior, but she doubted she would have been able to save the old man without his intervention. She wished she knew how much the boy had seen. He could hardly have missed the lightning but with any luck he would believe that it came from the man he fought.

Regardless, she could hardly leave him unconscious and she would need him to help get the old man back to the town, so she rubbed the last of the salve into his brow.

Gunnar's eyes opened. "Anike, are you a witch too?" he asked.

-2-

SUCCOUR AND SECRETS

Anike froze for an instant, then recovered herself. "Lie still, Gunnar. You were hit on the head. I want to see if the elixir has healed your injury fully." She lifted his hair to examine where the warrior had struck him and found the skin intact. The salve had done its work.

Witches were reviled, usually with good reason, and she did not want to be forced out of Kindiski as she had been from her childhood home of Trollgard. She had not finished the research that had brought her to the town in the first place.

Gunnar shook his head, dislodging her hand. "I am fine, Anike. I am not a child," he said a little petulantly. He looked around, his expression a mixture of irritation, curiosity and anxiety. "Where is that man? Did you kill him?"

"No," Anike said. "I managed to wound him, but he got away."

"Wound him with the lightning?

She laughed. "With my knife. You were hit on the head and a blow like that can make you see stars that might look like lightning."

"I am sure the bolt struck before he hit me. It made his blade miss."

"Injuries to the head can jumble memories, Gunnar." Anike did not like to lie outright. "You suffered quite a blow and I needed to use an elixir to wake you up."

She stood. "You did a very brave thing. Foolish, but brave and if you had not showed up, I probably would not have had a chance to hurt him. But, Gunnar, next time someone tells you to run, you really should run."

Gunnar refused to be distracted. "I am not a child. I know my duty, and I know what I saw," he said stubbornly. "The warrior was struck by lightning. He might have been a witch, but I don't think he would have aimed it at himself. It must have been you. If you weren't a witch too, he would have killed you after he knocked me out, wouldn't he?"

Anike could not help but smile at Gunnar's outpouring of thought, something his father would train him out of in time. His logic was sound, but any admission to using witchcraft would have serious consequences. Witches were rare, but the law was strict and hurting another with witchcraft, even in battle, was likely to lead to her execution.

She tried to divert Gunnar again. "He was not really interested in me, and it was only when he was carrying the old man away that I had the chance to attack him from behind. Perhaps not the most honourable way but I am a healer, not a warrior."

"Even so," said Gunnar. "It was a brave thing to do if you were not a warrior yourself. Or a witch."

"Gunnar," Anike adopted a slightly exasperated tone. "If I really were a witch, do you think asking me would be the safest thing to do? Witches are said to bring death and destruction to everyone around them, and I do not see anyone here but you and me. Leaders need to learn tact and discretion." She adopted a scary face and Gunnar instinctively pulled back, then she smiled and he laughed.

"Now help me get this man to my home so I can treat him."

"Of course, Anike. I wouldn't have minded if you had been a witch, you know? It could have been our secret."

"I know I can trust you, Gunnar, if I ever need to."

Gunnar smiled at that. The boy had failed to notice that she had not directly denied being a witch. For all that he liked to consider himself an adult, Gunnar had a lot to learn. His father, Rek Ranulfsson, was a thoughtful and honourable leader and she hoped Gunnar would grow to be like him. All in all, he was a likeable lad and he seemed receptive to the ideas about fairness, consideration and restraint that she had slipped into their conversations from time to time. The arl was a widower and she had been happy to provide the boy with a feminine perspective he might otherwise have lacked.

Gunnar looked down at the old man. "Anike, who are these people? And where did that other man, the witch, come from?"

"I wish I knew, Gunnar. Witches are rare." Anike recalled a woodsman from near her home town who had become a witch just days before she had, the only other she had met. She shuddered as she remembered her life being pulled out of her by the same spell that the black-clad witch had used on Gunnar.

"That one was very confident. We should inform your father. I hope the old man can tell us more after I get him back on his feet."

"If there is danger, my father will be able to deal with it," Gunnar asserted.

"I am sure he will," Anike agreed. "Now, help me make a stretcher and keep an eye out while we do so. I think the witch has gone for now, but he might return." Her demon was quiet, which made her sure he was no longer nearby but she could not tell Gunnar that.

As they fashioned a crude frame from branches to carry the old man, Anike turned events over in her mind. They had to tell the arl about the witch in black, and urgently. The man was extremely dangerous and, as a rule, witches behaved much as she had outlined to Gunnar, trying to kill everyone they met. She suspected that most were unable to resist their demons, which then took control and acted without human restraint.

It occurred to her that witches might not be as rare as was commonly thought, and it was only the weaker-willed who came to anyone's notice – those who could not resist their demons. This man seemed a lot more assured than that and he had not been hiding. The runes on his sword appeared to allow him to cast a strength spell, and while some warriors had runes etched into weapons, most patterns were little more than nonsense and amounted at best to vague calls for aid from the gods. Greatswords were expensive and rare, so he was either rich or had the favour of a wealthy patron. All of this suggested this man was even more of a threat than most witches and the arl definitely needed to know about him.

She was also worried that Gunnar would blurt out something about the lightning to his father and it would be much easier to allay any suspicion if she could talk to the arl first.

With the old man suspended between them, they made their way back to town. Anike had Gunnar take the front end of the makeshift stretcher. She wanted him to concentrate on the route and where he planted his feet rather than staring at her back and contemplating whether she was a witch. Fortunately, the old man was not far from skin and bones. While neither had a warrior's build, Anike was fit and Gunnar was showing signs of the strength he would soon grow into, and they carried him easily.

As they walked, Anike thought about what she had learned during the battle. Never having tried to combat another witch before, she had not considered that spells could be affected by someone other than the caster. She had thought the rune patterns that she used to channel the power had existed purely in her mind and it was only the effect that manifested in the real world. It was now clear that they had their own independent existence, one that actually touched the target of the spell, and if that target was a witch, they could perceive that pattern.

The conjured stone javelin had not registered to that sense, but it had missed her. Her own lightning spell could not miss because it connected her directly with the target, but that link was what had allowed the other witch to counter it.

If runes existed independently from her will, it explained why the law runes she set around the prison in her mind were more effective at containing the demon than images of what they represented and why they continued to confine it even without her active concentration, something she had previously noted but merely accepted.

Anike and Gunnar carried the unconscious man down the slope through the woods and out into the fields. Farmers were digging in the stubble left over from the harvest and reinforcing wood and grain stores against the coming winter. A few stopped and regarded them as they passed but the urgency of their work, or perhaps a reluctance to become involved, kept them at a distance.

Kindiski lay on the northern bank of a river with its buildings clustered on and around a small hill. Dwarves had constructed its stone walls and the buildings within them centuries before and the arlberg, the compound which contained the arl's hall, lay right at the summit. Outside the walls of the stone town lay the wood town, built by humans to house an increasing population in the years since the dwarves had been forced back to Svartalfheim.

Anike's house was near the outer edge of the wood town, which suited her well as it gave her easy access to the countryside to hunt for her herbs. She made a living selling elixirs and potent herbs. The only other herbalist was old Vanna, who was too frail to go foraging much and seemed unable to keep an apprentice long, so Anike sold excess herbs to her. The arrangement suited them both.

The arl owned a fair number of houses and Anike was fortunate to have found this one empty when she had come to Kindiski around midsummer the previous year. The arl had been happy to welcome another herbalist to town and take her as a tenant. She knew him quite well as he had visited her often, more frequently than one might expect from a landowner checking on his property.

Anike called for Gunnar to halt outside her door and set down her end of the stretcher. She walked past some plants in wooden troughs, fading in the late autumn chill, and opened the door.

The single room was set out with distinct areas, with her bed in one corner, topped with neatly piled furs. A large oak worktable dominated the other side of the room with several chairs set round it, and three cauldrons stood on top, lined up in order of size. A series of shelves containing small boxes and a variety of flasks were set against a nearby wall, and a tall cloth-bound broom stood in one corner.

Reaching beneath the bed, Anike shifted a large pine chest out of the way and pulled some extra furs to the middle of the room for the unconscious man to lie on. She and Gunnar carried her patient in, and the boy helped her lay him on the makeshift pallet.

Going to the shelves, she lifted out a small jar and, after a moment's thought, selected a second. She spread the contents of the first over the man's brow, chest and the remaining wound on his leg. The blood flow ceased as the elixir took effect and his flesh became a healthier colour. This salve would not heal him, but it stabilised his condition, preventing him from getting any worse. She spread the other elixir on his lips and opened his mouth to put some on his tongue. The second potion would bring deep sleep, administered partly to give the man's body time to heal and partly because Anike had to talk to the arl and did not want the man to wake while she was not there. His will would be weakened by his injuries and if he was a witch, his demon was more likely to seize control. She had no desire to come back to find her house a smoking ruin.

She thought she could stop the spells of another chaos witch if she was close enough to perceive the rune pattern. Spells, even those a demon created, were very precisely formulated and any defect in the design made them fail. She could not use the opposing form as she had with the warrior on the mountain, but placing the same form rune into the wrong place in the pattern ought to have a similar effect.

The man was near sixty and rather thin, though fit for his age. His beard and hair were matted and dirty, and his smell suggested a bath was not a common occurrence for him. Again, she found herself drawn to him and she let the feeling flow through her so she could study it. The demon was feeling empathy and perhaps satisfaction, both emotions alien to it in her experience. Her comprehension of its thoughts and feelings was vague at best so the closest analogy she could come up with was recognition of an ally. It reinforced her view that the old man was another witch with a chaos demon inside him.

Normally, she would have guessed his pursuer was a bounty hunter, trying to capture the old man and bring him to trial for some act of witchcraft, but that did not make sense if the man in black was a witch himself. She was missing something.

Looking at the old man, she was satisfied that he would sleep for some hours yet. "I think it is safe to leave him," she told Gunnar. "We should go and see your father."

Gunnar became more exuberant as the two of them got closer to the arlberg and when they passed through the gate into the stone town, he called out to another boy who was repairing the wall, "Ingak, guess what happened!"

Anike laid a hand on his arm. "Let your father decide what to tell people."

Gunnar looked abashed and nodded, but then glanced down at her hand and started to smile. She gave him a slight pull to move him on and let go. "I will tell you later," he called out as they moved away.

"If your father and the women let you!" Ingak called back.

Gunnar blushed and hurried on.

It took only a few minutes to reach the arlberg at the centre of the town. Within its stone wall, the imposing arl's hall loomed over the smaller, mainly wooden, buildings. Gunnar and Anike walked through the gate, then past the stables and the quarters for the thralls before detouring around a group of warriors practising with spears and axes. Gunnar waved at them and a few nodded back.

They passed a man and a woman walking slowly across the yard, both about Anike's age. She did not recognise them, but visitors were common and the arl was obliged to offer shelter to travellers whom no one else would put up. They were talking to each other in low voices, and each carried a drum. The man was flamboyantly dressed with a feather on his hat. The woman was blond but kept her eyes lowered so Anike could not see her face clearly.

Anike went up to a thrall who stretching after setting down a large bundle of firewood he was taking to the kitchen. "Where can we find Arl Rek?" she asked.

The man waved towards the hall.

"Thank you. Let me help you with that." She picked up a bundle of sticks while the man shouldered the rest.

Gunnar looked at her in surprise but made no comment, instead walking to the door ahead of them to open it. Once inside, Anike set down the wood to a grunt of thanks from the thrall then walked past the cooking fire into the main part of the hall, followed by Gunnar.

Arl Rek was standing at a table listening to Wulfnar, his steward. He straightened when he saw Anike and smiled warmly at her. Taller than she was and perhaps a dozen years older, he moved with the practised grace and poise of a warrior. His short blonde hair and beard were neatly trimmed and his blue eyes sparkled, though his features were a little out of proportion and his face could best be described as homely.

His smile faded when he saw her serious expression. "What brings you here, Anike?" he asked.

"May I speak to you alone, my lord? It is urgent," she said, trying to ignore Gunnar who was almost hopping from foot to foot in eagerness. She frowned. "Gunnar will no doubt have something to add. In a moment."

Puzzled, the arl looked from one to the other. "Of course," he said and led them to the middle of the room. The steward looked nonplussed.

"My lord, there was a witch in the woods this morning." She paused to let that sink in. "I found him attacking an old man. Trying to capture him, I think, or the man would have been dead."

She glanced at Gunnar, guessing that his father would be less than pleased that his son had got himself into danger but as the boy was unlikely to keep quiet, she decided to say more. "He used witchcraft on your son, my lord, but he also had a greatsword and wielded it like a veteran warrior. Gunnar fought bravely. We managed to wound him, and he retreated though not before Gunnar took a blow to the head which knocked him unconscious. Fortunately, I had enough of my elixirs with me to heal it. Gunnar and I carried the old man he was pursuing back to my house and I am worried that this witch might come back."

Arl Rek scowled. "That is bad news, indeed." He looked at Gunnar. "We will have words about you attacking a skilled warrior alone. Later."

"I wasn't alone. Anike was there."

Rek's expression became even harder. Gunnar gulped, and Rek turned back to Anike. "You mentioned an old man?" he asked.

"I did not recognise him, my lord. I have given him potions to keep him from dying and help him sleep. It will be a while before he wakes." She met Rek's gaze. "The warrior-witch appeared to be alone and he headed back into the mountains to the north, or at least he started that way. I managed to stab him in the leg so he may be more cautious next time."

"And there was lightning!" Gunnar put in. Anike winced inwardly, hoping nothing showed in her face.

"There was no lightning. Unfortunately, Gunnar took a blow to the head which made him see stars. I have healed that wound." The witchcraft that was used on Gunnar left no visible mark despite the harm it had caused.

Rek studied her. "Forgive me, Anike, but I am surprised – impressed, but surprised – that you and Gunnar fought off a man such as you described."

"We were lucky, and he was not really interested in us. He wanted the old man alive and when he was picking him up, I had a chance to strike him." Her brow creased. "One more thing. He did not say much, but I think he had a Larten accent."

"I doubt the Lartens would raid this far south. The mountains are all but impassable and there are plenty of towns on the coast, so he is probably a mercenary or an outcast."

Anike nodded. "Could the old man be an escaped slave?"

"You have not been here that long and there will be people living in and around Kindiski you have yet to meet, Anike. I will come and take a look at him now, with your permission. I may know him."

Rek was more courteous than most members of the ruling jarl caste would be when talking to someone from the middle caste of karls like her, and she was pleased he took the time to ask when he could have commanded. She nodded.

The arl spoke to Wulfnar, who looked alarmed and set off at what passed for a run. The steward was not a young man.

Turning to Gunnar, Arl Rek said, "You stay here, boy, and don't start spreading tales while I am gone." Gunnar nodded but his eyes danced with mischief and anticipation.

With Arl Rek at her side, Anike returned to her house. On the way, he enquired further about the witch and the battle. He accepted without overt suspicion that she had waited until the witch had picked up the old man and turned his back on her before she wounded him with a thrown knife. Many of the details she gave were correct in any event, and it was true that the witch had very much focused on the old man. Without that advantage, Anike was not sure she would have defeated him.

On reaching her house she opened the door for the arl and followed him in. The old man was still on the floor, his chest rising and falling as he slept. The arl looked down on him, frowning. "I do know him," he said at last, but he did not sound pleased. "This is Cairn Vinarsson, another witch. I have not seen him for about fifteen years."

Anike felt a tide of sympathy for the man swell at the words of confirmation. With an effort of will, she divorced herself from this reaction, coming as it was from her demon. Rek's words confirmed that the man had his own demon inside him, tied to chaos and destruction like her own.

"He has been a witch for all that time and not committed any crime?" Anike asked, impressed with Cairn's level of control. Had he hurt anyone with witchcraft, the arl would surely have had him executed.

"Cairn started a fire in the forest, but it was raining at the time and no great damage was done. He did not commit a crime against any person and after that, he headed up into the mountains. As far as I know, he has lived there since. People have seen him from time to time but mostly at a distance."

"Was he exiled?"

"No, he just left. He had no family, so no one really tried to stop him or bring him back. I think the town largely forgot about him, to be honest. He has been no trouble."

Cairn had been fortunate to have been far enough from others for the demon only to have trees as its targets. Memories of when she had awoken after her own demon had merged with her came unbidden to her mind. She saw a burning farm, bodies hurled by conjured wind, and lightning lashing from her hand to strike Bjord, the son of the arl there, a man who had been her childhood friend and potential husband.

She shook her head, dispelling the images. Despite his isolation, someone had clearly taken an interest in Cairn. Perhaps he had terrorised another town but Anike doubted that any arl would send one witch to catch another.

Worse for Anike was the possibility that the people of Kindiski would start thinking about witchcraft again and that might lead to suspicion of her.

Arl Rek was talking again, and she made herself focus on his words. "How long before he wakes up?"

"He should come back to some sort of consciousness tomorrow, perhaps early afternoon, but I doubt he will be coherent then. It may be a few hours longer before he fully recovers."

"I would rather not have it well known that there is a witch in town," Rek said. "It could cause panic or even a lynching. Can you keep him here safely? If you are worried, I can have some of my men move him to the arlberg."

Anike considered this. Cairn was dangerous, and all the more so in his current state. Pain interfered with her own ability to restrain her demon, and this seriously injured man would have great difficulty keeping any sort of control. If the feelings coming from her own demon was a reliable guide, it was likely that it would attack someone other than her.

"Thank you, but there is no need to move him," she told the arl. "I think I can look after him here. There does tend to be panic when witches are involved, and it might not be a good idea to have a witch inside your hall when he does wake. There are a lot of innocent people there."

"You are sure you will be safe here alone?" The arl sounded concerned.

"I am used to taking care of myself, my lord," she reassured him, "and now I know Cairn to be a witch, I will be very much on my guard. I will not be in any danger tonight, I am sure."

"Could you wake him now?"

"Not easily, my lord. I used a potion to make him sleep and give him a chance to heal. Most of the elixirs I have on hand are for light wounds – those are what people want." This was true as far as it went. While she did have some salves that might have worked, she wanted to be alone with Cairn when he woke up so she could talk to him, and her house was the best place for a potentially difficult discussion. She was also the only person with a chance to counter the demon's spells.

"Very well," Rek said, then his expression changed to something not so much worried as a little nervous. "In that case, Anike, would you like to come to the hall this evening as my guest? A skald arrived today and is going to give a performance. The little I have heard so far is exceptional."

Anike was surprised at the invitation. Worded as it was, it suggested some sort of courtship, but it was also possible that Rek was just suspicious about how she had defeated a witch armed with a sword and wanted to keep her close, perhaps hoping she would give something away. She chose to react as if the arl had meant the former. "Of course, my lord. I would be honoured."

"Excellent." Rek looked relieved. "I will expect you at sunset. I will set more warriors to be alert for this sword-bearing witch you saw but you should stay vigilant too."

"I will, my lord, and I will see you later.."

Rek smiled, nodded and left.

Anike stared after him, not quite sure what to make of the turn of events. Her place in Kindiski, built up by a combination of hard work, cordiality and avoiding conflicts, had been put at risk by the events of the day. She would not be safe in any town where she became known as a witch and she did not want to hurt anyone defending herself. Not again. The most prudent course of action would be to just leave.

She reminded herself that she had largely allayed Rek's suspicions, at least for the moment. Gunnar might not have been completely fooled, but he did not really count. He was unlikely to be believed even if he did give a full description.

The proximity of the law witch was a more serious problem. While it would have been hard to track her once she entered the town, he might be able to find her by consulting the runes. To someone skilled with them, runes could be used to reveal secrets and if he knew enough to inscribe a spell on his sword, it was quite possible he could read them. It was likely that he was still recovering somewhere so would not be back that day, but she had not hurt him that badly. He could very well return at some point and she could only hope that Arl Rek would set enough guards.

Despite these threats, she had weathered the first part of the storm and could anticipate what might come. Leaving Kindiski would be giving into fear, especially since she had still not gone through more than a fraction of the records the dwarves had left in the town, the cache that had brought her to Kindiski in the first place.

Anike checked on Cairn again, making sure he was comfortable and soundly asleep before she left. His breathing and pulse were slow, a normal reaction to the potions she had given him, allowing his body to heal. Arl Rek was well out of sight before she closed her door and took the route back up the hill herself. This time her bag held a blank scroll, a sharpened stick and some ink.

The Hall of Records was a small stone building within the arlberg. Humans had no written language, but the dwarves had used one. Two summers ago, several rune casts had led Anike to Kindiski and the best-preserved archive in eastern Gotlund. When they had held sway on the surface, the time humans called the Darkstone Occupation or simply the Occupation, the dwarves had worked metal and stone in ways men could only dream of. They had passed on some of their techniques to smiths and masons, but these skills had faded over the centuries. The Hall of Records mostly contained accounts of shipments, costs and diaries but among the mundane was some valuable knowledge, though it was rarely used. Few people cared what the dwarves had recorded and fewer yet took the time to learn their language.

Anike opened the door to the Hall of Records to see the only other person who spent much time there. When she had first come to the archive, Nangar, the master mason, had found her in the middle of the room staring at the documents in frustration. He had helped her learn the dwarven language, and in return for his aid and guidance, she had made a great many elixirs for him during her first few months in Kindiski. Nangar was always looking for ways to build more efficiently or with greater strength. Despite being hampered by a limp, he was young to be a master, and that was in no small part due to his studies here.

"Anike," he greeted her. "Come to look for more on underground plants?"

"Yes," she said, smiling at him. "One of these days I hope to find discussion of some that grow in shallow caves, rather than deep in Svartalfheim."

Nangar nodded and returned to the diagram he was studying. "Good luck."

"You too." As she crossed the room, Anike reflected on what she was really looking for, a different kind of knowledge, even harder to find. She wanted to learn about the origins of witches and the demons that had merged with humans to create them. There was little reliable human lore since witches tended to have short lives ending in execution once they started using their power. Her own demon had joined with her during witch weather, a sudden storm from clear skies that most people thought of as an ill omen, but that might not be the only way to become a witch.

In fact, she might not have been the demon's first choice. It had appeared in the form of a ball of fire or lightning and had headed for Bjord, the arl's son. Anike had pushed him out of the way and the demon had entered her instead.

She guessed that law demons would have a slightly different method as storm and fire were archetypal chaos, but had no idea what that might be. For a fleeting moment, she wondered if she would get a chance to ask the warrior in black.

She headed for a section of the archive dealing with dwarven interactions with humans, the place she felt was most likely to hold accounts of witches and demons. She had not found any reference to dwarven witches and could not imagine witch weather beneath the surface in Svartalfheim so doubted that dwarves had any witches themselves. Some of what she had read in the dwarf records had confirmed that there were two types of demons, law and chaos, but she had not found much else on that subject. However, there was still a great deal of the archive to go through.

"It amazes me how well the dwarven parchment has lasted," she said as she sat down.

"Much of what the dwarves made is finer and stronger than anything we have," Nangar said. "I hope someday to find the secret of making their paper in these pages. Human paper is rare and fragile, so we use vellum much more and there are many competing uses for skins. If we knew how the dwarves made this, we could devise a written language, more versatile than runes."

She frowned. "People need to be clothed more than they need writing, but I admit some things would be a lot easier if we did not always have to rely on word of mouth. I suspect the dwarves used some tough underground plant, but it was so normal to them that they haven't recorded it here."

"The passing of information is more deeply rooted in dwarf culture than ours. Look at this." Nangar lifted out a book and opened it. "Here they make records of transactions where questions and answers seem to have been used as currency. The true answers have value, perhaps because dwarves are quite capable of lies and trickery."

Anike read the page and nodded. "It is an interesting thing to do, to formalise that. Whatever their reasons, I am glad they chose to keep records."

"As am I, Anike. But I must get on."

She left him to the words and moved to a different shelf. Soon after starting to look through the records, she found a book she had not read before. Her dwarven had improved a great deal over the last year, and she found she was studying a critique of the human rebellion, as the dwarves viewed the time when humanity threw off the yoke of the Occupation and forced them back to Svartalfheim. She knew the history of course, as dates were measured from the time that Huppik the Clever had become the first High King after liberating humanity from the dwarves. He had invented sails and that had allowed him to deploy forces so rapidly that the dwarves had been unable to counter them. A dwarf was said to be a match for ten warriors in battle, but they were few in number and had been unable to resist him, even with their own human thralls.

The part of the account in front of her was recording the mechanics of sails but it was full of astonishment that humanity had rejected the benevolent stewardship of the dwarves, and Anike found this point of view interesting. She took the parchment to Nangar who looked up at her questioningly. "Found something?" He no longer assumed that she needed help to read the records.

"I think so," she told him. "It's a dwarven report on the human liberation and it contains their comments on sails."

Nangar looked over the page. "Not of much use to us now, though. They clearly did not understand them any better than we did." Nangar had a pragmatic mindset. "I suppose there is no wind underground or they might have invented those too."

"I wondered about that. There are legends of the dwarves that involve ships. The sons of Ivaldi, who made Odin's spear, also made the ship Skilbladmir for Frey and according to the legend it had sails."

"It was also supposed to fold to the size of a cloth," Nangar said, "so the whole story is probably just a myth."

Anike nodded. "Perhaps. I suppose the tale we know could be a more recent re-telling and the sails are a detail added later. After all, any imposing ship built now would have sails as well as oars."

Nangar's eyes skimmed down the page, reading it faster than Anike could have managed. "Huh! Looking at this, one would think that the dwarves were doing us a favour by conquering us, as if we could not be trusted to govern ourselves. Just because they could work metal and stone doesn't make them better than we are."

Anike thought of the raiding back and forth across the narrow sea between Gotlund and Lartenland and was not quite so sure that the dwarven view had no merit.

"You might find this interesting, Anike." Nangar had resumed reading. "It talks about a potion."

Anike leant over to read the page again. "You are right," she said, "but there are a few words in this passage I do not recognise." The dwarven language was more closely related to runes than human speech, but there were many differences.

Nangar ran his finger down the parchment. "The dwarf is talking about an oil humans used on their blades. I hadn't heard tell about that."

"Poisoned blades are not very honourable," Anike said. "Could you read this part for me, please? Some of the words are unfamiliar."

Sighing, Nangar set aside his own parchment and took hers in both hands. "Much of this is plant names," he said. He translated the passage aloud. "Do you know that recipe?"

"No," Anike told him. "From the notes it seems to be a poison that specifically affects dwarves, weakening them 'nearly to the fragility of a human' apparently. It sounds as if he was listing the elixir ingredients in the hope of finding an antidote but lacked sufficient knowledge of surface plants to make one."

She considered. "Dwarves were supposed to be much stronger than men, and they ruled us for hundreds of years before Huppik led his rebellion. Humanity might have needed such an advantage to drive them back. I would be inclined to believe all this, after all, Huppik was known as 'the Clever', not 'the Honourable'."

Glancing outside, Anike could see the afternoon was wearing on. She knew she should check on Cairn again before going to the arl, so she apologised to Nangar before taking the parchment back to its place, feeling a little guilty for taking up his time. Neither of them had learned much of use that afternoon.

Bidding him farewell, she went home. She found Cairn still sleeping and his condition unchanged, so she dripped a very diluted potion between his lips. He swallowed when the moisture touched his tongue and a little colour returned to his face.

Satisfied, Anike turned her attention to her own appearance. It would do no harm to make herself presentable for the evening.

Normally, she found her good looks a hindrance as it was hard to make men take her seriously, and women seemed to think she might have designs on their husbands. As a result, it was rare that she untangled her hair or removed the dirt that digging up plants left on her.

This evening, however, she wanted to distract the arl from recent events as much as possible. Wincing inwardly, she changed into a clean tunic and washed her face and hands. She found a comb and brushed her hair so that it fell evenly around her shoulders, then headed back to the arlberg to meet Arl Rek.

THE BEAT OF THE DRUM

The arl was standing in the middle of his hall, conversing with a man and a woman when Anike entered. The man's clothes danced with patches in all colours of the rainbow on his tunic with his feathered hat set at a jaunty angle atop his blond head. She recognised the pair with the drums that she had seen when she and Gunnar had walked through the practice yard earlier. The colourfully dressed male skald was doing most of the talking while the woman kept her eyes lowered, save for occasional glances around her.

When Rek saw Anike coming towards them, he brought the conversation to an end. The pair moved off to a corner of the hall while the arl came forward to greet her, taking both her hands in his for a moment. "You look beautiful," he murmured and led her to a seat.

She smiled at him. "Thank you," she said, inclining her head and taking the place he had indicated which had a good view of the performance area.

Rather than going to the arl's high seat overlooking the hall, Rek sat down next to her and leaned in. "I am glad you were able to come. Cairn is still asleep, I take it?"

"Yes, he is stable and mending. There is no reason why he should wake before tomorrow."

"Good. It gives us a chance for a longer conversation. I want to talk to you about Gunnar."

Anike was surprised at his serious tone so soon after the warm greeting and felt a tinge of worry. The disturbing possibility that Gunnar had said something more about the lightning came to the front of her mind, but she smiled and replied, "Of course, my lord. He is a brave child."

"Yes, he is a child," Rek said, "But sometimes too ready to think of himself as a man. I do not want to hear of him putting himself in harm's way to impress you again."

Anike drew in a sharp breath at the change in tone. She knew that Gunnar did not have anything like the experience necessary to fight a witch, and his rapid defeat had proved that. A little stiffly she replied, "I am not sure he wanted to impress me. He may have felt a duty to protect me." She recovered herself and continued. "Bravery and compassion are good attributes in an arl, are they not?"

"Yes, they are, but they need to be tempered by good sense and experience."

"That is another worthy trait, my lord. I am happy we agree."

Rek frowned. "He is not ready for real battle, Anike. It will be some years yet before he can stand as a defender of the people."

"Perhaps you should let him have a little freedom," Anike suggested. "You might be surprised at how capable he can be if you give him a chance."

"In a year or so that might be worthy of consideration. For now, he trains and nothing else."

Rek looked like he was going to say more, but then shrugged and shifted his gaze to the skald. "Lalfar has a powerful voice. I am looking forward to hearing his recitation."

The skald was talking easily with some of Rek's men, but Anike's gaze was drawn to the woman sitting on the floor behind the pair of drums. From her angle, Anike could see there were runes painted on them though she could not read them from so far away. "Who is that with him? His wife?" The pair looked about the same age as each other, and Anike.

"His sister, Enya. A quiet one, she has hardly said a word."

"A pretty girl, my lord," Anike said, then blushed slightly. The woman was lovely, but she usually kept that sort of observation to herself.

Rek looked askance at her. "I suppose so, but not the most beautiful woman I have seen, even today."

This was a clear, if oblique, compliment but the admonishment that she might have been responsible for Gunnar's reckless decision to fight the witch did not sit well with it. Anike felt that the arl had not entirely decided what his motives for the evening were.

She was saved from any further need to navigate Rek's train of thought when the skald came forward into the area that had been cleared for his performance. The arl rose. "I must leave you for a moment," he said to her. "It would be a discourtesy to the players not to take the high seat during the performance." He smiled at her and turned away.

Gunnar slipped into the place his father had vacated. "What did you and my father talk about?"

"Later," Anike told him. "I wish to hear this." She did not want to give Rek a chance to criticise either of them.

As the audience quietened, Lalfar started to speak and Enya began to beat on her drum, emphasising the rhythm of the verse. The tale was an old favourite about a giant who had built a wall to protect Asgard, the home of the gods and how Loki had tricked him, preventing him from finishing in time and saving the gods from having to pay the price – the hand of the goddess Freya in marriage.

Lalfar's telling was more exciting than any Anike had previously heard. The meter and rhyme were clear, and the drum matching the cadence of the words and the pace of the saga added to the atmosphere.

Behind her brother, Enya began to smile, perhaps at the pleasure of the performance or with pride at the attention her brother was getting. Her eyes danced and the expression lit up her face, framed by her golden hair. Enya was truly beautiful when she was happy, Anike thought.

When the scheming giant had fallen before Thor's hammer, Lalfar brought the tale to an end. The hall, more crowded now than when the tale had started, filled with applause. Anike drew out a few coppers and sent them to join the rain of coins landing in front of the performers.

Lalfar acknowledged the acclaim with a smile and a deep bow, then turned to whisper something to Enya, who nodded and started a different rhythm on her drum. The skald began another tale of Loki and the apples of Idun, fruit which gave youth to the gods. Loki had been one of their number before turning against them, and he had died at Ragnarok in battle with the god Heimdall. Anike wondered if Lalfar identified with Loki the trickster, as he was central in both these legends.

Lalfar told the second story as compellingly as the first, including clever alliteration in key passages. While the tale followed Loki to a giant's castle, Rek came down from his throne to stand beside Anike, who got to her feet to avoid making him bend down.

Rek leaned in close and spoke in little more than a whisper. "He is good, isn't he?"

"Indeed, my lord, but I think the drumbeat Enya supplies adds a lot to the performance. It gives the recitation a greater depth."

"You are right. Sometimes it is not the obvious performance that carries the day. That which lies behind it may also be important." He leaned closer. "For example, I still do not see how you managed to drive off a witch who so easily defeated my son by yourself."

While she had hoped he would let that subject lie, Anike was not too surprised. She turned away from the skald's recitation to look directly at Rek. "I told you earlier, my lord, I was lucky. He went back to Cairn after Gunnar fell, and I had a chance to get close while he was lifting him."

"Yes, so you said, but it seems a big risk to take for someone you didn't know. Unless you have a particular skill?" The tone was quizzical rather than hostile.

Anike looked at his face. He did not seem to be challenging her — if anything his expression was somewhat hopeful. Suddenly she realised what he was hinting at and smiled. "While my mother was a shieldmaiden, I am not. I am fast though, and I can take advantage of an opening when I see one."

Rek seemed a little disappointed. "Weren't you afraid of the witchcraft?"

"I was more concerned about the blade, truth to tell. I have seen the damage a sword like that can do. Luck was with me, but I took no undue risks." She looked back at the performers. "Oh, that was a good turn of phrase," she said.

Rek seemed ready to ask more but then drew back from a confrontation. "Yes, very clever," he said, giving a slight smile and a nod, and returned his attention to the tale.

Anike's gaze was drawn to Enya at the back of the room. She seemed caught up in the performance, beating a rhythm that caught and magnified the key words Lalfar was using, but then she seemed to feel Anike's eyes on her, blushed and looked down. Her hands faltered a moment before she recovered her poise.

Enya reminded Anike a little of her childhood friend Inge, a woman who had abandoned her out of fear after Anike had become a witch. Like Inge, Enya was pretty with pale blonde hair but where Inge had been outgoing, Enya seemed shy save when caught up in the joy of the performance. Anike felt some shivering of emotion inside her as she watched the woman perform and this time it had nothing to do with the demon.

When the skald's recitation came to an end and the pair had gathered up the coins at Lalfar's feet, the audience began to disperse. Some headed for their homes while others went to congratulate the flamboyant skald. Enya picked up the drums and almost seemed to fade into the background.

Anike smiled at Rek. "They were good. Thank you for asking me here. I hope they will stay for some time."

"They did ask to shelter here for a few days, but they should be willing to stay longer after this acclaim."

Anike felt unaccustomed butterflies in her stomach and wondered if she had enough courage to act on the sudden urge to speak to

Enya. She reminded herself that she had faced down a skilled warrior-witch earlier in the day, and this woman was no threat. Speaking to her could not work out worse than not doing so. "Excuse me a moment," she said to Rek and went over to Enya.

The young performer cast a panicked look towards her brother who was busy laughing with some men on the other side of the hall. Without any obvious way out, she stood and bowed slightly. Anike smiled at her, hoping to put her at her ease. "You play very well," she said.

"Thank you, my lady," Enya said, bowing again.

"My lady? No one has called me that before."

"I am sorry," Enya stammered. "I thought that was the proper form of address for the arl's wife."

Anike's eyes widened in surprise, and then she laughed. Enya looked even more nervous than before. "No, no. My name is Anike, and I am just a karl, a herbalist. The arl is a widower."

It was Enya's turn to look surprised. "I am sorry. I just thought... I noticed how the arl treated you this evening, and I saw you with his son earlier."

"Oh, I see." Anike smiled. "No, I am just the arl's guest this evening, nothing more."

Enya nodded, looking a little relieved, and Anike cast about for something else to say. Her eyes lit on the drums and the runes on them. "Your instruments are a work of art," she said. "May I have a closer look at them?"

Enya smiled and picked one up. "My mother made them." She handed it to Anike who turned it over, admiring the craftsmanship. A pattern of runes had been dyed into the taut hide and it took only a few seconds for Anike to see that despite a superficial resemblance, it was not a spell but a prayer to the god Tyr to guide the drummer. The wood was polished to a smooth finish and rich hues shone through. There was love in the care of the instrument.

"It's beautiful," Anike said as she handed it back. "How long do you plan to stay? I would like to hear more."

"Oh, I don't know," Enya replied. "Lalfar usually makes that sort of decision, but it will probably be at least a week."

"Is it not about time to shelter for the winter?" Anike asked, though there was still plenty of time to travel before the weather became really cold.

"We will have to see," Enya said, smiling a little and looking down at her feet.

"Do you tell stories too?" Anike asked.

"No, but I do dance sometimes and Lalfar drums to accompany me."

"I would like to see that," Anike told her. "I will wager you dance with grace and poise."

"I try," Enya told her shyly. "Perhaps I will dance tomorrow."

Anike smiled but was not sure what to say next. The short silence was interrupted by the arrival of Lalfar. Anike expected him to ask if she had enjoyed the performance. Instead, he said, "I hope my sister isn't bothering you, my lady."

"As I told your sister, master skald, I am only a karl. My name is Anike. I am pleased to make your acquaintance," she said, a little grudgingly.

"And I am not yet a master, Anike, just a journeyman." His tone was confident, almost belligerent as he came to stand beside and a little in front of his sister.

"Nonetheless, an inspired performance from you both." Anike could not quite keep all the hardness from her tone. Lalfar did not look like he was about to leave Enya alone again.

She was not sure what it was, but there was something about the young woman that fascinated her. Feelings were surfacing that she had not experienced since she was only a little older than Gunnar and had been worried about what her adolescent companions thought about her.

She cast around for something to persuade Lalfar to leave so that she could talk more with Enya. "I am sure some more of the men would like to compliment you," she told him.

"Anyone else who wants to do that can wait," Lalfar replied dismissively. "I wanted to see how my little sister was and find out more about her new friend." He moved a little closer to Enya as he spoke. Enya's mouth twisted for a second and she glanced up at her brother, but she did not move away.

Lalfar studied Anike and his mouth parted slightly as he looked her up and down. "And I am glad she found someone so lovely, especially as she is not married to the arl."

Anike blinked at the shift in attitude, then shrugged. "You are very kind." She supposed many women would find him handsome, and Lalfar radiated assurance and he seemed to expect her to be flattered. She turned back to Enya. "It must be comforting to have such a protective brother." She tried to make her tone pleasant.

"It is, especially without our parents around." Enya sounded sincere and a little sad. Anike thought of Enya's drum, once her mother's, and guessed that no parents were waiting for them to return. She had no wish to say something that would upset Enya.

"Well, it is late," she said. "Thank you both for such an inspired performance. I hope you enjoy your stay in Kindiski." Inclining her head she retreated, surprised at her irritation at Lalfar's interruption. She mentally checked the demon's bonds but found them secure. The annoyance was hers, though she also felt a sense of relief that she had not made a fool of herself. Enya had made her nervous, as well as intrigued and excited.

She had no wish to stay longer but it would have been discourteous to leave without speaking to Rek, so she went over to him. "This has been a very pleasant evening, my lord. Thank you for inviting me."

He took her hand in his. "Thank you for coming, Anike. I trust you will be my guest again soon?"

She smiled at him. "Of course. I look forward to it," she said, then addressed him more seriously. "If anything changes with my patient, I will let you know. Goodnight, my lord."

The air was cold when Anike left the shelter of the hall, and she drew her cloak tightly about her. As she walked through the night, she gently chided herself over how she had acted over Enya, more like an infatuated girl than a mature woman. She allowed herself to enjoy the feeling of attraction for a moment, then consigned it to the realm of fantasy. She had more pressing issues to address.

The guard at the stone town gate let her out into the wood town. Usually, anyone leaving so late would have to work the gate by themselves, but it seemed that Rek was taking the presence of a witch within his domain seriously and had set guards at key points. Whether a single warrior would be of much use was another question.

As she headed back towards her house, an image of Lalfar rose in her mind. It was an unusual name, but it seemed familiar and with a little thought she realised why. The elves called themselves the lios alfar, and the skald's looks and name had brought a fey image to mind. Unlike the dwarves, the elves did live on the surface and very occasionally met with men. They were said to be tall with fair hair and gifted in verse – much like the skald. Dwarves, she remembered, called themselves svart alfar.

On reaching her house, she found Cairn much as she had left him. She made sure he was comfortable and then thought about turning in, but knew she was not tired enough to sleep with the events of the day still chasing through her mind.

The battle with the warrior-witch had left her with unanswered questions. Concerned that she had no real idea of his motivation and purpose nor any sound basis to decide if or when he might come back, she reluctantly decided to cast the runes.

Anike pulled the chest out from under her bed. The wood was as smooth as ice and while it was shut fast, it had no visible means of opening. Anike had constructed it herself with the aid of witchcraft, which she had used to shear through timber more quickly than any carpenter. She had felt a peculiar satisfaction when she had been able to turn the demon's destructive essence into an act of creation.

There was a lock, but no keyhole or other mark to show where it was. Short of breaking the chest apart, only another witch would have been able to open it. She laid her hand on the wood, visualised a simple rune pattern and spoke the name of the movement rune, "*Prana.*" Under the command of her witchcraft, the hidden bolt slid back, releasing the lid.

The chest contained folded canvas, with runes dyed or inked on them. It was wrapped around sheets of vellum bound into a book with runes covering its pages too. Sitting atop those were jars holding elixirs she did not lightly use. She lifted all of this out and set everything on the floor, revealing a tunic and leather armour. The armour had once belonged to her mother, Isolde, who had died giving birth to her in a witch weather storm.

Having been raised by her father, Anike had been known as Dareksdottir most of her life. Since she had left her home town of Trollgard, she had taken the name Isoldesdottir. Anike was a common enough name, but rumours of the witch Anike Dareksdottir had circulated for many months following her spectacular departure.

Beside the armour was a small bundle of leather, which to her had a weight that was more than physical. It clinked as she carried it to her work table. She unwrapped the leather hide and laid it down to display a design of nine circles with lines between them, all labelled with runes.

Inside the hide was a cloth bag containing runestones, each a small pebble with a single rune on it. Hers had been inscribed by witchcraft, using the fire form to scorch each symbol into the pale stone.

Runecasts were not lightly performed. The information they imparted, though often obscure, was usually accurate. Her teacher in rune lore, Hilda the Seer, believed that the runes drew on the knowledge of the Norns, but wherever it came from, a payment was exacted for the answers and so Anike used the runes sparingly. The connection between runes and witchcraft was obscure lore, and runecasting was not viewed in the same light. Seers who used it were respected, though often feared for they asked for sacrifice from those seeking answers. A questioner who declined often found their luck altered for the worst. The world exacted its price for knowledge one way or another, and Anike preferred a sacrifice she could choose.

This cast was primarily for Cairn's benefit and the price for unselfish casts was usually less, but with Cairn staying with her, she was already involved and there was an element of self-interest. One of her more complex potions was a suitable sacrifice, she judged, like the one she had used on Cairn – it would take hours of searching to find the herbs to replace it.

As she was interpreting the cast herself, there was no need to speak the question aloud and she let it form in her mind. "Why does the witch in black I fought today want to capture Cairn?" Runecasts told of the present, and asking questions about the past and future was a sure way to add uncertainty to the answer.

Weighing the bag of runes in her hand, she was reminded of how real the symbols were, much more than just images. To her, each rune elicited an impression. The chaos runes were pleasant and the law runes unsavoury, and sensation tingled through her fingers as they brushed the stones inside. She drew some out, apparently at random but guided by fate, selecting them until she felt the answer was complete, and cast them onto the hide.

Her intellectual interpretation of the pattern was enhanced by the demon's intuitive understanding of the runes. 'The law witch wanted to capture a chaos witch to trade for someone he had a duty to protect.' She put the potion she had decided to sacrifice outside her door. The sacrifice was complete once it was placed beyond use for her or in her interests. It did not have to be wasted or destroyed, and she could take it to old Vanna.

As she closed the door, she considered the answer. She had learned quite a lot and there was an extremely high price for supplementary questions so it would not be wise to use the runes again soon, despite many details still being unclear.

It was useful if disquieting to learn that Cairn was not specifically the target and any chaos witch would do, including her. It was also clear that the warrior's task was not complete, and he would be back. He was also motivated by a duty, trying to save someone else so probably regarded his cause as just, or at least justified. Perhaps most intriguing was that he was trying to capture Cairn for someone else, though Anike did wonder who would entrust such a task to a witch.

Briefly, she considered taking Cairn out into the woods and leaving him there, just to keep trouble away from herself and the town, but that would be abandoning him to an uncertain fate. Her conscience would not let her forsake him, at least until he was well. In any case, the law witch ought to take a while to recover sufficiently to be able to make another attempt to capture Cairn, so his staying with her should not to be an immediate source of danger.

She could use runecasts to get an idea of the law witch's location, but the price might be too high and it did not seem necessary yet. She remembered how animated her demon had been when he had been close to her, aware of the proximity of an opposing demon long before she had seen the witch. It was quiet now, as it had been since the witch had retreated.

With a final check on the old man, she went to bed. Vivid dreams of fire and water, lightning and ice that could have originated with the demon woke her several times in the night, but faded in the dawn light, as dreams generally did. The demon, if not exactly quiet, was not so animated that she considered there to be any imminent threat. As the first pre-dawn light crept into the house, she gave up sleeping, rose and dressed.

Satisfied that Cairn was looking slightly better, she made a little tea, not a true elixir but a concoction of energising herbs. She spooned it carefully into his mouth and watched him swallow. While the potion she had given him would prevent him from dying from his wounds, it did not help with hunger or thirst.

After she had seen to Cairn, she made herself breakfast and then set about gathering what she needed for a visit to the forest to gather herbs for more healing salves. The old man had been quite seriously wounded and even if she could get him to drink a potion without choking, healing him completely would reduce her stock significantly.

Normally she only carried a knife when she went outside the town but faced with the prospect of meeting Cairn's hunter again, she took more precautions. Opening the chest, she removed the tunic. It had several layers of cloth on the arms which when unbound would reveal rune patterns. The handle of the broom in the corner of her house lifted out of the bundle of twigs at its base to reveal a staff, bound with cloth to hide the runes she had burned into the wood.

She rummaged through her chest until she found a spearhead that would fit onto the slightly tapered end and slipped it into her bag.

A knock on the door startled her. "Anike, are you there?" came Enya's voice.

- 4 -

ENDINGS AND BEGINNINGS

Anike's heart fluttered, though she could not tell whether it was from surprise, anticipation or nerves. Taking a deep breath to calm herself, she opened the door.

Enya was standing outside with a slight smile on her face but she looked down at her feet when Anike appeared in the doorway.

"Good morning," Anike said. "It is really nice to see you, Enya. How are you? I was just going out," then added in a rush, "I didn't expect a visitor so early."

"I can go if you like," Enya said quietly.

Anike's stomach sank at the thought. "No, no, I was just surprised," she said hastily. "Would you like to come in?"

Enya nodded, and Anike stepped back to allow her inside. As she crossed over the threshold, Enya's eyes darted curiously around the room, then she noticed Cairn on the floor. She let out a small gasp.

"A patient," Anike told her. "He was wounded yesterday."

"An accident?"

"No, he was attacked in the woods." At Enya's horrified look, she added, "He will live, though," and instinctively moved to try to block Enya's view. "What ... was there anything in particular that brought you to me?"

Enya pulled her eyes away from the old man on the floor. "Oh. Yes. Lalfar sent me to ask if you have any potions that keep people awake.

He was drinking very late last night and is worried about being tired this evening. He doesn't want to make any mistakes when he performs."

"Perhaps you could dance instead? I would like to see that," suggested Anike, and blushed.

Enya's cheeks coloured too. "I am not sure I would feel comfortable performing before some of the men Lalfar was drinking with last night."

"Ah, yes. Some men can be coarse when they see a beautiful woman." She bit her lip and Enya looked down. "Anyway," she continued. "I know that potion but have none made up right now. I was about to go and gather herbs, so I can pick up what I need for it too. Would you like to come with me?"

Enya looked panicked for a second, then relaxed and smiled shyly. "Lalfar hasn't managed to get up yet. I have nothing else to do, so if you are sure I won't be any trouble, I would like to join you."

"It will be pleasant to have the company." Anike picked up her staff and held the door open for Enya.

Farmers were already at work in the fields and the sky was brightening slowly, though cold mist still softened the colours and edges of the landscape as they headed towards the river, well away from the area of the previous day's encounter. Enya had solid boots which Anike supposed were essential for the life of a travelling player, and she kept pace as they walked down the hill.

To break the silence, Anike explained the recipe for the potion Enya had requested and where the herbs to make it might be found. After listening quietly for a while, Enya started to show interest, asking about which parts of the plants were needed and how they were prepared.

Anike had picked a few plants and was describing the uses of jarl's narrowleaf when Enya commented, "Lalfar doesn't usually let me go off by myself to learn about things like this."

"I noticed that he came over to check on you last night."

"Yes, he feels responsible for me. He is the oldest of us."

"Us? That sounds as if there are more than the two of you?"

"There were, once," Enya said in a tone of finality.

Anike let the subject drop. "Do you enjoy travelling?" she asked instead.

"It's what I know, and Lalfar enjoys meeting new people. We worked our way along quite a lot of the north coast and after we got to the eastern edge of Gotlund, we turned south and then back west again. I prefer being near the sea myself, but we are more popular inland. There are fewer travelling performers."

"I grew up in a town on the coast myself," said Anike. "My father is a fisherman and I always loved being near the sea."

"Why did you leave?"

Anike frowned. Memories surfaced, of burning buildings, a conflagration in the arl's hall, fire and wind mixed with the screams of men and women, and of holding a sword with the point pressed against Bjord's throat.

"I had a disagreement with the arl's son. It is in the past. Years ago."

Enya nodded. "I see. You seem quite at home here."

"I have been here well over a year but many of the townsfolk still think of me as a newcomer, though a useful one."

"I suppose a herbalist is welcome anywhere."

"Usually, yes. Much the same as good performers, I expect."

"Ah, but herbalists are not confused with thieves. We itinerant entertainers suffer from that sometimes, especially since Lalfar is fond of gambling. He is quite good at it so he is sometimes accused of cheating and we have to move on quite quickly when that happens."

They walked on, pausing occasionally for Anike to pluck herbs that grew along their route. They stopped when they entered the long grass of the meadow beside the river.

Anike bent down to pick some pink flowers. "Maiden's rose," she said, "The last ingredient of your potion. I have the others I need for it now, but if you are happy to walk with me for a while, I have some more herbs to find."

She paused to see if she could sense any unusual activity or emotion from the demon, but it was only radiating its usual contempt for humanity. The moment of stillness gave Enya a chance to refuse, but when she said nothing and smiled slightly, Anike pointed and said, "This way."

As they walked through the long grass, Enya's movements became more relaxed and her face brightened. "I don't get the chance to just walk for its own sake very often. Travelling between towns is much more, well, purposeful and hurried."

"Then you should take this chance to enjoy it," Anike told her.

Enya nodded. "It is pleasant to spend a little time outdoors like this."

"Something to make the most of before winter comes."

Anike led them up from the meadow into a small wood and across the mottled carpet of fallen leaves. She lifted some aside to reveal the plants she was searching for.

"It would be useful to know something about herbs," Enya said.

"If you stay awhile, I could teach you," Anike told her.

"I think we will be moving on soon, unfortunately. Lalfar prefers to shelter for the winter in a larger town than this."

Anike looked over at her. "What made you take up this life?"

"There was nothing left for us, after..." Enya tailed off.

"I am sorry. I did not mean to bring up bad memories."

"It's not your fault. Can we go back now?"

"Of course." The mood had changed, and they walked back to Kindiski in a brittle silence. Anike knew she had stumbled on to something painful from Enya's past, perhaps a Larten raid which had left Lalfar and Enya orphans with little choice but to start a new life on the road. Enya was obviously sensitive about the subject and Anike tried not to feel too disappointed that their walk had come to an end. She told herself it was no one's fault – the question had been innocent – but that did not console her when she looked at Enya's blank face.

When they reached her house, Anike said, "I will make the potion for you now, if you like. Do you want to come in and wait?" Enya nodded and followed her inside.

She came to a sudden halt at the sight of Cairn pushing himself up to a sitting position, looking as weak as a ghost and blinking at the sudden light from the doorway. He had awoken several hours earlier than she had expected.

"Do not try to move," Anike told him, stepping forward.

His gaze rested on her for a moment before he turned it on to Enya. "*Agni!*" he cried, and a bolt of fire flew from his eyes towards her.

Enya froze, too shocked even to scream. Anike leapt and shoved her clear of the path of the flames. The burst of fire caught Anike's arm and ignited her tunic. She felt her the stab of pain as her skin blistered, and smothered the flames against her body, desperately wondering how she could contain the situation without Enya finding out that there was not just one witch in the hut, but two.

The burn hurt but it was not disabling. Anike ignored the pain and launched herself at Cairn, bearing him back to the ground. Face to face, she could see something dancing in his eyes, the complete opposite of the dead gaze of a law witch, and she knew she was looking at the demon. As she had feared, Cairn had been unable to hold it back in his weakened state.

The demon stared back for a moment and then its eyes shifted beyond her. "*Agni,*" it said again, and the beam supporting the roof of her house caught fire, an act of pointless destruction.

Anike cursed silently. While she had perceived the rune pattern forming, it had not been directed at her and she had not realised what it was until it was too late to stop it. Now she knew what to look for, she was fairly sure she could block the next spell, but in the meantime she needed to do something about the fire.

"Get out! Find some water!" she shouted at Enya.

"I am not leaving you alone with a witch!" Enya shouted back.

There was no time to argue. The fire was spreading above her head, and the roof was in danger of collapsing and burying all three of them. Anike tugged the cord on her sleeve to release the cloth layers and pulled at them to reveal the one at the bottom. She read the pattern and spoke the form rune, "*Agni.*" Instantly, all the flames in the house vanished.

That action must have surprised Cairn's demon for it now looked directly at her. Anike sensed a pattern of runes form, joining her to Cairn, a simple spell to throw her away and in response she visualised the movement rune as well, adding it to the pattern taking shape. "*Prana*," they both said at the same time and the air between them danced with the released energy of movement, scattering her hair before it dissipated. Anike was surprised by how insubstantial the pattern had been in comparison to those created by the law witch or to the rune she had added.

The demon in Cairn's body struggled against her grip and simultaneously summoned another rune pattern, this one centred on the lightning rune. Anike found a weak point in the design and spoke "*Eneki*," just ahead of his demon. Electricity crackled around them both for an instant, a flash of harsh blue light.

Conscious that she had to block every single spell, without taking her eyes off Cairn she called out, "Get a piece of cloth to gag him." Even that small shift in her attention meant that his next spell, aimed at Enya rather than her, nearly got past, and flames danced in the air for a moment as she countered it.

Enya looked around, grabbed a bandage and knelt behind Cairn's head. His demon finally seemed to realise that Cairn was physically the same size as Anike and threw all his strength into pushing her off. Anike knew from personal experience that demons cared very little for the health of their body and were not deterred by pain, and Cairn was fighting harder than a human could have done in his injured condition. She heard a joint crack in his shoulder and his arm bent alarmingly as he struggled.

Anike began to topple. Enya dropped the gag and grabbed Cairn by the shoulders to hold him down. He flexed his body still further but suddenly seemed to lose all strength, and blood came gushing from his mouth. Her healing elixir had not prevented him from rupturing something under the enormous strain the demon had forced on his body.

He gasped once more and collapsed, going completely limp as his final breath left his body. Anike sensed a force surge around her legs, still wrapped around the man's torso, then rebound. An instant later Enya was thrown back and Anike saw her fall in a flash of multi-coloured energy, stunned by a cascade of colours that seemed to sink into her.

Anike pushed Cairn's lifeless body off her legs and crawled over to Enya. Alongside her own feelings of guilt and concern, she recognised the demon's sense of kinship was now being directed at the unconscious girl. Cairn's demon must have transferred to Enya, something she had never considered possible.

She looked down at the prone woman. After her own demon had entered her, she had been unconscious for hours, so there was no immediate threat. Just as she was wondering what to do next, the door burst open. "I smelt burning," Lalfar said. He stopped as his eyes adjusted to the gloom in the house and saw Enya lying motionless on the floor with Anike kneeling beside her. "What in Tyr's name are you doing?"

Knowing it would make little difference to the impression Lalfar had formed, Anike nevertheless stood and took a half step back. Explanations flashed through her mind, each inadequate to explain the scene as it must appear. She opted for asserting authority. "Come no closer, Lalfar. There is great danger here."

Lalfar regarded the bloody corpse of Cairn lying beside his unconscious sister. "From you, it seems. I knew I shouldn't have sent Enya here." He took a long stride into the room.

Anike fell back, poised to dodge and ready to scream if he drew the axe at his belt but Lalfar went to his sister and shook her. "Enya, Enya!" he shouted into her face.

Enya's head lolled. Lalfar looked angrily up at Anike. "What have you done to her?"

"Calm yourself, Lalfar," Anike said. "This is not what it..." She cut off in shock as Enya's eyes opened.

"*Prana,*" said Enya. Lalfar's head snapped back as if he had been struck a heavy blow, and he fell to the ground. "What...?" he managed, forcing himself to his hands and knees.

Enya sat up and looked about her, but Anike could see her eyes dancing with energy and fury. She was shocked that the woman had woken so soon, but perhaps because the demon was already used to being tied to a human, it had recovered much more quickly.

She hesitated, unable to see a way to intervene without either revealing herself as a witch or hurting Enya, and in that time Lalfar had pushed himself back to his feet. Trying to distract the demon, Anike moved forward and placed herself between them.

Enya ignored Anike and spoke again. "*Agni*," she said, and Lalfar's clothes burst into flames. He shouted in panic as the fire scorched his skin and started to beat at it ineffectually with his hands.

Hoping that in the confusion Lalfar would not be concentrating on who was speaking, Anike read the spell on her sleeve again. "*Agni*," she said echoing Enya and using her witchcraft to quench the fire.

The demon in Enya cast an unreadable look at Anike, while Lalfar stared in astonishment. "Enya?" he asked hesitantly.

"She is not in control of herself at the moment, Lalfar. We must restrain and gag her before she hurts you."

"No. Enya knows me. She won't hurt me," he said, somewhat against the evidence, Anike felt.

The demon in Enya paid no attention to his words but raised its hands and spoke "*Agni*," conjuring a ball of fire which it threw at Lalfar.

Without thinking of the long-term consequences, Anike reached out her hand and felt for the pattern that was guiding it towards the skald. "*Agni*," she said as she gestured to deflect the flaming missile into the ground.

"But..." said Lalfar.

"I told you that you were in danger." Given what she had just revealed about herself, she did not dare to turn her back on the man, though Enya was the immediate threat. Enya's demon made her body take a sidestep to try to get a clear line of sight on Lalfar and as Anike moved to stay between them, she felt a rune pattern form. "*Eneki*," she said at the same time as the demon, and lightning flickered in the space between them. Again, Anike could sense the relatively tenuous nature of the demon's pattern, but it seemed to have no need of rest. She had to find a way to contain it until Enya was able to recover.

"You can control the power, Enya, concentrate!" she urged, stepping forward and grasping the woman's wrists. Touching her, Anike could feel the next spell as it started to form. "*Prana*," they both said. A haze filled the air around them for an instant.

"Enya, listen to me." Anike spoke firmly, her voice carrying as much authority as she could muster. "The energy overwhelming your mind can be controlled. You have runes on your drum. Think of *Log*, the rune of law. Picture it in your mind."

Enya's body tried to pull free, but Anike held her fast. "The power you feel is at its weakest after... *Agni!*" She countered another spell and a wisp of fire flickered in the air around them. "Now, Enya! Concentrate on the rune and master yourself."

Submerged beneath the torrent of power that was the demon, Enya's mind and spirit gave no sign that she had heard. Her body continued to struggle against Anike's grip. Lalfar came forward, holding one hand out placatingly, and her head swivelled to look at him.

Anike countered another spell. She was about to tell him to get back again but realised that in his instinctive way, Lalfar might be right. While risky, his approach could help Enya in her struggle. The worry that she might hurt or kill him ought to reinforce Enya's will and help her break the demon's hold.

Anike wondered if she could help Enya more directly. A chaos demon would recoil from a law-aligned rune, and they provided the best means of confining it. Through her own demon, she could sense rune patterns so surely Enya's demon would be weakened by those Anike imposed from outside. She visualised the image of the rune of law, but her own demon recoiled and she realised that the rune had only existed in her own mind, intangible without the demon's power.

She let the image go so she could counter the next spell from Enya's demon and tried another way. "Enya, think of ice and snow, a blizzard burying the burning inside you. Enclose it in ice to keep Lalfar safe."

Enya's next rune pattern was even less substantial and faded away before the effect could manifest, then the impression of unnatural light and power faded from Enya's eyes, and her body went limp.

Anike let her down to the floor. "Hold her," she told Lalfar whose face was a mask of horror. "She will need you now." She stood back to allow him to reach his sister.

Enya was starting to cry, though whether through misery, fear or relief, she could not say. She recalled her own actions when the demon's fury had first burst forth and was glad Enya would not need to endure the same guilt that she had felt over the deaths of innocent people.

Lalfar looked up as he cradled Enya in his arms and allowed her head to rest on his shoulder. "I am sorry," she told them both. "There is no easy way to say this." She nodded at the corpse, "Cairn was a witch, and his power passed into Enya when he died. I had no idea that could happen. What I do know is how difficult it is to control that power to begin with."

She paused, considering whether to tell them about the demon, but Lalfar interrupted her.

"You are a witch too," he said. It was a statement. "Did you turn Enya into one to tie her to you?"

"Of course not. This man was here because he was attacked in the forest yesterday. I had intended to keep him asleep until he was fully recovered, but he woke sooner than he should have done. Pain makes it harder to control the power and his injuries must have sapped his will and made him vulnerable."

To Enya, she said, "You can feel the power, like a sea of fire?"

Enya nodded. "It burns in my mind. It made me think of Lalfar like a rat, to be exterminated."

"It will do that, magnifying fear and anger, and changing how you see things. If you are not careful you will lose control and start using witchcraft to destroy things that you would have always accepted before, on the slightest whim. You have to be on your guard all the time.”

"You seem to be in control, Anike."

"I have had a lot of practice."

"I can feel it again." Enya's voice rose in fear.

"Think of a blizzard," Anike told her, and went to her table. She emptied out her bag of runes, picked one up and returned to Enya who had closed her eyes in concentration. "Hold this and look at it," she said giving her a runestone inscribed with *Log*, the rune of law.

Enya opened her eyes and stared at the symbol.

Anike spoke slowly and reassuringly. "Keep calm. I can block what you do if I am close enough. There is no need to worry." Enya's brow furrowed in concentration, then she relaxed and her breathing steadied.

"You are doing better than I did," Anike told her.

Enya took a deep breath. "This helps," she said, clenching her fist around the runestone, and pulled her brother close.

The whole conflict had only taken moments, but it would not be long before a neighbour came over to see what had caused the brief fire and to check that all was well. This would inevitably lead to more questions and both Lalfar and Enya now knew what she was.

She turned to them. "You need to get out of town before someone finds out about this. So do I. It is not safe for you to be around people yet, and my secret is out." Anike went to her shelves and started to sweep jars into her bag.

"Wait," said Lalfar. "You can't abandon Enya now."

"Lalfar is right, Anike. I need you," Enya added.

"I am not going to be much use to anyone if I am put on trial for witchcraft, and no one will be able to help you if you burn something down with people inside."

Lalfar's face flooded with anger and Enya looked frightened and hurt. "You would really run off and leave me?" she asked in a small voice.

"Aside from what the townsfolk might do, Cairn was attacked because he was a witch. His assailant was a witch too, as well as a warrior. Once this man learns where I live or hears about you, neither of us will be safe. If he had wanted to kill me, he might well have succeeded. You are certainly not ready to face him. It may take a few days as I wounded him but I am sure he will return."

"It sounds like you are making excuses," Enya said. "You were happy to stay this morning when you had a sleeping witch under your roof. What has really changed?"

"You both know about me now!" Anike burst out. "If anyone knows my secret, it might as well be the whole town."

"Do you think we would do that to you? That I would?" Enya asked in a hurt voice.

The words tugged on Anike's heart, but her head ruled her. She looked at Lalfar. "If our places were reversed, would you trust me?"

Lalfar did not answer at once but thought about the question. "Yes," he said, surprising her, "because the arl would believe you over us if you told him that Enya was a witch."

He was right, Anike realised. Fixated on the idea that everyone would turn against her if they even suspected her secret, she had forgotten how useful a scapegoat could be. She was well regarded in Kindiski and favoured by the arl, while Lalfar and Enya were unknowns. Even if Rek was disposed to listen to Enya and Lalfar, he would be much more likely to believe Anike's accusation in return, making it very difficult for them to raise any charge or complaint.

"Can you at least stay long enough to help me?" asked Enya, eyes wide. "I'm frightened."

"Is that really what you want?"

"What else can I do? I know you weren't responsible. I saw what that man was doing. He tried to kill me. He didn't know me, so he must have been out of control just as I was when I attacked Lalfar." She turned to him. "I am sorry."

Anike looked at her, thinking. Despite Enya's words, Anike knew that she was responsible. She had allowed Cairn to wake and instead of insisting Enya leave, had asked her to help. While she could not have known the demon would transfer, she had been too sure that she could control the situation and that overconfidence had put Enya at risk.

The discussion had reminded her that when she had left her home town, she had intended to do exactly what Enya was suggesting, to find witches and teach them to control the demon inside them so that they could live without fear of hurting the people they loved. In the last two years, she had not come across any others and had almost forgotten that plan, delving into the lore kept by the dwarves instead.

She looked at the young woman shivering with fear, with her hand clenched hard around the runestone. Guilt and sympathy rose to match the sense of responsibility she felt. It would be cowardly to run. "In truth, I would prefer not to leave this town if it can be avoided. If we are careful, we can all stay for a few days at least." She looked at Lalfar. "Does that meet with your approval?"

"I think," he said slowly, "it is for the best. We will need to move on soon anyway and you can use the time to help my sister." He looked at Cairn's body and gave it a nudge with his foot. "First, though, we need to tell the arl about what happened here, don't we?"

"Tell the arl what, exactly?" asked Rek from the doorway.

- 5 -

TRAINING GROUND

"My lord," Anike said. "I was about to come to see you. Cairn is dead."

Arl Rek's gaze took in the room, flicking over the table to the scorched roof, Lalfar's charred clothes, the burn on Anike's arm until it finally came to rest on Cairn's body.

Gunnar peered in from behind Rek. "You aren't hurt, are you, Anike? We saw smoke. Oh!" He stopped suddenly when he too saw Cairn.

Anike relaxed a fraction. If Rek had heard her named as a witch, he would have kept Gunnar away.

The arl stepped inside. "You said he was going to recover, Anike. What happened?"

"He would have done, but he woke much earlier than I had expected. It may be that a witch can throw off the effects of an elixir more quickly. Anyway, he summoned fire that set light to my roof and Lalfar's clothes. I was trying to restrain him." She looked at Enya for support, and Enya nodded.

"He was fighting so hard that he broke open his wounds," Anike went on. "He tore something inside, I think. He was like a wild animal trying to escape from a trap, flailing around both physically as well as with witchcraft, and his body was not strong enough. See here." She pulled Cairn onto his back so Rek could see the blood on his lips. "He died before I could do anything to stop the bleeding."

"I hardly thought you had murdered him, Anike. One of your neighbours came running to the arlberg to say they thought your house was on fire."

"That is why we came," Gunnar added.

"They were right, though we managed to beat it out. I had not expected him to be able to do much when he was so injured, and my error cost him his life. I should have taken greater precautions to ensure he stayed asleep until he was better."

"Would that have helped?"

Anike realised that she was in danger of revealing more than she had intended. She was sure that his weakened condition had diminished his ability to control his demon, but she could hardly justify her opinion using her own experience. She changed tack. "Yes. We made his injuries much worse when we restrained him. If he had been stronger, we could have held him down without hurting him. Bound and gagged, he could have been taken back out to the hills. My guess is that he would not have been a threat since he had lived alone for years without giving trouble."

Rek frowned. "Perhaps, though if he had hurt you and lived, he would have had to stand trial."

He turned to Enya and Lalfar. "I apologise. It is a poor host that allows his guests to be attacked by a witch. Brave warriors have run when faced with witchcraft, and it does you both credit that you stayed to help Anike."

Lalfar, doubtless embarrassed to be standing in front of the arl in charred rags, still drew himself up. He looked from Anike to the arl and seemed to come to a decision. "You are gracious, my lord, but the credit belongs to Anike. She kept her wits throughout. It is not her fault that there was such a tragic outcome."

Enya looked frightened and Anike could see that her fingers were white as she clenched them around the runestone. To divert the arl's attention away from her, Anike said, "You told me Cairn had no family, my lord. What should we do with the body?"

Rek looked at her, more intently than she was comfortable with. He did not answer but instead said. "Another witch defeated,

Anike. I might have to find a title for you." He almost sounded impressed but Anike thought she sensed an undercurrent of suspicion.

Gunnar chose to intervene. "Anike is very brave, Da, the way she didn't run from the warrior in the woods. And now another witch."

"There ought to be a trial really," Rek said. "After all, you did kill someone. But I doubt it will serve any useful purpose. I can see the scorch marks on you and the roof. There is no question that Cairn was using witchcraft so anything you did would be defending yourself. I will have to think about whether it is really necessary to put anyone through that."

"You don't really have to put Anike on trial, do you, Da?"

"I said I would have to think about it, Gunnar," Rek told him sharply.

"There is no need to worry, Gunnar," Anike told him. "Any trial by your father would be fair, and I have no fear of it." To Rek, she added, "I await your decision, my lord. I am not going anywhere."

"She was just trying to stop me getting hurt," said Enya quietly, then shuddered.

"Enough." Rek's voice was firm. "Anike, I will let you know what I decide tomorrow. For now, I will send someone to collect Cairn's body. It will be left for the animals. Witchcraft has to be seen to be punished, and burning or burying would be too honourable an end. Gunnar, come."

He paused at the door and looked at her. "At least this should bring yesterday's matter to a close."

Anike shut the door behind him. After some initial formality when she had first arrived in town, Rek had been friendly and considerate but today he had been much more serious. Although Cairn had died whilst in her care, she had not thought the arl would even consider a trial, and his decision not to rule it out suggested that his trust in her was beginning to wane.

"Thank you," she said to Enya and Lalfar after the arl's footsteps had died away. Had they told him all they had seen, she could now be bound and awaiting trial.

Enya was still on edge and was muttering "Ice and snow, ice and snow," under her breath and her hand still gripped the runestone. Anike remembered what it was like when her demon had first merged with her, distorting and warping her perceptions. It would have been terrible if Enya had lost control of her demon while the arl had been there.

Anike wondered if it might be possible to bolster her resistance further. Returning to the bag of runestones, she realised that they had been scattered across the table when Rek had been there but he had not commented on them. He would not have recognised their connection with witchcraft but they were out of place in a herbalist's home. It was possible he had thought they were Cairn's.

Dismissing that worry, she found the rune of frost. Ice was easier to visualise than an abstract such as law, and Enya was still muttering about ice under her breath.

She handed it to the frightened woman. "This is *Ranak*, the rune of frost. It may suit you better than *Log*, but you should keep them both. Try saying their names too. The power within you is the essence of chaos, and these law runes should assist you in keeping control, just as they help me. Can you picture them in your mind? It will be more effective than thinking about snow."

"I know these runes," said Enya, "and I can feel something when I hold them. It is unpleasant but does seem to help."

"It is the power reacting. Chaos is woven through you, but this will keep your mind clearer, like bitter tea."

"I have the law rune on my drum too," Enya said. "I hope it doesn't affect my playing." She closed her eyes. "I cannot really picture it clearly with my eyes shut. The shape gets blurry but if I say *Ranak* to myself, it does help."

"When Cairn's body has been collected, we had best go out of the town for a few hours so that I can show you a little more," Anike said as she pulled out the makeshift stretcher she and Gunnar had used to carry Cairn the day before. "Help me get him onto this so he can be ready for collection."

She wiped the blood off Cairn's face, and Lalfar helped her load the slight body onto the stretcher. They had just finished when Wulfnar, Rek's steward, arrived with a burly assistant. They lifted Cairn between them and headed to the door. "Are you coming too, Anike?" Wulfnar asked.

Anike considered. Rek might want a chance to talk to her, but she did not dare leave Enya alone. "No," she told him, "I do not want to be reminded that I failed to save him, but please thank Rek for sending you so soon."

Wulfnar nodded, and the two men headed back to the arlberg.

When they were out of sight, Anike pulled out the chest from beneath her bed, put the slate and chalk in her bag and then picked up the runes and her staff. "Time for some training," she told Enya. "Come with me."

The three of them walked out of the town. Anike took the lead, with Lalfar and Enya following behind. Lalfar had his arm around Enya and was whispering to her in an urgent tone, too softly for Anike to hear what he was saying.

Anike made no attempt to interrupt, as she was trying to decide if she should tell Enya about the demon. Her instinct was that it was too soon for that, even though she had made life difficult for herself in the past by keeping information to herself. It had taken her about a week to understand that the power inside her was a sentient alien intellect and not merely a wellspring of energy warping her perceptions like a drug. In some ways, it had been a relief to know that all the terrible things she thought she had done had not been manifestations of her own subconscious desires and she could blame all those deaths on the demon. However, the realisation that she had a hostile passenger she could never leave behind had not been easy to come to terms with. As she had not seriously hurt anyone, Enya did not need that absolution and Anike meant to prevent her from ever being in that position.

They reached the woods and Anike took them to a sheltered valley, hidden from the town. The sky was overcast, threatening rain at any time. Today, Anike was hoping for the cold rain that was accepted as a matter of course by the inhabitants of Gotlund during autumn.

Water was a law-aligned element and would help suppress Enya's demon, as well as put out any fires.

Anike led them down the slight slope to where a shallow stream trickled through the centre of the little valley. "This should do," she said, stopping and turning to Enya. Her own demon stirred within her, perhaps in anticipation of interacting with its counterpart within the golden-haired woman. She ignored it.

"This new power will always be there, Enya. I am sorry to have to say that there is no way to remove it from you until you die, so control is the most important lesson to learn."

She looked at the blond girl, whose face was tight with worry. "You can control and contain the power with runes and images. Most witches are quickly put on trial and hanged because they fail to restrain it. The power is inherently destructive in nature so without control you become dangerous. You saw what Cairn did to my home."

"And I nearly did the same. I wanted to burn everything down."

"You can resist those desires more easily if you know they are coming and don't let fear or anger get the better of you."

Enya drew herself up. "I am not an angry person!" she almost shouted, then shock ran over her face and she looked at the ground. "That was so strange."

"I know. I felt so sensitive at the beginning too. I could take an insult from the slightest thing. It does get easier."

"Your staying has helped me. I cannot tell you how comforting it is to know there is someone who understands this."

She looked up again, "How did I become a witch?"

"I think the power is created during witch weather, originally. Mine came to me in a ball of fire when I was caught in it in the mountains, and I suspect something similar happened to Cairn many years ago. Rek told me that he burned down part of the forest."

Anike paused, less sure about the next part. "My guess is that when Cairn died, the power passed to you because you were in contact with him. Witches are usually hanged, so no one is touching them at the moment of death and the power has nowhere to go. I saw one executed a few years ago and there were no new witches following his death. I cannot be sure – most do not live long enough to understand much or pass on what they learn. If their first act as a witch is to set fire to buildings with people in them, they are caught quickly."

"I could be put on trial?" Enya asked. Her eyes suddenly seemed to shine.

"Stand back," Anike said to Lalfar and put her hand on Enya's shoulder. Enya's eyes danced over her, and Anike felt a pattern forming, a spell to throw her away. "*Prana*," she said, an instant ahead of Enya. Her will prevailed and the spell collapsed.

Enya frowned, closed her eyes and her hand groped in her pocket. Anike held her breath, watching the struggle mar the woman's lovely face before Enya relaxed and her eyes opened, this time clear and calm.

"You did well," Anike said.

Enya withdrew her hand and opened it to show the two runestones. "The smoke in my mind retreated when I concentrated on the feel of these," Enya told her. "I probably should have kept them in my hand."

"It will help. While strong emotions like fear and anger feed the power and make it harder to control, it is a thing apart and not an aspect of your imagination. It will recoil from law runes."

"How did you manage at the start? Did someone help you too?"

"I was knocked out by the ball of fire, and my companion took me to an isolated farm. When I awoke, I lost control and destroyed quite a lot of it. I had to leave the area to avoid the trial that should have followed." Anike left out the deaths from her account. "I came across a seer and while I was casting runes for her to read, I felt them as you do. I learned to use them to control the power, both to suppress and to harness it, like when I put out the fires." She thought of the battle with the law witch. "There are still things I do not know, though."

Her demon was becoming more animated, and she put this down to talking so openly about her witchcraft. She continued. "There are two types of power, chaos and law. You and I have the power of chaos inside us but there are law witches too, like the one who attacked Cairn. We can call on fire, lightning, wind and movement, while law witches command cold, water, earth and stasis. The most effective way to control your power is to use images of the opposing law-aligned runes. I keep mine locked in a stone chamber surrounded by law runes, and if I need it, I let it out and then force it back into the prison."

Enya was looking apprehensive again.

"We can work on how best you can stay in control," Anike continued. "It is not your fault if sometimes you fail. Remember that. It is as if someone had given you mead instead of water and you became drunk without noticing. What I am telling you will help but if sometimes it does not work, it is the will of the gods."

A chill wind blew the first drops of rain into Anike's face. Within her, the demon was struggling more vigorously as if the description of its ability was empowering it. She sensed flickers of its desire to be allowed to act, but she deliberately ignored them. "I can channel my power using chaos runes to make spells," she went on. "For that, I have to be able to see the entire pattern, and for most spells that means I need to have it on something in front of me, like this." She showed Enya the pattern on her sleeve.

"If the design is so simple that I can picture it clearly in my mind all at once, then I can cast a spell without it being written down. If you want to learn more about that, I can show you but if you just wish to stay as quiet as possible, we can focus on exercises of control."

"I am struggling to hold the power in, Anike," Enya said. "It is becoming harder, and these are not helping so much now." Her hand gripping the two runestones was white.

"It could be because we are talking about it," Anike said, then paused. Her own demon was now hammering on its prison. "Or..." she trailed off, looking around. From the far side of the stream came the sound of a branch breaking.

"Lalfar, ready your axe! We are about to be attacked." She unbound her sleeves and pulled the cloth from her staff to reveal the rune patterns. As the bindings dropped to the ground, the black-clad figure of the warrior-witch emerged from the trees.

"Run, Enya," Anike shouted, but an instant later she knew it was too late. Enya hurled the runestones down as if they were hot coals and when Anike turned, she could see the demon staring out of the young woman's eyes.

- 6 -

TREMORS

The man in black held his greatsword ready in both hands as he advanced slowly from the trees. The raindrops did not seem to touch him and the air around him glinted like crystal, even in the grey light of the day. He had no sign of injury.

Anike lifted her staff but before she could read one of the rune patterns on it, Enya's demon spat out "*Agni!*" in a tone of unmistakable hatred. In response, the man intoned "*Ranak,*" in a clear voice and for an instant fire shimmered around him before vanishing in a glitter of frost.

Anike read the inscription on the staff. This spell should have sent a blast of flame straight at the warrior, but she saw him frown in concentration as he sensed the pattern forming and felt an ice rune inserted into the spell's design. As she spoke "*Agni,*" he repeated "*Ranak.*" Her spell's pattern hummed with tension before shattering, sending another cloud of ice dust into the autumn air.

The warrior paused as he looked between Anike and Enya, his expression betraying a hint of puzzlement, nothing like the bleak, expressionless stare of a law demon. With the man in control, he would be without the unlimited selection of spells available to his demon. While his blade was covered in runes, there was only room for two or three spells and with Enya and Lalfar beside her, she ought to be able to defeat him.

The warrior clearly saw the odds differently. "Give me the girl," he said to Anike in what she was now sure was a Larten accent, "and I will not need to kill you and the man. Resist, and you will both die, and I will take her over your corpses. I will not turn my back on you again."

"Never!" she and Lalfar called back, almost at the same moment.

Enya ignored the ultimatum and called out *"Eneki!"* A jolt of lightning lashed out, only to be lost in a haze of mist as the man took one hand from his sword hilt, gestured and said *"Unda,"* almost dismissively before charging up the hill.

As he reached Enya, he swung his blade in a wide arc just below shoulder height. The blow was a little slower than Anike expected, and she saw that he was using the flat of the blade. Lalfar leapt forward to deflect the incoming sword with his axe. Anike moved to her left and thrust her staff like a spear, but the man in black stepped back and swept aside her attack with a smooth parry. Balanced easily on the balls of his feet, his eyes flicked between the three of them, weighing them up.

Before he could strike, Enya's voice came again. *"Agni,"* she said, and a ball of fire the size of a fist appeared in her hand. She threw it at the warrior's head. He ducked and let the fire pass over him, but as he did so Lalfar leapt forward to get inside the reach of the greatsword and swung his axe. The man in black dropped one hand from his own blade and blocked the haft with his arm as he straightened up. Taking advantage of her opportunity, Anike swung her staff at his leg as hard as she could. The stout wood slowed markedly as it passed through the shimmer surrounding his body but still struck the man's leather-clad thigh hard. He grunted in pain, but her satisfaction was short-lived as he swung his greatsword one-handed at Lalfar's neck. As Lalfar pulled his axe back to try to block the strike, the warrior took a double-handed grip on the hilt once more and redirected the swing beneath Lalfar's parry. The keen steel bit deeply into Lalfar's leg and he fell, crying out in pain.

Anike took a pace back, read the pattern on her staff again and shouted, *"Agni!"* The complex attack on Lalfar had taken all of the warrior's attention and he only managed a token attempt to block the spell. This time the bolt of fire struck him full in the chest and exploded, throwing him away from the injured skald. He staggered, and Anike could see the scorch marks on his face and armour.

The warrior regained his balance. "That was a mistake," he said coldly, and she saw his eyes go blank as the demon took control. "*Ranak*!" it hissed through his mouth as the rune pattern formed.

Anike felt for the weakness in the spell. "*Agni*," she countered and shattered the blast of frost before it fully formed.

Knowing that the demon would ignore pain and any wound short of a crippling injury while it was in control, Anike flicked through the multiple layers of cloth on her sleeve to find her next spell, even as it turned towards Enya and drew back the sword to strike. Enya's demon spat out "*Prana*," but whatever spell was intended, the law demon brushed it aside with a cold "*Ert*."

Enya turned and fled towards Anike. Her demon might not be concerned by pain but it did not want Enya to die, depriving it of its body and perhaps its own life.

With Enya darting out of reach, the law demon struck instead at Lalfar. The writhing skald managed to raise his axe to block the blow but the force behind it knocked the wooden haft back against his forehead. He dropped, out cold. The law demon raised the blade again to finish off the fallen man.

Enya's demon stopped and turned back, well out of sword reach. Presumably seeking to use any advantage, rather than acting out of a desire to save Lalfar, it pointed at the man in black and launched a dart of fire.

The law demon paused with the blade held high and turned its head towards her, intoning "*Ranak*," to nullify the attack.

Anike used the moment of distraction caused by the fire. She had found the spell she wanted on her sleeve, and the demon was too occupied to counter her. She surrounded it with a levitating force and lifted it away from Lalfar, into the air and beyond sword reach.

Before she could bring it to a dangerous height, it spoke, "*Ert*," shattering her spell and fell to the ground, landing awkwardly on hands and knees, several paces away from the skald.

Enya's demon evoked fire again, but the law demon countered as it rose. It charged again and this time the sword was poised for a killing stroke. Enya's demon took a step back and tripped, falling onto its back. The law demon reached it and raised the sword high.

Not having recovered enough energy to cast another spell powerful enough to be of much use, Anike started forward hoping to block the blow with her staff, but she was too late, too far away. She watched helplessly and saw the blade come down, then pause, as the black-clad man's face tensed in concentration. His expression turned from one of triumph to pain as he wrested control back from his demon and the effects of the scorching she had inflicted earlier registered.

From the ground, Enya tried to conjure fire again but the man blocked the spell with a sharply intoned ice rune, then kicked Enya hard in the head. She crumpled, knocked out cold.

Anike pulled up short as the law witch spun to face her, hurt but poised for battle. She picked another spell from her sleeve and spoke again, "*Prana.*"

She had not tried to cast this spell directly on the warrior and he glanced about him, trying to determine what she had done. Seeing nothing, he smiled slightly, raised the blade, turning to look at her. "Last chance," he said. "Leave. Let me take the girl now. You are no match for me alone and if you try to interfere again, I will kill you." Anike had no doubt that he meant it but held her ground.

The witch nodded, then raised his sword again just as Lalfar's axe, animated by her last spell, smashed into the back of his head. The crystal shimmer slowed the weapon but did not stop it, and he staggered. His blade faltered and Anike leapt forward, swinging her staff in a wide arc at his head. Again, the crystal shimmer slowed her stroke but could not entirely shield him, and this time he went down, leaving Anike standing beside three unconscious bodies.

Lalfar was the most seriously wounded. The cut in his leg was bleeding freely, so Anike found a salve in her bag and applied it. The immediate danger passed as the flesh started to knit together, so she moved to check on Enya. The woman was breathing, with a wide red welt marring the side of her face her only visible injury. Anike frowned and felt her pulse, which was fast but strong.

Deciding that the girl was not in immediate danger, Anike went to check on the warrior in black. He was also out cold, his face relaxed for the first time but reddened from her spell, which had left his beard singed and some of the leather armour cracked and buckled. The crystal shimmer still surrounded him. It looked to her as if he would be unconscious for a while but she reminded herself that she had also thought that of Cairn.

She could not let such a dangerous enemy go free but she could hardly kill him while he was helpless. Even if it had not been a dishonourable action in itself, he had given her a chance to retreat and she respected that. She would have to take him prisoner, even if that meant trouble once he woke.

She bent for his sword, but agony erupted in her leg as something small and hard struck it with incredible force. Anike felt her thigh bone snap and she fell screaming as the pain surged through her. She struck the ground face first, too focused on her inner struggle to consider the source of the attack.

The demon seemed to gather strength from her torment, and she fought to hold the image of its prison in place. The mental construct began to crack as the pain sapped her will. Fractures formed, joined and multiplied in the walls, the prison held together only by the ragged remains of her failing concentration, and she desperately pulled a potion from her bag and gulped it down.

The elixir numbed her pain as it spread through her body, and she rallied. She forced the fragmenting prison back together and felt the demon's blast of rage as she denied it its freedom.

Crippled but insulated from pain, she raised her head and looked around to locate who or what had attacked her.

Fifty paces away, beyond the stream, was a short but unnaturally wide figure, dressed head to foot in steel plates. It held something that looked like a small bow on a short staff in its hand. Her mind rebelled against what she was seeing. The shape seemed somehow inhuman. She blinked and shook her head to clear her vision, but the form was no figment of her imagination.

He was several inches shorter than she was but had broader shoulders than any human. The helmet hid most of his face, but a black beard hung from his chin and the little skin she could see was a pallid white. The interlocking slate-grey plates of metal covering his body must have weighed more than a grown man.

She could only be looking at a dwarf.

He advanced out of the trees, followed by another similarly accoutred and armed. As well as the staff-bows, at the waist of each hung an unfamiliar weapon, something like an axe or a war hammer. Both had shields on their backs, made of some dark metal rather than the wooden ones she was familiar with.

The second dwarf raised his own bow-like weapon and pointed it at her. There was no sign of an arrow, but he was sighting as if he were about to shoot at her. Blood flowed freely from her injured leg, and she could not walk or even stand until she healed herself, so she lifted her cloak to read and cast the spell of flight. As she willed herself off the ground there was a loud thumping noise from the weapon and something passed through the air where she had been, so small and fast that it was only a blur. She heard it hit the ground a few feet away but could see nothing but a small hole in the earth.

The dwarf leaned forward and pulled a handle on the weapon, tensing the bowstring again. His companion raised his own staff-bow, aiming at her in his turn. Anike had no time to attempt another spell, so turned sharply to her left. This time she had a brief glimpse of a small ball rushing towards her, glistening like polished metal, before it tore a deep furrow through the flesh of her side. It had not hit any vital organs but was still a serious wound and while her potion kept any pain at bay, the next shot might hit something critical.

In an effort to distract the dwarves, she willed the axe she had bewitched earlier to rise and sent it spinning towards them, but it landed short.

The second dwarf had reloaded and was starting to take aim. The weapons took longer to prepare than a bow, but the tiny missiles were heavy and travelled at tremendous speed. Although she had a spell that created a shield of wind to stop arrows, she doubted that it would deflect these deadly shots.

She could feel her demon struggling for release again, directing waves of hatred against the dwarves, but she resisted its bid for control. They looked impregnable in their armour and her demon would probably leave her exposed to their peculiar weapons while it mounted an attack.

Whatever their reasons, the dwarves clearly intended to kill her. She was no match for them and her heart sank as she realised that any further attempt to help Enya or Lalfar would surely lead to her death too, at least until she had time to think and plan. Even flying away was risky under the threat of the deadly dwarven weapons so instead she dived for the staff she had let fall when first struck. One of the dwarves tracked her flight, taking his time to ensure that he would not miss, and that care gave her time to escape. She grabbed the solid wood and read the second spell engraved into it, one that she saved for emergencies. While focusing on a point in the trees, behind and well beyond the dwarves, she named the rune of movement to invoke the spell of dislocation and vanished from the scene of battle.

The next instant she appeared at the point she had been looking at. She rarely used the dislocation effect as the idea of being nowhere during the eye blink of transition was unsettling, and the sudden shift was disorientating.

She glanced back at the dwarves, one of whom had given an oath of surprise, and she recognised the dwarven language.

They looked about them but she had already ducked behind a large fir tree and was peering carefully through the evergreen branches. She had no idea how acute dwarven senses were, though she hoped Svartalfheim was a dark place and they might find it hard to see clearly through the glare on the surface.

One of the dwarves turned back to the three unconscious people on the ground, then said, "Keep careful watch for the other witch. She may return," in a deep rasping voice before walking towards the prone humans.

Anike felt her strength draining away. Her last potion had blocked out the pain from her injuries but had not cured them. Her blood welled out, soaking the left side of her tunic and both of her legs. She did not know what the dwarf was going to do to the others but if she did not cure herself, she would bleed to death regardless. There were dangers in insulating pain away as it warned when the body was damaged, and hers certainly was.

She pulled a flask from her bag and drank. The bleeding halted and her wounds knit a little, but the gash in her side would reopen easily and her potion was nothing like strong enough to heal her broken leg as well. She carried a salve but she doubted even that would mend the leg completely, and one of the others might need it more, assuming the dwarves did not finish them off.

One was looking about him with his weapon held ready, while the other lifted both Enya and the law witch, slung one over each shoulder then bent again to pick up the man's greatsword. Their hands and feet nearly reached the ground. Anike marvelled at his strength. She doubted she could have lifted the warrior at all yet when the dwarf started to walk, he seemed scarcely more encumbered than if he were carrying a pair of rabbits. Still vigilant, his companion led him back up the slope.

It was not just the warrior in black that wanted Enya, it seemed. Anike recalled that the runes had told her that he had been looking to take Cairn for someone, and she wondered if the dwarves were looking to make the same trade, or even if they were the ones who really wanted the witch. It was not clear to her why, in either case, the dwarf had picked up the warrior as well as Enya.

In any event, she had to stop the dwarves from escaping. They had taken two humans and according to legend and history, dwarves had little regard for them, certainly as individuals and she could not allow Enya to suffer at their hands. The law witch might also be a victim and he was still human, at least in part.

The dwarven armour looked as if it would deflect a bolt of fire, but lightning might be another matter. Reading the pattern on her sleeve, she focused on the dwarf carrying the weapon and said,

"*Eneki.*" A blue-yellow flash struck down from the clouds, outlining the dwarf for a moment in a harsh light. Sparks cascaded from him in a fragmented shower but instead of falling as Anike hoped, he just halted. Cursing in what she hoped was pain, he looked for his attacker.

This time he saw her, and the bow-like weapon came up. Anike pressed herself against the trunk of the tree but the shot burst right through it and hit her in the shoulder. Fortunately, much of its force had been absorbed by the wood, but it spun her round and she would have fallen had she not been supported by the flight spell. The injury was nothing like as bad as the previous ones, but she was feeling battered despite the potion.

She flew to another tree, a stouter one, and rose up behind the thick trunk to the lower branches. The next shot slammed into the wood but did not penetrate through to her side. Hovering just above one of the tree limbs, she risked a glance, only to see both dwarves heading away at a fast trot.

Any desire to follow was brought to an abrupt end when her flight spell expired. She had to grab a branch with both hands to stop herself from falling a dozen feet onto her broken leg. Her staff dropped to the earth.

She could feel her injured shoulder weakening rapidly and she started to slip. Unable to lift her cloak to read the flight spell again, she recalled a simpler pattern, one of the first she had ever created, cast the spell and drifted slowly back to the ground. She picked up her staff and leaned on it.

Breathing more calmly, she realised that she could no longer hear the dwarves, and more than that, her demon had quieted. The battle had been so intense that she had paid little attention to the sense of antipathy it had been radiating, but now she noticed its absence. The reaction had been similar to the one the law witch engendered, though less intense. It might be that the dwarves were aligned with law as their association with stone was clear.

Now she had to make a decision. If she pursued the dwarves, she would have to leave Lalfar behind, and he might die from his injuries.

If the dwarves were to injure or kill her, he would certainly bleed to death before anyone found him.

And she had to admit she had no plan for fighting the dwarves. She had once defeated a monster, surely more dangerous than a dwarf, but she had been able to stay out of its reach and more importantly, she had known its weaknesses and was prepared for the battle.

With a final glance in the direction the dwarves had taken, she drifted over to Lalfar. On closer inspection, he was even more badly hurt than she had thought but at least the dwarf had not finished him off. While his axe had blocked the final blow from the greatsword, the blade had been deflected onto his arm after the axe haft had struck his head, and in her earlier haste she had missed this wound. His clothing was cleanly cut and blood welled up through the gap, as well as from the deeper gash just above the knee. She had little salve left so, after applying just enough to his arm and leg to staunch the blood flow, she bound the wounds and then spread the tiny amount that remained onto his scalp. His eyes fluttered open as the bruise shrank. "Enya?" he asked blearily, then he saw the blood on Anike's tunic and trousers. Shock registered on his face as he looked about him.

"I am sorry," Anike said. "She is alive but captured. I was able to stop the swordsman but then dwarves attacked. They took both Enya and the warrior away. Dwarves! I thought they had been gone for centuries."

"How far ahead are they?" Lalfar asked as he peered around unsteadily.

"They went off up the hill about five minutes ago." Anike looked him up and down. "Can you stand?

Lalfar pushed himself to his feet, staggered and grimaced. He closed his eyes again and pulled himself together. "We have to try and find her! Did they leave a trail?"

She gestured to where the scorched ground marked the lightning strike. "They started there."

Lalfar took a careful step forward, groaned in pain but then limped to where Enya had fallen. He looked at the ground carefully. "I think I can make out some tracks."

He headed towards the scorch marks and picked up his axe from where Anike's spell had flung it earlier. "Let's be off."

- 7 -

PATHS

"My leg is broken. There is no way I can walk," Anike told Lalfar.

"Can't you heal it with a potion?" he asked.

"I used the last that I had with me on you. I have some more at home." She peered into the trees ahead. "We should go back to town and inform the arl. He will bring Kindiski's best trackers, I am sure."

"We would lose a lot of time. If it has only been a few minutes, we might catch them."

"I suppose so," Anike said slowly. She had never learned to track herself, and she was also wary of catching up with the dwarves without a much greater force. She had some other spells that she could use but was a long way from being sure that she could defeat the dwarves or protect Lalfar. "I am not sure that is wise though. We are both wounded and could use help."

"The longer we wait, the further they get ahead of us."

"True, but they have a good lead already. I know the direction they set off, but I do not see any tracks."

"We can't let Enya be taken." Lalfar looked at the ground. "I think I see something like boot prints. We can try to follow them. It's our best chance to save her."

Anike nodded. It would not be the first time she had taken risks for others. "Very well, but if we do catch the dwarves up, do not just charge in. Stay hidden until we have a plan. They are exceedingly dangerous, well protected by their metal armour and they carry weapons a bit like bows that fire small missiles. They nearly killed me with those."

Lalfar looked at her in surprise. "Can't you just blast them with fire or something?"

Anike shook her head. "I hit one with lightning and it barely slowed him. I am a healer, and I have not dedicated my time to devising spells for battle. I might be able to do something, but any fight will be hard and that is why we need a plan."

She touched her leg to the ground and shook her head. "If we are going to follow them, I need to cast a spell or I won't be able to move."

She lifted the side of her cloak to reveal the flight pattern and then her eye caught something that made her pause. On the ground lay the two small runestones Enya had flung down when the demon had taken control of her. Anike had forgotten them in the battle. Enya would be terrified when she awoke and would struggle to keep control her demon without them. Anike shuddered at the thought of what she would go through.

This was her fault. Once again, she had believed that she was in control, that she could manage everything. Even knowing the law witch was a danger, she had led Enya out of the town and exposed her to attack and then she had fled before the dwarves. She had let the girl down and she would not do that again.

Anike swept the runes up and put them away, before looking at her cloak again, glad that her blood had not obscured the patterns on it. "*Prana*," she said and rose a few inches into the air. "Let us go then, if we are doing this."

The pair headed uphill through the trees, but if Lalfar had ever been following the dwarves' trail, it soon became clear he had lost it, so Anike tried to work out where they might have been going. There had to be a cave in the vicinity. She had briefly visited a dwarven chamber once before. After being caught up in the tumult caused by her becoming a witch, Hilda the Seer had taken refuge in one and a passage had led to Svartalfheim from it, until the dwarves had sealed the way after their retreat from the surface. She did not recall seeing any caves when she had surveyed the area for plants and if there was one with an obvious entrance or seal, Nangar would surely have mentioned it, so any route to Svartalfheim had to be hidden. The dwarves were cunning artificers who could have made the portal blend in with a cliff.

"What do the dwarves want with Enya?" Lalfar asked suddenly.

"They must have a reason for needing a witch. They might be acting for someone else, or perhaps they want witches for themselves. Maybe they were looking for one of each kind, but I have no idea what could have led them to the surface now."

"Each kind?"

"Law and chaos. The man who attacked us used law runes. Enya is a chaos witch. The dwarves have them both."

"Why did they not take you?" Lalfar's voice held more than a hint of accusation.

Anike felt the need to justify her withdrawal, both to Lalfar and herself. "I had to retreat. They were shooting at me, and for all I knew then, killing me was their objective. I was seriously wounded and had to find somewhere to heal. I did not know they were after Enya too, not for sure."

It occurred to her that Lalfar had apparently accepted what she said about the dwarves without question, even though the much more plausible explanation would have been that the law witch had taken Enya. She supposed that the day had piled so many fantastic events on him that he was prepared to accept one more. Anike had clearly been seriously wounded by someone and it would be odd to lie about who it was and no one was likely to make up a story about an attack by dwarves.

"Why don't you fly up high to see if you can spy them out?" Lalfar asked a couple of minutes later as they made their way up the wooded slope.

Anike came to a halt, chiding herself that she had not thought of this herself. Her imagination had been constrained by an innate sense of caution, as rising above the treetops could make her visible from the town. Now she thought about it, while the branches would hide the dwarves while they remained in the woods, she should be able to spot them if they moved out onto the slopes above the tree line. Unfortunately, they would see her too.

"If we get close to the upper edge of the forest without finding any sign of them, I will try that," she said, "but it would be a last resort. I do not wish to alert them."

"Can't you summon a mist to hide in?"

Anike shook her head. "Mist is water, and water is a law form. I can create smoke but that would look unnatural and be just as obvious as me flying. I do not have a spell which conjures a cloud of smoke that moves. I never saw the need." She looked into the distance. "There are a lot of things I did not see the need for," she added, a trace of bitterness creeping into her voice.

Dealing with other witches was proving complicated. Enya seemed to be struggling more than she herself had with the demon, though she might manage better with time. It might have been a good idea to get her out of the town, but she shouldn't have gone so far. It had been foolish to allow Enya to spend so much time with her in the first place when she should have been looking after Cairn. She had to try to make this right. She just hoped that she was not also making a mistake by following the dwarves without taking time to recover and prepare.

It took about ten minutes to reach the edge of the wood. The drizzle fell between the branches and soaked them, and she had to renew her flight spell twice. There was no sign of the dwarves.

The ground above the trees was moss and rock, and Anike doubted that anyone but a skilled hunter would be able to find a trail on it. After a few moments staring in vain for any clue, she squared her shoulders, recast the flight spell, and rose into the air. From only a little above the treetops the view of the valley would have been spectacular had the weather been better. She could not see the town through the drizzle so was probably safe from accidental prying eyes, but the swirling droplets limited her own vision too. She turned slowly in the air, scanning the slopes but with no sign of the dwarves, she returned to the ground. As she landed, she felt the first throbs of pain in her leg, telling her that the potion was starting to wear off.

"I see nothing," she told the skald. "We will have to go back to the town and tell the arl what happened."

"That could take hours," Lalfar objected.

"I do not see any alternative," Anike told him. "Do you?"

As Lalfar looked around, seeking any clue that he could use, Anike retied the bandage on her leg. Unwilling to complicate matters or worry him, she refrained from saying that excessive pain inhibited her control of her demon but she knew he would be at risk when she started to feel the full effects of the wound. Instead, she said, "I need to get back to my home too. The potion I used for pain is starting to wear off, and I will be of little use if I am in agony."

Lalfar gave her a hard look, clearly reluctant to give up the chase. "Very well," he said at last.

They headed back to Kindiski in silence. When they reached the edge of the trees near the town, Anike said, "You will have to help me from here. I cannot use witchcraft to move while anyone else can see me."

Lalfar nodded, so she landed and draped an arm around his shoulders. As they limped across the fields towards the town, a rumble sounded in the hills behind them. It was unlikely to be a coincidence, but Anike was not sure what it portended.

They attracted more than passing glances as they made their way across the fields. Farmers paused in their work and exchanged words and grim looks, perhaps about Anike's state or even wondering what had happened to Enya. When they reached the edge of wood town, Anike hailed a young man and sent him off at a run to bring the arl to her house. She needed to go home and treat her injuries but wanted Rek to hear of the threat to his domain directly from her as soon as possible.

Her strength was waning when they finally reached her home. Once inside, she stripped off her rune-covered sleeves and cloak and bundled them under her bed. Lalfar bound some cloth around her staff to hide the runes while she applied salves from her store to her leg and side. As the elixirs started to do her work, she lay back, feeling bones re-knit and her flesh heal. Tiredness overwhelmed her and she wished she had found the time to brew the potion to defer fatigue that Enya had asked her to make. She closed her eyes and let the darkness take her.

Hammering on the door jolted her back to consciousness. The arl, with Gunnar at his heels, did not wait for the door to be opened and flung it wide before she finished sitting up. "Anike, are you safe?" he almost shouted. On seeing her nod, his tone changed from anxiety to exasperation. "What possessed you to go out of the town again?"

She struggled to recover her equilibrium. "I needed herbs. That is not important. What matters is that there are dwarves in the hills and they have taken Enya."

"Dwarves? You can't be serious. There have been no dwarves on the surface for hundreds of years. If they still live, it is deep underground."

"Rek, listen to me. I am quite serious," Anike said quietly but firmly. Even the few minutes of rest under the influence of her elixirs had helped her, but at that moment she had no patience for honorifics.

"Where is Lalfar's sister?" Rek ignored her comment.

"Enya," Anike reminded him. "As I said, the dwarves took her."

"We were attacked by a man with a greatsword, lord," Lalfar put in.

"It was the same man Gunnar fought yesterday," Anike added. "Together we brought him down, but then the dwarves attacked and took both him and Enya."

"I knew you could beat him again," Gunnar said excitedly.

Rek silenced him with a wave and looked at Lalfar. "You say the attackers were dwarves too? Not brigands?"

"Well, I didn't actually see them, my lord, but I believe Anike. I lost consciousness just as she hit the warrior with her staff. That must have knocked him out, but when I came to, she was covered in blood and her leg was broken."

Anike was glad that Lalfar could think on his feet, but his trade was telling plausible stories.

"You didn't see them?" Rek persisted.

"Not as such." Lalfar shrugged.

Rek was having more trouble with the concept of dwarves than Lalfar had, so Anike tried a different tack. "You can see the blood. Someone attacked us, and even if I am mistaken and it was only the witch's men, they have still taken Enya and we have to get her back."

Rek looked at her, taking in the set of her features and the blood on her clothes, then nodded. "You can't be right about the abductors being dwarves, but I have a duty to my guests. I must answer attacks on those under my protection with the sword. Are you fit to travel, Anike? I want you to show me where all this took place."

"Yes. I just need a little rest, but I can do that while you are gathering a war party. Lalfar, I suggest you get your shield."

Rek looked at her, his expression now a mixture of worry, curiosity and admiration. "You have certainly made my life more exciting these last few days, Anike."

She smiled weakly. "Wrong place at the wrong time, my lord. It happens."

"Or is this the will of the gods, I wonder? Come on, Gunnar."

When he had led Gunnar and Lalfar out of the house, Anike lay back and let her eyes close again. If they were lucky, it would not be hard for a skilled tracker to follow the dwarves and they would find them on the open slopes of the high hills where Rek's men would be able to overwhelm them. Having seen their strength and resilience, and the strange weapons they carried, Anike knew that the dwarves were a match for many times their number of men but history told that when faced with a serious human rebellion, they had retreated underground rather than fight to the death. If the odds were too great, they might withdraw and Rek would not then need to fight them to free Enya.

At least that was her hope. As she could not use witchcraft in front of Rek, she would not be able to help, though nothing she had done had been that effective against the dwarves in any event. She had not created spells to fight such beings, and while she had some that might be more useful in her book, she would be very happy to have a group of armed men with her. There was certainly no time to devise anything new now.

Anike opened her eyes again. While she was not fully recovered, she was too much on edge to rest any more. She pulled her blood-soaked clothes off and dropped them in a bucket of water. Her skin had been healed by her elixirs, but she had to wash the dried blood off before changing into clean clothes. Wearing fresh garb made her feel better.

Still troubled by how easily the dwarves had defeated her, she tried to recover her equanimity. Her pride, and her confidence that her witchcraft would prevail against any foe, were dented. She thought she could have beaten the man in black alone and he certainly had not overwhelmed her as the dwarves had done. If this was now the measure of her enemies, she would need more power in the future.

The demon seemed to respond with pleasure to that thought, and she frowned as she remembered that Olaf, her former master in herbcraft, had warned her against such temptation – just before he had betrayed her out of fear of what she might become.

Olaf's fear had only been speculation, but the dwarves were real and she lacked the power to succeed against them alone. She had to hope that her wits and the men the arl gathered would be enough.

With her knife in her belt and her cloak wrapped around her, she took up her staff and went out to meet Rek.

He had gathered a warband at the arlberg over a dozen strong. There were warriors she recognised and hunters, not all familiar to her, but she was pleased to see that they were heavily armed with blade and bow. Rek was in ringmail now, a sword by his side. Anike was relieved to see that Gunnar was not one of the group. Lalfar stood with them with his shield slung on his back and the axe hanging at his belt. He smiled at her as she walked towards them.

Taking a place next to Rek at the front of the warband, she led them up through the woods to the little valley where the dwarves had attacked. The ground was muddy, but the rain had not managed to wash away all the blood that had been spilt there.

She pointed up the hill. "The dwarves left that way, but the fight was here."

One of the hunters bent to the ground and picked up a small object. He showed it to Rek. Anike could see it was a perfectly round ball of metal, about the width of a thumb, partly covered in a dark red substance.

"Strange," Rek said to the hunter. "Have you seen one of these before?" The hunter shook his head.

"This is what they shot at me," Anike said. Trying to judge the trajectory, she added, "This is the one that broke my leg, I think."

"It does have blood on it," Rek said, "like a good sling shot, but made of steel. Heavy." He turned to Anike. "What sort of weapon did they use?"

"I have never seen anything quite like it. It looked like a small powerful bow set on a heavy haft, and it shot these through a tube. However it worked, these balls flew so fast you could barely see them. The dwarves reloaded it by pulling a handle, faster than you could get a new stone into a sling."

"We will be cautious, then," said Rek.

"Do you believe me about the dwarves now?" Anike asked, hoping he was not underestimating the threat.

"Whoever attacked you was using very unusual weapons, and that makes them dangerous," Rek replied. "We will find out if they are really dwarves when we catch them."

"This way, my lord," said one of the hunters. "You can still make out some of the footprints. Someone heavy and in hard boots, I judge."

"Good, Ulfrik," Rek said. "Lead on."

The hunters nocked arrows, and the warriors readied shields and war darts as they moved up the hill. Ulfrik reached the place where Anike's lightning had struck. "Some sort of fire was set here," he said.

Rek looked at Anike.

She had been expecting this query and had a lie ready. "One of the dwarves was carrying Enya and the warrior, and the other one stopped here to strike his axe and shield together. Sparks flew off and landed on the ground. I could not say what he was doing, but afterwards he just set off again."

Rek frowned, then nodded to Ulfrik.

The war band followed up through the forest as the hunters moved steadily forward, occasionally conferring with each other as the trail led over harder ground. When they emerged from the trees, it was a few hundred paces west of where Anike and Lalfar had been earlier.

They halted and Rek looked questioningly at Anike. "I have no idea which way," she said in response to his implicit inquiry.

"The ground is poor for tracks here, my lord," said one of the hunters.

"Do your best," Rek told him.

The hunters spread out. "There is something here," another called. "It looks like a fresh scrape of metal on the rock."

"Heading for that corrie, I would say," Ulfrik said, pointing at a bowl-like depression in the mountainside at the head of a small valley.

"Then that is where we shall go," Rek decided.

The hunters scouted ahead again, picking up occasional signs of the dwarves' passage, with the warriors following behind with Anike and Lalfar.

Cresting a small rise, they looked down into the corrie. Anike remembered it from when she first arrived in Kindiski and had surveyed the area for the best places to find herbs, but it had changed dramatically. An overhang on one of the steep sides of the ravine had collapsed and the fallen rock covered much of the bowl near the steep mountainside at the far end.

"That is a fresh rock fall," one of the hunters said. "I was here last week and the cliff on that side of the valley looked stable."

"We heard something as we came back towards the town. Remember, Anike?" Lalfar said.

Anike nodded, recalling the rumble from the mountains behind them. Her demon had become a little more agitated as they approached the rockfall, though not so much as when the witch had attacked. She thought it likely that it was sensing him not too far away, and if he were alive, Enya probably was too.

"It looks like the trail goes up to that fall," Ulfrik said. "Either they are buried beneath it, or they crossed over it to hide their passage. If they did that, the trail should continue somewhere else."

He turned to the other hunters. "Spread out," he said, and they went to examine the ground around the edge of the rockfall. Lalfar paced anxiously as he waited.

The hunters reformed into a small group and spoke to each other quietly, and then Ulfrik came over. "Nothing," he said.

"There are no signs of any bodies," Rek said to Lalfar, in a tone Anike assumed was meant to be reassuring. "Even if they had been right up against the cliff, they would probably have been able to get away, or at least to the side, and we would see some trace of them. They must have come to this area after the rocks fell and used them to disguise their trail."

Anike was not convinced. One of those they were following was a witch with power over stone, and this fall seemed too much of a coincidence. "Were there any caves here?" she asked. She could not recall any, but she might have missed a small grotto, particularly if it had been behind bushes. "They might have taken refuge inside."

"No, nothing like that," Ulfrik told her, then to Rek he said, "I think you are right, my lord. We will look again."

While the hunters scoured the edge of the rockfall, Anike went up to it and climbed over the lower rock. Ignoring the arl's warning to be careful lest she dislodge the slide again, she poked through the rubble. Close to the top, she found one end of what looked like a thick bar made of stone, very smooth, and almost a perfect cylinder. It did not look natural. It was buried beneath several large rocks, far too heavy to shift, so she left it and went back to the others. "I thought I saw something, but it was just stone," she said to Rek though she was sure that the bar had been formed with witchcraft and suggested that the rock fall had been caused on purpose.

A quarter of an hour later, the hunters came back and Ulfrik reported, "My lord, we cannot find any sign of an onward trail. With the rain and all the disturbance from the rocks, I think we have lost them. I am sorry."

"I know you did your best." Rek nodded to him, then turned to Lalfar. "I will send riders to the nearby towns. We will not give up on your sister. Someone will have seen her, and we will get her back."

Lalfar managed to nod, though his face was set with pain and worry. "Thank you, my lord."

Anike understood how the arl had come to his conclusions and to voice her disagreement would have given too much away. If the dwarves had gone through an entrance disguised as a cliff wall and had not wanted anyone to follow, they could have had the law witch warp the rocks and bring down the overhang. The stone bar did not seem necessary but could have served some purpose in that scheme.

"Come," said the arl. "There is nothing else we can do here."

As they crossed the fields, Anike leaned into Lalfar and whispered, "Can you come back to my house? I have an idea."

"I have to go with the arl first, to make sure that the riders have a good description of Enya and the witch who attacked us, but I will join you as soon as I can."

Pleading fatigue, Anike took her leave of Rek when they entered the wood town and returned to her home. It took her a while to clear away the mess that the day's events had left, and she had only just finished when Lalfar knocked on the door. As soon as he had closed it behind him, she got out her bag of runes.

"What are you going to do with those?" he asked.

"I am going to try to find out where Enya has gone."

"Isn't it bad luck to perform divination?" asked Lalfar.

"It can be, but I do not see any alternative, and there are ways to mitigate the consequences by sacrifice." She laid the hide map out on the table. "I think that the dwarves went down a passage under that rock fall."

"If you are right, how does that help us? It will take dozens of men to clear those rocks, and the hunters said there was no cave there anyway."

"The entrance would have been dwarf-wrought, designed to look like the cliff, and probably overgrown by now too. If we could get to it, I could break through, but I have no idea where to look. Still, there are many entrances to Svartalfheim, and there is likely to be one we can find much more easily."

Lalfar looked puzzled. "Where?"

"First, let us be sure we need to go to the dwarf realm." She drew her knife. "I will need a blood sacrifice." Lalfar bared his forearm, but Anike shook her head and drew back her own sleeve.

Lalfar looked surprised. "Shouldn't I be the one to make the sacrifice?"

"You could, but as Enya means more to you than she does to me, the price of an answer to you will be higher. It is better that I ask." She opened the bag of runes.

"Runecasting is not witchcraft, is it? I have met seers before, and no one called them witches."

"No, not witchcraft, but it is related. Runes are a link to the true way to see the world and can be used to understand it but to change it needs witchcraft. It took a while for me to work all this out by myself. If there are loremasters of witchcraft, I have not heard of them."

She shook the bag. "The dwarves need Enya alive, or they would have killed her already. Let us go to the heart of the issue," she said, closing her eyes to concentrate.

"What route do Enya's captors intend to take to reach the final place they want her to be?" she said aloud and plunged her hand into the bag. She scattered a dozen stones on the rune map, opened her eyes and leant forward over them. "Can you read them at all?" she asked Lalfar.

"Not really," he replied, a little warily.

"This is not the clearest reading, and even I cannot be absolutely sure of the meaning," she admitted. "I think that is because it is referring to something I have no knowledge of. As best as I can work out, it says 'Enya is to be taken through Svartalfheim, past farm, ancient peril and craft to where the great ice waits'. Some of the images may be allegories, but it is clear that she has been taken underground."

"So we go back to the rockfall?"

"Only if we have to. It would be easier to use the other entrance."

"You mentioned there could be others. Where do you think the closest one is?"

"It should be in the arl's hall," Anike told him.

- 8 -

THE STONE SHATTERS

"Where in the hall? How do you know about it?" Lalfar asked.

"Someone once told me that the dwarves made passages to the arls' halls that they built. Kindiski has a particularly good selection of dwarven records from the time of the Occupation. I found a passing reference to a tunnel months ago, but I gave it little thought as the dwarves closed all the ways to Svartalfheim. It is probably in the main hall, but it will be sealed with stone."

"Let's go then."

Anike frowned. "We need to know the exact location of the entrance. It should be in the records, and my friend Nangar may know it already." Her eyes widened as a thought struck her. "There is something else there I want to re-read as well."

She was thinking about the potion used against the dwarves to drive them from the surface, an entry that she had previously considered just a historical curiosity. It was a great stroke of fortune that she had come across it the day before, so blatant a coincidence that she wondered if it was a price paid by someone else for their own reading of the runes, perhaps even the dwarves themselves. If so, she would be foolish not to take advantage of the opportunity.

With that thought, she remembered the sacrifice for her own cast and drew the knife over her forearm, then crossed to a bucket and let the blood drip into it. She winced against the pain before finding another salve to apply to the wound.

As the flesh healed, Lalfar said, "Why not just sacrifice the elixir?"

"The pain and blood are a greater sacrifice," Anike told him. "Even though I can cure them, they are worth more than just the loss of a potion. It is quite possible that acting on this particular answer will be a great enough price in itself but I am erring on the side of caution as I used the runes yesterday too."

"Will the arl let us use the entrance? Or even come with us?"

"He may not even know about it. I suspect the seal is very solid and I will need to destroy part of the floor to access it. That will shout 'witchcraft' for all the world to see."

She went to the door, then hesitated. The enormity of what they were about to attempt was becoming more real to her with every passing moment. For the sake of someone she had met the day before, she was trying to find a way to pursue two beings who had nearly killed her onto their home ground.

Lalfar looked at her. "You aren't having second thoughts about going after Enya, are you?"

"You were unconscious when the dwarves attacked. I have never seen anything like them. Of course I am questioning whether we should be doing this without help."

"By the time the arl believes you, it will be far too late. I am going after her, and you have to help me. If you don't, I will tell the arl about you being a witch."

Anike withdrew her hand from the door and turned sharply to him. "You gave your word not to do that."

Lalfar folded his arms. "And you agreed to help Enya."

Anike stared at him. He was clearly getting desperate. She could understand a brother's love for his sister and a desire to do anything to protect her. Enya had told her that Lalfar was a gambler, and trying to blackmail her was a high-risk strategy. She felt an urge well up inside her, a desire to destroy him to remove this threat, but she recognised the demon's touch.

She was worried about what the arl would say, but Lalfar had been right before when he said that Rek would believe her over him. Probably. It was more of a risk for him as if he did, he would lose any chance that she would help him. He could not afford that, though she did not dismiss the possibility that he would act out of anger or spite. Threatening her showed how far he might go.

The threat was real, but it was not the true issue. She had exposed Enya to the demon, then to the threats from the witch and the dwarves and let her be taken. She was responsible and she would not rest easily until she had tried to put those failures right.

"There is truth in that," she said. "I did agree to help Enya and she does still need it. We will go after her, but I need to check the archives first. Come on."

"Thank you. I knew you were a good person really. I wouldn't actually have told the arl, obviously."

Anike snorted. She had the sense that Lalfar would say almost anything and his retraction carried little weight. Still, his desire to help his sister seemed genuine and she would not have wanted to go to Svartalfheim alone.

As she led Lalfar up the hill, she wondered if she might have been overestimating the danger. While the two on the surface had attacked her without warning, history told that dwarves were not always ruthless, and they had not killed the law witch. They had ruled firmly but had not massacred the human population. It might well be that the dwarves they could come across would not be particularly hostile, and a single human was not much of a threat.

She was not a normal human though. The demon allowed her to sense dwarves and that would give them a chance to avoid contact. While she had not focused on using witchcraft in battle, she had devised some spells she had not had with her when the dwarves had struck. One would destroy weapons in the hands of her foes, created in anticipation of a time that she was named as a witch, and it would be particularly useful against the dwarves. The expedition would be dangerous, but it was not suicide.

Trying to put the blackmail attempt behind her, Anike took Lalfar to the archive hall. She had hoped Nangar would be there, but the chamber was silent so she walked down a row between piles of ledgers until they reached the area where he spent much of his time studying the dwarven principles of construction. Dwarven plans of the arlberg lay amongst these records. She assumed that long ago the arls had commanded the area from a wooden structure on the hill, but the dwarves had replaced it with stone.

"I had never been sure that the dwarves abandoned their designs for Midgard entirely," she said to Lalfar, trying to move on from his attempt at manipulation. "They could have destroyed the archive easily enough and if they had no intention of reclaiming the surface, I am sure they would have done so."

She set Lalfar to look for plans, something he could do without needing to read the dwarven language, while she concentrated on written accounts.

Ten minutes later, Lalfar waved a diagram at her triumphantly and she went over to look at what he had found. Sure enough, it showed a long shaft leading straight down from the arl's hall. It appeared to emerge just behind where the throne now sat and at the bottom of the shaft was a single word in dwarven, 'Home.'

"It does come out in the hall," Lalfar said. "You were right. It must be sealed or people would fall into it."

"I have never noticed that part looking any different," Anike mused, "but I wasn't looking for an entrance. Rek may well not know it is there. He will want to get Enya back, but I doubt that he will be willing to break through the stone floor on my say so. We will be on our own, I think. Can you go to the hall and see if there is anything which indicates an entrance? I would prefer not to have to tear up the entire floor to find it — we might as well go back to the rockfall if I have to do that."

"Tear up the floor?"

"I have a spell to destroy stone," Anike told him, "but it only works on quite small areas." She had created the spell to destroy stone tiles on the roof of another arl's hall so she could rescue her father. "I do not know how large the seal is but it must be several feet thick, at least. Try looking for a stone that does not quite match those around it."

"Aren't you coming too?"

"Before we go, there is something else here that I need. I will meet you at my house."

"Very well," said Lalfar. "This had better work. We have spent a lot of time here." With that, he left.

His tone did little to reassure her that he would be a good companion on this journey. It might have been all desperation and anxiety, but she suspected there was a very self-centred core to the man. However, he was motivated to find Enya and even his company would almost certainly better than none.

Recalling the notes of the dwarven retreat from the surface she had found the day before, Anike dug out those scrolls again. Not dwelling on the history this time, she went straight to the list of ingredients. It seemed that whoever had written the start of the record had found where the potions were made and listed most of what he had found. In places, annotations in another hand suggested that a herbalist had worked on devising a counter and had noted some proportions and antidotes.

There was enough information for her to duplicate the venom. Most of the herbs were common enough and where both names and properties were shown, the work was accurate so she had some confidence in dwarven herbcraft. The relative simplicity of the elixir may have been one reason it had been used to such great effect.

Lalfar was at her house when she returned to it. "Did you find the entrance?" she asked him.

"Yes, I did. There is a circular stone about four paces behind the throne. It's a slightly lighter grey than the ones around it and quite a lot bigger, nearly two paces across. It feels completely solid and would be easy to overlook. There is no way of opening it that I could see."

"There would be no reason for the dwarves to make it accessible from the surface," Anike commented. "Did the arl ask what you were doing?"

"He wasn't there. The hall seemed a little quiet."

"Odd, but maybe he was looking at the town's defences."

"Perhaps. As it is less busy, we should go now."

Anike considered. She doubted that it would be easy to penetrate the seal and expected to have to cast her spell several times before she could open the route to Svartalfheim. It would be safer to wait for night but if the hall were quiet now it would mean losing far less time.

"Yes," she decided. "I just need to gather some things."

She opened her satchel. "Hold this," she told Lalfar and dropped in bandages, jars, her small cauldron and other tools of her herbcraft. "I will sort it out once we are in Svartalfheim." She went to her herbs, selecting the ones she needed for the dwarf-weakening elixir first then, with a shrug, wrapped most of her stock in small squares of cloth and put them into her bag. It was more than likely that she would need to brew more potions before they were finished but there had to be some water in Svartalfheim.

Then she opened the chest and took out a book, pages of vellum she had sewn together on which she had recorded all the spells she had devised. It went into the bag with her slate, chalk and runestones.

Having checked that the spearhead was still in her satchel, she pulled out her mother's leather armour. She had not worn it in over a year and it took a few moments to put on. She was a little slimmer than her mother had been, but she had re-fixed the bindings and it fitted her well enough.

She picked up her staff and turned to Lalfar. "We can collect your gear when we go through the hall."

They set out towards the arlberg. Lalfar's pace quickened as if the knowledge that they were finally on their way had galvanised him. Anike's own emotions were mixed – she was apprehensive at the thought of invading the domain of an ancient race which had ruled the surface for centuries, two members of which had defeated her so easily.

But the desire to purge her guilt over what she had allowed to happen to Enya tugged her onwards, and there was something else too, the pull of anticipation about what she might learn in Svartalfheim. Even the remote possibility of discovering the origins of witches or unravelling some of the mysteries of the dwarves attracted her. They had made Thor's hammer, Mjolnir, and other powerful artifacts. While it was unlikely they would share their lore with a human, she could always hope. They could have been cooperating with the law witch over Enya's abduction so it was possible they would treat with humans and that might give her a chance to learn more.

The hall was quiet when they arrived with a few thralls preparing the evening meal under the stern gaze of Wulfnar. There was no sign of Arl Rek or any of the men who had come with them to find the dwarves' trail. Shrugging, Anike went into the hall, Lalfar at her side.

While he gathered his gear, she walked to the area behind the throne, a fair-sized section of the hall where the arl kept some of his more valued possessions, more like another room than a recess. The hides of powerful beasts, tapestries and half a dozen large carved wooden figures of gods were set neatly by the far wall.

Now she knew where the portal stone was, Anike was able to make it out. It was larger, slightly paler and set a little higher than the flagstones around it, though centuries of use had worn the edges down to smooth slopes. It seemed almost as if it was fused to the adjacent stone, or the mortar was so closely matched as to be indistinguishable from it. She doubted Rek knew there was a passage beneath.

When Lalfar came up to her, she said, "Can you cause a distraction? Perhaps recite some poetry? I need to set up a screen to hide what I am doing. That will be rather obvious, so it would be good if you could keep everyone's attention on you."

Lalfar smiled, nodded and went over to Wulfnar. "You don't mind if I practice?" he asked.

Wulfnar shook his head, and Lalfar found a place well away from the throne and cleared his throat. He started to recite a tale about the hero Sigurd and a dragon, and people paused in their work to listen and stare.

Anike lifted a couple of the wooden figures of gods, Vali and Idun she noted absently, and placed them between her and the throne then hung a light trophy hide between them. Hidden from casual glances, she opened her book to the spell she needed, laid a hand on the seal and spoke *"Prana,"* as she read the pattern. The top two inches of the stone turned to dust, and the spell scattered it over the floor towards the back wall. The lighter grey of the sealing block continued down. She tapped the stone but there was no hollow echo to indicate that she was close to breaking through.

She suddenly became aware of the silence. Lalfar had stopped his recitation, and she lifted her head to look about her. Over the hide, she saw that Arl Rek and his retinue had entered the hall.

Gunnar was at Rek's side. "Anike!" the boy cried and started forward but came to a halt when his father gripped his shoulder.

"What are you doing, Anike?" the arl asked as he walked towards her, his voice sounding puzzled but with a distinct undercurrent of suspicion.

Berating herself for not having waited until the night, Anike stood up and wondered how to navigate the situation. She saw Lalfar, trying to be unobtrusive, edge his way towards her, but put him out of her mind. It was too late to come up with a convincing cover story, so she simply said "I was looking for a way to get to Svartalfheim. The records show that there is one under the floor here."

Rek stopped in surprise. "The dwarves again? I considered you were mistaken before, but now I think you are lying to me. Gunnar took me to where the warrior-witch first appeared. Would you like to know what I found, both there and where Enya was taken?"

"Blood?" hazarded Anike, not liking his tone. She had a sense of deja vu, a man who had courted her discovering her secret and turning on her. She shivered at the recollection but used the moment to open her cloak a little so she could see the pattern on the inside.

"Scorch marks," Rek told her. "Blood as well, but I was expecting that. The ground was charred around where Gunnar fought the witch, just like the place that you said the dwarf struck sparks from his weapons. My son told me he thought he had seen lightning strike the man, but you persuaded him he was mistaken. I also found singed leather, once part of some armour, near the bloodstains where Enya was taken."

Anike regarded him steadily, waiting for him to finish. Lalfar was now behind the throne as well.

"Do you have anything you want to tell me, Anike?" Rek asked, his eyes narrowing.

It could have been worse. There might still be a way out of this. "My lord," she said, voice calm while her mind raced. "I have made oils that burn, and I carry these for self-defence. I threw one at the witch when he was fighting Gunnar and used my last while he was fighting Lalfar. The elixir is really made to coat blades, but it will burn for a while even without being applied to metal."

Rek's expression did not change. "Why did you not tell me this before?"

"It was not that important."

"Really? At first Gunnar seemed very excited when we found the scorch marks, but then went strangely quiet."

"But Anike," Gunnar put in. "You said I had imagined the lightning because I was struck on the head. You didn't mention anything about oil."

Everyone in the hall had stopped what they were doing to watch and listen.

"I have been told before that it would avoid misunderstandings if I were more open and forthcoming from the start," Anike said, "but really it only worked as a distraction, hardly worth a mention."

"Lalfar didn't say anything about it either."

"I wasn't sure it hit him," said Lalfar quickly.

Rek's eyes flicked over to him, but he returned his attention to Anike. "I would like to believe it, but so much has happened around you recently." He took another step towards her, close enough that he could look over the screen she had set up and see the new depression in the floor. He stopped, looked at it and his face darkened.

Anike sighed. "All I wanted to do is help, Rek. First Cairn, and then Enya. Please, just let us go to Svartalfheim."

Rek was still looking at the lip in the stone, noting its size and depth. It would have taken a mason hours to carve out. "How did you do that?" His hand went to the hilt of his sword.

"Rek, just walk away. Please."

"I want to understand, Anike." The friend and suitor displaced the ruler within him for a moment then his face and voice hardened again. "I trusted you."

"Anike is a good witch!" shouted Gunnar. There were hostile murmurs in the crowd.

"That did not really help, Gunnar," Anike called out to him, "but thank you for trying."

"You haven't admitted to using witchcraft," Rek said. "Leave town now and we can put all this behind us." There were mutterings at that, but they quieted quickly.

Lalfar was looking at her. His blackmail was useless now.

There was no way she could salvage her position in the town, but she could save herself and forget about Enya, closing this chapter of her life behind her. She looked between Lalfar and Rek, and at the emotions playing over both men's faces as they waited for her decision.

Lalfar's threat had never really been significant, save that it amplified her own sense of responsibility for what had happened to Enya. She could leave town with him and find the entrance to Svartalfheim that the dwarves had used, but that could take days. Even if they caught up with the dwarves, it might be too late to save Enya. No, the only real chance to rescue her was to descend here.

She either had to abandon the young woman with a demon inside her, kidnapped and held by unseen enemies of humanity or she could confirm to the town that she was a witch.

"I am sorry, Rek," Anike said sadly. "I thank you for that generous offer, but I cannot abandon Enya. Please do not try to stop me."

"I will not allow you to use witchcraft, Anike," said Rek and stepped forward, starting to draw his sword.

Anike lifted her cloak. "*Agni*," she said. Regret tinged her voice, but she pronounced the rune clearly, reading the pattern on the lining of the cloak. Smoke filled the room before her, created and held in the air by the spell, looming like an iceberg just beyond Lalfar.

Cries of alarm rang throughout the hall, but amidst the voices were the sounds of weapons being drawn. Lalfar, who had seen witchcraft several times that day, recovered the most quickly. He pulled over Rek's throne and shoved it hard into the smoke. Anike heard a loud curse as someone stumbled into it.

"Everyone get back," Rek shouted. "Gunnar, stand where you are. Do nothing. I won't have you taking any risks."

Anike flipped over another page in the book. "Do not panic," she told Lalfar. "This is not real. *Agni.*" A figure made of pale white flame appeared before them, a semblance of a human, looking as she imagined a ghost would.

Despite the warning, Lalfar took a step back. "You command the dead?" he said in an awed tone.

The image flickered, moving slightly from side to side with its arms raised. The fear of the unquiet dead was deep-rooted both in myth and history. Mothers frightened unruly children with tales of the draugr, walking corpses, and of the ghosts that had fought against the gods at Ragnarok. The terror of being trapped beyond the grave in Midgard and never reaching Valhalla cowed many stout warriors. Witchcraft was frightening, but the living dead were worse.

"I told you. It is just an image. Now let me concentrate." She turned back to her previous page, pressed her hand to the stone again and said *"Prana."* The spell disintegrated the rock and this time she willed the shower of stone dust into the smoke, adding to the confusion.

A warrior, axe in hand and wiping his eyes, stumbled out of the smoke and saw the foxfire shape. He screamed once, then turned and fled back into the haze. "The witch has raised a ghost! The dead have risen!" he shouted, his panic cutting through the general hubbub.

Anike reached down into the depression she had created and spoke again. *"Prana,"* she said to the stone for the third time, concentrating on making a much narrower but deeper hole. This time some of the dust fell away out of sight. The stone plug ended about five feet beneath floor level. There clearly was a chamber or passage beneath.

Another warrior emerged from the smoke and stopped on seeing the apparition, mouth open. Lalfar gave him a hard shove and he fell back. The crash told her that he had tripped over the upended throne.

"They will be on us in a moment," Lalfar called. "Can't you stop them?"

"There are limits to what I can do without hurting anyone, Lalfar. Duck down." She lifted her cloak. "*Agni*," she said again, this time creating a cloud of smoke that covered the area behind the throne but suspended three feet above the floor. The pale fire of the ghost figure cast an eerie glow through the murk. Crouching on the ground, they could still see a little, but anyone on their feet would not be able to make out anything through the smoke.

She turned to a different spell in her book. "*Prana*," she said again. A crack formed in a perfect circle in the stone as her witchcraft disintegrated the outer edge of a cylinder, allowing almost half of the sealing stone to fall away. There was a brief silence, followed by a tremendous crash as it struck something far beneath. In the gloom caused by her smoke, Anike could just see a metal ladder set into the wall beneath the stone seal.

Then the spell creating the seeming ghost expired and the figure vanished, taking with it the light she needed to read her spells. Lalfar crouched down beside her and the feathers from his hat brushed against her face, giving her an idea. She reached out and plucked one while bringing to mind a spell simple enough for her to visualise the complete pattern without it being written in front of her. "*Agni*," she said again and surrounded the feather with a nimbus of pale flames.

"I will climb down first," Lalfar called and put his legs through the gap before Anike could stop him. He deftly pressed his hands against the sides of the hole and let himself down until he was able to reach the topmost rung with his feet.

There was the sound of heavy steps coming towards her through the hall, more than one person. Anike looked down to see Lalfar starting to climb down the metal ladder. "Beware the hole, Rek!" she called out at the approaching boots, which paused for a second before coming on again.

Dropping her staff through the gap, she concentrated and visualised the rune pattern for her levitation spell. "*Prana*," she said and willed herself to drift down to the top of the ladder.

She had only climbed down a few rungs when a voice came down to her. "Anike, wait! What have you done?" Rek cried out as his face appeared above her, lit by the pale witchlight from the feather. He was on his hands and knees, crawling beneath the smoke, but he had a sword in one hand.

"What I had to do, Rek. Delay would have meant losing Enya."

"You have devastated my hall!"

"There was no other way. I am sorry."

"You do not make those decisions, Anike. You defied me to my face."

The smoke above Rek cleared suddenly as the spell expired and he looked up. As he did so, Anike let go of the ladder, relying on her spell to hold her up, and opened her book again.

"Even arls don't know everything, Rek, and sometimes we have to act in accordance with our consciences. If anyone was hurt, I am sorry."

She concentrated carefully on where she would cast her next spell and read the pattern. "*Prana*," she said with resignation, and the spell cut through the stone side of the well, slanting down steeply from the floor of the hall. The large piece she severed slid down at an angle into the entrance of the well under its own weight, coming to a halt inches above her head and obstructing the narrow way. The well was not sealed but the remaining gap was too small for anyone to pass through.

She let the witchlight feather fall. "Goodbye, Rek. I really do wish things had been different."

"Anike!" Rek called one last time, but she ignored him as she climbed down the ladder.

The feather had come to rest on a stone floor almost fifty paces below. In its light, Lalfar was looking about him with a puzzled expression. "There is no way out," he said.

Up above, the arl was calling for ropes.

"There has to be," Anike told him, examining the chamber. The shattered fragments of the slab that had fallen from above lay on a smooth stone floor but there was no sign of an exit. The dwarves must have sealed the lower end of the shaft too.

She considered. Anyone coming up the passage to reach the ladder would most likely expect it to be in front of them. "It should be this way," she told Lalfar and looked at the wall more carefully. Sure enough, when she brought the feather close, she could see a very slight depression in an arch shape.

She put her hand on the stone and disintegrated a hole a foot deep. "I was right – this stone is slightly different from the side of the shaft," she said.

There was a grinding noise from above as Rek and his men tried to shift the stone that she had dropped into place at the top of the well.

"Can you stop them?" asked Lalfar, looking up.

"They are not coming down yet," Anike said. "I will try to cut through before they get to us. *Prana.*"

The hole deepened but Anike could still not see the far side. "The dwarves definitely did not want humans following," she muttered, and cast the spell again, turning a longer, thinner cylinder to dust.

This time there was a breath of air from the other end of the hole. In relief, Anike used the other spell to cut a crack, angled downwards from just over her head. It bore out a cylinder that fell away into the passage beyond with a loud grinding sound. "Go on," she said, looking upward to check on Rek's progress.

There was a different scraping noise, then a loud clunk as the stone she had used to block the well was lifted away.

Lalfar disappeared through the gap, and she threw her staff after him before climbing through herself.

She found herself in a very well-worked passage, wide and arching above her. There was no time to admire it. Looking back, she focused on the roof area. "*Prana,*" she said once more, sheering off the stone above the hole she had created. A slab dropped from the ceiling with a crash, barring the way. She could see flickers of torchlight around the edges of the stone but it was wedged in tightly and the gaps were too small for a man to get through. She doubted Rek would be able to follow for many hours.

Satisfied, she turned to take her first step into Svartalfheim.

IMPRISONMENT

By the witchlight surrounding her hand, Anike could see a passage extending ahead of them. The walls were smooth, so finely carved that she could not see any tool marks and just above her head they started to arch together to meet about ten feet from the ground.

The light died. Lalfar said "I can't see. Create some more light, Anike."

Anike ignored the peremptory tone but as she concentrated on the rune pattern to conjure light, she noticed that they were not standing in pitch darkness. Subdued illumination was coming from widely spaced stones in the wall, enough to see a little.

"Look carefully," she told Lalfar. "These are glowstones, I think." She went to the nearest one. It was cold to her touch but brightened as it drew heat from her hand, casting a stronger light. "Yes, I thought we would see these." She recalled another beautifully carved cave with such stones set in the walls, drinking in light and heat during the day and giving comfort during the night to an old woman caught up in the turmoil she had brought with her.

"You know a lot, it would seem," Lalfar said.

"Just fragments of lore," Anike replied. "Let us see if these will glow brighter." She cast a simple spell to heat small objects on the stone.

Instantly, the light flared into a dazzling blaze, throwing the passage around them into sharp relief. A face appeared on the wall, and Anike recoiled before she realised that it was just a bas relief she had not seen in the dimmer light. An exquisitely carved bearded visage, too bleak and craggy to be human, looked out at her and beneath it were characters in dwarven script.

"Baran, Governor of *Dangat*, called Kindiski by humans," she read. "This is him, I suppose. There are some numbers underneath too, 410 and 720."

"There is another one," Lalfar said from a little further down the passageway.

Anike came to stand next to him. "This one is Grang. It also says Governor. The numbers beneath are 8 and 410." She looked further down. "There is one more, Orban, with 1 and 8."

"Do you suppose the numbers are years?" Lalfar asked. "Telling of the duration of their rule?"

"Perhaps. Dwarves were supposed to live all but forever, so hundreds of years as a governor might be possible. If this is what these carvings are saying, it looks as if these three ran Kindiski for centuries. How long did the Occupation last?"

"About eight hundred years, I think," Lalfar said.

Anike was about to comment further when the sound of voices reached their ears from behind them. Arl Rek had to have reached the bottom of the shaft. She looked again at the stone she had dropped into place. There was no way a grown man could get through any of the gaps, but Lalfar said, "Let's get out of here."

"Only one way to go," Anike noted. "We will take one of the glowstones with us, though." She opened her book of spells and read the pattern, concentrating on the wall around the glowstone. "*Prana*," she said aloud, and the normal stone surrounding the glowing cube crumbled to dust. She caught the glowstone as it fell forwards and handed it to Lalfar. It illuminated the passage clearly, and once he had a firm grip on it, he set off at a trot.

"Not so fast," Anike called after him. "We have no idea what is waiting for us."

Lalfar looked back, frustration written on his face. "As you said, there is only one way," he pointed out.

"I do not want to miss anything important. We know very little about Svartalfheim and we should be cautious."

"We have waited long enough. Come on!" Lalfar set off again with the glowstone held high, but he pulled his shield from his back and slid it onto his left arm.

Anike cut another glowstone from the wall and let its cold surface rest in her hand. The demon always struggled against being bound again after each spell but it seemed less vigorous here and her best interpretation of its mood was that of sullen resentment or apprehension. She supposed the presence of stone all around her was affecting it, though whether that would be good or bad was not yet clear. It had a tendency to strike out against structures it considered law-aligned.

She hastened after Lalfar, still just able to make out the glow that marked his presence. He was being rash, and she wondered if he was trying to mask fear. She hoped he would not crack under the pressure placed on him over the last day. It would take a strong will to stand firm in the face of what he had been through, and she doubted everything had sunk in yet. She herself was still coming to terms with the presence of the dwarves on the surface, and that was only part of what Lalfar was going through.

It was a pity that she had burned her bridges with Arl Rek but she could live with that. His interest had been flattering her vanity a little, but she was much more concerned about no longer having access to the Hall of Records than the loss of his good regard. On the other hand, she now had an outside chance to learn from the dwarves directly, always assuming that she could find any way to do so after rescuing Enya. Remote as it was, that was an opportunity she had never imagined having. Like Lalfar, she had to adapt to changing points of reference.

Lalfar had slowed and she caught up with him perhaps two or three hundred paces from the entrance. Distance was hard to estimate but the passage was definitely sloping downhill, taking them deeper into Svartalfheim. As she drew level, he said "I think there is a turning ahead, or this passage meets another. I didn't want you having to guess which way I had gone."

"There must be many junctions. Perhaps there will be some markings or signs to indicate which way we should go, but my best guess is that we are heading roughly east. Hopefully, we will come across a trail but if there is nothing obvious, I will consult the runes."

Lalfar took the lead.

Anike became aware that the demon was more agitated than it had been a few moments before. Something here was not to its liking. "Be careful," she warned.

Lalfar paused and that gave him a few vital extra instants to react to the clatter of metal on stone. He nearly cannoned into Anike as he leapt back, narrowly avoiding the swing of an axe wielded by a dwarf who had been lurking behind the corner.

The dwarf stepped forward and swung again. Anike jumped clear as Lalfar raised his shield to catch the axe. Not a small man, Lalfar was almost knocked from his feet by the force of the blow. He took a few paces back, recovered his balance then dodged back out of reach as the dwarf stepped forward, bringing his weapon back in a vicious reverse cut.

It was obvious even from those few moves that Lalfar was no match for the dwarf. To make the outlook even grimmer, the dwarf was encased in plates of steel armour, more than tough enough to turn aside any blow from Lalfar's own axe even if the skald did manage to strike past his opponent's shield.

Wishing she had set the spearhead on it, Anike thrust her staff at the dwarf, but he did not even bother to block. The end caught him in the middle of the chest, and it was as if she had struck the wall of the passage. The shock of the impact ran up her arm. He brought the edge of his shield down onto the staff, knocking it from her grip. She retreated, keeping her eyes on him.

Lalfar jumped in, trying to bypass the dwarf's guard with a high crossways strike. The dwarf ducked beneath the blow, thrust his shield against Lalfar's and threw him a dozen feet to land on his back behind Anike.

She drew further away, past the fallen Lalfar whilst pulling out her book of spells, trying to give herself enough distance so that she would have a chance to read one of the patterns. The dwarf charged at her but staggered and came to a halt when Lalfar grabbed his leg from the floor. He cursed, regained his balance and kicked Lalfar away, then turned back to Anike. Seeing that she had her book out and was reading a spell, he threw his axe at her, just as she spoke, "*Prana!*" aiming above him.

Her spell would do nothing to stop the axe, so she tried to fling herself out of the way as it flew end over end towards her. She managed to move just enough so that instead of the blade splitting open her chest, the blunt end hammered into her instead. Her own leather armour did little to absorb the force and Anike felt her ribs break. She staggered back, gasping in pain.

With a crack, the slab that her spell had almost severed from the ceiling, weighing about a ton, tore free and fell onto the dwarf, crushing him to the ground. Only one armoured hand was visible sticking out, stretched towards her. Blinking tears from her eyes and trying pull herself together, she still managed to breathe a sigh of relief.

Then her eyes widened and she gasped as the hand was withdrawn and, very slowly, the edge of the rock started to rise.

The physical shock and pain, together with fear on seeing the dwarf survive her attack, sapped her will, weakening the demon's prison. Driven by its own hatred of the dwarf, the demon broke free of the bonds that had held it in check for so long.

Its desire for destruction overwhelmed her, pulling her weakened mind along in the current of its rage, The demon's wishes blended with hers, surrounded, distorted and magnified that part of her that desired destruction, particularly of the creature of law before her.

A complex pattern of runes formed in her mind. Expressed in runes, the demon's thoughts could change reality and it needed to do little more than decide what it wished to happen and then channel power into that desire. Her consciousness, even tethered to the demon's will, could still read those runes and understand what the demon was about to do even before it opened her mouth to say "*Agni.*"

It conjured fire into the stone beneath the dwarf, who had risen to his hands and knees despite the boulder on his back. The rock under him melted into lava and the dwarf was forced down into it by the slab of stone on his back until only the top of his helmet remained above the burning liquid. A brief shudder was all he could manage before the heat vanished and the rock re-solidified about him. The slab settled on top like an enormous grave marker and the stench of law that the demon perceived and loathed vanished.

Amongst the demon's less comprehensible thoughts, Anike thought she detected a flicker of satisfaction. Her disgust at what the demon had just done, along with the fear that it might turn on Lalfar at any moment and do the same to him, ran through her and galvanised her will. She found the strength to flood her mind with images of water and froze them to form a sphere of ice around the demon's flaming core. The demon struck at the image as it formed, trying to shatter it with flame and fury, but she focused her will and held the mental construct firm against its assault, then compressed it to hold the demon tight within. The ice solidified and she turned it into a white durable pearl. Despite her wounds and the force the demon was directing at her, her will held and completed the prison by inscribing the rune of law on the image, locking the demon away again.

Agony flooded through her body and she collapsed to the ground. The demon had very little concern over what happened to her physical form when it was in control. Even great pain did not hamper it but when she shut it away again, all of her perceptions returned in full force. Despite the waves of pain, she strengthened the confining images, reinforcing them with runes until she was sure the demon would stay contained.

Now that it was safely shut away, she realised that the agony coursing through her body was matched by guilt over allowing the demon to escape. She had managed to hold it in check for nearly two years but now she had failed and allowed it to commit an atrocity. She did not want to imagine a worse way to die than the fate it had inflicted on the dwarf.

Lalfar pushed himself to his feet. "That was incredible."

"No. That was terrible," Anike said. "You don't understand. It was my demon that melted the stone. It has been two years since I last lost control of it. It has killed people before, innocents as well as the guilty, but never as cruelly as this. It just wants to destroy, and you were nearly next." She looked at the slab of stone she had cut from the ceiling and shuddered. The movement set off new waves of torment from her ribs so she opened her bag, pulled a flask from it and ignored Lalfar while she drank it. She felt the pain ease as broken bones knitted within her and then realised that Lalfar was speaking again.

"... mean, demon?" he was asking.

She frowned. "You need to understand. A witch holds a demon inside them and it is the demon who casts the spells. Most of the time, I use runes to force it to do what I want, and only what I want, but if it seizes control as it just did, it can do what it likes. It can make my body attack someone or use its power itself, and it can make up new spells in an instant. Fortunately, it hates dwarves more than humans or it would have been you sunk into the stone."

She looked him up and down. "Enough of that. How do you fare? You took a serious blow."

"I am fine." Lalfar shook his head, then a look of horror came over his face. "You mean that Enya has one of these demons inside her too."

Yes," Anike sighed. "It will be trying to take control of her every moment of every day, and she needs to know how to fight it. It can be done – I have not lost control like that since shortly after I became a witch. Once we rescue her, I can teach her all my techniques. She should be able to control the demon after that, unless she is severely wounded, like I was just then."

"I hope so." Lalfar gestured vaguely at where the dwarf was entombed. "Was this one waiting for us, or following us, or did he just happen to be here? He didn't ask any questions, just attacked, and now we can't ask him anything."

"Waiting for someone following, I assume. We may not be able to ask him," she said, shivering as she thought about what she had done, "but we can still look for a trail. They must have come this way if they set an ambush."

Anike raised her glowstone and conjured heat into it, illuminating the passage with a bright blue-white light. Now that she had healed her injuries, the demon gave her little trouble and she was relieved that its brief release had not strengthened it.

The corridor the dwarf had been waiting in was larger than the one they had come down. There was some dwarven script on the wall near the junction. She went over to it and read '*Dangal*'. On the other side of the passage were two other words, '*Thorlan*', which was on the left, and '*Undasan*'. Given what she had just read about the dwarven governors, she assumed they were place names. On the floor were a few light scrapes suggesting that someone in metal boots had passed that way, but whatever a skilled tracker might have learned from them, they gave her no clue as to the direction the dwarves had gone.

"Nothing clear," she said. "If I tried to draw any conclusion about their route, I would just be guessing." She rummaged in her bag until she found her rune map, laid it on the ground then threw the runes onto it. Intending to draw her blood as a sacrifice, she laid her knife against her arm but Lalfar stopped her. "Take the blood from me," he said. "It's at least as valuable as yours."

"Next time," Anike said. "I promised my own blood as I cast the runes, and I have to fulfil that bargain." She drew the knife over her arm and let the blood fall onto the stone in front of her before she bound the cut, then read the cast. "We go left," she said.

SHADES OF DESIRE

The main passage was over twice the height of her head and wider than the one they had come down, more like a road than a corridor, and Anike and Lalfar made their way along it at a fast walk.

"Do you think that the dwarves are close?" Lalfar broke the silence between them.

"I doubt it. If they were nearby, someone would have come to investigate the noise of that fight."

Lalfar nodded and they walked on. The corridor started to slope down, and they followed it for about ten minutes before Lalfar spoke again. "Could you trap the dwarves in rock too, when we catch up with them?"

Anike stopped and looked at him. "It is a horrible way to die. I could probably work out a spell for that but it is not something I want to know how to do."

"You are squeamish about death?"

She shook her head. "I have seen a lot of people die. I am a healer but some are beyond my help. No, it is the cruelty of that spell. If I do have to kill, I would not want them to suffer like that."

"Well, how about just trapping their feet? Then we can run."

"That I might do. It is an idea, but I am not sure how effective it would be if the dwarf could just step away. It takes time to devise a spell, but I could look into it when we rest."

She stopped and opened her bag. "I have suffered enough for that runecast now. I do not know what exactly lies ahead but it is probably better not to face it wounded." She found an elixir, drank a little and watched the cut on her arm seal.

"Could you find Enya with witchcraft?"

Anike thought about this. "Possibly, if she was close enough. Again, I will need to work out the rune pattern for the spell." She put the flask away. "We should make some progress before we rest though."

There were no junctions in the passage, but it seemed that the temperature was rising slightly as they continued downwards. Almost imperceptibly, the light from the glowstones became stronger in response.

Without the sun or any real change in the environment, it was hard to judge how far they had walked but Anike thought it was several miles before she noticed a different texture in the darkness ahead of them, perhaps an indication that the tunnel was opening out. She pointed it out to Lalfar and they advanced more cautiously until the outline of an arch appeared out of the gloom. The light seemed to disappear into the space beyond and there was a change in the texture in the echoes of their footfalls.

Once at the threshold, Anike saw that the corridor opened into a large area, a natural cave as far as she could tell. There were no glowstones but the area was lit by faint luminescence from the heads of some of the mushroom-shaped fungi, collectively giving off just enough light for her to see the floor. The cavern was larger than the arlberg and all its buildings, and she could see neither the far end nor the roof, though the points of some stalagmites were just visible. There was a faint babble of water from somewhere within, deadened by the soft shapes of the mushrooms and moss that covered many of the rocks. Perhaps because of the presence of plants, however exotic, Anike found the whole place rather more peaceful than the carved tunnel leading to it.

Lalfar held up his hand. When she halted in response to the silent request, he moved forward into the space, axe at the ready. He followed a bare path between the rocks and fungi running roughly through the centre of the cave. Anike quietly lifted her staff and stood ready to cast the firebolt spell. The circle of light from Lalfar's glowstone moved forward around thirty paces, then came back towards her.

"It looks safe," he said. "There is another dwarf-made tunnel leading up on the far side. Are you tired? This could be a good place to rest."

At his question, Anike felt the weight of the hours they had spent beneath the stone and nodded. She realised that she had no idea how long it had been since she had slept.

"I am too," Lalfar told her. "We will have to sleep at some point. There are some fairly comfortable-looking areas away from the path which are less exposed than the passageway."

"It would be sensible to stop," Anike agreed. "We do not know what lies ahead, and it would be unwise to face it tired." She crossed to one of the larger mushrooms. "I recognise this from the dwarven records. Its name translates to 'bread fungus', and the dwarves ate it and used it in curing elixirs, a simple recipe according to their notes." She pulled one and it came away from the ground with a slight tearing sound. "I can try to brew something with it later. There is water here too so it is a good place to work."

"Let's make camp then," Lalfar said.

They set down their bags, and Anike took out some roots. "I will cook these," she said. "I was hoping we would catch up with Enya quickly so I did not bring that much food. We may need to eat something that grows here if we have a long journey ahead of us."

"You can't use witchcraft to make food?"

"No. Everything I conjure is transient, and I cannot create anything living or dead at all. As I understand the principles, a law witch could create permanent ice or stone, but no one can make living or once-living things out of nothing. Life, flesh and blood are neither law nor chaos, so are beyond a witch's direct control. I can affect living things with forms such as fire, but they are inherently more resistant to witchcraft than inanimate objects. While I can reduce a block of stone to dust, I have nothing like the power needed to do the same to a man. Witchcraft has very real limits."

She smiled and handed him a small cauldron. "Fortunately, I can cook. Can you put water in this please?"

Lalfar brought it back filled to the brim. She smelt it then cautiously put it to her lips. "Very clean," she said. "It tastes a little odd from minerals in the rocks here but it is safe to drink."

She assembled a small tripod and hung the cauldron on it. "This moss should burn well," she added. In a moment, she had a small fire alight and dropped the roots into the water.

While the simple meal was cooking, she took out her slate and started to put together the spell to locate a witch. The basic principle was clear, and Enya had a chaos demon so she could use the chaos rune when defining the target of the spell. The range would not be large, perhaps a thousand paces, but sufficient to alert her when they were getting close.

The meal was ready before she finished the spell. Lalfar, who had been practising moves with his axe and shield, sat down next to her. "You fight well, Lalfar," she said. "Where did you learn?"

"From my father first, and I've picked up more on the road. Enya and I travelled a lot, and it was not always safe."

"Is there anything you can teach me? I have not spent a lot of time fighting hand to hand and I will need to be able to defend myself here. Outside, I could always fly away if there was a real threat, but that may not be possible in these tunnels."

Lalfar looked at her in surprise. "It would take a hero to fight a dwarf hand to hand, Anike."

"The witch is human. As for the dwarves, while I may not be able to hurt them, I do want to be able to avoid their attacks. An axe is a little heavy for me, but I can handle a spear."

"Running away is a good strategy for most women. I don't want you feeling overconfident and getting hurt or killed. It would be a shame to spoil your beauty." He paused. "That is, I don't think I will be able to find Enya without you."

Anike chose to ignore the first comment. "All the more reason to practice. I really do not expect to get through this without a fight. Do you?"

"I suppose not, but I can't turn you into a warrior overnight."

"People show the greatest rate of improvement when they start to learn new skills."

Lalfar sighed. "Well, I suppose you are quick and look fairly strong for a woman, so perhaps we can do something."

Lalfar did not seem to think anything of how he had referred to her gender. His offhand comment and his earlier remark about the value of her beauty revealed his view of women but it was her strength and speed that were important, not her sex. However, he had agreed to help her so she suppressed a sharp retort. "Thank you," she said, instead. "We can practice after we finish the food."

As they ate, Anike became increasingly aware of the slight illumination coming from the fungi. Her eyes were becoming more accustomed to the dim light, and that could only be to the good. Clearly, the dwarves needed some light too or they would not have set glowstones in the walls, but they probably needed less than she did and any reduction of the differential between her abilities and theirs was welcome.

When they had finished eating, she picked up her staff and gripped it like a spear.

Lalfar got to his feet and brought his axe and shield to guard. "A spear or staff is a good weapon for blocking, but it is better to keep your attacker at a distance if you can. If you have to parry, remember that the axe blade extends beyond the haft of the weapon." He swung forehanded before stepping forward to slam a sharp shield bash towards her.

Anike skipped back a pace and thrust at his shield. He deflected the blow and brought his axe down hard on her staff, knocking it aside before closing past the point. She shifted her grip and brought the staff up two-handed to catch his next blow just above her head but could not stop the downward sweep of his axe. Lalfar halted the blade just in front of her eyes.

"Well, that did not work out very well," she said, stepping back again. "I need more practice."

"You are not strong enough to block a blow that way," Lalfar told her. "A dwarf will strike a lot harder than I do. You need to let the force of the blow move you backwards." He smiled, and his breathing quickened.

"I need to stop you getting so close," Anike said. "Dwarves do not have your reach, so if I can keep them away that will work better."

She took a long stride back and thrust at him. As he raised his shield to block, she shifted the point down to aim at his exposed leg. He swept his axe down and knocked the staff to the side. She pulled back and stabbed again. This time he stepped forward, angling his shield to let the point skid off, then rushed her. She gave ground, trying to keep him at a distance. For a moment she thought she had fended him off but then her back came up against a large rock, and she stopped.

He beat her staff aside and came past her guard, and once again she just managed a double-handed parry, holding the axe above her head. This time he pressed forward, pinning her body to the stone behind her. Their faces were only inches apart, and she saw lust in his eyes as he leaned forward to kiss her.

Anike bent her knees and dropped, an instinctive response to threats that had served her well in perilous situations before, then straightened outside his arms, holding her hand palm up towards him. Lalfar looked surprised.

"What in the name of Thor were you thinking?" Her voice cracked like a whip.

"I thought you liked me."

"You are loyal to your sister. I admire that, but it is a far cry from wanting you."

Lalfar looked taken aback. "I don't understand. Why did you want to get close to me if you weren't interested? Why befriend Enya?"

"You need to take things at face value sometimes, Lalfar. It is not always about you. I actually like Enya."

"Don't you like me too?" he asked, taking a step towards her, a half smile contrasting with the hurt in his eyes.

Sometimes her looks were a mixed blessing. "You are not my type, Lalfar. You have some good points, of course, but I just do not see you that way. I am glad you are here with me as I really would not want to do this journey alone, but that is it."

"I thought you were doing all of this so you could get my attention," Lalfar said.

Anike had already marked the man as arrogant but this comment took her by surprise, even so. Men could think in such convoluted ways. "Is it so strange that someone can like Enya for who she is?" she asked.

"It's not how it usually goes. I thought you were angry with the arl and wanted to use me to make a point with him."

Anike stared at him. "That is an … interesting … way of looking at things, Lalfar."

"I didn't want to miss a chance with you if you were thinking that way."

She glared. "Nothing could have been further from my mind."

The remains of the smile drained away and he looked sheepish. "I am sorry, Anike, I misunderstood." He took a deep breath and held out his hand. "Friends then?"

Anike did not see her relationship with the man as friendship, but rather than doubt his sincerity to his face and insult him, she took the proffered hand and shook it. "Friends. It is fine, Lalfar, we can still work together to find Enya. That is what we both want."

Lalfar's face was shadowed. Anike could tell the rejection had wounded his pride, but she did not see what she could or should do to make him feel better. She did not intend to apologise nor was she going to pretend to find him attractive, so she opted for silence. They would need each other in this realm and though she was not afraid of him, there was no need to antagonise him further.

His hold of her hand had gone on a little longer than she found comfortable. She pulled away slightly and he let it go. "Once again, I apologise," he said. "You have done more for Enya than anyone else could have. I had no right to expect so much and I would not have got this far without you."

Anike relaxed a little. "We have worked well together so far and if we can continue to help each other down here, we have a chance to rescue Enya."

She went back to the fire and turned to him. "You had better rest first. I will keep watch while I work on my spells and wake you in a few hours."

He nodded and unwrapped a well-used bedroll, probably a necessity for a travelling performer. She was less well prepared, but she had slept under her cloak many times and the moss was thick and springy. As Lalfar settled down, facing away from her, she turned to her slate and chalk, and continued working on the spell to locate Enya.

The core of the description for a witch was chaos, a form rune and one of the fundamental elements of the world, and it had to be included in the spell. As she set down the runes, it occurred to her that the ability to find other things would be useful, like plants that she needed. She put that idea to one side as she did not want to get diverted. Without spending time she could not afford, she was not sure whether it was even possible to find a living thing as she could no more use the life rune than the law rune.

It took her a couple of hours to devise the proper pattern. When she tried it, she was not surprised to find that it did not detect anyone but her. It would have been extremely fortunate if Enya had been so close. Anike found a blank page in her book and copied the spell from her slate.

Lalfar seemed to have settled into a light sleep, his breathing slow and regular, and Anike considered him and his propositioning of her. Lalfar's advances were an inconvenient and unwelcome complication. She had skirted around her own attraction to Enya while talking to him. It was not something that she could really put into words, but she felt drawn to the woman. The brother and sister had little in common, but Lalfar was protective of his sibling and Anike was unsure how he would react to someone else wanting to get close to her.

Many men had made admiring comments to Anike and had to be politely but firmly deflected, but Lalfar seemed to expect women to welcome his attentions. That aside, emotions had been quite intense over the last day. She should have taken some steps to make her views plain earlier, but hindsight was a wonderful thing. Now all she could do was hope that their shared goal would allow them to work together. There was no one else here and she had to rely on him.

She was getting tired and was wondering whether to wake Lalfar or work on something else when a sound reached her ears over the ever-present murmur of the underground stream. It was a sort of scraping thump. She listened carefully, cocking her head to one side. A series of further noises followed, echoing from the direction they had come from. It could have been footsteps, but softer than the clank of metal dwarven armour on stone.

She bent over Lalfar and put a hand over his lips. He did not stir so she shook him gently with her other hand. He grunted, but she pressed her hand down and when his eyes opened, she put her finger to her own lips. He started to rise, and she whispered, "Something is coming from behind us," before letting him get up.

He shook his head to clear it and came to his feet, his axe in hand.

Anike put the glowstone under her bag to hide the light and looked back towards the entrance to the cavern. The noise was coming closer, and it sounded like the boots of one or two people on the stone. A flickering orange light was growing in the passage.

She and Lalfar exchanged glances, and both ducked down behind a moss-covered rock. They peered at the figure that came into view, a torch in one hand and a drawn sword in the other. Anike could not stop the gasp of surprise from escaping her lips.

It was Gunnar.

- 11 -

THE EDGE OF CHAOS

Lalfar looked from Gunnar to Anike in astonishment.

Anike caught his gaze. She shrugged her shoulders and raised her eyebrows.

As the young man took his final steps into the cavern, Anike picked up the glowstone she had hidden and came out from behind the rock. When he saw the light, Gunnar instantly went into a guard position, then his eyes lit up in recognition. "Anike!" he called out.

"Gunnar! How did you get here? Are there others with you?"

Lalfar joined Anike in the circle of light cast by the glowstone. "And why did you come?" he added.

"I am glad I finally found you," Gunnar said. "I was beginning to think that I would just wander down here forever. And for a time I was worried that the rock was alive. It looks like it ate someone back there."

"But how did you get here?" Anike asked, preferring not to talk about the dwarf she had entombed in the rock. "The passage was blocked."

"Almost blocked," Gunnar told her with a grin. "There was just enough of a gap for me to wriggle through, and I pulled my blade and other equipment after me. I had to wait until everyone was in bed though. Father forbade me to come after you."

"But why did you follow us, though?" Anike asked.

"I thought you might need my help," Gunnar told her. "And this looks like it will be a noble adventure, something that could even impress my father." He sheathed his sword. "You were amazing on the surface, Anike. You drove everyone off. My father said that if you want to get yourself killed down here, he wasn't going to stop you. He had Nangar start work to block up the top of the shaft and I had to get through before he finished. The passage will be sealed by now, though I know you can break it again."

"This is not one of your father's hunts, Gunnar. This is going to be dangerous." She took a deep breath and carried on. "That dwarf you passed, sunk into the rock? He would have killed us both if I had not managed to stop him like that."

"I understand, Anike, but if it wasn't perilous, how could I show my bravery? I want you to see that."

Infatuation mixed with foolhardy bravado was a combination that could get good people killed. Looking at Gunnar's eager face, Anike doubted that she would be able to dissuade him but she still had to try. "You should go back. Your father will be worried."

"He has to get used to that. He deserves better than a coward for a son."

"He just wants you to be safe until you are ready for battle, Gunnar. And I doubt anyone is really prepared for what we are going to face down here."

Gunnar's face shone in the light of the glowstone. "So that puts me in the same position as you. Neither of us is ready, and you are here anyway."

Anike frowned at him. "There are degrees. This is not a venture for someone unseasoned."

"Lalfar is here, and he isn't a warrior at all. Not trained like a jarl, and he doesn't have the responsibilities of one."

Anike glanced at Lalfar, who was keeping quiet for once. "It is his sister that was taken."

"And she was taken while a guest of my father. It was his duty to protect her. He might not believe in dwarves, but I do. And I will prove to you and him that I am a warrior."

The temptation to call him a foolish child crossed her mind, but from her that could crush him or make him either angry or doubt himself. Neither was likely to be safe in Svartalfheim. She tried another way. "You could tell Rek that you could not find us. He would have to acknowledge you were brave to try."

"But I have found you. And I am not going to let you go off alone again."

Lalfar chipped in. "My lord, Gunnar. This is no place for ..." He trailed off, apparently unable to think how to finish the sentence without giving insult and reluctant to take too familiar a tone with the young jarl, even in such a strange place.

Anike picked up his thread. She doubted the boy would be of much help, more likely just another thing to worry about. "This is no game. You saw what I did to the dwarf. Not only did he survive when I dropped that slab of rock onto him, but he had started to lift it. No man is that strong. I had to melt the floor out from under him to stop him." She skirted around the revulsion she felt for what the demon had done, what she had not been able to prevent the demon from doing.

"But you can overcome anything, Anike. Your witchcraft is really powerful, and I can protect you while you use it."

"I do not want anything to happen to you, Gunnar. I am not sure I can keep you safe. You are going back."

Gunnar put his hands on his hips. "No. I won't return to my father like that. I will show him I don't need to be wrapped in wool anymore. And anyway, I can't get out now my father has sealed the passage again."

"I will take you back myself, then."

"Anike, you can't," Lalfar interjected. "It will take hours and the dwarves will get further ahead. And how would you stop him coming back?"

"I could block the passage properly, but you are right that it would take too long." She turned back to the boy. "And it is not really my decision to make."

"Gunnar, you showed plenty of courage coming here, and independence of mind to want to help me after what you saw me do. I am not your mother. If it is really what you want, you can come with us." She frowned at him. "Just remember, I will be more impressed if you don't take stupid risks."

Gunnar looked triumphant. "Thank you, Anike."

"It is too late to go on now," Anike said. "I am tired, and we all need to rest. Gunnar, I want you to think about if you truly want to do this. It was a feat to find us and you can be proud of that, even if you do nothing more. We can make a final decision in the morning, or whatever passes for morning here."

Gunnar smiled, believing he had won. He was probably right. Even though he did not belong on such a hazardous journey, it was very unlikely he would change his mind and she could not force him. She briefly considered trapping him behind a rock fall so he had little choice but to go back, but he might still try and find his way around, and she could not bear the thought of his wandering alone and lost in Svartalfheim, unable to get home. They would have to make the best of it.

She closed her eyes for a moment and felt the delicious comfort of darkness. Turning to Gunnar, she asked, "How alert are you?"

"I am fine," he said. "A warrior has to be able to do without sleep." He sounded sincere and certainly looked more awake than she felt.

"Then you can take the next watch," she decided. "Wake Lalfar in about three hours, and both of us if there is any hint of trouble. You can rest when he takes over." This was something useful he could do.

"Yes, Anike." Gunnar seemed happy enough to take direction from her. Anike rolled herself up in her cloak on the moss.

She woke several hours later feeling a lot more rested. Sleep had come easily, despite the strange environment.

Lalfar was sitting by the fire with a sleeping Gunnar beside him.

Anike went over to the skald, who said, "Can't you make him go back? He is going to slow us down."

"You saw how keen he was, Lalfar. If he is resourceful and determined enough to follow us, he may be mature enough to decide what to do now. Whilst this is not what I had in mind, I did tell his father he should give Gunnar more freedom and I should heed my own advice. We do not know what risks we are taking either and I am not going to leave him here. We will just have to look out for him."

"Three is a better number than two," Lalfar admitted. "I might have chosen someone else but I suppose we can try to look on this as good fortune."

She nodded. "We ought to view it that way. I will make something to eat and we can wake Gunnar, if he has had enough sleep?"

"He has been resting for about four hours," Lalfar replied. "I scouted out a little further and there is one passage leading out of the cavern. It was clearly made by the dwarves and it slants upwards."

"I will take some of the fungi with me when we go. I think they will be of use, if only as food when our supplies run low," Anike said. She filled the cauldron with bread fungus, topped up her waterskin and was replacing the cap when she noticed a faint rushing noise. At first, she thought it was the stream in front of her but then realised it was coming from the far end of the cave, the direction that they had to go.

Lalfar came to stand beside her. "That is new," he said in a worried tone, and they cautiously approached the passage. The sound grew and by the light of the glowstone in her hand, Anike could see a thin sheen of water spreading over the ground. It flowed faster as she watched, running out of the passage before them into the mushroom cavern. She recalled that the way they had entered the cavern had been downwards as well, making this a low point where the water would collect. Looking up the passage, the flow did not seem to be stopping – if anything it was increasing.

"We need to get out of here," she said and headed back to the sleeping Gunnar.

"This does not look good," Lalfar said as he followed her. "Do you think it is aimed at us? Perhaps the dwarves are trying to block the passage, or to drown us."

"I think they would be more direct," Anike replied. "They probably think the dwarf who attacked us would have been capable of stopping any pursuit. This is more likely to be something natural, the equivalent of a storm for this realm."

She reached Gunnar and shook him awake. "Get up now!" she told him. He blinked, then saw the urgency of her expression and sat up. "Yes, Anike."

"We are about to be caught in a flood," she told him and looked about her. "I don't see any way for so much water to get out. This cavern is at the base of a trough and it will fill up soon. We have to go on or we will be stuck behind it."

"You are right. We certainly can't stay here," Lalfar said.

They splashed between the mushrooms and into the tunnel. The water was running faster now and came halfway up their boots. The force of it pressed hard on Anike's legs.

With Gunnar leading, the three struggled against the flow. It was now up to their knees and had become a veritable river. Behind them, the mushroom cavern was starting to fill up. The little stream had found a way out so Anike supposed it would eventually drain, but she had no idea how long that would take.

They fought to keep their footing in what was rapidly turning into a rushing torrent. "I did not expect to meet my end down here by drowning," Lalfar said grimly.

Gunnar laughed at that and half turned, but slipped and his right foot went out from underneath him. He shouted, almost a scream, and fell face-first into the water. His torch went out and he started to tumble as he was dragged down the slope.

Lalfar braced himself against the wall with one hand, set his feet and grabbed Gunnar as he was swept past. For a moment, the boy swung as the current threatened to pull them both loose but managed to get his feet under him once more and came up spluttering. He was shivering from his immersion in the cold water.

The chill was stealing the light from the glowstones too, and the passage was turning to black as the water rose.

Gunnar was still struggling to keep his balance, and Anike could feel the flow pressing harder against her own legs too. Whilst enough light from the glowstone in her hand remained for her to see, she lifted the cloak to read the pattern dyed into the right-hand side. "*Prana*," she said and rose out of the water.

"Hold on," she called to the others and hunted in her bag for the spellbook. Turning quickly through it, she located the page she needed and read the spell there. "*Prana*," she said again to surround Gunnar with the energy of movement and lifted him clear of the water.

Gunnar gave a cry of excitement as he rose into the air and flapped his arms, trying to fly. She cast the same spell on Lalfar, who looked angry and frightened as she lifted him. He grimaced and he put a hand on the wall, trying to stop himself rising even if it meant staying within the torrent.

"Not a good idea," Anike told him. She slipped the book and the dimming glowstone into her bag. "It will be quicker if I tow you. The spell supporting you only allows me to move you very slowly, and it does not last long. Each of you reach towards me."

She held out her hands. Gunnar took one eagerly but when Lalfar eventually grasped the other, his grip was like a vice, matching the set of his face.

With the water still rising beneath them, Anike pulled them both along near the ceiling of the sloping passage. After a hundred paces or more, and a recasting of the spells, the glowstones in the wall became brighter. Ahead there was a change in the sound of rushing water, more as if it were a river passing over rapids.

They came to a cross tunnel. The water was pouring out of the branch to the right, but it was the cross tunnel itself that caught her attention. In both directions, it was almost a circle around five or six paces across. Its floor was not flat but a part of the circle with the lowest point about three feet above the floor of the passage they were in, and every part of its surface glinted as if coated in dark glass. The water was pouring into their passageway with only a small amount splashing across to the other circular opening.

Anike set them down on the dry ground past the strange circular cross tunnel then went back to look at the junction more carefully. She could feel heat coming from the stone of the unflooded passage.

"What has happened here?" she asked. "This is not at all like the finished tunnels we have seen before. This rock looks as if it has been melted recently. The power needed to do this with witchcraft would be enormous, far beyond anything Enya could have managed, so it cannot have been her."

"Perhaps this is how the dwarves make their tunnels, at least to start with," Lalfar suggested. "They could burn through the rock with some artifact, then use the water to cool it."

"I suppose so," Anike conceded. "The rock is still warm and if that is what the dwarves are doing, then they are still working in this area and we probably should leave. We do not want to be caught by any dwarven builders."

"Which way?" asked Lalfar.

Anike considered the passages. Water was gushing from the passage to the right, and it filled much of that tunnel. It would be very difficult to go that way, and she would have to use witchcraft to keep them above the dark rushing liquid. The other circular cross tunnel slanted very slightly downwards and if the rock became even hotter, it would be impossible to pass on foot. More importantly, if there were dwarves working on the cross tunnel, either way might lead to them.

"We go on," she said.

The three hurried on up the passage away from the water, Lalfar in the lead now. A few hundred paces further on, he held up his arm and they all stopped. From ahead of them came a noise, not easy to make out but it sounded like a voice.

Lalfar and Anike exchanged looks. It was quite a long way off but had definitely come from in front of them.

"What is it?" asked Gunnar.

"Quiet," Anike whispered urgently. "There is someone up ahead."

"Oh," said Gunnar, and loosened his sword in its sheath.

They craned their ears, but no further sound came to them.

"We cannot go back," Anike said. "The cavern is flooded, and I do not want to walk down a tunnel that has just been melted."

"It might have been Enya calling out," Lalfar said. "We should go on but keep quiet in case there are dwarves."

"We may not be able to avoid dwarves forever," Anike said, "and at least this way we probably will not run into a group with a device that can melt rock. We should have the element of surprise with us too."

Gunnar smiled. "A fight at last."

Anike frowned at him.

"Did you make the spell to find Enya?" Lalfar asked her.

"Yes, I used it last night and she was not within its range. I can cast it again." Anike found the pattern and spoke "*Izik*," naming the rune of chaos to trigger the spell. Again, there was no sign of Enya, and she shook her head. "She is not that close, Lalfar. If the noise is a dwarf, we should avoid contact if we can. It could be another guard left to ambush us."

"I want to see a dwarf." Gunnar fingered the hilt of his sword.

"We do have to go on, but let us try to be stealthy," Lalfar said. He looked pointedly at Gunnar. "No rushing to attack, my lord. You haven't fought the dwarves and we have. We need to be careful. Fighting is a last resort against these creatures."

"Creatures?" asked Gunnar.

"Legend has it that the dwarves were created before men," Anike told him. "They are quite different to humans. I am not sure I would have said 'creatures' though. They are supposed to be more intelligent than us, and very cunning, and they are certainly many times stronger."

"They are sometimes called 'creatures' in the tales," Lalfar said in a wounded tone, then continued in a more normal voice. "But those stories are often told from the gods' point of view. The gods did respect them, but hardly thought of them as equals. Let's not argue about that. The point is that they are not human and they are really dangerous."

He looked at his hand. "I think we should rely on the glowstones in the passage so we don't give away our approach."

"Sensible." Anike nodded and put her own in her bag.

The three started up the passage cautiously, guided by the occasional glowstones in the walls. After a while, their eyes grew accustomed to the dim light, and they were able to go faster. She could feel a growing sense of antipathy from the demon, another sign that they were approaching dwarves.

Ahead of them, the sound came again, now clearly words, and this time it was answered. Anike thought that the second voice was not quite so deep as the dwarven voices she had heard before.

There was a slightly lighter patch ahead where the passage opened out. Carefully, they approached the threshold and peered through. What might have started as a natural cavern had been worked with smooth walls and there were three passages leading away in various directions, each dimly lit by glowstones. The floor, some twenty paces below them and the size of a field, was flat and level. Stone steps set against the wall led down to it from each passage, including the one they were in. Fungi grew in neat rows and many gave off light, making the hall brighter than anywhere they had been before. While the details were unfamiliar, Anike recognised a farm.

In the centre of the hall, two dwarves were bent over different rows of mushrooms, picking them and dropping them into baskets. One stood up and Anike took in her long hair, lack of beard and body shape, and realised she was looking at a dwarven woman. The other was shorter, barely four feet tall, and almost as slim as a human. He also lacked a beard and had short hair, and could have been a child a fair way short of adulthood.

Something that looked like an axe or small mattock was tucked into the belt of the taller dwarf.

The three humans pulled back into the passage. Lalfar beckoned them closer and they put their heads together.

"What do we do now?" asked Gunnar in a low voice.

"They are not the ones who took Enya," Anike said. "The cavern is quite big. We could try to slip past them."

"There is not enough cover," Lalfar whispered back. "We are completely exposed on the stairway, and they will hear us if we make any noise."

"We could attack them," Gunnar said, fingering his sword. "They don't look ready for a fight."

"That could work," Lalfar agreed. "They're not heavily armed."

"I think one of them is a child," Anike pointed out.

"They are dwarves, subjugators of our people, and he looks nearly full-grown to me," Lalfar said. "And after the fight that single warrior gave us, I doubt even a dwarf child is helpless."

"They have not attacked us and if they did not take Enya, we have no quarrel with them. And I do not want to get into a fight that we can avoid."

"We don't know that they weren't involved in taking Enya but regardless, they are in our way. Do you want to abandon her just because someone might get hurt?"

Anike glared at him. "That is unfair. I am happy to battle those who took her, but these look innocent to me. I see no need simply to attack."

"But we raid Larten villages," Gunnar pointed out. "My father sends warriors to the coast for the summer raids, and I will be going with them next year if he thinks me worthy. We all kill people and take slaves and most of those haven't attacked us either."

Lalfar stiffened at that. "I don't approve of taking slaves," he said in a flat voice.

Most people just accepted slavery as part of the fabric of life, particularly in the coastal towns, and Anike cast a sharp glance at him. To Gunnar she said, "I know we do that, and the Lartens raid us too, but I do not approve and I would not do it myself. And I agree with Lalfar about slavery."

"I wasn't suggesting we take them as slaves," Gunnar said quickly. "I only meant that people are attacked all the time, whether or not they seek it. That is just the way of things."

"I approve of raids about as little as I approve of floods, but we know both might happen and we guard against them. These two might not be expecting anything. No human has raided Svartalfheim before.”

She paused, wondering if that was actually true. The dwarves had taken a lot of effort to seal the entrances, and that suggested they had reason to do so. It was also quite possible that the seals had been breached in the hundreds of years since they retreated back to Svartalfheim. “At least, I have never heard of it,” she amended. “But even if I was prepared to attack without provocation, it might not be wise. They still could be more than a match for us, and suppose one of them runs off to get help? We could be trapped.”

“We have the advantage of surprise, and you can use witchcraft to block the exits,” Lalfar said.

“We could try talking to them,” Anike said.

“I like the sound of attacking,” Gunnar put in. “It has all the making of a great battle.”

Anike could not remember being so bold or foolhardy herself at Gunnar’s age, but others had been. Before starting her apprenticeship in herbcraft, she had been content gutting the fish her father had caught, but the Arl’s son Bjord had dreamed of battle, always thinking of glory and never of pain or loss. Some people grew out of those dreams, but others did not. And such dreams meant that there were those who never had the chance to grow up.

“No,” she said firmly. “We will not fight unless we have to. I am going to talk to them.”

“You will give away our advantage,” Lalfar said.

“I will go by myself. If it comes to a battle, you will still have the element of surprise, perhaps more so as they will be focused on me.”

“That might work,” Lalfar agreed grudgingly. “Especially if you can get them to turn their backs to us.”

“I will try,” Anike said. “We will need every chance if they are hostile. Just because I would prefer to talk does not mean that they would.” She set the spearhead on her staff and handed it to Gunnar. “I will keep my knife but leave this with you. Throw it to me if we have to fight.”

She looked hard at him. "Wait here until I need you or until everything is resolved."

Gunnar nodded, but his face was eager.

Anike went down the passage to the light of the closest glowstone and read the flight pattern on her cloak. "*Prana*," she said and cast the spell on herself then walked past Lalfar and Gunnar and down the steps into the hall. She made no attempt to hide.

– 12 –

MOTHER AND CHILD

Anike walked at a steady pace with her head high, hoping to give an impression of confidence whilst not appearing to be a threat. The smaller dwarf caught sight of her before she reached the floor of the hall and tugged on the other's arm. The larger dwarf, who Anike was now sure was a woman, looked up and got to her feet, her hand going to the mattock at her belt.

Slowing a little, Anike called out "Greetings," in dwarven. Both dwarves looked surprised though whether it was just because she was human or because she spoke dwarven, or perhaps because she spoke it so badly, she did not know.

When she reached the bottom of the stairs, Anike found that the floor was completely flat, unlike the now-flooded cavern they had rested in. The mushrooms were arranged in precise rows, growing on rock of a different colour and texture.

The dwarven woman stepped forward. In the dim light, her skin had a greyish hue and now that she was closer to her, Anike could see she had a short, thin beard. She wore a green-brown tunic which looked as if it could have been made from the heavy strands of some plant and a basket made of the same material was on the ground nearby, half filled with fungi.

"Greetings," she said again. "I mean you no harm."

The dwarven woman drew the tool at her belt. On one side it had a short heavy pick with a sharp point and on the other was a hammer. While it might not have been forged as a weapon, there was no doubt it could inflict a serious wound. The dwarf held it easily in one hand but did not attack, nor did she go into any sort of defensive stance. If she were human, Anike would not have taken her for a warrior but she reminded herself that she was not dealing with a human.

"What do you want then?" the dwarven woman asked. Her voice was very heavy and slow, like the tolling of a large bell. The words were not pronounced quite as Anike had expected, but she understood them well enough.

"I just want to pass through," she moved forward, hoping to draw the dwarf's attention away from the entrance behind her.

"Humans do not come here unaccompanied," the dwarf said. "The entrances have been closed to them. How did you get in? Where do you think you are going?"

Anike doubted that she could deceive the dwarf successfully, knowing so little of Svartalfheim. "I followed some of your people. I am looking for someone. Another human woman. They brought her down here from Midgard," she said, unable to think of a better explanation. She hoped that dwarves, like humans, might have differences of opinion and that not everyone would support the kidnap. "I do not know where she is now. I think she was brought this way." Her words were halting as her tongue wrapped itself around the ancient language.

The dwarf looked Anike up and down, and her eyes lingered on Anike's sleeves, where some runes were visible. "Are you here alone?" she asked. It was hard to interpret her tone, but it did not sound friendly.

"There are others with me. They are watching," Anike said, not wanting to be caught in a lie. She hoped she might be able to win a little trust with honesty.

The dwarf's eyes shifted to the passage where Lalfar and Gunnar were waiting, and she nodded slightly. "Call them down," she said. "I will not talk to you while I have to guard against others." She let the mattock rest on her shoulder.

The element of surprise was gone, but Anike had the impression that the dwarf already knew about Lalfar and Gunnar. "Come down," she called back in Norse. "The dwarf knows you are there." She kept her eyes on the dwarf's face as she shouted, and she thought she saw the dwarf relax slightly.

Lalfar and Gunnar walked down the stairs. Both had weapons ready, and Gunnar held Anike's spear in his shield hand. The dwarf watched them approach, then brought her pickaxe back off her shoulder and felt the sharp spike with her thumb.

The men came up to them and stopped just behind her. Gunnar passed Anike's spear to her, and she set the base on the ground, leaning on it and trying to appear less threatening. She held out her other hand, palm open. "Do you know where our friend is?" she asked. "Have you seen her?"

"I have not," the dwarf replied, "but my heart sings to know that Barodar found a suitable human."

"What does he want her for?"

"She. Barodar is a woman. She is taking your friend to the Giant."

"What giant? Why does he need our friend?"

The dwarf smiled. "Your friend should be proud that her small life can assist in a great purpose." She folded her arms. "I will tell you nothing more."

Anike frowned and translated for the others.

Lalfar lifted his axe. "Tell her that if she doesn't help us, we will kill her and her son."

"I understand you," the dwarf said in heavily accented Norse. "I speak both human tongues. You are not in a position to make demands. A threat made by a human has no weight."

For a fleeting instant, Anike wondered what the dwarf meant by 'both' human tongues as she knew of only one but pushed her curiosity away and forced herself to focus. Lalfar's rash approach was leading them towards a fight they could ill afford.

Rather than back down, the skald moved forward to her side and hefted his axe. The dwarf did not retreat but unfolded her arms so that her mattock was ready.

"Then I will beat the answers out of you," Lalfar declared and swung at her head.

"Lalfar, stop!" Anike shouted, knowing it was futile as the words left her mouth.

The dwarf raised her left arm and blocked the haft of the axe. A human might have suffered a broken arm, but it was as if Lalfar had struck a tree. The blade came to a halt well short of the dwarf's head. Her pick swung through the air, hammer side leading and struck Lalfar's shield a resounding blow but he had shifted his weight and was only knocked back a pace, though the wood started to crack.

Gunnar, who had hesitated for a moment when Lalfar attacked, stepped forward and swung his sword low at the dwarf's body. She did not even try to block it, and the blade passed beneath her arm and struck her side. It left a small rent in the tunic but if it had inflicted any injury, there was no sign of it.

Gunnar brought his blade back and readied a thrust but the dwarf child leapt on him. Despite being much taller, Gunnar staggered back, fighting to stay on his feet. The dwarf pulled the youth's shield out of the way and closed inside blade reach. Gunnar cried out as a blow from the child's fist took him in the stomach.

Anike's flight effect was still on her so she willed herself into the air to get clear of their reach. As she rose, she considered the firebolt spell but doubted it would really hurt the tough dwarves. Instead, she put her head through the carrying loop of the spear to free her hands and pulled out her book of spells.

Lalfar swung his axe and stepped back to avoid the counter. The dwarf woman advanced, moving to her right and leaving her left side exposed. Lalfar struck at it but the move had been a feint, and the pick came back in an underarm sweep. The haft caught Lalfar's arm and even coming from an awkward angle, the blow contained enough force to jar his axe from his hand.

Beside him, the dwarf child pushed Gunnar to the ground. Unable to use his sword in such close quarters, Gunnar dropped it and pulled his dagger from his belt, but the young dwarf grasped his wrist while hitting the boy repeatedly with his other hand.

Hoping to turn the tide of the fight, Anike cast her spell, not at the dwarf woman but at the child. "*Prana*," she said, surrounding him with the energy of movement. Dwarves were more solid than humans and she had not been certain the spell was powerful enough to lift him but was more confident of it working on the child than the woman.

Her will and witchcraft raised him into the air. The roof of the cavern was a long way up and a fall from that height ought to be enough to injure even a dwarf, perhaps prove fatal. She did not want a death on her conscience though. The dwarves had not started this fight.

"Look up!" she shouted at the dwarf woman, who was advancing on Lalfar. "I have your son."

In her urgency, she had shouted in Norse, but the dwarf understood. She looked up at the dwarf child who was still rising, stopped and let her weapon fall to her side. "I surrender," she said in dwarven. "Let my son down, and I will allow you to pass and give you three true answers."

"She has surrendered," Anike informed the others as she descended to the cave floor, recognising the value that the dwarf was placing on her son's life by offering truth. "Do not press the attack," she added as Lalfar and Gunnar both bent to retrieve their fallen weapons. She brought the dwarf child back down to the ground while Lalfar scowled at the woman. Gunnar still held his sword at the ready.

The dwarf woman turned to face her, keeping one eye on Lalfar. "Ask your questions," she said.

Anike did not trust Lalfar to come up with a sensible enquiry, so she asked, "Which way should we go to find the human that Barodar brought to Svartalfheim?" She did not want to waste a question asking whether she had seen Enya, as it seemed clear the dwarf knew where she was being taken.

The dwarf indicated a passage, the least information that could amount to a proper answer.

"What does Barodar plan to use the human for?" She asked her second question, trying to phrase it so that the dwarf would have to give more than a mere location, which would mean little to her.

"She intends to use her to wake Hrym."

Lalfar, who had not understood the answer, nevertheless looked up sharply at the last word.

Anike translated for him and Gunnar. Lalfar's face paled when she told him about Hrym but he pulled himself together. "We can get the answer to one more question," she added. "What else do we wish to know?"

"How long will it take Barodar to reach Hrym?" Lalfar asked. To Anike, he added, "We need to know how fast to go to catch them."

"They should reach Hrym's Hall in what you would call two days," the dwarf answered Lalfar without waiting for Anike to translate. She put a hand on her son's shoulder and guided him behind her. The dwarven boy shook his fist at Gunnar, but his mother said firmly, "We are finished here."

Gunnar made as if to approach the dwarf child, but Anike put a hand on his arm. "They surrendered, and have met the terms. We should go." Gunnar looked rebellious for a moment, then nodded.

They headed for the passage the dwarf had indicated. As Anike looked back, she saw the woman staring after them with cold eyes.

They hurried up the passage, as much to put distance between themselves and the dwarves as to catch up with Enya and her captors. Anike had little doubt that the dwarves could call on each other for aid, and they could be pursued if they lingered near the farm cavern. Her sense of urgency infected the others and they set a fast pace.

After a few minutes, they came to a crossroads. "We need to rest for a moment," Lalfar said, "and then we can decide which way to go."

Anike turned to him angrily. "What were you thinking? You did not have to start that fight. You know how dangerous dwarves are."

"We were not getting anywhere. She wasn't going to tell us anything, and she wasn't a warrior."

Anike fought to keep her voice level. "Perhaps not, but she was still more than a match for you. We could have just walked past. You put our lives at risk."

Lalfar crossed his arms. "We have to take risks if we are going to succeed. And we got those answers, which we wouldn't have if we had just walked past her."

Anike's hands whitened on her staff. "You were reckless. It could have gone a lot worse, but that is the point. We were lucky, and we cannot keep relying on that, particularly if we have to use the runes again. They can affect our fortune."

"I will do what I must to bring Enya back."

"Admirable. But putting us in unnecessary danger does not help."

"I think it was necessary."

"No, it was stupid. You let your frustration get the better of you." She glared at him.

For a moment, Lalfar looked as if he would argue more, but then his expression cleared and he looked at his feet. "You are right. I am sorry. I won't let it happen again."

Not entirely trusting the sudden change, Anike said, "Good. I hope it doesn't."

"Who is Hrym?" asked Gunnar in the sudden silence, "and how can your friend wake him up?" He looked at Anike, but it was Lalfar who answered.

"Hrym was a giant, the king of the frost giants, according to legend. He is mentioned in a few old tales but he is mainly known for being the captain of the ship of ice that brought the frost giants to fight the gods at Ragnarok. History does not record what happened to him specifically, so I thought he had died there with the gods and other giants. Almost every creature who fought in that battle was killed, along with everyone who lived on the northern islands of the archipelago."

"We do not know, do we?" Anike put in. "It is not a name I recognise, so perhaps he was not that important."

"Anyone who is mentioned by name in the sagas of Ragnarok is important," Lalfar said firmly.

"This goes someway to explain my runecast. 'The place where the great ice rests' must have been a reference to Hrym. I should have interpreted it as 'Where the Lord of Ice sleeps'. The king of the frost giants would be the Lord of Ice."

"How can Enya wake him?" Lalfar asked.

"Now that I do not know. I will have to do a runecast when we next rest to learn more."

Anike thought, but did not say, that the dwarves were likely to be planning to sacrifice Enya to the giant. Blood was a potent force.

"Can you ask the runes what would happen if the giant wakes up?" Gunnar asked.

"We can be pretty sure we do not want that to come to pass, even without any runes. Now that the gods are just spirits, he must be one of the most powerful beings in the world and an enemy of the gods will not be a friend to humans."

"That won't happen," Lalfar told him. "We are going to save my sister."

"Yes, we are," Anike said with optimism she did not entirely feel.

"Why would the dwarves want to wake this giant anyway?" asked Gunnar.

"I have no idea," said Anike. "Perhaps they have just found him? That seems unlikely though."

Frowning, she thought back nearly two years to the first dwarven chamber she had set eyes on. Bjord's hunt for Anike had started to involve other people and Hilda the Seer had taken refuge there to avoid being caught up in it. Anike had found the cavern and there had been a carving on the wall which depicted what she had taken at the time to be men bowing to a giant on a throne, but dwarves would make more sense. If that had been a representation of Hrym, then the dwarves had known about him for many hundreds of years. "Or perhaps they have only just worked out how to do it," she added.

"The dwarf might have been speaking in allegory," Lalfar commented. "A story, or an idea of frost and ice so significant that it is referred to by name, as we sometimes refer to thunder as the sound of Thor's hammer. She might not have been speaking literally."

"Surely the dwarves wouldn't use a historical figure for that?"

"Why not? We do. And he might not even be real. Ragnarok was a long time ago, and humans had largely abandoned the northern islands of the archipelago before the giants and the gods fought their final battle there," Lalfar said. "Parts of what we think of as history could be just myth."

"The dwarf would not have referred to 'waking the giant' without naming him unless he was real, would she? In any case, now I have a better idea of what we are going to face, I could do a runecast to find out if Hrym is more than just a legend, but it is not the most pressing issue. He is still two days away, and we need to pick a path from here." She went to look at the signs on the wall of the junction.

"What do the legends tell about giants?" Gunnar asked Lalfar

"There were fire, frost, mountain and sea giants. They were terrible creatures of great power. Their kings were the equals of the gods, and they could change their shape, or disguise castles with seemings, illusions that made them appear to be something else."

"There is a rune for seeming," Anike put in. "It is a law rune, so I cannot use it but a law witch like our black-clad warrior could create a spell to make him appear to be someone else. If Hrym was a frost giant, he would be aligned with law. Dwarves are as well. I can feel that when I am close to one. Perhaps they have decided to wake a leader or figurehead?" She frowned. "Though why now?"

"They could intend to retake the surface," Gunnar suggested. "We drove them back before, and they may think they will be able to defeat us if they have a giant with them."

"Perhaps. Who could oppose such a being now?" said Lalfar.

"All the more reason to find Enya," Anike said.

She had been studying the names on the wall. They meant little to her. The only one she recognised was '*Undasan*' which was a name she had seen on the wall near Kindiski, but they had travelled away from it. There were three other choices and nothing to guide her. With a sigh, she reached into her bag and drew out the runes. Using them too often would invite disaster, but there was too much at stake to guess.

Anike finished laying out the rune map on the ground and cut her arm to sacrifice her blood. "Which is the safest route to take so that we can reach the place Enya is being taken to wake Hrym, that will not take us longer than two days to travel?" she said aloud and cast the runes, letting the blood drip onto the stone. The reading told her to turn left towards '*Da Valdi*' but after that became more descriptive rather than indicate specific turns.

"We will need to pass through a repository of some sort, but the path there is guarded," she interpreted, "It does not sound easy but if that is the safest way, we should take it."

She gathered up the runes and paused, as from the passage ahead came the unmistakable sound of metal boots on rock, coming their way.

- 13 -

PERSPECTIVES

The three humans looked at each other. The sounds were of many feet, and they were coming closer. They were not running but they were not strolling either.

Anike cursed their ill luck. The dwarves had found them very quickly, perhaps a cost of a runecast which was more useful to her than the blood she had shed to pay for it.

"We should go," Anike said and headed up the passage to *Da Valdi* at a run with Lalfar and Gunnar following. A hundred paces on, she paused to listen. The sound of the dwarves had not diminished, so she hurried on.

After another couple of minutes, they came to a crossroads. The runes had told her to continue straight ahead but if there were dwarves following, she had to delay or mislead them. She indicated the passage opposite. "Keep going that way, and I will catch up. I need to slow our pursuers down. I will be able to find you if you take every right turn. Do not stop until you can no longer hear anything behind you."

Lalfar and Gunnar exchanged glances. "I will stay and help, Anike," Gunnar offered.

Anike smiled at him. "Thank you, but no. I can fly faster alone. Go on, and I will be with you again soon. Go."

Lalfar guided him away, and she watched them disappear behind a bend in the tunnel.

Raising her cloak, she read the flight spell. "*Prana*," she intoned, knowing that it would be to her advantage to be in the air. Dwarves had to be used to how sound travelled underground but flying made very little noise.

She turned to a page in her book, drew in power and focused on the ceiling above the passage they had just come down. *"Prana,"* she said again and sheared off part of the ceiling just before the junction so it fell in a thunder of noise to block most of the passage. She doubted it would delay the dwarves for long and if they had not actually been looking for her before, they surely would be now, but she needed a few extra moments to prepare her plan. She did not want to have to fight. The gods had tricked giants and dwarves in many legends, and she chose to put her faith in a ruse.

The clatter of metal-booted feet on stone was getting closer, so she turned to the passage to the left and used the spell again. She hoped the dwarves would think it made no sense to block this passage unless it were the one they had taken. With another crash, tons of rock fell, not quite sealing it but presenting a significant barrier.

Before the echoes had died, she was flying silently away from the crossroads, desperate to be out of sight before the dwarves reached the first rockfall. As soon as she turned a bend, she landed and listened. Stone was being shifted behind her, but she did not dare look back around the corner. With her spell nearly expired, she walked cautiously on, confident that the dwarves were making enough noise to cover the sound of her footfalls.

She paused as the grinding of rock on rock stopped and heard dwarven voices, too distant to make out the words, then more noise of stone being shifted. The clank of metal on stone grew fainter and vanished.

Anike smiled. It seemed that the dwarves had been taken in. She hurried down the passage and came to another intersection. Hoping that Lalfar and Gunnar had done as she had asked, she turned right. The spells had not taken her long but before she caught up with the men, she heard voices ahead of her. Anxiety, mixed with guilt for sending them into the unknown alone, washed through her. She cast the flight spell again and pressed on to reach them.

As she grew closer to the source of the voices, she was relieved to hear they were speaking in Norse. She rounded a corner and came on Lalfar and Gunnar facing each other, their faces set and grim. "What is going on?" she asked.

"It's nothing," Gunnar said, turning to her as his expression relaxed into a smile.

"Nothing?" she said. "I could hear you almost as far back as the junction."

"This one wanted to go back to help you," Lalfar said.

Sighing, Anike shook her head. "Thank you, Gunnar, but there was no need. This was something it was easier for me to take care of alone."

"We heard crashing," Lalfar said.

"I thought something had happened to you," Gunnar added.

"That was my work," Anike told him. "I brought down the roof as I did at the entrance to Svartalfheim, but I blocked a decoy passage. The dwarves seemed to have been fooled and went that way."

Lalfar looked at Gunnar. "You should listen to me more," he said. Anike noted that his tone was becoming less respectful to the young jarl, perhaps the result of being further from the domain of human custom.

"We have to go back to the last junction and take the other direction," she told them. "I only got you to turn right so I could find you. If there had been a fork, it might not have been clear which way was straight on. We need to go on a little further and then we should join a main passage."

She frowned. "After that, it is a little unclear. Hopefully, we can get some assistance from the wall markings, but I might have to use the runes again. I want to delay doing so as long as possible though, to avoid incurring the displeasure of the Norns."

While they returned to the junction they had just passed, Anike wondered at how empty the corridors were. They had met dwarves, it was true, but she had expected there to be more since there was not as much open space as in the forests and mountains on the surface. She supposed they had just not found a town yet, perhaps because the runes had set them on a path that would avoid such places. For all she knew, there were great dwarven cities, and their people rarely ventured out. Or perhaps there were just not that many dwarves.

As they walked, Anike became aware of her demon becoming more agitated. "Hold on a moment," she said and drew her book out. She turned to her latest spell and incanted, "*Izik*," reading the pattern she had devised to find a chaos witch.

There was no suggestion Enya was close, but the demon was exerting itself more than it did in the presence of dwarves, more as how it had done when she had fought the law witch. She frowned. Surely if he were nearby then Enya would have been with him and close enough for her spell to have found her.

It was possible that the demon was feeling the distant giant, undoubtedly very strongly connected to law, but even a legendary being would surely not stir that response from two days away. It had to be something else.

Their passage ended when it reached a broad corridor which stretched both left and right. The indication to *Da Valdi* was to their left, and she was about to tell the others when the demon made a serious attempt to break free from the shackles within her. She closed her eyes to reinforce its bonds, then opened them again to see a lone figure walking towards them from the other direction. A greatsword was held ready in his hands, and the black armour was now familiar. Her demon clamoured to be allowed to attack the law witch.

The leather-clad figure advanced at a measured pace, his boots making little sound on the stone floor.

Gunnar drew his sword and Lalfar hefted his axe. By unspoken agreement they took places in front of Anike, who opened her spellbook. The witch paused, his gaze passing over each of them in turn.

Anike did not want to underestimate the danger he posed. The first time they had fought, he had been overconfident and had turned away, and the second time she had defeated him, she had been free to fly. More importantly, in both confrontations he had wanted to take a chaos witch alive so had only allowed his demon control for short periods.

The witch's face was not as blank or cold as it had been the last time she had seen him. If anything, he had a look of apprehension though he could not have been surprised by their presence any more than she had been by his. He was not attacking, so he was still controlling his demon even as she was, but there was a glint like the shadow of a crystal in the air around him and she realised he was using a stasis effect to enhance his armour, and that showed that he was prepared. He had chosen to have this meeting but his purpose did not seem to be to fight.

Lalfar and Gunnar were tensed, and it would only be moments before Lalfar started another battle which they might be able to avoid. It was easy for him to blame the witch for the loss of his sister. Furthermore, both he and Gunnar had been defeated by this man and would likely want revenge.

She reached out and laid a hand on the skald's shoulder. "Wait," she told him, then to the witch, "Stay back! What do you want?"

Gunnar glanced back at her in surprise, a foolish move when facing an experienced warrior, but the witch made no attempt to take advantage of the opportunity.

"To talk," the man said, as she had expected.

"Then say your piece." She kept her eyes on him.

The witch relaxed ever so slightly.

To Lalfar and Gunnar she said, "He is holding back his demon. If he had wanted to attack, he could have let it loose. He wants to negotiate."

The witch lowered his blade, but Anike was conscious that a skilled warrior could bring it back to guard in a flash.

Lalfar tensed, and Anike sensed he was still on the verge of attacking, of trying to exploit the momentary advantage. Gunnar seemed ready to follow his lead but not only did Anike's conscience recoil from an attack against someone willing to parley, she knew it was too much of a risk. More importantly, here was a chance to find out some real information.

She tightened her grip on Lalfar's arm. "Let him speak first. He may be able to tell us something that will help us find Enya."

Lalfar stared at the black-clad witch fiercely. "For Enya's sake." He lowered his axe.

"A sensible decision," the witch said. "Down here, any human needs all the allies they can get." He sheathed his sword on his back. The practised motion left Anike in no doubt that it could be in his hands again in a flash. She caught a glimpse of the runes on the blade and guessed that they were spells to use in battle.

"My name is Karak Skymirsson." The name meant nothing to Anike, but the accent was definitely Larten.

The man continued. "I need your aid. The dwarves have someone I have to rescue too." He paused, looking for reaction, but the three regarded him silently, so he continued. "I am sorry I tried to take your friend, but I was forced to do it by the dwarves."

Lalfar looked sceptical, but Anike said, "Go on."

"I serve Arl Aedan of Orestad, and I am the bodyguard of his son Hrost. Do you know Orestad?"

Lalfar frowned, but Anike thought she recognised the name.

Gunnar shook his head, and Karak continued. "It is a Lartenland town. The Arl was hoping to find a way to Gotlund through Svartalfheim, so he sent some men to find a route."

"For raiding?" Anike asked.

"Yes," said Karak levelly. "But we encountered dwarves in the tunnels and were captured. The dwarves wanted a witch from the surface, one tied to chaos. They decided to use me to find one. They had been casting runes but knew I could do it more quickly once they had a general idea of where to look. They threatened to kill Hrost if I refused to help them and put our two companions to death to show they were serious."

Gunnar gasped. "It is dishonourable to kill defenceless prisoners."

Karak nodded. "The dwarves seem to have little sense of honour and they don't regard us as equals. History tells us that they were clever and scheming, and I think that is right."

"How did you come to be in our hills?" asked Gunnar. "We are a long way from the north coast."

"They took me to the entrance their runecasts had told them was closest to a witch. I went to look for him. After a while, I felt his presence." He looked at Anike. "It was the old man you first saw me chasing. I tried to capture him, but he got away. The dwarves needed him alive, you see."

"Why?" asked Anike, relieved to know that this meant they would likely keep Enya alive for the same reason.

"They need the chaos inside to wake a giant. If the witch dies, it disappears. You would have done as well," he added, "but you seemed more powerful and might have been too much to handle."

Anike nodded thoughtfully. This accorded with what she had worked out.

"After I failed the first time, they followed me on my second attempt and took your friend when I could not. They only needed one witch."

"So why are you here now, alone?" asked Anike. "I can tell that there are no dwarves anywhere nearby."

"By the time I had recovered from our battle, we were deep in Svartalfheim. Because of my nature, they thought I would want to come with them to the giant, but my duty to my arl comes first and I told them to release Hrost. They refused, saying that as I had not delivered the witch to them, they were not obliged to keep to their end of the bargain. When I insisted, they grew hostile and I retreated. My runes tell me that they have kept Hrost alive as a hostage in case I return and attack. I doubt they feel very threatened, but they could be concerned that I might thwart them by killing your friend."

"So you are here, seeking to ally yourself with us?" Anike asked. "Looking for our cooperation so we can both save people."

"Essentially, yes. Together we may be able to save them both. I have learned a little about them and I know where they are going.

"So do we," Gunnar said. "Hrym's Hall."

It was perhaps not the wisest move to tell Karak that piece of information, Anike reflected. She could have used it to test his veracity.

"You have attacked us all, and for all we know this could be all lies," Lalfar said. "You just expect us to trust you now?"

The man called Karak regarded him calmly. "You may or may not," he said, "but all I have lost by trying is a few minutes."

"A few minutes? I doubt that," Anike countered. "Our friend is not that close."

"No, but some dwarves did pursue me, and I was fleeing in this general direction anyway. If you don't agree, I will just keep running until I am sure I have lost them."

"Suppose we kill you instead?" Lalfar said, hefting his axe again.

Karak touched the hilt of his sword. "Then the sound of battle will lead my pursuers to your corpse."

"Think for a moment, Lalfar," Anike said. "Violence is not always the best answer." She glanced at Karak. "Necessarily. It is just one option. We will discuss it."

Karak shrugged and crossed his arms.

Anike led the other two a few paces away. "We do not have to trust or like him to enter into an alliance," she said.

"Yes, but how do we know any of this is true?" Lalfar asked.

"It makes sense to me," Gunnar said. "I don't have my own guard, but my father has talked about it for when I am older."

"I agree," Anike said. "His accent is Larten. He is probably not telling the whole truth, but I suspect his story is basically accurate. And if he did not have a falling out with the dwarves, why would he be here alone?"

"I do not like the idea of having him at my back, especially with that sword," Lalfar said.

"Then let us make him hand it over to us, at least until we meet enemies," Gunnar suggested.

Anike nodded. "He may not do it, but I agree we need to take some precautions. Remember, he is still dangerous without it and his demon needs no weapon or written spell to kill."

"You can protect us though, can't you, Anike?" Gunnar's voice rang with trust and confidence.

"If I am awake, probably. Let me see if we can use our indecision to our advantage."

She turned to Karak. "If you truly wish to ally with us, tell us something we do not know."

"A further sign of good faith? This is beginning to look one-sided."

"You came to us."

"Very well." Karak considered. "I will tell you why the dwarves want to wake Hrym."

"Go on," she said.

"The dwarves venerate him. It's not exactly worship as they don't expect anything in return. They seem to have decided to protect him while he sleeps, and he is under threat."

"What could threaten a giant, even if he is asleep? Other dwarves?" asked Lalfar.

"No, it is the Nidhogg."

Gunnar looked blank, but Lalfar and Anike both gasped. A legendary creature from the dawn of time, the Nidhogg was supposed to gnaw at the roots of Yggdrasil, the World Tree, trying to make it fall. It was not mentioned in tales of Ragnarok, so Anike supposed it might have survived.

"How can such a creature really exist?" asked Lalfar.

"I haven't seen it, but the dwarves talk about it. They think it is real, though they speak as if there were more than one. They say 'this Nidhogg', not 'the Nidhogg'. Whether there is one or many, it is a great wyrm, tunnelling through rock. The dwarves say it is usually much deeper down in the earth but now it has come close to the surface and is heading towards Hrym. If it reaches him while he is still asleep, it will kill him."

"Can Hrym fight it, if he is awake?"

"No, or at least the dwarves don't think so. I imagine he would be weak after slumbering for so long. They want him to awaken and escape."

"So that is why they plan to sacrifice Enya now," Lalfar said.

"Yes. Until now, they had been content to leave Hrym be. Now they need to give a chaos witch to him, to wake him up. I assume that releasing her chaos familiar is the key to that," Karak said. "She is not my enemy and if we can rescue her as well as Hrost, I will not object."

"Why did the dwarves tell you all this?" Anike asked, noting that Karak referred to Enya's demon as a familiar.

"Hrym was king of the frost giants, after Ragnarok perhaps the most powerful law-aligned being in the world. They thought I would want to save him because of my law familiar, the source of my witchcraft."

"Are they wrong?" Anike asked quietly.

"I have no loyalty to a giant, whatever his history or powers. I serve Arl Aedan."

"It seems a fantastic story," said Gunnar.

"This was not just what they told me. They talked about it among themselves too."

The dwarves would not have spoken to each other in Norse so Karak must be able to speak dwarven, at least a little. She would have to remember that he would understand anything she said to the dwarves.

"If you are telling the truth," Lalfar challenged.

"You walk in Svartalfheim and have fought dwarves," Karak pointed out. "Are you really doubting that there is truth to our legends?"

Lalfar looked at him, then shook his head.

Gunnar piped up, speaking to Anike. "That tunnel we found that looked melted. I wager the Nidhogg did that."

Karak's story suddenly seemed much less fanciful. Anike shuddered, thinking of the size of the tunnel. Gunnar was probably right, and she did not want to meet a creature that could burn through solid rock. The stone had still been warm, so the Nidhogg could not have been far away when they found that tunnel.

She gestured Gunnar and Lalfar closer. "I think this alliance is worth a try. He has been willing to share information. Are we agreed?"

They nodded. "He gives up his blade if he wishes to come with us," Lalfar added.

Anike turned back to Karak. "We have decided that we will work together, but if you wish to travel with us, you will have to let me carry your sword. I will return it if there is danger or we need to fight."

"My sword? Surely you are not serious," Karak said. "I cannot fight without it, at least not in a way which is safe for you. If I have to unleash my familiar, it will be you that is the target, not the dwarves."

"Yes, we realise that your demon is law-aligned," Anike told him, "but you have it under control."

"I noticed you call it a demon. Interesting. Yes, I do, but without my sword, I will have to release it if I am threatened. And there is nothing to prevent you attacking me." He looked pointedly at Lalfar.

"Save that we know you would release it if we did, as you would have nothing to lose," Anike told him. "While we could kill you, it might come at a cost. The sword is another matter. You could strike me down without warning and the others would be defenceless against your witchcraft."

"You are asking a lot. A moment's delay in returning my sword to me could prove fatal, and not necessarily for me."

"You are free to act on your own then. We will not have you close unless you disarm. I will carry the sword – I have no training in it – and I will return it if you need it."

Karak held her gaze. "I have your word that you will not attack me if I give it up?"

"Yes," Anike told him before Lalfar could speak. "Unless you attack first or betray us."

Gunnar nodded. Lalfar still looked unhappy but then shrugged and dipped his head in acknowledgement.

"I agree then," Karak said, "provided I carry your spellbook. I will let you read spells from it if you need to, but I will keep it unless we have to fight."

The spellbook was useless to Karak, but she would be placing a great deal of her own power in his hands. Karak could not use any of the spells and indeed so many chaos runes might make it uncomfortable for him to hold, but he could destroy it. She shuddered instinctively, then paused to consider his condition more carefully.

She did rely on the spellbook. It was the result of many days of hard work and it was wishful thinking to imagine she could find a way to use anything but simple spells without it. The prospect of losing it brought home to her how dependent she had become, and it was not a pleasant realisation. Overreliance on any single thing, even something she had created, was not a good idea. If she allowed it to become a crutch, she could be helpless if it were lost or destroyed. She had other resources, including her wits and here was a chance to affirm that she was more than her witchcraft.

In any case, Karak would be mad to destroy it after he had come to her for help. He might be lying, but he was clearly neither stupid nor insane.

"That is fair. I agree." She held the book out towards him.

Karak raised an eyebrow, perhaps having thought she would refuse, then slid the scabbard off his back. For a moment they both were holding book and blade. There was a brief hesitation then they both let go, completing the exchange.

"I hope I have not made a mistake here," he said.

Anike felt the weight of the keen-edged blade and silently agreed.

From the distance behind Karak came the sound of steel on stone. "It seems that my pursuers have not yet given up," Karak said.

"Any suggestion on which way to go?" Anike asked him.

"We should try to get past them, but the side passages do not always lead straight or true. Let us go back the way you came and find another route. Unless that is, you are also being hunted."

"It would be safe enough to retrace our steps a little, as our own pursuers took a different passage, but I think our route would have to lead us back here. How far have you come since you left the dwarves?"

"I have walked for several hours," Karak said.

"Then we need to hurry," said Lalfar. "We cannot let them get too far ahead."

"Let us take the other main way, then find a side passage and somewhere to stop where we can cast the runes again," Anike said. The sounds of metal footfalls were definitely louder. "Come on."

She led them along the broad passage neither they nor Karak had yet taken. Lalfar indicated for Karak to go next. If he was worried about being followed by two armed warriors, he did not show it. Anike reminded herself to tell Gunnar to keep his distance. She did not trust the boy to be able to hold onto his weapon should Karak try to seize it, but there was no time for such admonishments with dwarves approaching.

She could not help but wonder whether allowing the Larten to come with them was wise, but nothing about this venture was certain.

THE GUARDIAN

Anike set a fast pace and it was not long before they found a side passage. It led to the right and slightly in the direction Karak had come from, and she turned into it, hoping they were not heading towards more trouble.

After a few more minutes they reached a larger tunnel, wider than any they had come across before. The roof arched up to more than twenty feet above their heads, and numerous glowstones were set into the walls.

There were no words of guidance at the junction, perhaps because the passage they emerged from was too small to warrant them. She glanced at Karak. He was looking about curiously, but she asked anyway. "Do you know which way to go?"

He indicated right. "This way leads more towards where I came from, I think, but it is easy to become turned around down here, and I don't remember crossing this passage."

"We had better move away from this intersection until we are out of sight, then consult the runes again," Anike said.

Lalfar nodded, and the others were silent.

She turned right and went a few paces down the road-sized corridor. For a moment she considered asking about Karak, but the need to pick a direction was more urgent. She could not think of a single question that would deal with both issues properly and did not want to risk two casts with the attendant price the runes would demand. The best she could come up with was, 'Which way should Lalfar, Gunnar and I go to reach Enya as safely as possible before the dwarves give her to Hrym?' If Karak was planning betrayal, the runes might provide at least a hint within their answer.

She was unwilling to make the cast without a sacrifice and did not want Karak to overhear how she worded the question. It was better not to give him any more information than she had to. Beckoning Lalfar over, she asked him, "Are you willing to sacrifice your blood this time?"

He nodded, and she leaned close to him and whispered the question to him. Pulling back, she said, "Do not say it out loud. Just think of it as you cast the runes and bare your arm."

Lalfar threw the stones and allowed Anike to draw her knife over his forearm and guide the blood onto a cloth so there would be no stains on the ground to mark their passage. She read the runes and noticed that Karak looked at them too.

She saw no indication that he intended to betray them. Their safest course was to turn right along a path to an archive or repository but even on this least dangerous route, there was an obstacle that they would need to overcome. She frowned. The runes could be referring to a dwarf guard though the answer read more as if it was something inanimate, perhaps a locked door. She hoped the latter was the case. Breaking through a door would be easier than defeating a dwarf.

Dwarves could read runes too and could track them in the same manner, so it was better to keep moving. She gave Lalfar a potion to heal his arm. Injuries had begun to accumulate, and they needed to stay strong.

"We go this way," she said, "but there is something in our way. It is not clear what it is, but this is still the safest path to take." She dropped the runes and the map back into her bag.

As they set off again, Gunnar said, a little hesitantly, "Anike?"

"Yes, Gunnar?"

"What did you mean about a demon?"

Anike stopped short. She had forgotten that Gunnar had not been present when she had explained the source of her power to

Lalfar. The boy must have been more than a little puzzled by her conversation with Karak, perhaps even frightened.

She placed a hand on his shoulder. "There is no need to worry. I keep the source of my power in check and control it with runes, but it is an intelligent and destructive being. It merged with me a couple of years ago and made me a witch. Karak is in the same position."

Sighing, she continued. "Most witches cannot restrain their demon consistently and that is usually why they do such terrible things – it is the demon that does them. People are right to be cautious of witches. When we reach Enya, I will need to work with her so that she can stay in control, like me."

Gunnar looked at her for a moment and then smiled. "I always knew you were a good witch, Anike."

She squeezed his shoulder. "Thank you, Gunnar. Let us be off now."

This corridor was large, seemingly more of a road. The few side passages they saw were mostly unlit, not part of the path indicated by the runes, so they passed these by. As they progressed further, Anike became aware that they were now walking over a slight covering of dust and while they were leaving a trail, there were no other footprints.

She looked back but could not think how to the erase signs of their passage. Wind would clear away the marks of their boots but just leave a different sort of trail.

It was also concerning that the dwarves did not seem to use this route and she could not help but wonder why so major a road had been abandoned. She began to wish she had phrased the runecast differently.

After another fifteen minutes, the passage ended in a flight of wide stone steps which led gently downwards, and the walls and ceiling were even more brightly lit.

"This does look like the way to somewhere, doesn't it?" Lalfar commented.

"This archive must be very grand," said Gunnar.

"A place long abandoned, it seems. This route does seem suitable if we wish to avoid trouble," Karak said.

They descended cautiously, alert for any sign of life, but the area appeared to be deserted. After about fifty paces, they reached an enormous hall, wider and higher than any worked area they had yet seen. From the foot of the stairs, Anike could see the length of the hall, some twenty paces wide and perhaps four times that length. At the far end were great double doors on which was set a bas relief in a crude image of a man or dwarf, some fifteen feet high and bisected by the gap between the doors.

Set throughout the gallery were over twenty plinths around two paces tall. Atop each was a statue and above every one, a glowstone hung from an elegant bracket that seemed to grow from the wall. The statues showed all manner of men, or perhaps they were gods or dwarves, and some inhuman creatures. They formed two rows, like a stone honour guard for those approaching the doors.

The closest pair of statues were wolves, one carved from white stone, the other as black as pitch, both standing in poses so lifelike that they looked as if they might spring from the pedestals. "Look at those," Anike breathed. "They could almost be real."

"Maybe they are," said Gunnar. "Turned to stone by the dwarves."

"I doubt that," Karak told him with a short laugh and pointed to a figure a little further on. "Look at that one – it is Odin. He died during Ragnarok." The statue he had indicated was unmistakably the All-Father with his spear raised in a salute or challenge, and his one eye seemed to dance with a hint of light.

Anike walked slowly between the statues, her footsteps raising small clouds of dust. Some she recognised as gods by what they held. Vali the Avenger was armed with his bow and Idun carried her casket of apples, but many of the others were unknown to her. Some seemed to be dwarves, others giants. She looked at Lalfar.

"I don't know them all," he said. "There is Sigyn, the wife of Loki, and that one is Hel with her half skull face, but I do not recognise the dwarves."

Gunnar had stopped by another statue, an elegant and stunning woman. "Her hair is actually made of gold threads," he said, looking up at her.

"That must be Sif, Thor's wife," Lalfar said. "Loki stole her golden hair and he had some dwarves make her more out of gold. The Sons of Ivaldi, they were known as."

"The runes said to go through the archive," mused Anike. "Is this it? Dwarven feats and legends recorded in stone?"

"I would say that is the entrance to somewhere," Karak said, gesturing at the giant double doors at the far end of the hall.

As they drew closer, Anike got a better view of the bas relief. It was not, as she had first thought, a crude depiction of a man or a dwarf, but a simple and elegant figure, created with the same incredible workmanship as the statues in the hall. She could make out runes covering the figure but not on the rest of the door. The pattern was large and complex, with the forms of earth and movement both prominent. If it had been a spell, it was much more intricate than anything she had ever conceived but she doubted that it was, as it featured forms of both law and chaos.

There were no obvious handles or other means to open the doors. The dust before them had been undisturbed for years, and she was about to step forward to examine the runes more closely when Karak put up his hand. "Wait."

Anike halted. She had been ignoring her demon, which had been constantly struggling to break free and attack Karak, but now she suddenly felt it lash out hard against its bonds, its attention directed at something in front of them. She suspected Karak had just felt something similar.

Ahead of her there was a suggestion of movement, and it took her a moment to believe what was happening. Barely disturbing the dust on the floor, the two sides of the figure, one on each door, were bonding together. Gunnar gasped as he saw it, then let out a cry as the entire image stepped out from the door, leaving a hollow behind it.

It took a single pace forward and spoke in dwarven. "Ivaldi forbids entry on pain of death. I am the instrument of that will."

"How is it doing that?" Anike said in amazement, before realising that Gunnar and Lalfar had not understood the words. She stepped backwards, put a restraining hand on the arm of each and translated.

Karak glanced at Anike. "Perhaps it was just triggered, and this is all it does."

Anike had never worked the contingency rune *Rea* into a spell but she knew it could be tied to certain events, such as the presence of life. "It would be a lot of effort just to speak a warning aloud," she said, "but go ahead if you want to test that theory."

Karak started to edge around the stone figure but its head pivoted towards him, more smoothly than Anike would have suspected from a statue. There was no sound of grinding – the stone in the neck almost seemed to flow like water changing course in a stream when a rock was placed in it. Karak pulled back.

"I think it will carry out Ivaldi's decree if we give it a chance," Lalfar said.

"Ivaldi? That name seems familiar," Karak said.

"Yes, I spoke of his sons earlier," Lalfar reminded him. "Ivaldi was a dwarf, though his own deeds are not recorded in any tale I know. His sons made hair for Sif and Odin's spear, Gungnir. He was probably a crafter too. Perhaps he made a guard for his home."

"We may have to fight it then. Here." Anike reached a decision and handed the greatsword back to Karak. "Let me have my spellbook. We will exchange them again when the danger is passed, but we will need all of our strength here, and I do not want to risk unleashing your demon."

Karak nodded as he took the hilt of his blade and passed the book back.

"So you are not trying to avoid this fight?" Lalfar asked.

"It is not a living creature. It is just an obstacle we must pass."

Karak drew the sword from its sheath, flourishing it as he did so. Anike had her first chance to look at the runes inscribed on the blade properly. Her demon recoiled from them. Even on a few seconds inspection, she was sure they were spells.

She lifted her book. "It is just stone, and I have a spell to destroy that," she said. "I need to touch it though. Can you draw its attention?"

"I can," said Karak, looking at his blade. He flipped it over and read the runes on one side, "*Ert.*" A crystalline shimmer surrounded him as the stasis field formed.

"I want to help," said Gunnar, sliding his shield off his back.

"Just be careful," Anike told him.

Karak moved towards the left of the stone figure and when it turned to face him, Gunnar angled towards its other side. Its head rotated to keep track of him. Looking up, Anike saw the stone stretch as it did so, and she recognised a warping effect. Strange as it was, the figure could be animated by witchcraft, or something closely akin to it.

The rock form moved towards Gunnar and swept its right arm out in his direction. Caught by surprise, Gunnar dodged back but Karak stepped forward swinging his blade. It clanged against a stone leg. The figure swung its other hand at him, ponderously but more swiftly than Anike would have wished. Karak blocked but the force of the blow sent him sprawling and the animated statue advanced towards him. He collected himself and started to roll away.

Before it could reach him, Anike leapt forwards, reaching towards its right leg. "*Prana,*" she said, reading the spell to reduce stone to dust as her hand hit it. Power flowed, but it had no effect on the figure before her and she barely had time to fling herself clear before an arm like a tree trunk swept through where she had been standing.

She scrambled to her feet a few paces away, ready to run, but the stone figure had returned to immobility. It looked as if it had no interest in them unless they approached it or the door.

"So, that did not work," she said.

"Did you actually cast the spell?" Karak asked.

"Of course I did," she told him crisply. It would not do for Karak to believe her craft was erratic. "Whatever animates it must be protecting it somehow."

She stared at the figure. When she had touched the stone, there had been a sensation. The runes on it were active, like a spell but as solid as the rock. She could not imagine being able to interrupt it as she had Karak's spells.

Trying to get close enough to examine the runes that covered the body without causing it to react, she took a cautious step forward. Law runes, stone in particular, were prominent within the complex pattern. There were many instances of the warp effect too, particularly near the joints but the most striking rune was on its forehead.

"It has been given life," she breathed in wonder. She had never thought to see *Vit*, the rune of life, a force beyond law or chaos, used in a spell. It was much harder to affect living creatures than inanimate matter and if this rune imbued the stone with life, it was no wonder that her spell had failed. She could never cast a spell powerful enough to turn a human to dust.

Her other offensive spells would not work either. She could not call lightning from the sky while underground, and fire would be useless against something made of stone.

"I do not believe any of my spells can hurt it," she told the others. "You have nothing either, I assume?" She addressed Karak, and he shook his head.

She drummed her fingers on the shaft of her spear. "Smoke could work. We might be able to pass it if it cannot see us."

When no one dissented, she opened her book and found the spell. "*Agni*," she said clearly, covering the area where the figure stood in thick, grey smoke. She moved towards the side wall, keeping well beyond the limits of the cloud, then headed towards the doors.

The thud of stone on stone told her that the figure had taken a step in her direction. Whatever its means of perception, it was not blocked by the smoke. She pulled back.

"It is not being fooled, is it?" Lalfar said as they waited for the cloud to disperse. "And it seems quite dangerous."

"Dangerous enough to keep dwarves away. From the look of the dust on the floor, no one else has been here in many years," Karak said. "It is not pursuing us though, so we have time to think through our strategies."

"How can we kill something that can intimidate dwarves?" Gunnar asked.

"It may be respect for Ivaldi that prevents the dwarves from coming here," Anike suggested. "This animated figure just emphasised his desire. I expect they could deal with this if they really wished to."

She turned to Karak. "The runes are not just decorative. They seem to be doing something. I felt that when I touched it."

"How does that help?" Karak asked. "You don't think you can dispel it, do you?"

"No. I wish I could study them properly, but the inscribed runes are likely to be what animates it and give it the trappings of life. If we can erase them somehow, we might be able to stop it."

"How could we do that?"

"Do you have a spell to create stone? You conjured a stone javelin when we first fought."

"I can see where you are going but I don't know such a spell myself. My familiar, my demon as you call it, did that."

"Perhaps I can do something then," Anike said. "I need a fair-sized cloth. Does anyone have one?"

Lalfar pulled a bright blue rag from his belt. "Will this do?"

Anike suspected he used it for juggling. "Yes, I think so." She spread it on the ground next to the wall. The dust on the floor was a paler colour than the animated figure, and she wanted something that would match the stone that made it up. She used her witchcraft to destroy a small part of the wall and channel the dust into a large pile on the cloth.

"The stone creature is reacting to us without anyone to direct it, almost as if it is intelligent. It may have something to do with the life rune on its forehead. As far as I can see, it is the only place that rune is inscribed on it. If I can erase it, even for a moment, it may stop it."

"Really?" said Lalfar.

"I am not sure, of course, but when I touched it, I sensed that whatever is making it move is akin to witchcraft, and a spell can be made to fail if the pattern creating it is disrupted. I cannot imagine how this figure can act as if it were alive if it has no life rune, so if I can block it then it ought to interrupt the spell."

Anike lifted the corners of the cloth to stop the dust from escaping, turned to another page in her spell book, and lifted the cloth into the air with her witchcraft.

"Get ready to run past it if it does not react to me," she told the others and willed the cloth towards the stone figure.

The construct ignored the rag, and Anike wrapped it around its head, letting the dust fill the life rune, then edged forward with her back pressed to the wall.

The stone figure did not react.

"Run!" she called as she passed it and made straight for the doors. She reached them and pushed, but they did not move. There was a clatter of feet as the others joined her. "Together," she ordered and all four of them shoved, but the portal still refused to budge.

"It doesn't pull, does it?" asked Lalfar, looking at the edges.

"No, there are no hinges," Karak told him, looking back at the stone figure. His mouth became set, and Anike heard a whisper of sound. She glanced back too and saw dust seeping from beneath the cloth. The massive hands of stone came up to pull the rag away and stone dust fell all around. The construct turned to face them with the life rune clear on its forehead once more.

Anike flipped to the previous page and placed her hand on the door. "*Prana*," she said urgently, and a section in front of her collapsed to leave a hole through the door. Without waiting to see what lay beyond, she pushed Gunnar through and dived after him, followed by the others with Karak barely evading the massive fingers. He rolled clear and they watched the stone figure turn and seal itself back to the closed door.

Anike turned to look at where they had found themselves.

- 15 -

LORE

The chamber was not as huge as the gallery they had come from but was still the size of an arl's hall. Half a dozen stone tables were dotted around, some with benches next to them and others surrounded by chairs made from metal and stone, all a little lower than might be comfortable for a human. Set on the walls were shelves and hooks, many empty but some holding hammers, chisels and more complex devices that Anike could not put a name to. Intricate designs were carved onto most of the surfaces, many of runes but in other places were diagrams or pictures.

In the very centre of the room was an enormous device made from stone and dark metal with multiple compartments. It stood only five feet high but exuded a sense of solidity. With a start, she realised that it was a forge, cold after ages of inattention but with a weight somehow speaking of contained power, a now dormant force which had once helped shape the world.

Unlike the hall outside, there was almost no dust, and no sound or movement of air either. Anike had the feeling that they were the first to enter this room in a very long time.

Leaning on her spear, Anike took a moment to let her heartbeat return to a normal pace. There did not seem to be any danger here, or at least no immediate threat. The place looked like an abandoned smithy or mason's workshop.

Still amazed by the skill that had created the stone figure that guarded the entrance, she wondered if it had been made in this room.

In the two years since she had become a witch, she had gained considerable skill and knowledge but it was based on what she could work out from the runes themselves. The stone figure told her that there could be so much more to learn. The idea that witchcraft created many hundreds of years before could still function awed her.

Ivaldi was a name from legends, from long before Ragnarok. She had not really believed the stories telling of the works of his sons and the dwarves Eitri and Brokkr who made Thor's hammer, Mjolnir, but seeing the stone figure made her wonder if they were actually true.

Even more amazing was the use of the life rune, *Vit*, something she had not believed possible. It was clear from her demon's reaction that dwarves were aligned with law and she had not imagined that a dwarf could use *Vit* in a working. It was conceivable that the legends had preserved the name of a dwarf of exceptional skill and power, even by the standards of that race. No dwarf she had seen had used witchcraft, and from what Karak had implied, none of those he had encountered had either.

There were three other doorways in the workshop, one as large as the one through which they had entered, but Karak would probably have to duck slightly to pass through the other two.

Lalfar had already started to walk towards the smaller one on the left, axe and shield at the ready. Anike looked around the chamber again and followed him, with Karak and Gunnar close behind. Karak still had his sword, but she was not sure the danger had passed so she made no protest though she kept an eye on the warrior and a firm grip on her spear as they went to the next chamber.

Lalfar pushed the heavy metal-bound stone door open to reveal another room, larger than the workshop they were standing in but with a lower ceiling. Most of the floor was filled with shelves. She could just see over the top of those in the middle but the ones against the walls were nearly fifteen feet high. Each held what appeared to be stone tablets, most about a foot tall with dwarven words on the narrow edge facing out into the room. In the centre were set some low tables, but no chairs. There did not appear to be any other exits.

"Best be sure we are alone here before we look at these," Anike said.

Lalfar took her cue and led them back to the other small door. They found it opened onto another room, also without other exits and a little smaller than the workshop, containing about thirty pedestals around three feet high and a foot across at the top, and on every one was either a statue or a small device. The statues depicted animals or humanoid figures, and were exquisite, some in stone and others in what looked like precious metals. In the centre was a horse with eight legs, about two feet long, but the rest were almost as marvellous.

They would be extremely valuable but were little use in their current situation and no doubt rather heavy. Anike left them and went back through the workshop to the double doors that had to lead onward. They were the same size as the one that had held the stone figure but on this side were handles and the carving was abstract patterns. Contained within the patterns were some runes, though not enough to create any sort of spell and they seemed to be just decoration. She put her ear to the door and listened. There was no sound beyond.

"This seems safe enough," she said.

"As much as anything in Svartalfheim can be safe," said Karak. "That looks like the way we must go."

"I think we should rest a while," Anike said. The battle with the stone guardian had been draining. "I would like to take a look at those stone tablets too. There could be something there which we can use, or something we should know." The image of Enya held by the dwarves rose before her, but she had wanted to learn the lore of the dwarves for much longer than she had known Enya, and this was an opportunity she could not imagine having again. "We can spare a little time, and I am tired."

She turned to Karak. "Your sword," she said, holding out her book for him to take in exchange.

"I had hoped you would trust me by now," Karak told her.

"Hand it over!" Lalfar said and Gunnar appeared at his side. Both had weapons drawn.

Karak looked at them and shrugged. With exaggerated courtesy, he sheathed the blade and passed it hilt first to Anike. She exchanged it for her book and went into the room of tablets with the others behind her. Karak moved off to look at titles, while Lalfar and Gunnar went to the central table and started to get out food and water.

There were tablets beyond counting on the shelves. Dwarven letters were engraved into the stone on the edge of each, and Anike wondered how much effort it had taken to do that for every single one. Near to her was a tablet on which was inscribed 'Creation' and she reached for it, curious. For a moment she thought it was attached to the shelf, but then realised that it was just heavy. She put more strength into the lift, and nearly dropped the stone when it writhed in her hands. She realised that what she was holding was a book with a stone cover and carried it to the table to look at it more closely.

The edges of its spine flexed despite being stone, much as the stone figure had turned its neck. There was no controlling rune visible to the naked eye, but when she concentrated, she perceived a complex rune pattern woven into the cover, a spell that was still in operation and made the stone flexible in specific locations so the book could be opened. A permanent spell. It would have taken a great deal of skill and power to create this, though unlike the stone figure it might have been within the capabilities of someone like Karak.

Curious, she set the book down, turned and brushed her hand along the closest row of books. She sensed the same spell was cast on each of them as if whoever had done this had regarded it as a mundane act. There was a vast amount of knowledge in this room, perhaps the accumulation of wisdom of an ancient being who had centuries to gather it.

Gunnar and Lalfar seemed to be squabbling and she paused to listen.

"Don't you find this journey hard, my lord?" Lalfar was saying. "It is a far cry from your hall."

"A warrior has to be able to put up with the hardship of travel, my father says. This is much easier than some of the things we have done together. No biting wind, no rain."

"You have the best of everything when you are at home, though." Lalfar's tone was mildly accusing.

"It is not so different. When you were staying with us, I ate what you did, and I have to practice with the sword each day. I have the bruises to show for that. We all have our ordained place and everyone has to work to fulfil their duty."

"But your life is certain, you know where you will be each day and that there will always be a roof over your head."

"Unless I am called to fight, to protect my people. My father does not want me to risk my life yet, but I am ready. When I defended Anike against Karak on the mountainside, I knew that was what I was supposed to do, and if I have to give my life for someone under my protection then I will."

Lalfar paused, and his voice became more reflective. "Now that is something I understand. I suppose the number of people I would do that for is just smaller."

Relaxing as the conversation between the two moved onto the mundane business of food, Anike turned her attention back to the book. She could see that the pages were also made of stone, no thicker than a sheet of vellum and with dwarven script on them. The dwarves had not shared with humans the skill to make stone so fine without shattering. She did not see how it could have been chiselled into something so thin and again she felt witchcraft within as she touched a page, a spell to strengthen it. The creation was more than a physical act but again this was something she could comprehend. She had burned the runes into her set of stones and this was analogous, a warping of the stone to create letters.

Setting aside her wonder at the construction of the books, she turned her attention to the contents. She was familiar with the legend of the creation of the world, where Odin had killed the giant Ymir whose body formed the islands of the archipelago but this version of the tale was different and she found herself reading with interest.

In the beginning, Ymir formed this world out of stone and ice, something she had done many times before. At Surtur's command, Dra turned from his path through the emptiness to tear apart what Ymir had created as he had done many times before.

Ymir and Dra contended over and around the world, with Dra striving to break through Ymir's guard and shatter the world back to dust. Many had been the times they had contended since the beginning, and they were evenly matched. Many times, Ymir had repelled the assault of Dra and sent him back into the void between the stars and leaving a new world to travel on in silence, and many times had Dra broken past Ymir to tear her new world apart.

Anike's mouth clenched in a line. The dwarven was difficult for her but caught up in this new story, she persevered.

Mightily they struggled, and Dra drove Ymir back to the world. It looked as if he would be the victor in this particular battle, but Ymir braced herself against the cold ice and stone and grappled with Dra as he descended. Dra strove to throw Ymir out of the way and they both bled profusely from the blows they rained on each other. This time, the primordial beings were so evenly matched that neither could triumph and they fell together into the world of frost and rock, blending into one another and quickening the stone and ice they touched, infusing it with life. Ymir and Dra were no more and now the world knew its name, Yggdrasil.

And within Yggdrasil, the spirits of Ymir and Dra were blended but the blood of both that had been shed during the battle had fallen to the centre of the world and there it formed terrible wyrms, and these wyrms were called Nidhogg and they gnawed through Yggdrasil. Those of the blood of Ymir sought to sunder Yggdrasil's life and where they passed the stone was left cold and dead. Those of the blood of Dra burrowed through the substance of Yggdrasil, destroying it, and Yggdrasil trembled at their passage.

Anike reached the end of the page and frowned. There were some similarities to the story she knew, but a lot of significant differences. She had understood Midgard, the world, to rest in the branches of Yggdrasil but the dwarven tale painted it as part of the World Tree.

There was more in the book and she was about to turn over the page when a sharp gasp from Karak made her look up.

He had another of the stone books open on a table and was following the dwarven script with his fingers. His runes lay on a worn cloth next to him. Anike moved so she could see the book too, and so intense was his focus that he paid no attention to her approach. It took only a few seconds for her to see why he had reacted so strongly to this passage.

The spirits of law and chaos that reside within occasional humans always seek domination, and some succeed in suppressing the human entirely to become the purest physical incarnations of law and chaos. The humans name these Abominations. They have forgotten that these spirits can be harnessed, brought to heel and compelled to servitude. The humans who now direct the spirits with runes are but pale shadows of their forbears who could dominate the spirit and use its power as if it were their own, for they have lost the spell that will bind the spirit to their will. They are the lesser for its loss.

Karak turned the page to see if the passage continued but there was no more. Anike read the words again, then glanced at the runes Karak had cast. Without knowing what he had asked she could not be sure of the meaning, but it looked as if he was seeking knowledge that would be useful to him.

The ability to dominate a demon would certainly fall into that category.

"By Thor," Karak muttered under his breath. Anike silently agreed, the rush of possibility and implication cascading through her. The demon was a part of her but the passage made it clear that there was a way to control it, not by constant battle and the complex formulae of rune patterns, but completely. She had spent two years continually on guard, learning to control and use the demon's power with painstaking study. She had often idly wished to be able to do what it could, to make something happen merely by thinking about it, and more so since she had come across Karak and Cairn. While the book did not say exactly how it was achieved, it referred to a spell and they were inside a room with centuries of accumulated lore. It could be right next to them.

Karak and Anike looked at each other. She could see the longing in his eyes, the hope written plainly across his features, and had little doubt that it was mirrored in her own.

Lalfar was looking at them both in puzzlement. Anike turned to him. "Karak has found something in this book. It tells of a way for a witch to fully control and draw on the demon inside, without the need to spend hours creating spells."

"Can you do that?" Lalfar asked.

"So it seems, though the exact means are not detailed here."

Anike thought back to the first moments after the demon had fused with her. Her will had been subverted and the demon had taken complete control without her even realising it. She had struggled to master what she had thought were her own darker impulses until she had finally recognised the demon within her, and the quest to learn more had brought her to Kindiski, hoping to find lore older than that retained by humanity. Now she was among the works of Ivaldi, a figure so famous that his name had come down through thousands of years even to humans.

In this room could be knowledge that would make a real difference to her, and to Enya too. If she could find a binding spell, neither of them would have to struggle with their demons anymore, and no longer would she have to spend many hours trying to devise a spell to meet an unforeseen need. That would be true power. It would give them a much greater chance of defeating the dwarves. In the longer term, it might also be a means to end the ostracising of witches, if she could find and give them full control before their demons made them hurt those around them.

Her eyes took in the numerous shelves, wondering where to begin in the vast store of knowledge, then paused. It would take years to read every book and even if she focused on the most likely titles it would certainly take weeks. Enya did not have weeks, or even days. If she took the time to search, Enya would be sacrificed to Hrym.

Her gaze fell on the runes on the table. She could cast them herself to find the book, but the thought of the price that she would have to pay brought her up short. What sacrifice would the gods demand for something so important? This could be one of the most significant runecasts in centuries. Karak might have already incurred a tremendous debt to the Norns for the last cast as his demeanour after he found the passage made it clear he had not anticipated something so momentous, out of all proportion for any sacrifice he was likely to have made.

If she had merely been exploring and come across this place, she would not have hesitated to delve into the books, but she was here to rescue Enya, and a wave of guilt washed through her. She drew herself up.

"We cannot stay to look for the spell the passage alluded to," she said. "It would take far too long. We must press on."

This decision sacrificed a crucial opportunity for witches but even the chance that she could still save Enya was worth the sacrifice. If she let someone, let Enya, die then she would not be worthy of the power she might gain.

Karak ignored her and turned to look through the adjacent books.

- 16 -

THE WYRM

Anike went cold. The idea of Karak being able to dominate and control his demon chilled her to the core. Even without that degree of power, he was incredibly dangerous, cold and ruthless, not showing any hesitation in harming others to achieve his goals or in the service of his lord. The fact that he could justify his actions did not make him any less lethal.

"We must move on," she said. "This is fascinating, but now is not the time to look for it. We have people to save."

"You can't be serious," Karak said, pausing and looking straight at her. "This is the discovery of ages, and you would leave it?"

Anike's heart sank at his words. Suddenly the worry that Karak might find the binding spell matched her own desire to have it. "Look at this room." She gestured around. "How long would it take to find anything here?"

"The titles will help. It is worth the time to learn what the secret is, how the spell works."

"Anike is right," Gunnar piped up.

Karak ignored him. "Imagine how much easier it would be to help your friend if we had free access to our familiars' full power."

She could not deny that, but despite the advantages, she did not want him to have such power. Then she paused, considering. It might be sufficient if she had equivalent ability and could hold him in check. Perhaps.

There was still the time factor. "There is no guarantee we will find anything," she told him, "and we do not have years to waste."

"Have you got so used to your familiar that you don't want to control it?" Karak asked.

"Hardly. We just cannot afford the delay."

"I agree with Anike too," said Lalfar. "The further we let the dwarves get ahead with Enya and your Hrost, the harder it will be to rescue them."

Karak looked sceptical and showed no sign of moving. His eyes glittered as he looked around, and she wondered if he would refuse to leave with them. Anike doubted Lalfar and Gunnar could fully appreciate the danger Karak might present if he mastered his demon, but she did not want to tell them within his hearing and so let him know how much that worried her. There was no doubt that he would also be an asset when they did catch up with the dwarves so she wanted to resolve this in a way that would keep Karak with them.

She sought a compromise. "We do need a short rest though," she told him. "We can spend half an hour looking through the books, and if we find a solid lead, then we will discuss it again. Otherwise, we will move on."

Karak looked at her levelly. "Very well," he said after a moment, shrugged and turned to the shelves again.

Anike watched carefully to see that he did not reach for his runes. She was sure that using them again would have spelt doom for him, bringing down a dire fate that would encompass them all. Fortunately, he also seemed to have reached that conclusion. He had been right when he had referred to this as 'the discovery of ages.' She could not think of any lore that could be more significant and shuddered at the price that a runecast would require. Karak had moved away, looking at other books on the shelves.

She turned to Lalfar and Gunnar. "Have something to eat," she told them, then checking that Karak was out of earshot, leaned in towards Lalfar and added in a low voice. "We cannot leave him here alone. I doubt he will find anything, but we must not risk him letting him be the only one to gain that sort of power. I hope he will come with us when we have rested but if not, we will have to force him."

"He is right that it would help to defeat the dwarves though, isn't he?" Lalfar whispered back.

"Probably, but we could be changing one potential enemy for another. I do not trust him."

Lalfar nodded slowly and turned away. She saw him speak quietly to Gunnar as they started on the meal. The boy looked surprised for a moment then set his mouth in a grim line.

She set the book she had found down on the table and looked at the one Karak had found – 'The Power of Gelda.' Returning it to its place on the shelves, she went the other way and started looking through the titles but keeping a close eye on him. The section appeared to contain works on men, or more likely dwarves, that she had never heard of. Given the likely age of the room this did not come as a surprise. Karak had already looked at a couple of volumes and set them aside.

The book titles gave her little immediate cause for celebration or concern. The most promising that she found, 'Acts of Empowerment', contained complex instructions for creating artifacts beyond her comprehension. From what she could work out the author, Ivaldi presumably, was able to find natural sources or concentrations of law or chaos and bind them into objects, though how he was able to accomplish this was written in dwarven too obscure for her to understand.

She lost track of the passing minutes and was caught unawares when Lalfar announced "Time's up". When she glanced at him, he said, "We had a look at the double doors while you were searching through the books, and they just push from the inside. We opened them a few inches and they look out onto another entrance hall. No one was there."

She straightened. "Come on," she said to Karak. "We have found no clues. It could take weeks, and we can rest here on the return journey and search properly."

Karak tensed and turned to face her. "I think we are close. We should keep searching a little longer."

Of course, he could be right and Anike's desire to keep the spell away from him at all costs had wavered while they had been looking for it. She was coming round to the idea that as long as they could both gain mastery over their demons, allowing him that power would not be too bad. The dwarves were a more certain enemy, and she found the idea of much more flexibility in using her witchcraft against them tempting.

The delay while they located the spell remained a bar, however. "No," she told him, picking up her spear. "You agreed to a deadline. It is far too easy to keep saying 'just a little longer' and if we keep doing it, we will be having the same discussion in an hour, or six. I do not know exactly how long it has been since we slept, four hours perhaps, but we have a lot of the day left and we have spent enough time in here for now. There will be another opportunity once the prisoners are safe. Living dwarves obviously do not come here."

Karak was silent, but she felt the tension rising. He glanced over her shoulder and she sensed Lalfar and Gunnar had come up behind her, perhaps even preparing to draw weapons. Anike regarded Karak steadily, running her fingers over the runes on her spear.

"Very well," he said and looked away. "Let us go then." He thrust the book he had been holding back onto the shelf.

Despite its great weight, the door moved easily when Lalfar pushed it, and he led the way out into another hall covered with the dust of ages. Karak followed, then Gunnar and Anike brought up the rear. Wary of having to retreat rapidly should a new threat confront them, she left the door open. A glance at the outer side of the still-closed door showed half of a bas relief figure, similar to the one that had given them so much trouble on their way into the archive. She hoped that if the complete figure were split into two parts it would not be able to animate.

This hall was similarly constructed to the one on the other side of the archive but showed off a different type of art. There were no plinths with statues set atop them, but the walls had intricate images within bas relief frames. Colours ran through them, perhaps from ores woven into the rock. They depicted various scenes that Anike did not recognise and she presumed they came from a part of dwarven history that humans knew nothing of. Once again, she could not help but be awed by the quality of the work. Like the statues in the other hall, the images seemed to almost leap from the stone as if a moment had been captured by the eye of the artist and set down for everyone to see.

While she did not know the context, there was one picture showing the crowning of a dwarven king, and present among the respectful throng were figures that she could identify as Odin and Freya. If accurate, the dwarves stood high in the estimation of the gods, but there was no way to tell if this was history or myth.

At the far end of the hall, a broad stairway rose, taking them up and away from the archive of Ivaldi. Footprints in the dust marked their passage until they came to a junction with a corridor where the floor was clear. The sign for '*Da Valdi*' was pointing the way they had come, and Anike did not recognise any of the other place names.

"Your turn to cast the runes," she told Karak.

The warrior grimaced. "You seem to be getting more out of this alliance than I am," he muttered.

"I think not," Anike replied. "I made the last cast, and it was my witchcraft that gained us entrance to Ivaldi's archive."

Karak's brow furrowed but he did not disagree. He opened a pouch at his belt and drew out the worn, patterned cloth he had used in the archive. He spread it on the ground and his lips moved slightly as he cast stones from the pouch.

Anike leaned forward to examine them. 'The right fork will take from away from your goal, but the left will take you closer to danger,' she read. The meaning was sometimes unclear if you did not know the exact question, but she could guess at what Karak had asked.

Karak looked up at her. "Left," he said.

"The runes warn of danger ahead, so we may be close," Anike added. She looked at Karak, "No sacrifice?"

"I made a vow," he replied. "It is not your business." He stood and gathered up the runes and cloth map. Clearly, he trusted Anike no further than she trusted him.

The little group turned left and as they travelled further, the passage rose slightly. By Anike's best estimate without the sun or stars to help her, they had been walking for half an hour when she noticed Karak starting to glance anxiously about him.

"What is wrong?" she asked, and even as he shook his head and held up his hand for them to halt, she felt something too. The demon was radiating satisfaction, perhaps even joy, something she had never known it to do before. Even when it caused chaos, scattered men in panic or turned ancient constructions to dust, it had not felt as exultant as it did now.

Her natural senses told her nothing. Lalfar and Gunnar had stopped and were looking at the two witches in puzzlement.

"There is something," Anike told them, "but I do not know what it is. It may be the danger the runes warned of but if so, it is something new." They started forward again more cautiously.

This way was clear of dust and curved slowly round to the right. A side passage led off to the left, unworked and unlit. Mindful that it might conceal the danger the runes had warned of, they passed it carefully but there was no indication that it contained any threat.

The demon seemed to be getting stronger even as it became more exultant, and it was testing its bonds again. Anike could still feel the hatred for Karak oozing from it but that was dwarfed by the other sensations it was radiating. She reinforced the images that held it in check.

Karak was looking more and more concerned. He was clearly concentrating intensely, and Anike called for a halt. "Something is happening to our demons," she told Lalfar and Gunnar. "Mine is gathering strength."

"Mine is ... worried," Karak said. "I would say it was terrified, if I had any idea what could make it feel fear."

Ahead of them, perhaps a hundred paces away, the light from a glowstone swelled like a star, dazzling them, and then beside it the wall started to glow. It turned red, then yellow and then melted and ran. A blast of white-hot fire burst through the stone and blazed across the passage carving a deep furrow in the other wall. As the flame died, it was replaced with a terrible light shining from the newly formed entrance, flickering but incredibly bright, shifting from one colour to another so fast that it was impossible to tell them apart.

Then the reptilian head came into sight, pushing out from the stone. It was perhaps ten feet from the lower jaw to the tiny eyes atop it, with a partly opened mouth that seemed to drip liquid fire from between teeth that glinted like diamonds. Every scale on the hide scintillated with brilliant, oscillating light. Anike had only seen something like this once before, in the ball of fire that had fallen from the sky and brought the demon to her, but that display had been like a candle compared with the bonfire before her.

As the head thrust out from the wall, an eye swivelled to regard them one by one. It was black, but within burned a spark so bright that it was hard to look at.

All semblance of bravado stripped away, Gunnar screamed and fled back the way they had come, and Lalfar seemed frozen in place. As the burning gaze swept over her, it took all of Anike's will not to break into a run herself and follow Gunnar in sheer panic, but it was on Karak that the eye lingered the longest.

Then the creature seemed to dismiss them, and fire burst from its jaws again. The rock before it dissolved, some melting but most simply vanishing under the incredible heat. The head disappeared into the wall, and, propelled by legs too small for the great bulk, perhaps a hundred feet of enormous snake-like body followed it.

Anike was slowly letting out the breath she had been holding when she heard Karak say, "*Ranak*," and agonising cold exploded in her chest.

She staggered, then rolled forwards in case Karak was following up with a hand to hand attack. She was distracted, part of her struggling to hold back her own demon, empowered far beyond its usual strength and on the verge of breaking out of its prison. Its exultation flowed through her, mixed with the desire to destroy Karak's demon.

Anike came to her feet, threw Karak's sword well out of reach behind her and levelled her spear at him. Karak was advancing towards her slowly, his body balanced and ready to attack. As with the very first witch she had encountered, two years and a lifetime before, his eyes were cold and his expression dead.

For a moment, she was tempted to give in to her demon and let it loose, something she had only deliberately done once before. On that occasion, she had barely managed to re-cage it and now it felt stronger than ever, as if it were drawing energy from the proximity of the wyrm, the Nidhogg. Nevertheless, in the face of Karak's advance and despite the demon's demands, she resisted and reinforced the images of law holding it back.

Suddenly, Karak leapt at her. He knocked the point of her spear aside with his hand and reached for her neck. Anike barely had time to shift her grip to keep the haft between them, and tried to hold him away from her, but he was too strong and his fingers closed on her throat.

Fear washed through her. The demon in Karak would kill her with pleasure as it tried to destroy her own demon, and even unarmed and without the demon's power, Karak was very dangerous.

She felt a pattern of runes form around her, a stasis spell to drain her life, and struggled to find the will to counter with a movement form. "*Prana*," she said, barely able to force the word out past the hands around her neck, just as Karak spoke "*Ert*," in a cold voice, and spectral images of crystal formed and shattered around them.

She twisted the spear, breaking his grip, but his hands closed on the spear shaft. He recoiled as he touched the chaos runes inscribed on it, and in that instant she let go of the spear and got her hands up to his face, trying to push him away. Her witchcraft was useless in this position – she knew no spells that could hurt him that were simple enough to hold in her mind.

Karak dropped the spear and his hands closed on her wrists. She stared into the dead eyes of the demon as he forced her arms apart and pushed her back against the wall.

Then Lalfar came up behind Karak and struck his left arm hard with an axe. Karak gave no sign of pain, but his grip loosened.

Anike opened her mouth. "Do not..." she started but then felt another net of runes closing around her and changed the last word to "*Agni*," just as Karak's demon said, "*Ranak*." The frost spell collapsed in motes of fire.

Karak gave no sign of disappointment and struck Anike in the head with his left fist, making drops of blood fly from her mouth, but the blow was weaker than she had expected. Lalfar's strike must have injured him, hampering him even though the demon cared nothing about pain.

Anike managed to gasp, "Do not kill him," to Lalfar who was raising his axe again. Karak suddenly shifted his weight and his right hand shot towards Anike's waist to reach for the dagger belted there. His fingers closed around it, and Anike wrapped both her hands around his wrist to prevent him drawing it. Lalfar brought the axe down again, this time with the flat striking Karak's head. Karak took a step sideways and Anike managed to squirm away from him, but her dagger glinted in his hand.

Anike was beginning to think that they would have to kill the warrior. He was crouching, ready to attack again and her demon desperately wanted to destroy him where he stood. Empowered by the Nidhogg, she sensed it would be able to do just that.

The power running through her gave her an idea. "Hold him off for a moment," she told the skald and stepped back. Lalfar, with his axe and shield, ought to be able to keep the injured warrior at bay for a few vital seconds. Karak had dropped her book of spells on the ground when he attacked her, and she circled away from the two men to reach it. As she had expected, Karak tried to sidestep Lalfar so he could get to her. His demon wanted to destroy hers more than anything else and had no real interest in Lalfar while she was so close.

She grabbed her book and opened it to the page she needed. Quickly scanning the pattern, she said *"Prana,"* fixing her gaze on Karak. He spoke, *"Ert,"* as the spell closed on him but with the Nidhogg still within the vicinity, she was the stronger and his attempt to disrupt the spell came to nothing. She lifted him into the air, away from Lalfar. He did not try to struggle but fixed her with a cold glare.

"Ert," he said again, directing power against her spell, but Anike held it steady against the assault and he remained suspended in midair. She picked up her staff, ready to read the firebolt spell if she needed to.

Karak suddenly slumped, closed his eyes and then pain transfigured his face. "I have control again," he said. "I am sorry." Blood dripped from his scalp and arm.

Anike lowered him to the ground as she dug out a potion from her bag, one that numbed the pain. Karak's wounds would need to be tended but he had to contain the demon first. She could sense that the Nidhogg was further away now and that her demon's strength was diminishing back towards normal. In a few moments Karak and herself would be too evenly matched for her to defeat him with witchcraft again.

"What are you doing?" Lalfar asked. "He attacked you, betrayed us!"

"His demon, not him," Anike said, handing a potion to Karak who downed it swiftly. "That wyrm, the Nidhogg, made our demons react. Karak's panicked and overcame his will. He needs something to dull his pain or it might happen again."

She looked Lalfar in the face. "Thank you," she added. "He would have killed me if you had run like Gunnar did."

Lalfar held her gaze, then nodded and gave her a brief smile in return.

To Karak she said, "We have to find Gunnar, but to do that, you need to be able to walk, and you look battered. Drink this too." She gave him another potion, one that would give him strength and start to mend his wounds.

Karak swallowed that too. "I am surprised you didn't kill me," he said. "In your place, I would have."

"I know you would," she said. Karak was so different from her in some ways but in others, he was more like her than anyone else she knew.

She had been able to overpower him with witchcraft because the Nidhogg had empowered her demon. This rather seemed to confirm the accuracy of the dwarven creation myth and that the Nidhogg was formed out of the blood of Dra, a living creature of nearly pure chaos, a primordial force in tune with her own demon.

She shook her head – this was no time for cosmic introspection.

"We need to get after Gunnar and find him," she told them both.

Anike was surprised when Lalfar shook his head. "He shouldn't have run off like that, and he will come back as soon as he manages to shake off his panic."

"You would leave him behind?"

"I'm just saying that he knows where we are, and we don't know where he went. It will be easier for him to find his way back to us."

Anike had to acknowledge that did make sense.

Karak was looking down the corridor towards the newly-melted tunnel. Light still flickered within it, but it was now much fainter than the brilliant display they had witnessed when looking directly at the Nidhogg. The wyrm must have travelled some distance away from them.

Anike looked back at Lalfar. "He would have come back by now if he was going to. Something has happened to him."

"I agree," Karak said as Lalfar opened his mouth to argue. "He is almost certainly dead or hopelessly lost. We should forget about him."

"I wasn't suggesting that," Lalfar told him, aghast. "I meant we should just wait for him here. We could make a little noise, and that might guide him back."

"Along with the dwarves," Karak said.

"Now that is a concern I do share," said Anike. "There may not be many dwarves close by, but it would be taking a chance to draw attention to ourselves. I am not going to abandon Gunnar, though and I will go to search for him alone if I have to."

Karak and Lalfar exchanged a look, each no doubt a little surprised to find the other more on their side than hers.

"Very well," said Anike, looking between the two of them. "Before we do anything, we need to know for certain." She opened her bag and got out her runes, then held out her hand towards Karak. "My knife?"

Karak, who had set her dagger on the ground while he drank the potions, picked it up and handed it to her wordlessly.

She bared her arm before throwing the runes on the hide, asking "What route should I take to get to the living Gunnar?" If he had died, the runes would tell her.

Blood fell onto her leg when she slashed her arm and grimacing in pain, she read the response. 'Take the tunnel into the natural caverns then descend,' was how she read the answer.

She pulled out another potion and drank it, worried about the rate they were getting through her elixirs but with little choice but to heal herself after the sacrifice, and the effects of Karak's attacks.

"He is alive, but probably trapped after a fall," she said, gathering up the runes. "I'm not going to leave him. Are you both coming?"

Seeing that his argument was defeated by the message from the runes, Lalfar nodded.

Karak stood still a moment longer. "This is a mistake," he said. "You were the one that wanted us to hurry, and the boy is not worth the detour. You are letting sentiment control you. But I will come," he added as he saw Anike's scowl.

"My sentiment, as you call it, is what makes me human," Anike snapped. She dropped the runes back into her bag and set off, picking up Karak's sword and her spear.

They went back to the junction and Anike turned into the unworked passage without hesitation. They had not passed any natural caverns for a long while and she reasoned that the runes were telling her that Gunnar had taken this path in his flight. Blind panic made for poor choices and sometimes there was a primal need to find somewhere dark to hide.

She admitted to herself that she was upset at the delay, and with Gunnar for causing it. She wanted to get to Enya as soon as possible and the detour was costing valuable time, as Karak had rightly pointed out. However, she was responsible for the boy being there in the first place and she would not easily forgive herself if she allowed harm to come his way, but that did not stop her from being annoyed. Concern that she might grant the demon some advantage meant that she usually kept her darker emotions under tight control, but sometimes frustration could creep in.

She pushed the feeling aside. Gunnar had seen a creature out of legend and nightmares, part of the myth that went as deep as the story of the World Tree. Even if the book she had read was right and this was not a unique creature but one of many, it was hardly less frightening. She should not blame him. He was young, but he had shown bravery on this journey.

About fifty paces on, the passage ended at a ledge that overlooked a natural cavern. She could not see the far walls in the light of the glowstone she held. Ten paces directly below, a river ran along the cave floor before it disappeared into the walls, perhaps twenty paces to each side of her. She was surprised she could see that far down at all, but then noticed there was a glowstone lying next to the river, much fainter in the cold than the one she held. Gunnar must have dropped it. It looked as if he had run right off the edge of the cliff.

She looked around. There were unlikely to be any dwarves here. "Gunnar!" she called.

"Here!" The voice came from somewhere beneath her.

She could not see him so shouted again, "Where are you?"

Gunnar's voice came from somewhere below and to the right, echoing strangely. "I fell into the river, and now I can't get back. I am so sorry."

The light from the glowstone Gunnar had dropped revealed little save that the base of the cavern disappeared into darkness on the other side of the river.

Gunnar's voice from below again. "Anike?" he quavered, though whether from fear or cold or both, she did not know.

"I'm still here, Gunnar."

"I knew you would find me."

"Stay still, and I will get you out," she said. Pulling out a coin from her pouch, little use as currency here, she brought a rune pattern to mind and said, "*Agni*," to surround it with pale white flames that gave off light but no heat. She threw it towards the sound of the boy's voice.

The coin bounced on the rocks below and came to rest next to a large outcropping near the wall. In its light, she could see Gunnar, clinging to a stone spike that jutted above the water, close to the nearside cliff. Both of his arms were wrapped around the rock and his legs trailed in the current. The water disappeared into the cave wall just beyond him, presumably flowing through a large hole.

"I am going down," she told Karak and Lalfar, holding her glowstone tightly in her hand as she raised the side of her cloak to cast the flight spell sewn into the lining.

"Hold on, Gunnar," she called and flew down to the bottom of the cavern. She could not land anywhere close to him as the near side of the river was nearly vertical at that point. Hovering above him, she considered whether she could pull him out of the water, but the spell would not support them both and there was nowhere she could brace herself. The current was tugging at his legs, making his hold precarious.

"I can't climb up, Anike," Gunnar said, looking up at her, and she could see the fear in his eyes. "It's taking all my strength to hold on."

"Don't worry, I can use witchcraft to lift you," she told him, "but I need my spellbook. Just hold on a little longer!"

Rising up to the cavern entrance, she addressed Karak. "Give me the book," she told him. "I will have to use a spell to lift him."

Karak looked pointedly at his sword, still strapped to her back.

It was part of their accord, but Anike still felt a flash of trepidation at the thought of leaving him armed and alone with Lalfar, even for a few moments. She leaned it against the wall next to the pair of them. Karak's mouth became a flat line, but he made no further protest and passed her the book. She put the glowstone in her satchel and took it in both hands. Renewing the flight spell, she descended to the base of the cavern once more to hover above Gunnar.

As she turned through the pages, the foxfire surrounding the coin went out and plunged them both into darkness. Gunnar cried out in alarm, and there was a splash. His voice was cut off in a bubbling noise.

Anike cursed. She had lost track of when the witchlight would expire. Pulling the glowstone from her bag, she caught a glimpse of Gunnar being swept against the wall before he was dragged beneath the surface.

- 17 -

CURRENTS

With her heart in her mouth, Anike watched the place where Gunnar had gone under. There was no sign of him, so she flew across the surface of the water and reached down into it. The icy fingers of the current tugged hard at her arm, bitterly cold, but there was no living hand searching for hers. He had vanished.

Her flight spell was of little use underwater. She had designed it to fly through the air, and it would not function properly if she were submerged. She took out another coin, cast her foxfire spell onto it and dropped it into the river. Before it disappeared beneath the rock wall, she made out a wide channel, at least five feet deep. There was no sign of Gunnar.

For a moment she considered just dropping into the river to go after him, but she had no idea what awaited her. If the underground tunnel had no air, she would be following Gunnar into Hel's realm of death, so she rose back to Karak and Lalfar. They had been looking down, Lalfar rather anxiously, but Karak's face was stern.

"I told you this would be a waste of time," he said.

"I am not giving up," Anike shot back.

"But Anike," Lalfar said, a little hesitantly, "Gunnar is gone. It is sad, but that is the truth of it."

"In war, men die," Karak added. "He ran, and this is what happens when men break and flee."

"Be quiet," Anike said, spreading her rune map on the ground. "I made him slip, so I have to put it right." She was angry at herself, and too much anger empowered the demon. Taking steps to remedy the situation channelled that emotion into something more positive.

"It was his own fault," Lalfar said, but he subsided when she glared at him.

"Surely you don't mean to use the runes for the same question?" Karak asked incredulously. "You must know how dangerous that is."

Anike paused, knowing he had a point. Another question relating to Gunnar so soon after the last would carry a heavy price, but she saw little choice. While she did not want to bring misfortune on anyone else, she did not want Gunnar to suffer for her mistakes either. She had failed to prevent Cairn's death by not being careful enough and had doomed Enya to possession by a demon and then to the dwarves' clutches as a result. Moreover, even after nearly two years, she carried the guilt of the murders the demon had committed before she had finally realised what it was and restrained it. No, while there was a chance Gunnar was still alive, she had to act.

Therein lay the cost. If they went after Gunnar, it would at the very least take time and put Enya at greater risk. It could also be dangerous. The price was high, but she would not trade Gunnar's life for Enya's when there was still a chance to save them both.

She formed the question in her mind, 'Is Gunnar capable of surviving long enough for me to reach him and treat his injuries so that he will recover?' and decided on the sacrifice, a vow before the gods to save him if she could. She cast the runes.

The answer came back. Gunnar was alive but seriously injured. His life force was ebbing away, but there was still time for her to reach him.

"He is not dead, but he is badly hurt," she said. "We still have time to rescue him."

"You didn't ask how to get to him safely, did you?" Karak asked.

"There is no time to find a safe way," Anike said. "We will have to follow the river."

"That would be suicide," Lalfar told her.

"Gunnar survived it," Anike replied. "I can try to break through the rock so we can fly over the water."

Without waiting for another response, she renewed her flight spell and descended to the river. She focused on the rock where it met the water and read the spell she had devised to shear through stone. "*Prana,*" she said and a wedge about a pace wide and ten paces long fell away and sank.

She looked into the gap but still could not see through to the other side, so she changed the angle and cast the spell again, cutting a horizontal half-cylinder that broke away with a loud cracking noise.

There was no sign of the river emerging into another cavern, or even of an air pocket, so she flew back up to Lalfar and Karak.

"We will have to swim," she told them.

"No," Karak said. "We should leave the boy. It is too dangerous. Even if he lives long enough for us to get there, the water will be freezing and there might be rocks. I can see how swift the current is."

Anike looked at Lalfar, who would not meet her gaze. "I don't swim well, Anike. Karak is right this time. You can't save everyone."

Anike looked between them. What they said made sense, but she could not give up now. Breaking the vow she had just made would probably doom them all, so she no longer had any real choice. "That remains to be seen, but I have to try. Give me two hours, and if I am not back, go on as best you can. I will just have to catch up."

She dropped into the river before they had a chance to argue further and let the icy current draw her downstream.

The chill sang through her but the winter sea she had known while growing up had been colder, and she steeled herself. Just before the current pulled her under, she took a deep breath and let herself go. Fighting against the flow would be a waste of energy. It was better to let it take her, and concentrate on remaining calm, but the looming reality of being sucked into a tiny cave in the dark strained even her will. She made herself relax, concentrating on preserving her breath.

The water dragged her down, then along. The glowstone had gone out when it had been immersed in the cold river and without any light, the speed felt tremendous. She kept her arms up to shield her head and felt the scrape of rock against her hand when she raised it to find out if the river had brought her to an air pocket.

A childhood by the sea had taught her respect whilst removing any irrational fear of water, but that did not stop the demon from reacting to the presence of the opposing element. It was radiating anxiety from its prison in her mind and combined with a rational worry about the unknown time before she would be able to breathe again, it was starting to push her towards panic too.

Reminding herself that Gunnar, who had grown up inland with no experience of the sea had survived, she visualised her fear being carried away by the current and the image calmed her. Then her lungs started to burn, and the uncomfortable possibility that his survival had been an immense stroke of luck grew inside her. She focused her will to resist trying to draw breath.

Just as she felt she could last no longer, her head broke the surface. Gasping, she trod water and tried to get her bearings. The current had slowed and she could sense that the ceiling was well above her head. After two more breaths, she concentrated on the brooch holding her cloak, the only small object she could easily locate, and spoke, "*Agni*," to surround it with cold white fire. In the pool of illumination, she could see that she was in a cave. On one side was a tiny beach, and above it the rock face appeared climbable. At the very limit of her vision, it looked as if a tunnel led away from the top of the rock face, some ten paces above her.

There was no sign of Gunnar.

While the river did not pull on her so fiercely in this wider area, she could feel herself drifting towards another rock face under which the water disappeared. Anike thought it unlikely that the boy would have tried to climb the rock in the pitch dark, but she had to check. She swam to the tiny beach to look for any sign that he had washed up there, but there was nothing. He had to have been dragged further on and she could only hope he had managed to catch his breath while he was here.

For a moment, she looked up at the rock wall and the opening she could just see. It was about the same distance above her as the natural passage that had led them to the river. It would be possible to abandon her chase after Gunnar, climb it, and try to find her way back to Lalfar and Karak.

Of course, she couldn't do that. She renewed the flight spell, useless under water but might help her get out of the river later, and took out the glowstone. She found the spell in her book to heat an object, something that she had devised to boil potions without starting a fire, and cast it on the crystal. It flared into life, dazzling her and she had to shield her eyes.

As prepared as she could be, she replaced the spellbook in her bag, held the stone in her left hand and swam to where the river disappeared beneath the rock.

The gentle tugging sharpened to a harsh pull as she followed the water down and into the next passage, but this time the light in her hand made the experience more bearable. Once again, she reminded herself that Gunnar had lived through this.

A jolt against the ceiling threatened to pull the stone from her hand, and she had a momentary flashback to another time when she had been struggling in the water. Aged about ten, her father had taken her out in his boat to teach her to fish. The wind had risen unexpectedly, and the boom had shifted. Working a net, Anike had not seen it and it struck her on the head and shoulder, knocking her over the gunwale and into the cold sea. She had been so disorientated that it had taken her a moment to work out which way was up, and she had gulped down a mouthful of seawater before her head cleared the surface.

Her father was calling out to her. The boat had been blown downwind, and he struggled to tack back towards her against the gale. At that moment, she knew that she could not wait for him to rescue her and despite the rising waves, struck out towards the boat. She caught up with it and her father pulled her back onto the boat with his single arm, and held her close.

She was not frightened of water. She understood it.

The river sucked her through a small hole, then out into a larger area. The current slowed again, and she headed upwards. Her head broke the surface and in the light of the glowstone, she could see that she was in another enormous cavern. There was a steep bank to her left, and she willed herself into the air. The spell struggled to move her with so much water surrounding her body and soaking her clothes, but after an anxious moment, she lifted clear and flew the four feet up to the bank. She found herself on a long shore leading up to a vast cave whose walls were beyond the light she carried, shivering with cold and without any sign of Gunnar. She clenched her chattering teeth, then called out his name, but her only answers were faint echoes.

The glowstone suddenly went out as the spell heating it expired, plunging Anike into darkness once more, and the cold bit at her. She concentrated on the foxfire pattern again and cast it on her brooch, giving her enough light to read the heating spell.

As she turned the pages, she came to another pattern and paused. This one created a bonfire that burned without using fuel, and that seemed like a much better idea while she stood wet and cold by the river. It might also guide Gunnar to her if he could move. She cast the spell, then spread her cloak to catch the heat from the conjured fire.

Warmth seeped back into her body as she stood there and after a few minutes, she felt ready to continue. The idea of jumping back into the stream did not appeal but the shore was fairly flat and she could continue on foot for a while. When the fire went out, she conjured heat into the glowstone again and moved forward in the centre of the circle of light.

The river seemed to be running faster here, and she was going slightly downhill. To her left, the wall of the cave came into view as the cavern narrowed to little wider than the river.

In the distance ahead, she saw something moving, a large shadow shifting at the edge of her vision. She recast the flight spell, grasped her spear in one hand and then moved forward again. If it were something hostile then, unless it was blind and deaf, it already knew she was there.

As she advanced, she saw that what was moving was not living, but a vast artifice made of stone. A series of blades over fifteen feet wide were dipping into the river in a never-ending cascade. From beyond the blades, there came a continuous low rumble.

Getting closer, Anike could see that the blades were positioned like spokes of a vast wheel around ten paces tall, dropping into the river as it turned. Suspended above the whole device was a bridge crossing from her side of the river to a door in the wall on the other side, and it was from behind this that the rumbling sound was coming from.

The cavern closed in further as she approached the construction, and she could see that if she wanted to follow the river further, she would have to swim again, but there was a stair leading up to the bridge cut into the rock. The wheel seemed to block the whole river and she had a vision of Gunnar being trapped helplessly beneath it. She bent forward to look underneath and saw that a net stretched between the two banks, just in front of the wheel. Had the boy been carried this far by the current, he would surely have been caught in it. She touched a strand lightly with a finger. It was thinner than the ropes that supported the sails on her father's boat but felt similar, supple and tough.

There were no tears in the net and it seemed unlikely Gunnar would have clambered over it to jump back into the river. The fact that he was not caught there suggested that he somehow managed to get out of the water. She judged that by the time she had cast the runes, he could well have been carried this far by the current. Her best chance of finding him was to see if he had taken the stairs.

There was no sign of anything hostile, but the whole area was clearly dwarven work and it paid to be cautious. Carefully, Anike ascended the stairs and crossed the bridge.

She stopped to listen at the stone door. There was a tiny hint of orange light coming from beneath it, and around its edges, but she could hear nothing except the rumbling.

There was no choice. She pushed the door open.

The room beyond was another well-worked chamber, an oval shape with smooth walls some twenty paces across. In the centre was a metal device that resembled a forge and it was from this that the orange light came.

In front of the forge was a bed, and Gunnar lay propped up against a stone headboard atop it. Next to him sat a dwarf, feeding him something from a bowl.

Anike had not made much noise and the door had moved almost silently but as she pushed it open the dwarf paused with a spoon halfway to Gunnar's mouth and looked round at her, or rather in her general direction. His hair and beard were snow white and his face was lined, but most striking were his eyes. They were covered by the milky film of blindness.

Gunnar sat up. "Anike!" he called out, then collapsed back, the effort seemingly too much for him.

The dwarf did not rise but addressed her in Norse. "Your friend told me you would come for him."

"How is he?" Anike asked, instinctively taking a step forward.

"He will recover soon," the dwarf told her. "He was drowning when I felt my net stir, close to death before I pulled him from the river. I have given him something that will restore his strength."

The dwarf paused for a moment, then continued. "You are surprised that I helped him, I sense."

"A little, yes," Anike told him frankly. "Those of your people we have met have not been particularly friendly."

The dwarf nodded slowly. "Given our past, that is not surprising. The last humans any of us saw were rather hostile."

He paused again. "But that was a long time ago by the standards of your people. I imagine a dozen generations of humans have passed on the surface since we left you to your own devices in Midgard."

"More, I think," Anike said, wondering slightly at his phrasing. She had been taught that the dwarves had been driven from the surface, and the poison recipe she had found tended to support that.

"My name is Morsali," the dwarf said. "You are Anike, I take it from your friend's greeting."

"I am," she acknowledged. "Thank you for helping my friend."

"I am responsible for this place, and I do not care to allow harm to creatures that come here."

"We are both grateful," she told him and came forward. "How are you?" she asked Gunnar.

"Getting stronger again," the boy said. "I was terrified when the water swept me away, but I knew you would find a way to get to me. Then I blacked out and the next thing I remember is waking up in this bed."

"It is fortunate that you humans float when you are unconscious," the old dwarf told him. "If you had been one of my people, you would never have been swept into my net."

He laid a hand on Gunnar's forehead then stood and came towards Anike. He was a little smaller than the dwarven woman she had met in the farm, coming only up to her chin. "What brings humans to Svartalfheim, after so many years? A hunt for dwarven treasure, or a search for secret lore, perhaps?"

Anike paused. The dwarf had been cordial, even friendly, but he was still a dwarf. "Neither of those. We are looking for another friend, though I always welcome the chance to learn more."

She looked about. At the far side of the room, beyond a rail, stairs led downwards. "If I may ask, what is this place?"

"It is a rock mill," the dwarf responded. "Here, I channel the power of the river to grind ore-bearing rocks to powder."

"I see," said Anike. She wondered if this was part of the process of making the vivid colours that she had seen in Ivaldi's art. Perhaps water could be used to power other things too, like grinding wheat into flour. Nangar would probably be fascinated.

Morsali grunted and turned to Gunnar. "You will be strong enough to leave soon, if fortune favours you. The potion would have worked faster on a dwarf, but it will strengthen humans too."

"I am feeling better," Gunnar said, sitting up. "Warm inside too."

"Why would it work faster on a dwarf?" Anike asked, curious and prepared to take a chance to learn something more about dwarves. "I thought your people were resistant to such things."

"It contains a little *dazarak*," he said. Anike did not recognise the word.

He touched Gunnar on the shoulder. "You seem better. It is almost time to think about you leaving."

Looking at Anike, he added. "But there is a price to pay."

– 18 –

MOTIVATIONS

"I understand," Anike said, "though I am not going to agree without knowing what you are asking for. It seems to me that you have already completed your side of the bargain, and without payment."

"Canny," Morsali replied. "But the improvement will not last without another potion. *Dazarak* is too strong for humans without mitigation. I was going to ask your young friend here for payment but you will do better, I think."

Anike pressed her lips together. The dwarf had not said that *dazarak* was poisonous to humans but that was the implication. "What price do you seek then?"

"I will come to that. Are there more humans in Svartalfheim? Are the seals to Midgard shattered then?" He sounded concerned.

"No, the seals are intact, for the most part," Anike told him. "I had to break one to get inside, but the arl closed it behind me. There are only half a dozen or so of us."

"Ah, yes. You are a *vafieigervaettir*. It would not be too hard for one such as you to break the seals."

Anike frowned. *Vafieigevaettir* was a dwarven word she had not come across before but some of the component parts meant 'chaos' and 'spirit'. He was identifying her as a witch, presumably able to feel the demon within her just as she could feel his connection to law. It was a different word to that she had learned from the archive in Kindiski, and somehow sounded older.

"I am," she said, cautiously.

"The *eigervaettir*, witches as the humans called them, were not highly regarded while we were shepherding Midgard."

The dwarven perspective of the Darkstone Occupation clearly differed from the human view. "That remains the case in general," she said, "but it does not stop me from having friends."

"So I see, and half a dozen friends seems a lot to me. Dwarves are few in number compared with humans," Morsali said. "In truth, I have little interest as to why you are in Svartalfheim, provided your presence is transitory. A wholesale incursion would be a different matter."

"There is little chance of that," Anike told him. "Our people have no interest in being so far beneath the surface."

"Humans have always been very insular," the dwarf said. "Any objective assessment would have shown that humans benefited from our collaboration. However, they thought differently." He sounded slightly regretful.

"We recognise that the dwarves taught us how to work steel," Anike said a little defensively.

"Despite that and the peace we brought, humans still prefer to be in thrall to other humans, rather than guided by us," the dwarf said. "It still surprises me that a supposedly intelligent species can turn its back on the benefits of cooperation just so they can say that they are ruled by members of their own race, with their petty rivalries and jealousies, rather than embrace stability and calm."

The dwarf paused for a moment, then continued. "Which brings me to the price. It is nothing immediately onerous. I have something that belongs to a human and I wish it returned to their successors. The price is your vow that you will try to deliver it."

"And what is this thing?"

The dwarf rose and moved to the edge of the room. At his touch, a small panel in the stone wall swung open. He reached inside and removed something, then touched the wall in another place to reveal a second cavity. From this, he took a stone flask before returning to stand by Gunnar, who was looking worried. Anike could see that his face was flushed.

"This potion will solidify the gain from what I gave your friend earlier." The dwarf set down a flask, then opened his other hand to reveal a golden brooch. "This is the item I wish you to deliver."

Anike stared at it. It was probably the most beautiful piece of jewellery she had ever seen, the form of a long dragon winding back over itself, finely worked and inset with gems. Her mouth fell open and she shut it hastily. "Who does it need to be delivered to?"

"The successor to Huppik, the first High King of the humans."

"But there is no High Kingdom now," Anike protested. "It collapsed centuries ago." The rule of Huppik the Clever had lasted many years but his successors had been lesser men, and after his death, the islands of the southern Archipelago had eventually fragmented into separate kingdoms.

Morsali nodded. "I am not surprised that happened, but still there will be a successor, or a descendant, either of him or his successors. In any event, someone with a better claim to it than I have."

Anike frowned. "How is it you have this, and why make this request after all this time?"

"I made it for him, but I did not finish it before we left Midgard. I would not have left an incomplete work behind and you two are the first humans I have seen since."

There did not seem to be any harm in agreeing, though Anike had little idea how to find the right person to give it to. "I can try," Anike said, "but I cannot promise I will succeed."

"That is acceptable," Morsali said. "We have an accord."

He unstopped the flask and gave it to Gunnar. "Drink this. It will keep you healthy."

Gunnar grabbed the potion and gulped it down.

The dwarf smiled. "I am glad we were able to reach an understanding. I did want to save your friend." He held the brooch out to Anike.

She took it and turned it over, eyes taking in the wonderous work. The wrought gold was etched with tiny scales and a ruby was set as the eye. Each of the claws held a tiny diamond, glinting in the light. It was a work fit for a king, undoubtedly. Even more intriguingly, she felt a similar sensation to that from her bag of runes, tingles of both attraction and antipathy.

"It feels like runic work," she said, "but I do not see any on it."

"I inscribed them into some of the layers of the metal," Morsali told her. "They are inside."

Anike concentrated, but she could not sense any energy flowing. "What do they do?" she asked.

"They are not witchcraft, such as you would perform," the old dwarf told her. "I set within it an invocation to help the brooch stay with its owner. You might liken it to a prayer."

"I see. I am surprised you pray to the gods."

"Men do, and this is meant for a man to wear."

"Very well," said Anike. She found a piece of cloth, wrapped up the dragon and put it at the bottom of the pouch at her waist. "I will try and find the right person to give it to. How did you know Huppik, may I ask?"

"I was one of the first dwarves on the surface," Morsali said, a little wistfully. "I went there with hope, and for a while we built something. There was peace for many of your generations, more than you had had in a long time. But the history of your race has often been driven by the actions of a small number of ambitious men."

Gunnar frowned as Morsali continued. "Huppik was one of them. He was a liaison between my race and yours and we svartalfen regarded him highly. In the end, we found out that his diplomatic demeanour masked a man of ambition and cunning. It was clever of him to devise the poison he used against us."

"But Huppik is famous for inventing the sail," Gunnar said before Anike could respond. "That allowed us to move large numbers of men around quickly. Poison would not have been honourable."

Morsali regarded him. "I was there when we first went to the surface to restore order, and I was one of the last to leave. Sails made some difference, but the poison that he devised to weaken us counted for more."

"You came to restore order?" Anike asked.

"By that time, your ancestors, the humans from the north who had fled south to avoid Ragnarok, had all but eliminated the Southrons, who used to live on these islands, and were turning on each other. We wanted to preserve what remained."

"If you dwarves were acting in our best interests, why did humanity rise up against you?" Gunnar asked. "The stories from that time tell us that your rule was oppressive and restrictive."

"Your people chose freedom over security, struggle over prosperity, self-determination over advancement. They valued intangible feelings over pragmatism," Morsali said. "Of course, there were personal interests too. The uprising was good for Huppik, but short-sighted for humanity. We accepted the rejection once it was clear how much humanity valued rule by its own."

"Accepted?" Gunnar queried, picking up on the word Anike had noticed earlier.

"The poison Huppik devised had some effect on us, but it took a little time to work and we could have chosen to fight. We did not have to leave humans to their own devices, but took the concerted uprising as a sign that they would rather destroy each other than live in peace, so we left. We were not in real danger. "

"It sounds as if Huppik betrayed you," Anike said. "Why do you still want the brooch to go to his successor?"

"I had promised him a gift," Morsali said. "It was not conditional on his behaviour, so there was no accord that could be breached."

"I doubt most humans would think of it like that."

"We see things differently to you."

Anike nodded. "Stability and calm are not the most important things for some humans. Many prefer to fight." Her tone had turned slightly bitter. "We still have prejudices, unfortunately."

Morsali sounded sad. "But as it was, we accepted that humanity had taken a position and decided to leave you to your own devices and sealed the entrances so no one would come to Svartalfheim to trouble us. And we would not have to consider what they were doing to each other in Midgard."

Anike nodded and went over to Gunnar. He was looking healthy, stronger and most of his cuts had faded as if he had drunk one of her potions. "Your elixir was potent," she said to the dwarf.

"The *dazarak* enhances the effectiveness of most potions," Morsali told her. "It is just too strong for humans without mitigation."

"I have never heard of it."

Morsali nodded. "I would have been surprised if you had. There is none on the surface."

It was almost as if Anike heard the clink of falling runes in her mind. In a stroke of fortune that surely was the cost incurred for a runecast by someone hostile to her, Morsali had just revealed something truly useful. The history was fascinating, but she had to get away in case she or Gunnar said something that made him realise what he had done.

"That has given me a lot to think about," she said. "We have trespassed on your time long enough, and our friends will be worrying. Is there a way to rejoin the river upstream? We cannot make our way back against the current."

The old dwarf nodded and turned his face towards her again. "Yes. It has been interesting to meet a human again and I am glad to have been able to pass the brooch onto you, but I do not wish to be reminded of my time on the surface any more. Come. I will set you on the way."

He rose and walked towards the stairs leading down. He moved confidently but his hand brushed against objects as he crossed the room and his head tilted slightly as he walked. She and Gunnar followed.

The stairs wound through a large room with moving shafts of rock running into a central intricate construction, the source of the grinding noise. Anike could see a large bowl at the bottom of the device, where the dust of some green crystal was collecting. They came to a door, which Morsali opened.

"Take this way, then turn right at the junction. It will go up slightly. Take the next right turn and you will then be in a long passage that runs parallel to the river. You should be able to find your way back to where you entered it."

Anike nodded. "Thank you for your hospitality." She led Gunnar out into the passage and the old dwarf closed the door behind her.

"Come on," she said, leading Gunnar down the corridor.

Morsali would not have known she had the recipe for the elixir that Huppik had used, a formula that did not contain *dazarak*. If she could find this underground plant, she could use her skill and if necessary the runes to find a way to strengthen that potion.

"Why was he lying about Huppik?" asked Gunnar.

"I doubt he was," Anike said. "He probably did know him."

"But Huppik was a hero, fighting for freedom. The dwarves were keeping us as slaves."

"We only know the stories told by our ancestors," Anike said. "Of course they would celebrate our new ruler as a hero. The dwarves see us as less than them, sort of like horses or dogs, and we need to be trained with a firm hand. Perhaps he thought they were helping us, like when he pulled you from the river."

"But we aren't dogs, Anike."

"No." She smiled at him, but she felt there was some truth in what Morsali had said. How many lives were wasted during raids, and how much could be done if people turned their skills to construction rather than fighting? And the suggestion that her forebears had essentially exterminated the race of humans who had first lived in Gotlund was unsettling too.

She put that to one side. History was interesting but the knowledge of *dazarak* was important now.

"One more thing, Gunnar," she added. "Please do not mention the brooch to the others."

"Why not, Anike?" Gunnar asked.

"They might try to steal it. I mean to keep my promise to Morsali." She did not add her agreement with the old dwarf felt too personal to share with them, for some reason that she could not put her finger on.

Gunnar looked at her solemnly and nodded.

They followed the corridor. After the second turn, they passed the tunnel the Nidhogg had burned through the rock. The stone was slightly warm, but no light flickered from the direction the wyrm had taken. It did not tunnel quickly through solid rock, certainly slower than a walking pace, but it had long since passed beyond their sight. She wondered if it had turned at all. It was hard to imagine what could divert it.

They walked past the area where Karak's demon had attacked her then took the passage towards the cavern with the river.

Lalfar and Karak were where Anike had left them. Gunnar ran the last few paces towards them, and clasped Lalfar's hand. Both grinned broadly and a small smile even touched Karak's face.

On the ground between Lalfar and Karak lay something like the claw of a giant crab.

Anike looked at it, then between the two of them. "Are you hurt?" she asked.

"We were attacked by something like a giant spider after you left." Lalfar glanced down at the claw and shrugged. "It fled after we wounded it. We were about to give up on you, though."

"A dwarf rescued me," Gunnar said. "He was strange. Anike found me and brought me back."

"A dwarf rescued you?" Lalfar asked.

"He pulled me out of the river and fed me a potion," Gunnar told him, glancing at Anike as if seeking approval.

Lalfar looked surprised.

"Dwarves like order," Karak said. "Your being in the wrong place might have offended his sense of right and wrong, so he wanted to get you away."

"His name was Morsali and he was old," Anike told them. "Old enough to remember the start of the Occupation. He didn't seem interested in what we were doing here, only that we were not part of an invading force." She looked at Karak. "Do you know what *dazarak* is?"

"I haven't heard that word," Karak said. "Why?"

"The dwarf mentioned it. A plant they use in their potions." She did not yet want to say that it might be useful in making the dwarf-weakening poison better. It was something she needed to think more about first. Instead she asked, "Is the spider you fought going to come back?"

"Probably not," Karak answered. "We hurt it quite badly and if the dwarves had considered it any significant threat they would no doubt have closed the tunnel."

Anike reflected that what might not be much of a threat to a dwarf could still be very dangerous to a human.

"We should go," she said. "Thank you for waiting for us."

They passed the hole that the Nidhogg burned and then the turning that led towards Morsali's mill, this time keeping to the main passage. They followed it for several hours and it ran without major intersections, slanting slightly downwards and Anike thought it curved very slightly to the right.

The smooth walls occasionally featured dwarven script forming numbers or words, though these were of little use. '*Avendas* Twenty Four' did not carry any great meaning for her. Twice they passed rectangular basins of water at about waist height, fed by small spouts from the wall.

Lalfar walked next to Anike. "I never thought I would be part of a story," he told her. "I bring tales to life for an audience, I don't live them."

"This is no story," Anike told him.

"But it is, and more than that because it is real too," Lalfar told her. "I am grateful to you and glad you liked Enya enough to do this."

Anike felt a flash of guilt at Enya's name. "Tell me more about her," she said.

Lalfar looked askance at her. "What would you like to know?"

"I suppose I want to learn a little about how you came to be living the life of travelling entertainers." The cold dark environment was starting to seem hostile and impersonal, dulling her sense of empathy and suddenly it seemed important to remind herself that it was a real woman they were seeking. The temptation to go back to the archive and seek the binding spell was still there and she wanted an anchor to help her resist it.

"Well," Lalfar began, "when we were children, we lived on a farm near Karastag. It's a town a long way to the west," he said at her quizzical expression, "on the southern slopes of the mountains that run along the spine of Gotlund. I'm not surprised you haven't heard of it. We grew cabbages and potatoes – hard work, but we managed. Sometimes barely, but we got by. There were a few farms clustered together, almost a village, and we played with the other children and made music. I found I had a gift for stories, and Enya and Auda could dance like willows in the wind."

Anike noted the name of the second girl and questions flooded into her mind, but she did not interrupt. Lalfar was being more forthcoming than he had been before and she wanted him to continue talking about Enya.

"About five years ago," Lalfar continued, "A dire puma attacked the community. Winter was coming on, and it was hungry enough to risk taking some of our livestock. We tried to drive it away, those of us who were old enough. The arl's warriors could never have reached us quickly enough to help."

Having seen a dire bear and fought dire wolves, Anike appreciated how much bigger dire creatures were than the normal animals and how dangerous a cat standing as tall as a man at the shoulder would be. She found herself grudgingly impressed at Lalfar's bravery.

"My parents were both killed during the fight," Lalfar continued, his voice catching just a fraction. "Two other farmers as well. A terrible price to pay for a few cows."

"I did not mean to open old wounds," Anike said quietly.

"I am at peace with that now," Lalfar told her. "For the most part. At the time it was torment. Other families helped as best they could, while we grieved and tried to keep the farm going. I was the oldest so I became responsible for Auda and Enya. Enya was the youngest. Is the youngest."

He was silent for a moment, then continued. "The next spring we found we could not cope with the farm. There was too much for the three of us to do. We thought about trying to marry to bring in others, but Enya was too young and neither Auda nor I had time to look for matches. The farm belonged to the arl rather than us of course, so we gave it up and took to the road as travelling performers."

He smiled slightly. "It was a difficult life, but we were good at what we did. We were happy and managed to make a living for several years, though I had to be watchful to keep the girls safe. Sometimes that was difficult and on a few occasions I had to fight in earnest. After a while, I became good enough that we were bothered less, and Auda and Enya found ways to stay out of trouble. Auda was feisty and brave. She would never suffer a fool, or someone trying to take something from her or get her to do something she didn't want to."

He stopped and looked at Anike. "That was what got her into trouble."

"What happened?"

"When we were in Skellett on the north coast, there was a Larten raid, and it was a large one with five ships. We were travelling with some other performers at the time and we all took refuge in the circle of wagons. Together we fought off the raiders. Performers are a tough breed. When the Lartens retreated, a couple of the knife-throwers went after them to try to recover some of what they had managed to steal, and Auda went too. To my eternal shame and regret, I stayed to protect Enya in case any returned. If I had gone with Auda..."

Lalfar trailed off. Anike waited while he pulled himself together and continued. "She had an axe that a raider dropped, but her bravery exceeded her skill and one of them knocked her senseless. I could just see her in the distance and tried to reach her, but before I was close she had been picked up and carried to their ships."

Instinctively, Anike put a hand on his arm.

He looked at her, his face grim. "I assume she was taken as a slave, and perhaps she yet lives."

"And you feel responsible." Anike said it as a statement.

"Of course I do. She was... is... my little sister and I failed in my duty to protect her."

Anike doubted that there was anything he could have done but she knew what it was like to be powerless, and the guilt someone could feel even if there was nothing they could have done to prevent a disaster.

"Some slaves are treated well," she said, trying to find a grain of comfort for him.

"A wilful slave is not a good slave." Lalfar sighed, and Anike could see him blinking back tears.

"I couldn't save Auda so I concentrated on looking after Enya. When the others would not go south, away from the coast, I took her and we went our own way. I won't let anything happen to her now."

Anike nodded. The loss of a sister explained both Lalfar's overprotective attitude and Enya's caution.

"I have always been afraid to let anyone get close to Enya," Lalfar continued, a little hesitantly. "The thought that she would leave me for someone and I would no longer be able to protect her has worried me since Auda was taken. But seeing all you have done, perhaps I was wrong to keep her from making friends for herself."

Grudging as that was, Anike recognised that Lalfar had just admitted that he could not always be Enya's entire world. "Thank you," she told him.

He gave her a small smile then turned away to start down the tunnel again.

Anike followed. What she felt for Enya did not seem to be friendship, exactly. It was more intense, and yet ephemeral. She thought about how Enya moved, the way her hair fell and the sound of her voice. The surge of emotion she had felt when Enya came to her door was something she had never felt with friends as she was growing up, though she could not put a word to the sensation.

However powerful that feeling was, what had really driven her to Svartalfheim was a desire to put right the unwanted consequences of her decisions, something she was all too familiar with. She had let too much pain into the world already.

Turning her mind to Lalfar's story, she wondered what had happened to Auda. She could find out if the woman still lived with her runes, and it must have occurred to Lalfar that she could do that. He had not asked her to try a runecast and neither did it sound as if he had been to a seer before. She assumed that a fear of finding out that his sister had perished or lived in terrible conditions far away prevented him. If it meant telling Lalfar and Enya that their sister was dead, or deliberately keeping that knowledge from them, she did not want to know either.

Gunnar, who was walking ten paces ahead, too far to have heard exactly what Lalfar had told her, stopped suddenly and waited for them. When the others reached them, he pointed ahead. "There is a doorway."

Anike could see he was right. There was a deeper darkness where the tunnel opened up into a greater space, but there was no sound or light coming from it.

Gunnar advanced cautiously to the entrance, taking care to make as little noise as possible. "It is an empty chamber," he announced. "This might be a good place to rest."

Anike realised that she was tired. "That sounds sensible," she said. "We cannot walk forever without taking a break."

The chamber was about a dozen paces across, with benches seeming to grow out of the walls, and three small stone tables next to them. One corner held another of the raised rectangular pools with clear water flowing through it. There was no dust on the floor and next to one of the tables were some strands that might have once been part of a larger rope. When Anike looked carefully, she also saw some small pieces of what looked like mushroom and there was a very slight organic smell in the air. All the signs were that someone had passed this way recently, perhaps even the dwarves they were following.

"Can you cook something?" Gunnar asked her.

"Are we going to stop for the night?" she responded. "I have lost track of time."

"I am tired," Lalfar told her. "I think we have been walking for most of the day."

"We might go a little further," Karak said, "But I doubt we will find a better place to rest. We can start earlier tomorrow."

"Very well." She turned to Gunnar. "There is not a great deal to burn but I can create a small fire with witchcraft to use for cooking, and it would be sensible to replenish our supply of potions." She hung her small cauldron on its little tripod and put some of her herbs into it, together with some water. Water was one thing that did not seem to be lacking in Svartalfheim and it seemed safe enough to drink and use in elixirs.

She conjured a fire on top of one of the tables and set the water to boil. As chaos was incapable of manifesting anything permanent, the small fire had to be renewed several times before she was finished. She was glad she had thought to create a spell with such utility, though had been thinking of cooking in wet moors and forests rather than barren caverns. She got Gunnar to chop roots while she assembled the other ingredients for a stew.

After the meal was cooked, she cleaned the cauldron and set it up again to brew some elixirs while they ate. Gunnar was talkative during the meal, asking questions of Karak about the battles he had been in. Karak answered briefly, and Anike wondered how many of his fights had been with the Gots near her home on the north coast. When they were done, she advised Gunnar and Lalfar to try to get some sleep and let Karak decide what to do for himself.

Without any real hope, she cast the spell to detect Enya and was not surprised when it did not find her. Keeping one eye on the cauldron and the fire, Anike took out the slate and chalk and started to work on a new spell, something that might help against the dwarves when they reached them.

Karak gave her a curious look. "Why do you rely so heavily on these written patterns in battle?" he asked. "They are unwieldy, very time consuming to create, and largely unnecessary. Your familiar will generally act in accordance with your needs during a fight."

Anike looked up at him. "Yes, I saw how you use your demon, but even you have rune patterns on your sword."

"That is my point. It took a lot to create those and they are only there to give me the edge in battle when I have to be careful. It is much more effective to get into an advantageous position and let my familiar use its powers." Karak smiled wryly. "But my familiar does not worry too much about my taking wounds and I would prefer not to suffer them if I can help it. I do sometimes channel its power myself, especially if I am fighting with others."

"The stasis shield you use is quite obvious though. Your fellow warriors must have suspected you are a witch."

"Of course, but the arl knows how useful I can be. I saved his life when we were boys. I have his protection and he has my service. While I stay within his arldom or raiding Gotlund, he allows me to use witchcraft if I need to."

Anike nodded. She had once entertained notions that her own arl would see sense in having her support, but his hatred of witches had been too deeply ingrained. She felt a slight tinge of envy.

"I take it you were not a witch when you saved his life."

"No, not then. How long have you had your own familiar?"

"I have borne the demon for a few years," Anike told him. She did not like the term familiar – it felt too personal for the chaos inside her. "I was caught in some witch weather."

Karak frowned. "I had supposed chaos was trapped in stones like my law familiar was."

"A stone? No, it was more like lightning striking me."

"That was how it felt when I picked up the blackened stone and released my familiar."

"So you chose to become a witch? Was there anything special about this stone?"

"It was jet black with flecks of silver, and very smooth. Unusual enough for me to pick it up but I had no idea that the familiar trapped inside would join with me when I touched it. I am happy that it did though. It has given me strength and power beyond that which I would have had as a man."

"At a price though. In the end, every demon wants to kill," Anike said flatly, "It does not care if there are innocent people nearby or even what side you are on. Mine does enjoy causing panic and chaos first, but I suspect yours is more direct."

"There is skill in choosing the right place to unleash it," Karak told her. "I am a warrior, and I am good at it, even without my familiar. With it, I am nearly invincible. Having to open a book in the heat of battle would make me vulnerable."

"So you let the demon loose on people who have no defence."

"Is that so different to a battle with a sword? I outclass most warriors I face, and they are just as dead whether I kill them with the blade, or my familiar helps me."

"I do not approve of killing the helpless."

"My enemies know how to use weapons."

"Helplessness is relative."

"Is what you do any better? Your spells can kill and you fly beyond your opponent's reach, safe from any reprisal."

"I rarely use witchcraft against people and if I have to, I am the one who decides how and who I attack, and more importantly, when to stop. I am not subject to the whims of something that just wants to kill."

"I broad terms, I do as well," Karak told her. "I only release my familiar when I choose, and when it has accomplished what I need it to, then it is brought to heel. While it chooses the detail, if I disagreed strongly I would retake control."

Anike looked at him with disapproval, but it was mingled with interest. She had inferred that this was what Karak did but it was useful to have it confirmed.

He met her gaze. "You are hampering yourself, and when we catch up with the dwarves, we will need every advantage. You chose not to spend time searching for the spell that would allow us to fully master our familiars, and I can see why you did that. I think you were wrong, but there is nothing to be gained by that discussion now. Since we are where we are, we need every advantage."

As a matter of ruthless effectiveness, Anike could see his point. "How do you do that so successfully? I once released my demon deliberately and it was a horrendous struggle to cage it afterwards."

Karak shook his head. "You do not choose to let it go, you simply do not try as hard to contain it. At this very moment, my familiar is struggling for release so it can strike at you, and no doubt yours is doing exactly the same. It would be easy to relax just enough to let it act but still keep a hand on its leash so it can be reined in again. The bonds are loosened, not broken."

A frown crossed his face. "But the balance is delicate and you need a strong will. It took me a lot of practice to achieve that level of control, and I have been a witch for over twenty years now."

He leaned back. "I remember attacking an arlberg on the north coast about fifteen years ago. I fought alongside other raiders for a while but when I was able to get to a place where my comrades were not endangered, I was able to let my familiar loose. There was a shield maiden who I could not defeat quickly enough so I allowed it to kill her. It froze her in place, then drained the life out of her. When the arl attacked me, I realised from the curses he was shouting that she was his wife, but I feel no guilt over that. She was a skilled warrior, but I would have killed her with my blade in time. While my familiar also killed a woman and a boy who had been caught up in the fighting, they should not have been there. Innocents do die on raids, as you well know. It is how things are."

Anike felt herself go cold as the tale tugged at a memory. "Did you kill the arl too?" she asked.

"No. He was nearly my match in battle, and the melee pushed us apart."

Anike shivered. She knew this story. Two years before, she had heard a tale too similar to be a coincidence but told from another point of view. Before she could stop herself, she asked "This was in Trollgard, Karak? I have heard about that raid."

If Karak thought the question odd, he didn't show it. "Yes, it was. We raided Trollgard some years. Does it matter? It was one of the first times I used witchcraft in battle."

Anike forced her mouth into a tight line. She should have realised who Karak was sooner. There could not have been many people matching his description. Before she had left Trollgard, her former master in herbalism, Olaf had told her of this raid and how a black-clad witch with a greatsword had killed his wife and son as well as the arl's wife. These deaths had ultimately led to the collapse of her relationship with Olaf after she had become a witch herself, and to the hatred of witches that had driven the arl and his son Bjord to pursue her so fervently.

Of course, raids were a fact of life for the coastal towns like Trollgard and deaths were common. Anike had not thought about the man who had killed Olaf's wife and son as a person. She had just seen the event as part of history, and how it had influenced those she knew.

She had realised that Karak must have killed a lot of people over the years, but until now she had not considered them as individuals and had been able to avoid thinking about those actions. It was quite different to find out that he had slain people that were connected to her, who she might even have met when she was too young to remember. It was suddenly much more personal.

Her demon felt her anger rising and drew on it. Anike closed her eyes so she could hold it back. She reinforced the prison in her mind, focusing on the runes that kept the demon shackled. She hoped that Karak would not see the struggle, or not realise the cause if he did. She did not want to give him leverage over her.

Her breathing slowed as she mastered herself. Karak was still a valuable ally and it would be wrong to send him away simply because she could now name some of his victims. It would be even worse to attack him, risking her life and undoubtedly leaving them both weakened.

She reminded herself that she was not a slave to the destructive desires of the demon. Arl Svafnir and Bjord, and even Olaf, would want vengeance on Karak but they had all been unable to accept her as a witch and had turned against her. Their vengeance was not hers to take, nor was she bound by Karak's past deeds.

It was, however, clear that he had no remorse for his actions and remained exceedingly dangerous. His past was of less concern to her than his present state.

Anike stayed awake while Karak took advantage of their lack of trust in him by resting. The seasoned warrior seemed to have mastered the art of sleeping when he had the chance, or at least pretending to. Anike let him be and finished off the healing elixir, then turned her attention to the rune pattern she was working on, a spell that allowed her to move a small body of liquid. After completing it and testing the spell on some of the water, she started on another but was too tired to solve the pattern, so she woke Lalfar to let him take his turn on watch.

The night passed without incident and the next morning, when they started off again, Anike felt better for having even a few hours sleep.

After they had been walking for perhaps half a day, the corridor rounded quite sharply to the left, and they followed it to find that it now intersected a glassy bore, circular and some five paces tall. Anike could imagine the Nidhogg's fiery breath burning through the stone. It was only slightly warm so the creature must have passed by an hour or two previously. It seemed to Anike that they were encountering the route of the Nidhogg remarkably often, almost as if it were going the same way that they were.

The wyrm had come from the left but its fire had cut through the other wall as well. That hole ended in a dark void after a few paces. All she could see through the gap was emptiness, as if the hole had pierced into some great cavern. If there was a floor, it was far below and the only thing she could make out was a pillar of some dark rock at the very edge of their light.

Perhaps unable or unwilling to cross through the expanse it had broken into, the Nidhogg must have turned to follow their tunnel, for the floor had been melted and its incandescent claws had left deep gouges in the stone. They followed for a couple of hundred paces before reaching a junction. The slick circular tunnel continued straight on but the dwarven passage turned to the right and quickly became a bridge which spanned an enormous chasm, about forty paces across. It was sturdy and had a very solid handrail but was only two paces wide.

"The Nidhogg could never have gone over this," Anike observed, "so it continued straight on. We should cross though."

"Are you sure?" Lalfar asked.

"Yes, there was no passage ahead before the Nidhogg made one. It drops slightly and there is no dwarven working left exposed."

Karak nodded, took a pace onto the bridge and glanced over the edge. "It is perhaps lucky there is no light," he said, his voice sounding strange in the void. "I don't think I want to know how far down the floor is."

They crossed, and went into the passage on the other side, which led into the cliff then turned sharply right to run parallel to the chasm. After a few hundred paces, the wall on their right was replaced by another balustrade and they found themselves looking out over depths below and at the pillar of rock that Anike had seen from the other side. It rose from an unseen floor like an island with its top some twenty paces about them. It was closer to this side of the chasm, and as they approached Anike could make out a ledge running around it at about the same height as the floor of their passage. A moment later, they came to what appeared to be the remains of another bridge. It must have once led to the pillar but now extended only a few paces before ending in melted rock.

When she looked towards the pillar again there was a dwarf on the ledge, regarding them curiously.

- 19 -

THE BARGAIN

It was not instantly obvious to Anike what the dwarf was doing on the rock pillar but he clearly had no way of getting back now. The bridge had gone.

Karak led them back so they were behind the solid wall again. "We should follow the Nidhogg tunnel and stay clear of this dwarf," he said. "Either that, or we should go straight past."

"I am not so sure," Anike replied. "He is trapped, and we might be able to help him."

"Anike, he is a dwarf," Lalfar objected. "His own people will come for him and they will have some way of getting him back."

"Why would you want to help him anyway?" asked Karak. "The dwarves are our enemies. They have kidnapped people we need to save. If I had a bow, I would shoot him where he stands to ensure he could not follow us, or send word of our presence."

"He is unarmed," Gunnar pointed out. "That would not be honourable."

"Honour is for human opponents," Karak told him.

"Why?" asked Gunnar. "Should not all opponents be treated honourably?"

"Honour is a means to stop your enemies becoming too savage," Karak said. "If you behave honourably, you can expect the same in return so honour only matters where conflicts are long or will be repeated. We will not be fighting the dwarves again, so there is no need to treat them honourably."

"That is cold," Anike told him, and Gunnar nodded, but she thought of what she had recently learned about the human use of poison to push the dwarves back to Svartalfheim. Most people thought poison was dishonourable, so much so that it had been held against her when she had used an elixir to try to put a monster to sleep outside her home town. If Morsali was to be believed, the High Kingdom had risen upon a foundation of dishonour and the ambition of Huppik the Clever. Karak had expressed a view that the first high king might well have held, and history had made Huppik a hero. History was written by the winners.

But she was not bound by history or a warrior's honour. She was a healer. "I disagree with you, Karak. The dwarves could have killed Lalfar when they took Enya. I would not have been able to stop them."

Karak grunted. "It is not the same. They didn't see him as a threat, not worth killing. Anyway, I would be happy just to leave this dwarf where he is. We could be in danger if he is carrying one of those weapons that shoots those metal balls."

"That is not the point," Anike said. "My conscience requires me to protect people, and from everything I have seen the dwarves are people too. True, we may have to injure or kill some when we rescue Enya and Hrost, but those individual dwarves have become our enemies by their own actions and choices. This one is not."

She looked Karak in the eyes. "Morsali saved Gunnar's life when he could have let him drown in the river. The dwarf woman we spoke to kept her word and that is a form of honour. Dwarves are tied to law — to structure and order, and that is a better base than your view of human honour, which is basically self-interest."

"He may not want our help," Lalfar said.

"I have no intention of forcing it on him, but I am going to offer it."

"This is unwise," Karak said, and Lalfar looked doubtful too.

Anike looked from one to the other. "Then I will help him without your assistance. Are you going to try to stop me?"

"Not me," said Lalfar, "but I think it is taking too much of a risk."

"Let me have my sword back," Karak said. "You will need your spellbook to have any chance of helping him. If you agree that we can keep our own possessions again, I won't interfere."

"Certainly, while there is a dwarf in the vicinity. He might be a threat."

"No. For good." Karak stated this firmly.

"I am not bargaining, Karak. Your sword stays with me unless there is danger, I say otherwise or you leave us."

For a moment, Karak looked as if he would push the issue, but then he said, "Give it to me now then, if you insist on proceeding with this idiocy."

"I do." Anike handed over the blade and received the spellbook back from the reluctant Karak. She led them past the balustrade to the end of the bridge. There was still a little heat coming off the rock and she saw the ledge on which the dwarf stood ended in a wide furrow several feet deep which had been melted into the side of the spire. She assumed that the Nidhogg's fire had burst through the wall on the far side of the chasm and burned it away.

"We shouldn't waste time on this, Anike," said Lalfar. "Enya could be getting further out of our reach while we delay."

"It will not take long, in the scheme of things," Anike replied. She nevertheless felt a stab of guilt, and added, "We may learn something useful. This is not a wholly selfless act on my part." She hoped she was right. There was a balance between convenience and principle and though she thought it important to do what she believed was right for its own sake, there was a chance that a grateful dwarf could help them.

Regardless, it was not her way to abandon those in need. She went up to the edge of the bridge, and ignoring the pebbles that fell into the depths of the chasm, called out, "Sir, may I assist you?"

Undoubtedly already surprised at seeing humans in the passages of Svartalfheim, the dwarf's expression became plainly astonished at being addressed in dwarven. He called back, "What could you possibly do to help me, human?" Anike wondered if he had intended to sound as disparaging as he had come across.

With a glance at the drop just in front of her boots, she lifted her cloak and read the flight spell. "*Prana*," she said and rose a little off the ground. "I can attempt to bring you back with witchcraft," she called across. Dwarves seemed to weigh a lot more than humans and she was not sure her spell would work on him.

"How can I be sure you will not drop me when I am above the gap?" the dwarf asked, though whether he meant deliberately or by accident, he did not say.

Anike considered. "I will come over and let you hold my arm. If you fall, I will be dragged down with you."

"Really?" Karak asked, in Norse.

"Agreed," the dwarf said, after a moment's thought.

Gunnar looked at Karak questioningly and Lalfar asked, "What?" Karak explained quickly, and Lalfar looked shocked.

Anike ignored the exchange and floated towards the dwarf. She selected the proper spell from her book to lift a person. "*Prana*," she said again as she aimed the effect at the dwarf on the ledge. Invisible energy surrounded him and while he must have felt it for he put his hand on the rock behind him. Anike thought for a moment that his fingers actually dug into the stone as they tightened.

She moved closer, and with some nervousness, held out her arm. The dwarf took it, and Anike had to suppress both the rush of anger from her demon and the fear that the fingers would crush her flesh or bone. She shivered, then looked more closely at the dwarf. His beard and hair were shot through with steel-grey and his face was wrinkled but his hand on her arm felt like iron.

Anike willed him to rise but as she had feared, he was too heavy and the spell did not move him. She shook her head. "I am sorry, I had hoped that would work, but it was not so simple." Seeing his mistrust, she concentrated and inserted a stasis rune into the spell she had placed on him, naming it and disrupting the flow of energy to bring the effect to an end.

The dwarf let go of her and the wall before she could tell him what she had done, and she filed away the knowledge that he too could sense the runes.

"I cannot lift you," Anike told him, "but that does not mean I cannot help." She looked up and around. The column extended nearly twenty paces above her, a greater distance than that between it and the end of the bridge.

"Why is a human witch in Svartalfheim?" the dwarf asked in a tone more curious than hostile.

"I am on a quest," she told him shortly. "The bridge was destroyed by the Nidhogg?"

The dwarf nodded.

"I think I see a way to help you." She flew up to the top of the column. The rock seemed solid and though the surface was partly covered in a purplish moss, the structure looked intact. The moss itself was a carpet of delicate strands and the ledge ran upwards in a spiral to the summit save where the Nidhogg's fire had burned it away.

As she came down to the level of the dwarf, she saw that there was indeed a mark in the wall where his hand had gripped it, not crushed but melted without heat.

"I can break off a section of this column and let it fall to create a new bridge." Conscious that there must be a reason why he was on this column at all, she added, "Would that be acceptable to you?"

The dwarf thought for a moment, then nodded slowly. "As long as you do not damage the *dazarak* with your witchcraft."

Anike gave a start at the dwarven word Morsali had used for the enhancing ingredient. "You mean the moss?" she asked.

"Yes."

Anike strove to stay calm and hide her reaction. "I can do that," she told him. "I will break off part of the pillar facing the bridge, and it will fall. You had better stand back." The dwarf nodded his understanding.

Renewing the flight spell, Anike rose to the top again. She had only promised not to damage the *dazarak* with witchcraft and had said nothing about harvesting it, so she grabbed a handful as she hovered above the spire. Having slipped it into her bag, she studied the edge of the rock before opening her spellbook. "*Prana*," she said, cutting a deep furrow in the rock. She moved to the side of the pillar and hung in the air to cut another one, creating a crack that sheared off a slice of the corner from the top all the way to the ledge, angled so that the bottom was larger than the top.

She had thought that the severed shard would fall but it remained held in place by its own weight, so she flew to its lowest point and disintegrated some of the base. With agonising slowness, the corner started to fall away from the wall. "Get back!" she shouted at Lalfar and the others. She had been so caught up in her task that she had forgotten about them. They scrambled back up into the passage.

As the rock fell, Anike saw that she had slightly misjudged the direction and distance and instead of forming a new bridge, the span fell against the side of the chasm. For a moment, she wondered if it would shatter, but the shard was thick enough to withstand the impact and halted with a cracking groan that must have been audible for miles. The end came to rest a dozen feet above the passage and a little to its right.

The dwarf looked at the span and placed one foot on it. He pushed down and when it did not move, he added more weight. The rock shifted a little and he froze, but it settled into a slightly different position and then held firm. He stepped full onto it and walked swiftly along.

As he passed halfway, Anike saw the span shift again and a crack started to spread from the end resting against the wall. "Hurry!" she called, though he must have been as aware of the danger as she was. The dwarf took two further steps and then leapt. She watched with her heart in her mouth as his jump carried him towards the cliff.

He struck the rock wall and to her amazed relief held onto the sheer face for a moment, before he swung himself sideways and dropped onto the ledge. He landed, flexing his knees slightly to absorb the impact. Anike could see impressions in the wall where he had held on, the solid stone having been moulded like clay under his hand.

Anike landed beside him.

"I am glad you are safe, sir," she said.

The dwarf glanced at the men in the passage before turning back to her. "I am in your debt, witch. I do not care to owe anything to a human so I will repay you now. In return for your aid, I will answer one question you may have truthfully and to the best of my ability."

Anike nodded. Questions and answers did seem to be a form of currency among the dwarves, perhaps unsurprising with the mineral wealth all around them. "I will consult my companions," she said and walked past him.

While not as ancient as Morsali, this dwarf looked old and he gave her the impression of restraint and wisdom. He also had some power over stone to judge from how his hands had shaped the rock he had touched.

She wondered if he knew of the spell that a witch could use to master her demon and if she would ever get the chance to ask another dwarf. The breaking of the span had shown her the limitation of what she could do with improvised witchcraft. She had sufficient power for a spell that could lift an adult dwarf but she had devised the rune pattern to lift a human and until a few days before she had not seen any reason to modify it, and even since then it had not seemed that important. The demon could have moved him if it had chosen, but the only reason it would have done that would have been to drop him into the depths below. If she could master the demon, as the book they had found suggested was possible, she could have rescued him from the pillar without taking the risks that came from dropping tons of rock against walls.

Then she saw Lalfar looking at her expectantly and remembered that he had not understood a word of what had been said.

She could see Enya's face echoed in Lalfar's features and it reminded her of what had brought her to Svartalfheim, not the quest for knowledge but a rescue. Of course, if she found a way to tame her demon, that would help Enya and this might be a way to learn that without spending weeks in Ivaldi's archive.

Karak must have also seen that possibility. "Ask him about the binding spell," he said. Like Anike, he obviously assumed that the dwarf would only answer a question directly from her.

"Now you see the value in altruism," Anike commented, drily.

"What about asking for directions?" suggested Gunnar. "Hrym's Hall should be famous and it cannot be that far away. This dwarf must know where it is."

Karak glared at him, but Gunnar had made a good point. Using runes at every major junction did work, but the sacrifices hurt and there was only a limited supply of healing elixirs.

She looked at the black-clad witch. "I thought you wanted to rescue Hrost."

"I do, but I know what we are up against. Mastery of the familiars would make the battle much more even. It would be a tremendous stroke of fortune if this dwarf knew the binding, but he might be able to give us more information such as where we could find it or a clue to locate it in the archive. I think it is worth taking the chance to ask."

"Suppose he has no idea about the binding spell?" Lalfar put in. "We would have wasted the question. The words you read were set down hundreds, if not thousands, of years ago and they wouldn't have been directly relevant to the dwarves."

Anike made her decision. "Enough. Lalfar, you are right. The chances of finding out enough about the binding spell to help us in time is too small."

She went back to the dwarf, who was waiting with his arms folded. "What is the route you would use to get to Hrym's Hall if you were only as capable as a human and had to get there without wasting time."

The dwarf smiled, but only briefly. "A good question. Perhaps the spirit of the god Kvasir has inspired humans since our departure." He gave Anike a series of directions, complex but she would be able to follow them.

When he had finished, he added, "You made a wise choice. I do not know where you would find a copy of the binding spell."

Anike started. This last remark was made in good Norse.

The dwarf regarded her, considering. "Hrym would be able to help you though, so I suggest you ask him," he added.

"Why are you telling us this?" Karak asked, in a cold voice edged with suspicion.

"One question only," the dwarf said, and set off up the tunnel, then took a turning which would lead him away from the path he had indicated to Anike.

Anike looked at his retreating back. "Well, that was odd."

"He must have been very grateful," said Gunnar.

Karak looked at him scathingly. "He wants Anike to go to Hrym so she can wake him. He may not know that his brethren have already captured a chaos witch." The warrior frowned. "He may have no idea whether or not Hrym knows the spell. He could not have knowingly given a false answer to the first question by any measure of honour but he was not bound to tell the truth when he volunteered other information."

Anike saw a small smile on Karak's face, quickly hidden, which belied his words. Despite what he said aloud, she was sure he thought there was a good chance the dwarf was telling the truth. It was conceivable that Hrym would aid the law-aligned Karak, the giant would hardly be inclined to help her. He was much more likely just to kill her than tell her anything at all.

"We should move on," she said, "but there is something I should do first." Glancing up the tunnel to check that the dwarf was out of sight, she renewed the flight spell and went back to gather more of the *dazarak*.

"This moss could be useful," she told them when she returned. "It is supposed to enhance the effect of elixirs on dwarves."

"So it will work with the poison?" Lalfar asked.

Karak frowned slightly, and Gunnar said. "What poison?"

"You remember that Morsali told us that Huppik the Clever had devised a poison that weakened dwarves?" she asked.

When the boy nodded, she continued. "I have the recipe for that, and from what he told us, this moss should make it even more effective."

She went up to Karak, frowning. "Your sword," she said.

Karak's face grew hard. "I think I should keep it," he said.

"No. Not yet. The journey the dwarf described will take many hours, perhaps even overnight. You agreed."

"If I didn't have my blade, the spider would have killed us."

"If you had held it when the Nidhogg passed by, I would be dead now."

Karak nodded, acknowledging the point. "Very well. It would be dishonourable to go back on our bargain." He gave a brief, mirthless smile that did little to reassure her as they exchanged sword for book.

They walked on, following the route the dwarf had given them by the place names on the walls. When they found another chamber with water and stopped for the night, Anike stayed up brewing potions and finalising the patterns for new spells while the others slept. Her first task was to make a potion to defer fatigue, something she could risk taking now their final destination was close. With that simmering away, she considered the recipe for the dwarf-weakening poison and the *dazarak*. If they could avoid an outright battle with the dwarves, so much the better but she doubted that would be possible and wanted to even the odds against them.

The moss was similar in texture and smell to several she knew and when she touched her tongue to it, very cautiously in light of what Morsali had implied, the taste reminded her of oakheart lichen, which could be used in several elixirs to speed up the brewing process. She could not be sure exactly how the *dazarak* would interact with the other ingredients without trying, but the prospect of strengthening the elixir was far too good an opportunity to pass up.

Drawing on her herblore, she decided on the best way that *dazarak* could be used, then drew out her runes. Carefully holding the recipe in her mind, she made a vow to sacrifice two thirds of the elixir she would make along with more of her blood, then asked the runes how effective the elixir brewed from her recipe would be against the dwarves. It seemed that the thought process she had used to design spells had sharpened her ability to improve elixir recipes too as the runes confirmed that she had devised an elixir that was more potent than that Huppik had created.

She cut a long shallow cut down her calf and let the blood flow before binding the wound and turning to the potion. When the elixir to banish fatigue was finished, she cleaned the cauldron and mixed the ingredients for the poison.

While the runes confirmed that the recipe should work, it still had to be brewed properly and she had no way to test it conclusively before they went into battle. She was forced to make some educated guesses about some of the aspects of the process and the preparation required her full concentration.

She poured the lesser part of the finished elixir into a large flask. It flowed sluggishly, like honey. The original creators had clearly considered it would not be possible to get a dwarf to drink it, so it had been formulated as a contact poison, viscous and designed to be coated onto weapons. She wondered if Huppik had struggled to get his warriors to use poison, or whether they had accepted it readily. She emptied the rest of it into the basin and watched it dissolve.

A comparable conflict had been fought in Karak when he tried to decide whether to rescue Hrost or risk abandoning him so he could find the spell to get true mastery of his demon. She had felt the temptation too, but it seemed compassion or guilt drove her to save Enya more than Karak's honour motivated him to rescue Hrost. She admitted to herself that in the absence of the urgent need to reach Enya in time, she too would have wanted to find the binding spell.

Eventually, she roused Gunnar and instructed him to wake her after two hours, but it was Lalfar who shook her by the shoulder.

She was still tired but decided to save the potion that would defer fatigue until they were closer to the dwarves.

After walking for another couple of hours, a mixture of anger, foreboding and excitement started to flow into her from the demon as if it sensed something ahead, something it wanted to confront and destroy. She looked at Karak and recognised the telltale signs of excitement in his usually controlled manner.

They reached an arch leading into another vast hallway. Above the entrance was a picture of a giant sitting on a throne surrounded by smaller figures, vibrant with colour that seemed to be part of the stone. When she had seen this image before, at a different sealed entrance to Svartalfheim two years before, she had taken the figures for men but now realised that they must have been dwarves.

They had to be getting close. While the others looked at the fresco, she cast the spell to detect witches and for the first time there was a response. Enya was no more than a hundred paces away.

- 20 -

THE END OF THE ROAD

Anike wondered how large Hrym really was. If the painting was an accurate representation, he had to be over thirty feet tall. The myths she remembered were usually a little vague on the size of giants and Lalfar had not known. Those who had married gods were not much bigger than humans, but others were the size of a small hill, like the one who had built the walls of Asgard or the giant king who had guided Thor to the land of Jotunheim.

Beyond the arch, the hall extended before them, similar in shape to that outside the archive of Ivaldi, but much larger. It was empty and reminded her a little of a road leading up to an arlberg. At the far end, closed double doors some fifteen feet tall would have required the mightiest giant to stoop, and above them were set arches which seemed to be filled with ice.

This was not a fortress in the way that the archive had been. The walls surrounding the door were decorated with bas relief images of mountains and sea, surely foreign to the dwarves of Svartalfheim, and the doors themselves were covered in intricate abstract patterns. There was a sense of grandeur but no threat, at least in the construction.

With her eyes on the door, Anike cast the detection spell again. The sense of Enya's presence was clear, only a little beyond the great doors.

"Enya is still alive," she told Lalfar, who sighed in relief. She glanced at Karak. "Let us hope that Hrost is too."

"There could be someone on watch just beyond those doors," Karak said. "Remember, the dwarves can read runes too, and they may well know we are nearby."

Anike remembered the sense of runes falling when she had been with Morsali and wondered if that had just been her imagination or whether she had somehow sensed the World Tree reacting to a dwarven runecast.

"We need to plan an attack and we have to know what is on the other side of those doors for that," she said. "I will scout ahead. With luck, I should be able to get an idea of what lies beyond by looking through that ice. Enya is only a few paces beyond the door, and I may even be able to see her from there."

"If someone opens those doors, they will see you flying across the hall," Karak observed.

"Only if they look up," Anike replied. "I think it is time to return your sword to you. I will need my spellbook."

Karak handed it back and she gave him his blade.

Anike tucked the book away in her bag and lifted her cloak to read the flight spell. The walls rose to meet in a high arch and the light from the glowstones near the base barely touched the peak. It was dark, at least to human eyes, Anike reminded herself.

Alert for any sign of movement, she rose as high as she could and flew down the hall.

The demon had stepped up its assault on the bonds restraining it. She could sense its desire to attack a force of law ahead but she thought there might be a note of something else within its rage and desire, fear perhaps or at least caution. The Nidhogg had elicited a similar response from Karak's demon so she could only assume there was something nearby that was extremely dangerous and aligned with law, perhaps Hrym himself. She reinforced the prison.

As she approached, she heard faint sounds from beyond the wall. There was a sort of rushing noise, rising and falling, familiar but she could not place it. From a distance, it had looked as if the arches were filled with ice but now she was closer, she saw that they contained a translucent white crystal. There was a slight glint within them as they reflected some light on the far side, but she could not see through them at all.

She opened her spellbook. So high up, there was barely enough light to read the rune pattern and she had to concentrate to make out the shapes before putting her hand against the crystal and speaking, "*Prana.*" She willed the dust outwards as a hole formed in the crystal and peered down into the room below.

She was some forty feet above the floor, looking down on a chamber perhaps twenty paces long but twice that in width. There were no dwarves in view, and she could not see either Enya or Hrost, but there were signs of recent activity. A stone table was set with foodstuffs and some bedrolls lay on the ground, six in total.

In each of the walls to the left and right was a single stone door around seven feet tall, but the view was dominated by a pair of double doors over twice that size directly ahead, and the surges of rushing noise were coming from beyond them. All were closed, but the joins of the double doors were lit from the other side by a white light, bright by the standards of Svartalfheim. It reminded her of daylight but so far underground it had to have a different source.

With no dwarves in sight, she renewed the flight effect on herself and then cast the spell to detect witches. From her angle, it seemed that Enya was only a few paces beyond the double doors, and off a little to the left. She had some information now but wanted to find out more. Opening the doors immediately below her might attract attention so she used the disintegration spell again to reduce more of the crystal next to her to dust and the tiny crystal fragments fell behind her like glittering snow. She squeezed through the newly formed gap and flew down to the ground. This chamber was decorated with bas relief in much the same style as the outside. In several small alcoves were images of mountains and ice fields, and one showed a giant, presumably

Hrym, approaching a battle at the tiller of a ship made of ice. She was sure that she was looking at an image of Ragnarok, perhaps even made by someone who had been there.

Taking care not to make any noise by touching the ground, she moved to the double doors and put her ear to them. She could just hear dwarven voices on the other side but they were not loud enough for her to make out words over the slow ebb and flow of the rushing noise.

Stepping away from them, with their sound and the peculiar light seeping from beneath, she went over to the doors beneath where she had come in. There was no lock or any other means of holding them closed and they swung inwards so would not be hard to open from the other side. She flew back to the men and told them what she had seen.

"We have reached our destination," said Lalfar.

"I suspect we have little time," Anike told him. "My guess is that the dwarves are engaged in some sort of ceremony, a prelude to sacrificing Enya to Hrym."

"I doubt we will get a better time to attack," Karak said. "The dwarves are distracted."

"I suppose there is no chance we can reason with them?" suggested Anike, though without much hope.

"No," said Karak. "They have no respect for humans, a task to complete and no reason to bargain. If we do anything other than attack with all our strength, we give up surprise, and that is our greatest weapon."

"I know you are right," Anike said sadly. "I would prefer not to risk anyone's life, particularly one of ours, but it seems that we have no choice. Diplomacy is unlikely to work if they already have all they need."

"How will we get through the doors?" asked Lalfar.

"The place is not a fortress, and I did not see any way of holding them closed. They will be heavy for humans, but I think we can push them open. If not, I will make a hole."

"Should we poison the weapons now?" Lalfar asked.

"Yes, that would be wise. The oil should last the best part of an hour before it evaporates though it will probably only work for one strike."

She got out the venom she had made the night before and coated the blades. "It should take effect if you can get even a little of it into their blood but you will have to get past the armour, so aim your strikes carefully. And I am not sure how long it will take to work either, so do not assume someone you cut will go down at once." She put some on her own spear point and her knife. There was some left, but she hoped they would not need it.

They advanced cautiously up the hall, keeping a careful watch on the doors ahead of them. When they reached the far end, Karak drew his blade and read the runes on one side. '*Barak*,' he said aloud and pushed on the door.

It opened without a sound despite its weight and solidity, and they entered the chamber. The double doors ahead were still closed, outlined by the light beyond. Lalfar and Gunnar looked, their eyes wide in wonder while Karak's were narrowed as he surveyed the room for threats.

Anike raised a finger to her lips and pointed to the door ahead. "Enya is just beyond," she whispered.

"What are we waiting for?" Lalfar asked quietly. He looked around at the bedrolls and the food. "They might come back in at any moment."

"There are two other doors," Karak said. "I think we should be sure there are no dwarves behind either of them first. I do not want to be cut off when we retreat."

"We don't want to get into a fight we don't have to though," said Lalfar.

"We are about to make a lot of noise," Karak told him. "Anyone close is going to come out. If we hear something on the other side, we will block the doors. Anike, can you cut some stone wedges we can use?"

"Yes," Anike said, grateful for Karak's tactical acumen. "Gunnar, stay here while we investigate these side doors. If you hear anyone approaching, signal us." She concentrated on the edge of the table and used her witchcraft to remove three wedge-shaped pieces. It might have been her imagination but she thought the rushing noise rose in pitch for a moment as she cast the spells.

The three of them went to the door on the left. Anike held up her hand, then pressed her ear to it. There was no sound, so she opened her book, found the spell she needed and disintegrated a small hole. Through it, she could see a smaller chamber with books displayed on pedestals. There was no sign of anything living.

"It looks safe," she said and pushed the door open. The ceiling was much lower than the main hall, with a superficial resemblance to Ivaldi's archive. The books here were not made of stone but of something that looked like leather, and there were far fewer of them. One was propped up on the top of each pedestal and there were others on shelves beneath. The covers were works of art in themselves, some rich with colours of winter showing scenes of giants and dwarves in vistas of ice and snow but others reflected what Anike assumed to be Ragnarok, with prominence given to the frost giants and their role in the battle.

She frowned. Dwarves had dealt with the gods throughout history and legend, but the images suggested that at the last they had picked a side, and it was that of the giants. She had thought Ivaldi's work showed support for the gods but that probably predated Ragnarok by thousands of years. Dwarven attitudes might have changed, or perhaps the dwarves were not one people with a unified view but had differences of opinion or were even on different sides.

There was no threat here, so she led Karak and Lalfar to the single door on the opposite wall. The room beyond was also small and just as empty of life, but was semi-circular with a series of alcoves in the wall. Within each was a bas relief scene, coloured stone that seemed to grow out of the wall to create pictures, again mostly of giants. On one, a ship made of ice with an enormous frost giant at the helm, the artificer had depicted his features skillfully enough for her to see an expression that was somehow both noble and ruthless at the same time. This was not a place where anyone lived, but more like an enormous shrine to Hrym.

She pulled the door closed. "No danger in either room. It is time to face the dwarves."

They went back to the double doors. She put her hand on one, read the disintegration spell to cut a small hole through and put her eye to the gap.

The chamber beyond was wider and longer than the one in which they stood but her gaze was instantly drawn to another set of double doors directly ahead of her. These stood open, and it was from there that the bright light issued. What she saw beyond was so unexpected that it took a moment for her to comprehend what she was looking at.

She could see water, not an underground lake but the surface of an ocean, and it was day. A blizzard filled the air, and she could see ice flows being tossed by waves in the storm. The rushing noise was that of wind and waves hurling themselves against the shore.

The snow did not come in through the doorway at all.

Four dwarves stood in a loose semi-circle facing the sea. Two were helmed and dressed in the slate-grey heavy metal mail she had seen when they had first attacked her and the other two were clad in something resembling leather armour.

Just off to the left were two humans, both bound and with their hands tied in front of them. One was Enya, and the other was a young man of similar age.

She lifted her eye from the hole and whispered to the others. "Each of you take a look but be prepared for a shock. Make no noise." She stepped away, trying to understand how they could be looking at an ocean when they were deep underground. She could only assume that there was a cavern so vast that it looked like a sea, with enough glowstones to rival the sun.

She shook her head. It did not matter what they were looking at — they were not going there. What was important was getting the prisoners away. The sea was another mystery of Svartalfheim that she simply did not have time to solve.

"Let us make a plan," she said as Karak stepped back to allow Gunnar to look through in his turn.

"Our aim is to free the hostages. We do not need to kill the dwarves," she said, keeping her voice low. "It suffices if they are unable to follow us, so we should not stop for revenge."

Karak nodded. "They are hard to kill, so we shouldn't waste time finishing them off unless we need to. We don't know if this venom will work yet."

"Justice is found in revenge, though," said Gunnar. "It brings balance."

"Not at the risk of failing," Anike told him in a sharp whisper. "We are here to save lives."

Within her, the demon was straining at its bonds, trying to get to the dwarves and the giant. She held it back but it reminded her of something. "Karak, keep your demon under control. We do not need it turning on Enya or me."

Karak nodded. "Of course. That would be a distraction."

"The hostages have their hands bound and they are gagged, but their legs are free. I imagine the dwarves are concerned about Enya's demon but not about anyone running away in Svartalfheim. When we burst in, Gunnar, you go to them and get them out." She looked at Karak and Lalfar. "I will use my witchcraft to destroy their weapons while you attack. After everyone is clear, we can retreat and I can collapse the archway once we are back through the door."

She looked at their faces. "Agreed?"

Lalfar was worried, Gunnar eager and nervous at the same time but Karak nodded calmly. To him she said, "Cast the spells you need," and took out her spellbook. She placed the spell of flight on herself, and the animation spell on her poison-covered dagger.

Karak renewed the strength spell and on his word of, "*Ert,*" was surrounded by the shimmer of his stasis shield.

Her spear would not be as useful as witchcraft in this battle, so Anike slung it on her back by the carrying strap and opened the book to the pattern she planned to use first.

"Ready?" Karak asked and at their nods, opened the door. They charged.

The dwarves broke off their chanting and reached for weapons. Anike flew upwards and sent her dancing knife flying at a leather-clad dwarf who was picking up an axe, and the sharp edge cut a graze on his hand.

Karak swung a broad stroke at another dwarf who met it with a hard block, but the warrior-witch used the motion of the parry to swing himself around in a wide circle, and brought the blade in again, beneath the dwarf's guard. With strength enhanced by his witchcraft, Karak's sword cut through the leather-like armour and dug into his opponent's lower leg. A human might have lost a foot but the dwarf did not even fall, and Karak had to jump back to avoid the countering strike.

The two dwarves in full metal armour were a little slower. Gunnar took a wide path around them to reach the captives. Enya raised her face to look up at him with tired eyes and showed no sign of moving. "Get up," he shouted at Hrost as he pulled Enya to her feet. The young warrior got his legs beneath him and managed to stand.

One of the heavily armoured dwarves advanced on Lalfar, attacking the skald with a series of short, savage swings of an axe. There was no obvious gap in the armour for Lalfar to aim at and, unable to use the venom on his blade, he fell back, dodging out of the way rather than trying to block or counter.

Anike looked at the spell on the open page before her and visualised the rune pattern. "*Agni*," she called, concentrating on the weapons the dwarves held. At her command, the axe hafts burst into flames and turned to ash, while the metal blades melted and fell onto the stone. The strange staff-bow held by the other armoured dwarf collapsed with a sharp report, sending a metal ball flying into a wall. Lalfar took advantage of his foe's sudden loss of weapon to press his attack and the dwarf fell back, blocking with his steel sleeves.

The two dwarves who had been cut by the poisoned weapons were slowing, less sure in their movements, but the others were unfazed. Lalfar's opponent kicked at him, then stepped back and grabbed a long knife from the ground nearby, while the one whose bow had burned away drew an axe.

Karak pressed his attack on the weakened and unarmed dwarf before him, this time cutting him on the arm before turning to strike at the axe wielder from the flank.

Gunnar cut Enya's bonds and pushed her towards the entrance. "Run!" he told her. She blinked at him, puzzled, then drew herself together and followed Hrost towards freedom.

The leather-clad dwarf Anike had cut with her dagger picked up the other bow-like weapon from the ground and aimed it at her. She sent the knife at him again, aiming at the weapon, and knocked it slightly aside. The dwarf grunted in frustration and sighted on her again. Anike flew up towards the ceiling but he tracked her and she knew she would never be able to dodge when he fired. Desperately, she looked down at the spell again, trying to place the runes that would destroy the weapon, but she knew that she would never finish in time, and at that range the shot would kill her. The demon surged in response to her rising fear.

With a war cry on his lips, Gunnar brought his sword down on the weapon just as the dwarf fired. The metal ball slammed into the wall and relief flooded through her, carrying the demon back into its prison.

Anike drew a deep breath as she looked down on the melee below. The dwarf flailed at Gunnar with the weapon but he caught the blow on his shield as he retreated.

In the time he had won her, she concentrated and cast the spell again to destroy the weapons the dwarves now held, profoundly glad to have melted the second bow. However, the two in heavy armour were still very dangerous, with their fists able to strike with the force of a mace, and her spells had little effect on a dwarf at full strength.

Gunnar had retreated and the weakened dwarf had not followed after his bow had melted. The boy grabbed Enya's shoulder as he ran past and dragged her through the doorway after Hrost.

Karak was pulling back too, keeping one armoured dwarf at bay with powerful blows from his long blade. Lalfar was striking at the other armoured figure, but it would only be a moment before the dwarf decided to accept a blow in order to land a fist, and that would probably be the end of him.

Anike drew in power. "Run!" she shouted, then cast the spell of smoke. The haze covered the dwarves. Lalfar was caught in it too, but he had seen this spell before and he quickly emerged from the cloud and headed for the door. Anike flew above the grey surface, her spear sweeping through randomly. It clanged on armour, setting up confusing noises within the smoke cloud, and then she too headed for the doorway and dived through.

Karak and Gunnar were already pushing the doors closed. Anike knew it would be a few moments before she could cut through the stone above the arch and instead conjured another cloud of smoke to cover the area just beyond the doors, and Lalfar stuck wedges beneath them when they slammed shut.

Karak stepped back and closed his eyes in concentration. The sound of impact against the doors covered the word he spoke but a series of runes appeared on his arm, silver embroidery on the cloth that Anike had been sure was plain black. He read them and said *"Ranak."* A wall of ice formed against the doors, binding them tightly shut.

"That should hold them for a moment," Karak said, "but we have to get out of here."

Anike realised that despite her suspicions, she had underestimated him. She had assumed from his conversation he did not carry written spells save those on his sword, but it seemed he had developed more than he had admitted to. An ice wall would be very useful for an outnumbered warrior or someone facing archers with no cover. Somehow he had hidden the runes. Later she would have to think about how he had managed that, and what else he had been hiding.

Karak cut Hrost's bonds and the two gripped forearms in a warrior's greeting. Lalfar and Enya were hugging each other, and Gunnar was looking on, smiling. Anike felt a twinge of something, jealousy perhaps, and put her hand on Enya's shoulder. Enya turned her head and gave her a wan look, and the feeling vanished as Enya said, "Thank you."

A thousand responses flashed through Anike's mind but she settled for smiling and said, "We are not safe yet. I hope you can still run."

She was about to bring down the archway behind them when Gunnar cried out, and she looked back to see the double doors of the exit being pushed open by a dwarf armoured in metal scales.

Karak's sword came up to guard. Lalfar let go of Enya and stepped in front of her. The men looked at each other, then charged.

The dwarf pushed the doors wide and drew his own vicious looking weapon, about the size of an axe but with a scythe-like blade a foot long. He wore an open helm, and the metal scales of his armour glinted silver in the light of the glowstones. He had no shield but still moved forward eagerly to meet the attack.

Taking advantage of his longer reach, Karak struck first but the dwarf blocked and caught the sword between the scythe and haft of his own weapon and forced it down. He stamped hard on the blade, tearing it from Karak's hands.

Lalfar jumped forward and swung his axe but the dwarf just blocked with his free arm, letting the axe bounce off the metal, and the skald danced back to avoid a cut from the dwarf's weapon. Karak tried to recover his fallen sword but had to dive away to avoid being impaled on the scythe, with his stasis shield slowing the strike just enough to allow him to evade the deadly point.

The two men moved apart to flank the dwarf, who seemed quite happy to stand by Karak's sword and wait for the attack. Gunnar passed his dagger to Hrost and started forward to help.

Hrost grabbed Anike's arm. "I recognise that dwarf. I think he was sent to gather others of his kind when we reached this place." His Larten accent was more pronounced than Karak's and it took a moment for his words to register.

"Then we had better defeat him quickly before more arrive." Moving to the right so she had a clear target, Anike read the firebolt spell on her spear, "*Agni.*" The dwarf turned his face towards her just as the flames hit and he staggered, covering his eyes. His exposed beard and hair flared briefly as they were consumed and he took two steps back, swinging his weapon in Lalfar's direction as he struggled to see. Taking advantage of the distraction, Karak darted in to retrieve his sword.

The dwarf shook his head to clear it. His skin was reddened and blistered but he did not seem to have suffered any real harm.

Another figure stepped into the hall through the open doors ahead of them. Anike recognised the dwarf she had rescued from the pillar, now dressed in scale mail like his companion. He held a long, wide and slightly curved sword easily in one hand.

There was no time to consider the dwarven view of gratitude or honour. From behind her came the sound of splintering ice as the dwarves who had held Enya and Hrost began to break through. They were overmatched. While some venom remained on their blades, in a moment they would be facing four dwarves at full strength, and there could be more coming. Even Karak's blows could not penetrate plate armour and against such opponents, now ready for battle, their chances were slim. Even though she had the means to escape for herself, Anike could not see a way out for the others and needed time to find one. She looked about her. "Run! This way!" she shouted and headed for the door to the library.

Enya, Gunnar and Hrost followed her but halfway to the door, she realised that Karak and Lalfar were still trading blows with the dwarves. Karak was hard-pressed. The older dwarf was swinging his sword with frightening speed and Karak had only escaped serious injury because his opponent had not quite compensated for how the blade slowed as it neared his body. Lalfar was retreating from the short scythe, the dwarf appearing to be in no hurry. He was fending off the axe with ease while making occasional swipes, though whether he was holding back to enjoy the battle or waiting for reinforcements, Anike could not tell.

The ice wall shattered as an armoured dwarf finally pushed the doors open.

"Get into that room," she told Enya and lifted her cloak so she could see the smoke spell. "*Agni*," she called out, trying to catch all the dwarves within the cloud but leaving Karak and Lalfar outside it. She could not quite cover the one by the ice wall, but the two men took advantage of their opponents' momentary loss of sight. Lalfar turned and ran, while Karak dropped to one knee and spun in a complete circle with his blade outstretched a few inches above the floor. There was a crash as it connected with something metal. By the time she heard the louder clatter of a dwarf hitting the floor, Karak was already following Lalfar.

Anike preceded them into the library, flipping pages in her spell book. The door to this room opened inwards and the position was much more defensible than the main hall. Getting out again would have to wait. In the entrance hall, she could see the dwarf in full armour approaching

As Karak pushed the door closed, Lalfar kicked in the last wedge. Karak pulled him back by the shoulder and read the pattern on his arm, calling out "*Ranak*," to create another wall of ice over the doorway. He looked at Anike. "What now?"

There was a slam against the other side of the door. "Hurry, Anike," urged Gunnar.

"Stand back," she told him, and read the spell. "*Prana*," she said cutting a vertical crack in the arch above the doorway. With a crash, the wedge of stone she sheared off the arch fell and shattered on the floor, burying the lower half of the door behind a barrier of rubble over two feet thick.

"Being trapped is an improvement, is it?" Karak asked her.

"We would never have beaten them in the open," Anike told him. "You may be happy to earn a place in Valhalla by dying in battle but I am trying to save everyone."

"If you have a plan, put it into action quickly," Karak told her, pointing to the door. The wall of ice shattered into shards and they could see through the gaps in the rubble that the solid stone door was beginning to bow as if it were made of wood.

- 21 -

BREAKTHROUGH

Above the rubble that hid its lower half, the stone of the door was warping inwards towards them. Someone was using witchcraft or a similar power on it.

"It's the dwarves," Hrost said, pointing. "I saw them do this before. Some of them can shape the stone just by touching it!"

The dwarf she had saved from the column had done something similar when he grabbed the rock and he was one of those outside. With such an ability, they would be able to part the stone but from the rate the door was bending, it looked like it would take them a little time.

The roof was much lower in this chamber than in the hall where the dwarves were. "Get back," she ordered. "Duck down behind those pedestals." She looked up at the ceiling and cut a fissure deep into the rock, then moved back to join the others before cutting another. A great column of rock came down with a crash and buried all but the top few inches of the door behind rubble at least five feet thick. "That should hold them for a while."

Lalfar and Enya stood up, arms around each other. As she went over to join them, Anike saw Karak go to speak to Hrost. Gunnar looked about, then shrugged and followed her.

When Lalfar let go, Anike drew Enya into her arms and gave her a warm embrace. "How are you faring?" she asked.

Enya shook her head. "I was terrified. Every moment I thought the dwarves would kill me, and half the time I was so frightened or angry I couldn't stop the witchcraft running through me. After a while, the dwarves got tired of it and gagged me so I could not say those rune words anymore, but I kept trying and eventually they made me drink something that sent me to sleep. I only woke up a few hours before you found us."

Anike realised that she still had her arms about Enya but felt no urge to let go. Instead, she stroked the blonde hair. "There is no need to worry about that any more. We have you now and I will teach you how to control your power."

Gunnar came up to join them, smiling. Hrost was less demonstrative with Karak, releasing him after a brief embrace.

Enya's eyes fell on Karak and she whispered, "What is he doing here? He attacked us! He was working with the dwarves."

"He was acting under duress," Anike said, keeping her voice low, "but that does not mean he is to be trusted once we are out of danger."

Karak was coming over, and Anike reluctantly let her arms fall away from Enya. "You have a plan, I assume?" he asked her.

"Yes," said Anike. "We will go through there." She pointed at the wall closest to the way they had approached Hyrm's Hall.

Suddenly, she heard Enya cry out, "No!" and turned just in time to see the woman's eyes snap open, lightning seeming to dance behind them.

Enya, or rather her demon, had its gaze fixed on Karak. Terrified that an attack would trigger a fatal retaliation from him, Anike stepped forward and stretched out her hand to touch Enya's shoulder so she could feel the rune pattern that was forming.

All three of them spoke at the same time, and Enya's fire spell collapsed before it could manifest. With her hand grasping Enya's shoulder so she would feel the next spell form, Anike looked over her head at Karak. He was wary but calm. His sword was still on his back and his eyes were hard but it was his human coldness and not the dead eyes of his demon.

Without looking at her, Enya tried to shrug off Anike's hand. Anike kept contact, disrupting the lightning that Enya was trying to conjure. Enya's demon thought quickly but its spells were not complicated and the rune images had rather less substance to them than Karak's. Anike hoped its relative weakness would make it easier to confine than her own.

She whispered urgently to Enya, hoping to reach the woman within. "After the next spell, concentrate and imagine being plunged into icy water, then freeze your demon within it."

Enya's demon tried to create an effect connected with movement, but Anike countered it and then felt Enya's slight form tense under her touch. She pulled the woman around so they were face-to-face and when Enya's eyes opened, they were her own again but they were full of fear.

"Demon?" she whispered.

Anike cursed herself and the relief she had just started to feel evaporated. She had become used to talking openly about the demon and had forgotten that the trembling woman had not been part of those discussions and in her haste to help Enya regain control, she had been careless. It had not been the time for that revelation.

"I am sorry," Anike told her. "I did not mean it to come out like that. The sources of our power, yours, mine and Karak's are alive, not just wellsprings of energy. I call them demons. Karak calls his a familiar, perhaps because he is more comfortable with its desires than I am."

"It's alive?" Enya's shoulders slumped. "And I can't get rid of it, can I?"

"No. I am sorry. It will be a part of you for as long as you live. Although it is a thinking being, it is so strange that it might as well be an impersonal force, so perhaps you can think of it that way?"

Enya looked at her. "I don't think I can live like that," she said and collapsed to the floor sobbing.

Glancing at Lalfar, Anike moved back and let him crouch and hold her close. Crying was probably good.

"It is not easy to accept that you have an enemy passenger," she said, "but it will help to make sense of any bad things that you might feel yourself wanting to do in the future. It would not be you." It was only a crumb of comfort but Enya did not need to carry the guilt over the desires of her demon, or its acts if it got loose.

She looked down again at Enya sitting with her head against Lalfar's chest. Her sobs were getting fainter and Anike crouched down in front of her. Enya looked up at her through the drying tears and Anike placed a hand on her cheek. "We will find you a way through this, together. I will keep you safe," she said, meaning every word.

Enya nodded, and the ghost of a smile appeared on her face.

A noise of falling rock from the direction of the door made Anike jerk her head around. She could not see any change, but it sounded as if something had shifted. Time was running short.

She got to her feet. "Now to get somewhere safer," she told Enya. Turning to a different page in her book, she went to the wall closest to the way they had originally come. "*Prana*," she said, blasting a hole into the rock.

"Why not use the other spell?" Lalfar asked her. "The one that you used to block the entrance. It's quicker."

"It will not do very much if any stone I cut loose cannot fall away," Anike told him, then put her hand on another section of the wall. "*Prana*."

The hole was now big enough to crawl into. She had devised this spell years before and had to touch the rock to affect it. It was another spell she had never felt any need to modify until now.

The effect did not send the dust very far and she coughed, then called back to Lalfar, "Clear the passage behind me or it will fill up." She heard him grunt a reply. From further away came more sounds of rocks shifting, telling her that the dwarves were making progress.

She had to get the glowstone out so she could see what she was doing. Breaking through stone was slow even with witchcraft. She heard Karak invoke his demon to create another wall of ice over the door and trusted he could slow the dwarves enough for her to finish. Behind her, Lalfar was using one of the beautiful dwarven books to shovel dust out of the passage.

She pictured the layout of the halls, not wanting to emerge in the room with the dwarves and after a few minutes and over a dozen casts later, she broke through into the enormous approach hall. Her passage had dipped slightly and she was now a little below the level of the floor. The ground in front of her sparkled with multi-coloured dust, the remains of the crystal she had disintegrated to first gain entrance to Hrym's Hall.

Carefully, she raised her head and looked about. While there were no dwarves in sight, she could see that the double doors leading into Hrym's Hall proper stood open. It was fortunate that only two had come as reinforcements and they were both inside the Hall.

She destroyed another part of the rock to make the entrance large enough for them all to pass through, then climbed out. To Lalfar, who was just behind her, she said quietly "I am through. Pass the word back and get everyone out, quickly and quietly."

One by one the others funnelled through the passage. Karak brought up the rear. "They are nearly into the book room," he told her.

Anike cursed under her breath. It had taken too long to create the tunnel and if the dwarves broke through the door and found the other end, they would catch them quickly. She would have to take another risk. "I am going to go back," she told him in a whisper. "I will provide a distraction to give you time to get everyone away."

She turned to the others. "Go on," she mouthed, making shooing gestures with her hands. "I will catch up with you soon."

Karak regarded her with a strange expression, suspicious perhaps, then he gave her a nod, took Hrost by the arm and led everyone away.

Anike went back into the tunnel.

Once at the other end, she spread her cloak and read the flight spell. She breathed a sigh of relief as she emerged into the book room. Most of the rubble still lay in place, though there was a hole near the top of the door. It was not yet large enough to get through but a pair of hands on each side of the hole were slowly tearing it open as if it were a heavy canvas.

As yet, the dwarves could only see a small part of the room and they probably thought everyone was hiding out of sight, or perhaps preparing an ambush. She quickly covered the mouth of the tunnel with some books then crossed the room to the wall adjacent to the hall where Enya and Hrost had been held. As she ducked past the doorway, a dwarven voice called out, "I see the witch!"

She did not dare assume that she had destroyed all of their missile weapons so she moved out of sight before any of them could aim something at her.

It had been part of her plan to be glimpsed within the book room but she worried that the absence of noise might give the dwarves a reason to look elsewhere for them, so she opened her book, intoned "*Vata*," and was surrounded by a whirlwind. The roaring winds flung the dust from the tunnel into the air and tumbled books from their pedestals, but if there had still been people within the room, the dwarves would no longer have been able to hear them.

If she was not to be trapped when the dwarves broke through the door, she had to hurry. Standing opposite the escape tunnel, she turned the page back to the disintegration spell and cut a narrow hole right through to the next room. It was far too small to get through but sufficient for her to see into the chamber beyond by the peculiar daylight emanating from the ocean. After a final glance behind her, she read the spell from her spear and said aloud, "*Prana*," dislocating herself to a point that she could see in the next chamber. This was far faster than breaking through a wall several paces thick, and the dwarves would not be able to follow her directly.

Fighting down the wave of nausea that accompanied the use of dislocation, she took stock. The room was empty save for the residue of the battle but once the dwarves heard the winds from inside the room they would surely come, and that was what she wanted.

Ignoring the strange vista of the ocean through the door and the iceberg that she could see in the distance through gaps in the blizzard, she rose quickly to the ceiling. "*Prana*," she said and cut a plane through the upper part of the arch above the double doors then conjured smoke to cover the middle of the room before descending to hover just above it.

"Get ready," she shouted at her non-existent allies. "Make sure your blades are coated fully and make each strike count." A little desperate perhaps, but it conveyed a message.

When a dwarf came into view at the doorway, Anike called in Norse. "Not yet – There is only one. Wait for my signal."

The dwarf looked at her, then at the smoke which for all he knew was hiding her allies, and he shouted back over his shoulder. "They have broken through the walls. In here." There was a sound of running feet.

Anike had thought there were six dwarves but only five came to the door. They paused, assessing the situation, and then one dressed in plate armour, a woman by her voice, called out an order. "Take them."

Five was the most she was going to get it seemed, so Anike called out, "*Prana*," and cut the rest of the arch clear from the wall. A lump of stone weighing many tons fell towards the dwarves.

This was a threat even to them, and they dived away. The stone fell between them, catching the legs of the slowest as he tried to fling himself clear, then shattering on the ground and sending fragments from one side of the room to the other. Taking advantage of the chaos, Anike shouted "Attack! Now!" and dived forward, raising her spear so she could see the dislocation pattern.

Before she could read it, she was amazed to see Karak appear behind the dwarves, running towards her. He gripped his greatsword in one hand and carried something large over his shoulder. At first, Anike thought it was a sack but as he came through the doorway, she saw it was Enya. Karak must have used his witchcraft to magnify his strength for he carried her easily. Zigzagging between the dwarves that were starting to get to their feet he ran straight towards Anike.

She dropped down so that she was in front of him. "What are you doing?" she shouted at him, but Karak did not reply. Instead, he lashed out at her one-handed with his sword.

Caught by surprise, she barely blocked the blow with her spear. The heavy blade passed through her wind shield without slowing and the force of the strike knocked her sideways before she focused her will and steadied herself with the flight spell. She brought her spear back, ready to block the next blow but Karak had run straight past her, heading towards the door into the ocean without showing any signs of slowing down. From behind him, she could see Enya was unconscious.

Anike had just begun to reach for her book to find the spell to lift Enya away from him when he leapt through the doorway and into the ice-covered ocean. There was a splash, and he disappeared under the water. A flurry of snow covered the area, blinding her to his location and giving her no way to target him.

She was about to start forwards when a blow caught her on the back of the head, sending stars cascading through her mind.

Anike struggled to hold onto consciousness through the wave of pain. She had been so surprised by Karak's appearance that she had not paid enough attention to the dwarves. She was still suspended in the air by her flight spell and as her vision swam in and out, she saw a fragment of the stone arch on the ground beneath her, with a lock of long dark hair stuck to it by fresh blood. She was aware of movement, then strong hands grasping her, forcing her to the ground and binding her, and a gag being shoved into her mouth. There was pressure and the ripping sound of cloth tearing.

The flight effect ended and she slumped, dimly aware that she was being laid on her side. A dwarf held her head up and looked into her eyes, then let her fall. She felt the impact of her head on the stone, but it added little to her world of pain.

Drifting in and out of consciousness, she felt the demon struggling within, but it needed her will to bridge the gap to reality and she had so little coherent thought that it could do nothing, even though her own desire to strike out against the dwarves was a mirror of its own.

Sometime later, minutes she thought, rather than hours, her grip on consciousness began to strengthen and despite the pain in her head, she started to rally and become aware of her surroundings again. She forced the demon back into its prison and with her eyes still closed, tried to sense what was around her.

The first thing she became aware of was that she was gagged and bound so tightly that the bonds stung. She did not dare give away that she was conscious again so could not test them, but they were certainly not flimsy. The dwarves knew her capabilities and were taking few chances.

Voices came from nearby and trying not to react to what she was hearing, she focused on them. At least three were involved in the discussion.

"This one may have to do. We won't need to hold her long, since she has come to us here."

"Humans have such surprising loyalty, and they are confident in their own abilities, even in the face of hopeless odds."

"Like their dogs. It doesn't matter. Karak must be going to use the other one to wake Hrym. What other use would he have for her? It fits with what I told this witch."

"Will he be able to find his way through?"

"Probably. It is more his domain than ours."

"We only need this one alive in case he fails, but until we know what he has done, we had best not kill her."

"There is not a great deal of time, you realise?"

Anike felt her concentration wavering and reinforced the bonds holding the demon, then let herself drift for a moment before rallying. Karak's betrayal had not been for the sake of the dwarves but it still served their ends. It looked as if he had seized Enya once Hrost had been safe, taking advantage of her own absence. She hoped he had not killed Lalfar and Gunnar. He was quite capable of it, but she had thought his blade had been clear of blood when he had swung it at her.

One of the dwarves, presumably the one she had rescued from the chasm, had hinted at Karak's motive and it was not hard to put the pieces together. He had told them that Hrym could help with the spell to bind the demon and Karak had apparently decided the chance to learn that was worth more than escorting Hrost back to his father. He had taken Enya to wake the giant and wanted to do it without the dwarves being there, presumably because he doubted that they would just let him leave afterwards.

She turned her awareness to her body. Her only significant injury seemed to be to the back of her head but she was bound with her hands behind her back and her feet tied together. From what she could hear, it seemed that her captors, or at least some of them, were still talking in front of her. From one side came the crash of ocean waves.

Opening her eyes a fraction, she could see four dwarves. None of them were watching her, though two were facing towards her and would surely notice if she opened her eyes further or shifted position. Her spear and book were on the ground a couple of paces away, probably where she had dropped them, and her bag was lying nearby, next to her cloak and the rune-covered sleeves torn from her tunic.

She closed her eyes again to stop herself blinking and considered. Karak might have attacked Lalfar and Gunnar, and they were either dead or they were not. If they were alive, the dwarves would have no interest in them unless they mounted another rescue attempt, and if they were dead, she could not help them.

On the other hand, Enya needed her. The young woman would be no match for Karak even if she regained consciousness, and he could already be preparing to sacrifice her. Anike's blood ran cold at that thought and she forced herself not to shudder. It was clear what her course should be. She might still be able to help Enya but there was little that she could do for Lalfar and Gunnar.

In any case, she had to escape. Without moving, she tested her concentration, forming a rune pattern in her mind. The pain was a distraction, but she forced herself to ignore it. She held the spell's pattern, unable to stop it wavering a little, but it was clear enough to use.

She had been bound and gagged before. Nearly two years ago, she had been held in the arl's hall by Bjord after her former master Olaf had turned on her. That time, she had played on Olaf's guilt to get him to remove the gag and once her mouth had been free, she had loosed her demon, the only time she had ever chosen to do so. The demon had wreaked havoc in the hall and she had barely regained control before it killed everyone there. She had decided never to deliberately release it again, but she had also realised that she needed a way to escape from bonds. The law decreed that witches should be gagged when captured and it was still done, even though the reason might have been forgotten.

It had always been quite possible that some arl would discover that she was a witch and hold her for trial, so she had spent hours with a gag in her mouth, practising speaking a rune clearly enough to cast a spell. Most of the runes were too difficult to name precisely but one could still be formed through the gag and she had eventually taught herself to pronounce it properly. She had devised a simple pattern that she could hold in her mind to use in that situation to remove the binding and the gag.

She pictured what she would do and fixed the location of the spear, bag and book in her mind. If the dwarves had emptied the bag, that would be unfortunate but there was nothing she could do about it. If she stopped to search for anything, they would have her.

Cracking open an eyelid, she saw that the dwarves seemed to have reached a consensus and for all she knew their next step might be to pick her up. She could wait no longer.

She visualised the pattern and directed it onto her restraints. "*Agni*," she said, wincing as the bonds and gag burned away and seared her skin and lips, but she rolled to her feet and took a step forward. Her legs screamed as blood came back into them and she stumbled.

The dwarves turned to her. "No!" one said, a woman fully encased in metal armour but now with her helm removed, and took a step towards her.

There was not enough time to get to her equipment and she made her choice. Two dwarves reached for her, but she forced herself into a staggering run and leapt through the doorway and across the threshold into the freezing ocean.

- 22 -

THE SEA OF ICE

There was a moment of disorientation as she passed over the threshold and into the blizzard, then Anike struck the icy water. Her arm hit a concealed rock and the impact jarred her, nearly making her gulp in the brine before her head cleared the surface again. The shock of the cold had sharpened her senses and the pain lanced through her.

She glanced over her shoulder to make sure she was not about to hit any ice, and then started to swim away from the entrance on her back so she could watch the doors she had come through. She could just about make out figures there but they were hidden by the storm as she pulled away.

The cliff rose into white clouds that clung to the rocks, and snow and hail lashed land and sea alike. She could not see far upwards. The clouds were very low, hanging like a bank of fog, and if it were not for the light and falling snow, she might have believed she was within an enormous cavern.

The blizzard hid her from the dwarven eyes, and spotting a head between the waves and foam would not be easy, but she would have to get out of the water quickly. The sea around Gotlund had ice floes in the depths of winter, and she knew she would not be able to survive in the freezing ocean for long. It was much colder than the tunnels and halls of Svartalfheim.

The demon was struggling inside her, wanting to take some action against the environment. While it was hardly the most pressing matter, Anike found this odd as being in water usually suppressed it.

She looked around, trying to work out which way to go. The cliff was still intermittently visible between snow flurries and she could only suppose that she had to cross the ocean to find Hrym, or perhaps reach an island. Karak and Enya had to be here somewhere as well. There was no sign of them, but she had not expected that following them would be easy.

Enya was the key. Anike could use the spell that detected chaos witches to find her, once she found somewhere to write the spell down. If she could reach solid ice, she could perhaps scratch it into the surface.

A wave splashed her face. She could not concentrate sufficiently to cast even her simple levitation spell while swimming. Her arm was bruised from the contact with the rock she had hit but her body was not yet numb from the cold. She looked around and headed for the closest ice floe.

She reached the edge and tried to pull herself out of the water, but she could not get a firm enough grip and slid back in. She was still able to feel despite the temperature of the water and appreciated this surprising good fortune. The cold would steal her sense of touch soon enough.

Clinging to the ice to brace herself against the waves, she concentrated and managed to hold the pattern for levitation clearly enough to risk invoking the demon. "*Prana*," she said and felt the energy of movement surround her so she could lift herself out of the sea and onto the ice floe.

Her senses still rebelled against where she was. This place could not exist underground. They had walked downwards rather than up and had not travelled far enough to reach the coast. The only thing she could think of was that the doors were a portal created with dislocation witchcraft which had taken her somewhere a long way north. A chill ran through her at the thought of how much power must have been involved, many times greater than her demon was capable of. Her teeth started to chatter.

She looked around for a level space where she could scratch out a rune pattern. While she did so, she noticed that despite the sea and the wind, she was not really all that cold. She shivered, but did not feel the bone-chilling aftermath of being in water she had expected and neither was she numb as if on the point of death.

Relieved not to be about to expire but puzzled as to why, she felt a strange sensation caress her, something she found it hard to isolate against the storm.

Shaking her head, she dismissed the feeling. There were so many odd things around her, and she had to focus on finding Enya. Escaping from the dwarves had cost her much valuable time and Karak would have a good lead, even if carrying Enya had slowed him down.

The dwarves had taken her weapons and her cloak, so she could not use the sharp needle which was part of the clasp, but she still had the pouch of coins at her belt. On opening it, her fingers brushed the cloth she had wrapped around the brooch that Morsali had entrusted to her. She unbound it and freed the pin, knelt and tried to inscribe a rune into the ice. While the surface did not seem that hard and the metal scratched it easily enough, the marks did not stay but merged together again as if the ice was healing or warping back together again. She stared at the frosty surface and tried harder, but the same thing happened. Mystified, she returned the brooch to her poach and stood up. It was too cold to keep repeating something that did not work.

The only landmark she could make out through the driving snow was the iceberg she had glimpsed before, a single spire rising from the storm-tossed sea, then the blizzard closed in again and hid it from view.

Without any other obvious destination, she crossed over the ice floe and cast the levitation spell again so that she would not have to re-enter the chill water. Heading slowly forward through the blinding flakes, she heard the sound of ice cracking a little to the right of her course and changed direction. A billow of wind cleared a view through the falling snow, and she watched a side of the iceberg break away and crash into the sea, sending up a great spray of water.

In the moment of quiet that followed, Anike felt the odd sensation around her again and she realised that it was to this that the demon was reacting, struggling to oppose it. At last, she recognised what she had been feeling. All about her was the caress of runes, diffuse but definitely present. She was inside a spell, a weaving of law. As she concentrated, she perceived more of it and her eyes widened in shock as she made out the pattern. All about her was a seeming, an illusion, giving her the impression she was on an ocean in a storm.

Ilun, the rune of seeming, was law-aligned and she had given it little thought. There were legends of the giants using seemings to confuse the gods. In one tale, the king of the giants, Utgard-Haloki, had tricked Thor and Loki with illusions, deceiving Thor into striking a mountain with his hammer Mjolnir instead of the giant himself and even disguising the Midgard Serpent, Jormungand, as a giant cat. From the middle of an illusion of a blizzard-covered ocean inside a cavern, those legends suddenly seemed much more believable.

She wondered if Hrym was awake and had created an image of his home, then frowned. That could not be right. The dwarves had still been talking about Enya and herself being used to wake him and they had not advanced beyond the doors, so this image had likely been in place when they had first arrived at Hrym's Hall, perhaps even set in place centuries before by other dwarves to protect the giant. It did not seem likely that Hrym had been roused yet.

The dwarves must have known this was a seeming but had been unable or unwilling to do anything about it, perhaps not even wanting to risk entering it. In reality, she was probably only a couple of dozen paces away from them, even though she could no longer see the cliffs. She rubbed her injured arm. The chill she felt might not be real but the bruises certainly were. When she had jumped in, she must have hit something in the hall rather than a submerged rock.

Feeling vulnerable, she drifted forwards, trying to determine what was real and what was illusion. She headed in the direction she had last seen the iceberg, but it was little closer when it came into view again through another gap in the driving snow. By accident or design, the seeming was making it impossible to make much progress.

She landed, feeling as if she was floating in the water, and reached out with her mind to touch the runes around her, sensing the structure of the pattern. It was not particularly complicated, and she could understand how it was constructed. While the runes were more solid than something she could create, they were nothing like as implacable as those that had animated the stone guardian. She might be able to disrupt the spell and dispel the illusion surrounding her.

In principle, it ought to be no different to countering one of Karak's spells, but there were be additional challenges. The runes surrounding her had a greater presence and carried more weight, as if more power was invested in them but the difference was not so vast that she could not comprehend it – it would be like trying to wrestle Karak physically.

The other difference was that this rune pattern was stable, already invested with power rather than the sketchy designs that she had countered while fighting him. It was a fully formed and active spell, without the ragged edges of a pattern being cast.

These were just problems of degree, though. She had dispelled the flight spell she had placed on the dwarf at the chasm without really thinking about it, and that was the first time she had broken an ongoing effect. Of course, she knew exactly how her own spells were formulated but unlike trying to counter a spell that was being cast on her, she had time to analyse the structure of the seeming.

She felt through the pattern, hunting for weaknesses. While powerful, the structure of the spell was actually quite simple and it was extended over a wide area by repetition. She could not sense the outer bounds but the edges of each copy of the pattern were vulnerable. *Osc*, the chaos rune of veil, was directly opposed to *Ilun* so she inserted it into the pattern and named it aloud to channel power into it.

The illusion wavered for a moment as the force of her witchcraft jolted it, but it held. Anike was not too surprised that the first attempt had failed, but she had felt it give a little under her assault. There was no sense of adjustment or reinforcement in response to her witchcraft, no hint that someone was trying to hold the spell in place. She shifted the veil rune to a different setting within the pattern, gathered her will and struck again. This time, the rune pattern fractured. The fabric of the spell started to dissolve and the scene about her wavered as the illusion evaporated.

She was standing on a stone floor towards one end of a vast hall, larger than any she had yet seen. It was lit by dozens of glowstones, mostly set in the ceiling. Arches spanned the roof far above her, and carvings or bas relief adorned the walls. The hall was more than eighty paces long and over half that wide and its floor was inlaid with patterns of coloured stones. The double doors she had entered by lay behind her at the far end of the hall at the top of a short flight of stairs bordered by balustrades. Statues were set throughout the vast space, and she had the good fortune to be standing next to one when the seeming fell. Halfway down the hall on the opposite side wall was another set of double doors, some twenty feet high and over thirty feet wide.

The last of the illusion dissolved and the iceberg ahead of her became a giant sat on a throne. Even sitting down, his head was at least twenty feet off the ground. A white beard and white hair, looking like they were formed from frost rather than due to age, framed his face and his skin was the pale blue of ice.

She had no doubt that she was looking at Hrym, king of the frost giants.

Hrym was dressed in furs and boots, all covered in glistening ice dust. His eyes were closed but Anike could see movement beneath the eyelids. He was starting to wake.

Even from twenty paces away, she could feel the aura of majesty and power radiating from him and her demon was clamouring for release, to either attack or flee.

So awestruck was she by the giant that she did not see Karak until he shifted position. He was standing on a ledge near Hrym's shoulder, looking up at the great head above him and holding Enya tightly by the arm. A staircase climbed from the floor to where he now stood and there was a doorway in the wall behind him. Somehow, he had made his way through the seeming while it was still active and dragged Enya with him.

Then she saw that the giant king's lips were moving, and while she could hear he was speaking, the voice was too low for her to make out the words.

Karak turned and looked straight at her, then his gaze shifted to something behind her. She cast a glance back over her shoulder to see the dwarves coming down the steps into the hall.

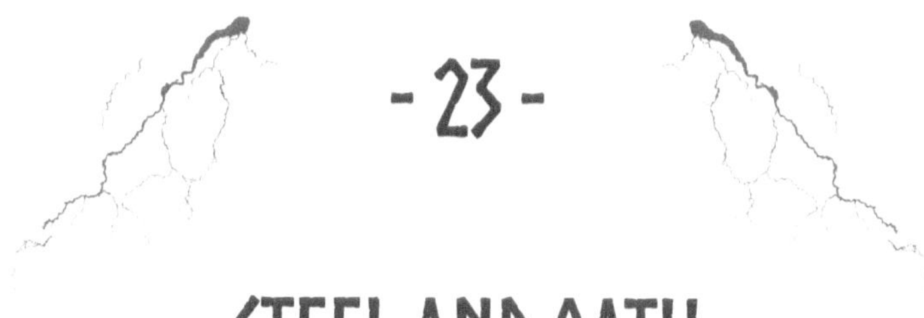

- 23 -

STEEL AND OATH

Pressing herself tight against the base of the statue, and hoping it would conceal her, Anike watched the dwarves advance. There were just five of them, the one whose leg had been crushed by the falling arch had presumably been left to watch against the possible return of Lalfar, Gunnar and Hrost. They were advancing slowly and their attention appeared to be focused on Hrym.

She was a little over halfway down the hall and they would not reach her for a few moments. There was dust on the floor, but she had left no trail that would reveal her position when she had flown over it.

Looking back towards Hrym, she saw that Karak was standing on the ledge beside the frost-coloured head and was facing the great ear, speaking to the giant. Enya was slumped against his legs with her fair hair covering her face, either unconscious or pretending to be. Karak had one hand resting on her arm as he spoke.

Anike measured the distance. Unarmed and without her spells, she was no match for the warrior, especially as he knew she was there and would be ready for her. With the dwarves in the hall, there was little she could do against him without giving away her whereabouts, but their low opinion of humans had worked in her favour. They did not seem particularly concerned about what had happened to her and were making no effort to keep their conversation quiet even though at least one of them knew perfectly well that she spoke dwarven.

"It was good to be given a chance to see Hrym's home as it was before Ragnarok," one was saying.

"It seems that the proximity of the witch stirred him and the dream collapsed as he started to wake," another replied, a woman. "We did not need the spare. Karak has decided to serve Hrym's ends, after all."

"There is not much time," a third dwarf said. "The witch's presence is quickening Hrym, but the Nidhogg draws closer by the minute."

Anike had forgotten the Nidhogg in the press of events but it was not her immediate concern. Karak had Enya and could sacrifice her at any moment but the conversation added to her concerns.

At that moment, she wished she had full access to the demon's power. She was overmatched by her adversaries and there was no reason for them to hold back any more. A dwarf in scale mail still held one of the bow-like weapons and could kill her from across the hall.

If she only had to imagine an effect for the demon to make it happen, it would have given her a better chance against the five dwarves. But she did not have that ability and there was no way she could get it in time to help, even assuming Hrym did know the spell, and would give it to a chaos witch. Karak was closer to that goal than she was.

She could release her restraints on the demon, as Karak had told her he did. Almost everyone within Hrym's Hall was an enemy and the demon would strike at the dwarves, Karak or even Hrym rather than at Enya, within whom a kindred spirit dwelt. Tempting as that idea was on the surface, there were two practical flaws, beyond betraying her vow to herself. Firstly, the only time she had let the demon take control, it had been very hard to bind it again and while Karak had given her hints on how he managed it, she was cautious about trying. The second problem was that the demon had little regard for her body and she was worried it would consider sacrificing her a valid trade for the mere chance to hurt Hrym. She had to rely on herself.

One of the dwarves was carrying her bag, and another had wrapped her cloak around the spear. If she could recover some key spells, she would have a chance. The bag looked full and she did not see her spellbook anywhere else, so it might have been still inside.

The book and cloak recorded patterns that were too complex for her to cast without the whole image set out before her, but that did not mean she could not recall them. She only needed some way to write the runes down so she could read them back.

Her eyes fell on the dust covering the floor all around her. Crouching, she sketched the pattern she was most familiar with, her flight spell.

She glanced up. The dwarves were passing her now and Hrym was starting to stir. His eyes were still closed but the fingers on his right hand were flexing and his head turned slowly towards Karak, who was still not making any move to complete the sacrifice.

Her spell was finished. Anike checked the pattern once more to make sure it was correct then read it and spoke, "*Prana*," aloud. The energy from the spell surrounded her and she lifted silently into the air.

Aloft and feeling more in control, she considered changing her plan, ignoring her equipment and going straight for Karak. If she went up to the ceiling, she could make her way to Hrym unnoticed then drop onto the warrior. Despite his greater strength, she might be able to push him from the ledge if she could surprise him.

But even if she could knock him off it, the fall might not be enough to incapacitate him, and unarmed and without any more witchcraft, she had no way to get an unconscious Enya past the dwarves. The flight effect was not strong enough to carry someone else unless they were supported by a separate spell. Attacking him now would just lead to their defeat and probable deaths.

Hrym's head was now turned directly towards Karak, and the giant's eyes had opened. Enya too had woken and she was looking up at Hrym. Anike realised what was about to happen before Karak did. Enya stared at the giant and said "*Agni!*", doubtless so frightened that she had lost control of her demon. Jets of flame leapt from her eyes towards the great face only a few feet away but they had about as much effect as water striking an iceberg. Hrym's lips slowly formed into a slight smile. His movements were still slow and accompanied by a cracking noise as if he were actually made of ice.

The dwarves had halted at the sight of the fire and were watching the drama playing out above them. Anike saw her chance and flew silently towards the one who held her bag. As she got closer, she realised that it was looped over one of his shoulders and she would not be able to get it off him before he could react. Her spell to lift small objects was simple and did not need to be written down, but she would have to be so close to the dwarf to use it that he would hear her speak the form rune. She would have to extract her book from inside the bag.

Ahead she could see, and just about hear, Karak speaking but he stopped as Enya launched another attack at Hrym, this time sending bolts of lightning at him. They left only a trace of a scorch mark on his face and if they hurt the giant at all, he gave no sign.

Hrym looked down at Enya and his lips moved. "*Ert*," came the long slow syllable, naming the form of stasis.

Enya screamed, "*Prana*," in a vain attempt to counter the spell but to no effect, and the giant's witchcraft froze her in place.

Anike was not surprised that such a being could use witchcraft as giants in legends had many supernatural abilities, but it gave her pause to note that his power was still strong, even after thousands of years. However, that was a problem for later.

She returned her concentration to the dwarf in front of her who was still focusing on Hrym. Warily, she drifted up to him, raised the flap on the satchel and very slowly started to lift out her book. If she could get it without being noticed, then she might try to reach a potion as well.

Hrym was talking now, in Norse, and Anike could make out the last of his words "...so I grant you a boon, human." Distracted, she let the book slip and caught at it. Her movement caught the eye of one of the other dwarves who glanced away from Hrym, and then turned his head sharply towards her.

Without waiting for the cry of warning, Anike closed her hand around her spellbook and flew straight up.

The demon's frustration was palpable as Anike pulled away from the dwarves, but she did not plan on letting them be. They had all seen her now and their focus had shifted from Hrym and Karak to her.

The dwarf she had rescued from the chasm was pulling one of the metal-throwing bows from his back, ready to aim at her. Anike had already turned to the page with the spell she had devised to destroy weapons. She called out, "*Agni*," and directed the energy into the bow and the axes that two others had in their hands. Fire consumed all three weapons and a steel ball shot down the hall to draw sparks from the steps near the entrance doors.

Any notion that she might have had that she was safe was soon dispelled. Two of the dwarves bent down and slid their hands into the stone, scooping up solid rock as if it were thick mud and then hurling the stones at her. Once again, she was reminded of their strength as the missiles flew through the air with astonishing speed. She dodged one but the other struck her in the side, winding her through her armour. The two dwarves bent to pull more stone from the ground.

She looked up at the ceiling. If she stayed high up, she would present a very difficult target, but that limited her own options. She could not even approach Karak without exposing herself to their attacks and there was little she could do to the dwarves from that distance.

She glanced at the black-clad warrior. Hrym was speaking again, something about witches, but her concentration was taken up by avoiding another volley of missiles. She had to deal with the dwarves first.

Her bag now lay on the floor behind the dwarf who had dropped it when he started throwing stones at her. The potion to weaken them might still be within and if it was, her best chance lay in retrieving it. She had devised a desperate plan to use it should she no longer have allies about her.

She turned to a different page and swooped down, avoided another rock and slowed when she was a few paces above the dwarves' heads. "*Vata*," she cried out and around each dwarf, the air solidified before fracturing into invisible knives which bit at their flesh. The wounds were shallow, but they were painful even to a dwarf and blood welled up as the spectral blades cut across bare skin. Her demon had shown her this effect when she was being hunted by a group of men intent on her death or capture, and she had recreated and refined it as she had travelled through Svartalfheim.

While it would not inflict serious injuries, the spell was still a potent distraction. She dived for her bag, lifted it clear of the ground and retreated up out of reach.

The flask containing the blade venom was still there, and by the weight she could tell there was still a little left. She hoped it was enough and pulled the lid off. With her other hand, she opened her book to the final page. The dwarves were only just starting to rally from the daggers of air and were not yet ready to strike at her, so she cast the spell on the oil. Created the previous night, this was intended to suspend and animate a liquid in the air. She had been reluctant to test it on the poison for fear of wasting it, and when tried out on water, that had leaked away quite quickly. She had not intended to rely on the spell in battle but now she had no choice. If it did not hold the venom, Anike had no idea what she would do next.

The spell worked better on the thick elixir and she sent the sphere of poison down behind the dwarves, who were looking up at her again, then flew sideways to distract them. As they sighted on her, she willed the sphere into the face of one dwarf in scale mail, the one she had rescued from the chasm, then off again towards another. He tried to parry with a shield, but she dipped the bulb of poison beneath his block and then up to catch his hand. As it entered their bloodstream, the dwarves sank to the ground, unable to lift their armour in their weakening state. One dwarf in lighter leather remained upright, but she had cut him with her dagger in the first fight and he would not be so much of a threat without superhuman strength.

Anike dropped towards her spear.

There were two other dwarves, both in plate armour, and the viscous liquid was shrinking with each strike. One rushed towards her, and she flung the last of the venom at his face, the only part of him that was exposed. The knives of air had opened only a few slight wounds but it was enough for the poison to enter his system. Anike grabbed her spear and dodged out of the way, watching him slow and collapse as he went past her. The spell had worked as well as she could have hoped for, but the final dwarf, the woman, still stood.

She was in armour but with her head bared. Holding a double-bladed axe in one hand, she advanced towards Anike. She bore cuts on her face too, but there was no more poison.

Keeping her eyes firmly on the dwarven woman, she landed next to the dwarf she had rescued in the chasm and placed the point of her spear against his throat. He tried to rise, but she pressed down and a trickle of blood joined that running from the small cuts on his face.

The dwarven woman froze.

"You are the leader of these dwarves?" Anike asked.

The dwarf stared at her. "Yes," she said. "I am Barodar."

"I do not wish to kill your warrior," Anike glanced down, "especially having rescued him from where he was stranded, but I will do so if you and I cannot reach terms."

The dwarf regarded her levelly. "What terms do you propose, human witch?"

"Your men are vulnerable. I can kill them, with spear or witchcraft but I see no gain from their deaths if we are not in conflict. Give me your word to bind yourself and all you lead, both here and elsewhere in Svartalfheim, that you will neither attack any human within this realm nor hinder their departure unless they attack you first."

She pushed the spear point in a little deeper for emphasis. "If you do so, I will let your comrades live. Decide now."

The dwarf looked at her, then over her shoulder at Hrym. "We have what we need now. I will forgo the pleasure of punishing you for your hubris, this time. Let my husband up and we have an accord."

Anike looked down at the dwarf she had rescued, frozen against the point of her spear. Little wonder this man had come to help the dwarven leader. She withdrew the weapon, ignoring the demon's rage.

Barodar made no move to attack her so Anike took a step back to look at Hrym more carefully. His body was half turned to Karak now and he was holding out a slab of rock, perhaps two feet by one but tiny in the blue-white hand.

Karak took it, looked straight at her and without warning turned and ran through the doorway on the ledge, dragging Enya behind him. Hrym pursed his vast lips, and Anike saw his forehead crease into a frown.

She picked up her cloak from the ground and set it about her shoulders before casting the flight spell from it, planning to fly past the giant and after Karak.

Hrym turned his head to watch her coming closer. Anike had no wish to confront or deal with him, even if he was barely awake. Fortunately, he did not seem very mobile yet, moving too slowly to stop her as she flew straight for the passage.

As she came level with his head, his eyes followed her and he spoke, "*Ranak.*" A wall of ice appeared directly in front of her, blocking the route Karak had taken.

- 24 -

THE GIANT

Anike pulled up sharply, coming to a halt on the ledge next to Hrym's head. The giant did not want her pursuing Karak, it seemed. She looked up and saw that his eyes had closed again.

Having the personal attention of a being thousands of years old should have filled her with awe but it was buried beneath frustration that Karak was getting away and worry for Enya, who was amazingly still alive.

The stone Hrym had given Karak must have shown the rune pattern for the binding spell, so Karak had surely assumed Anike would pursue him and taken Enya as a hostage. Ironically, his action guaranteed that she would follow as she could no more abandon Enya now than when the dwarves had taken her. Karak could easily kill her or leave her to die.

The wall of ice blocked her path. She reached out to touch the glistening surface and felt the tracery of runes within. Closing her eyes to sense the pattern more clearly, she found a place where she could disrupt it. "*Agni,*" she said, inserting the rune of fire into the pattern. The wall shattered and collapsed to ice dust which vanished as the power holding it in existence was disrupted.

Even before the sound of her voice had died away, Hrym spoke again, "*Ranak.*" Another wall appeared in its place.

Frustrated, she touched the new barrier and once again sought the pattern holding it. "*Agni,*" she repeated when she found it, but again the giant spoke as the wall collapsed. "*Ranak.*" His voice echoed around the hall, and yet another wall of ice blocked her way.

Hrym did not have a rune pattern in front of him and while the ice wall was not the most complex spell, it was more involved than anything she or Karak could have managed without a written pattern.

Anike put her hand up to the barrier again but paused. She could keep trying to break through, but the giant might take some more direct action against her if she did and she wondered why he had not done so already. A demon would have tried to kill her by now, so Hrym had to be casting the spells himself, but that did not explain why he had not simply frozen her in place as he had Enya. Her own demon wanted to act directly against Hrym, though whether it would have more success than Enya's demon was a moot point.

Whatever his situation, he was not going to let her pass and if he had wanted her dead, he would have been trying a lot harder. She would have to deal with him, but she wondered if he wanted something from her too.

Anike turned to look into the face of the giant king.

Hrym opened his eyes and spoke in a voice at once deep and sharp, like the cracking of a vast block of ice as it shattered. "It took you only a little time to accept the futility of your position. I am impressed. Humans used to be such simple creatures."

Up close, Anike could see the giant was not made of ice as he had seemed from further away. His skin was a bluish-white, but it moved in the manner of living flesh when he spoke. In some ways that was reassuring as it meant that Hrym was a living being, not an elemental like the stone guardian of Ivaldi's home.

"Why are you preventing me take that passage?" Anike asked, her tone betraying a hint of exasperation. She was becoming used to beings looking down on humanity as a species and while she no longer took offence, it would not do to let the giant think her frightened.

Hrym slowly flexed his arms against the throne he sat on, but did not answer the question, so she went on. "I assume you mean to ensure Karak has a good lead, for some reason. If you just wanted him to escape, we would not be talking."

"So fierce for such a small creature." The giant's tone contained a hint of amusement. "In my day, your people ran and hid whenever one of my kind came into view."

"I had thought your day was long past," Anike snapped before she realised what she was going to say. The demon's hatred and fear of Hrym were seeping into her thoughts, adding to her own frustration over being prevented from following Karak. She frowned and reinforced the barriers in her mind. The giant had not yet acted directly against her but given what it had done to Enya, there was no doubt he could and she did not wish to goad him. She modified her tone and added, "It seems I was wrong."

Hrym's lips twitched into what might have been a smile. "I do indeed wish the Law witch to have a chance to escape, but I also want to talk to you. You are repressing the Chaos shard within you even though it limits you to do so." Anike could hear the capital letters given to Law and Chaos.

The giant continued, "Despite having been able to dispel my dream and defeat the svart alfar, and knowing that I was preventing you from proceeding, your decision was to speak to me rather than to fight. I am curious."

It surprised her that the giant thought her worth talking to, and that he had not actually dismissed her as a threat. Her demon was a lot stronger than Enya's but Anike doubted that it was really capable of hurting the giant even though he could only be partially awake without the sacrifice of a chaos witch.

She glanced at the ice wall, chaffing at the delay but abandoned the idea of trying to dispel it again. It was clear that Hrym would not let her pursue Karak yet and if they had the chance to talk, she might be able to persuade or trick him into letting her go or find out something useful, such as what the giant had told the warrior. She also had to admit that she was intrigued at being able to talk to someone thousands of years old, and the prospect of learning something new was tantalising. If she was not allowed to leave yet, she would make the most of the opportunity.

"Since you wish to talk, let us talk," she said. "Perhaps we can trade questions."

"Very well," Hrym said, his words coming slowly. "You may start. I am curious to see what you will ask."

Anike was struck by a recollection of Hilda, the seer who had set her on the path to understanding runes. Never asking a question herself, she listened to those asked by others for what they revealed about the inquirer, and the giant was indicating something similar. The memory struck a chord and warned her that she should be cautious.

Hrym had seemed impressed that she was able to adapt to a new situation so she decided not to ask about Karak first. Instead, she said, "You called the demon inside me a chaos shard. Where does it come from?"

The giant's words were slow, like the roll of a wave. "The shards come from the void beyond the sky."

"What do they want?"

Hrym looked at her. "I will answer after you have told me something in return. What was the outcome of Ragnarok?"

Anike supposed that he must have been incapacitated before the end of the battle, assuming that the tales that placed him there were true. She answered carefully, "It was many human lifetimes ago, so what I know is only legend. Almost all who were involved in the battle were killed, so the tale goes. Most of the gods died, though they are still with us in spirit. Surtur is supposed to have burned away any who were not killed in battle, so I suppose that made him the victor. I have never heard that a giant escaped. Humans only survived because we fled the northern islands of the archipelago before the battle."

Hyrm nodded slowly, then addressed her last question. "Surely you know what your Chaos shard wants?" Again, Anike could hear the capital letter. "Chaos wants to destroy the world, to break it to dust and let the dust vanish. Law wants to kill all living things, freeze everything in place and leave the world in a pristine, unchanging state. The shards are small parts of these forces, able to function independently. Minions if you will."

"Demons."

"That word serves."

"Why do...?" Anike caught herself before she asked another question. "No. It is your turn." She wanted time to think about how to get the most from this discussion.

Hrym paused before asking his next question. "What races live in Midgard now?"

"Humanity mainly. The dwarves do not any more. As far as I know, they are only found here in Svartalfheim. There are some elves deep in the old forests, but I have never seen one and I think there are very few of them. There are supposed to be trolls in some mountains too, and there are some other monsters, like nokken."

She looked at the ice wall again but Hrym frowned slightly. Anike resisted the inclination to inquire whether he would let her go and waste a question, so she asked, "Why do the demons join with humans?"

"They cannot exist for long within Midgard or any world embraced by Yggdrasil, without bonding to a human." Anike noticed that he said 'human' and not 'being' which suggested there were no dwarven witches. "In order to explain, I will need to tell you of the beginning."

Anike leaned forward slightly. If she was being forced to listen, she did not want to miss a word.

"Long ago," Hrym started, "the forces of Law formed a world out of dust and ice and hung it in the void. They had been building them since the beginning of time. The fury of Chaos tried to tear each new world apart. Sometimes Chaos won, and the world was reduced to nothing, and sometimes Law stabilised it, making it resistant to Chaos. Then the cycle repeated itself with a new world.

"Ymir and Dra," Anike said, recalling the creation story she had read in Ivaldi's archive.

"In truth, they were nameless until the svart alfar, the dwarves as you call them, chose to refer to them so. As I said, this contest over worlds has happened many times before in the void, but in this one, the aspects of Law and Chaos that contended were too evenly matched. During their battle, they began to both fragment and merge as they strove against each other, and eventually they became a single force. We call it 'life', or Yggdrasil, the World Tree. Life is the child of Law and Chaos and both despise it, each one seeing it as corrupted by the other.

"So that is why no witch can use *Vit*, the rune of life," said Anike. "The law and chaos demons have no power over it."

"Indeed." The giant was talking a little faster now, caught up in what he was telling her. Perhaps because he had been asleep for long ages with only his dreams for company, he seemed eager to volunteer more information.

"Life is unique to this world and permeates its very essence. The forces of Law and Chaos in the void are repelled by the aura of Life and usually cannot reach the world. But sometimes there are ripples, branches of the World Tree moving in the wind if you like, that give Law and Chaos glimpses and paths to Midgard. If one opens, one force or the other can try to reach the world and work its will. They send the shards, the demons as you call them, through those ripples to the surface, clothing them in power to preserve them until they can find a human host to bond with. Witch weather is the product of the force surrounding a Chaos shard as it tries to reach the world. You will have seen that."

Anike nodded. "What of law demons?"

"They are carried by falling stars. Law requires a more stable home than Chaos. In both cases, the power that lets them exist here until they find a host may warp life nearby. Many of the creatures from your legends were formed by that backlash of power, a side effect of getting a shard into the world. Dire creatures were once normal animals but have been enhanced by Law, whereas draugr are those on the point of death who have been transformed by Chaos."

"You said the shards need a human to bond with but the dwarves have witchcraft too. So do you, and your power closely resembles that of Karak's demon." Hrym shifted slightly on his throne and Anike paused, deciding that it would be appropriate to show a little more respect. "Much less powerful than you, of course," she added.

"Witches are only as old as humanity. Humans are empty," Hrym said, lifting a finger slightly to forestall any protest. "I mean that they have no inherent connection to Law or Chaos. The older races are aligned to one or the other. Life did not form in an even surface but more like the sea with waves and troughs, and there are concentrations of Law and Chaos. Dwarves are formed with more Law, just as the Lios Alfar, the elves, have more Chaos within them. The giants, older than either, have deeper connections. Unlike you, I am a single being, alive but with Law running through me. The fire giants are the opposite, scions of Chaos. Humans are the only sentient creatures that are neutral and without any natural power. A shard may inhabit another creature but it will create a different sort of being, like a nokken."

"And the ancient witches worked out a way to bind the demons?" Anike could not resist asking.

"Yes, though it is a difficult process."

"How does it work?" Hrym was being surprisingly forthcoming, so she decided to press further, hoping to take advantage of his need to talk. He seemed to have forgotten that he was trading questions with her and this information might be worth the delay.

"The shards are not all equal in power and intellect. I can feel that the shard within you is much stronger than that within the Chaos witch who was here a few moments ago. Few humans would have the will to hold yours in check, but there are some shards that are so powerful that they overwhelm any human they join with and control them as if they were puppets. These are the beings that Law and Chaos most desire to create but in some ways they are less dangerous than you might be. Without the experience of true life, they act rashly and without understanding that living creatures cooperate and resist such blatant use of power. But you are limited in a different way and binding the shard would remove that constraint. When I ruled my frozen realm, I had witches in my service and they were more useful to me if the human was able to act with strategy but had mastered the shard within."

"How is the binding done?"

"Is this then the core of your being, witch, the desire for power, as it was with the carrier of the Law shard?"

Hrym's incisive question caught Anike off guard, and she looked at him sharply. "Power can be a means to protect those I care about, but it is not the only way. So, no, the desire for it is not the core of my being," she told him.

The giant frowned. "I wonder. I gave knowledge of the binding to him, the man you pursue. Your adversary, your enemy?"

Anike nodded. Her alliance with Karak was clearly over. "Will you let me pursue him now?"

"Not just yet. It will take him a while to understand the spell I have given him, and while you will not be able to cast it yourself as it uses the Law form, as you were able to dispel my seeming I have no doubt that you would be able to create a Chaos version, given enough time."

Hrym leaned towards her a little, and his tone became more menacing. "The spell I gave to your adversary breaks apart the Chaos shard inside a witch as it departs a dying body and uses the fragments of it to bind the caster's own Law shard. Of course, this destroys the essence of the human in the process, as her soul is still bonded to the Chaos shard." Hrym smiled, but his expression was as cold as he was.

Anike felt her fear and anger rise inside her, against Karak who would kill Enya to forward his own aims and against Hrym who was holding her here, letting him get further and further away. With it came her demon's renewed struggle for release.

Hrym watched her. "Go on, let the shard dominate you. We shall see if that helps you save the girl." He flexed his great shoulders. "It is certainly helping me."

Anike focused on the demon, but its force continued to grow within her, its strength increasing as it drew on something outside. Suddenly, she realised why Hrym had been keeping her there. There had never been any need to sacrifice a chaos witch. She had assumed that blood would be required, but all that Hrym had really needed was her presence.

The giant nodded as he saw comprehension dawn in her eyes and rose to his feet, towering above her. "Now you see the ruse. Your adversary took the other Chaos witch away before I was fully awake, and I needed you to remain in my presence long enough to thaw my old bones. And just in time, it seems."

He took a step away from the wall before turning to look down on her. "Do not worry, witch. You will not live long enough to avail yourself of the knowledge I have given you."

He raised one vast hand and formed it into a fist.

- 25 -

FROST AND FURY

Anike's demon screamed wordlessly as it struggled to free itself and attack the giant, its power beyond anything she had felt before.

The wall behind Hrym glowed red, brightened swiftly to white then vanished in incandescent fire, and the head of the Nidhogg burst into the hall.

Hrym looked over his shoulder and paused as if judging the distance, then back at Anike. He hammered his fist down towards her.

Brief as it was, his distraction had given her a chance and she had read the first rune pattern she saw on her spear. As she shouted, "*Agni!*" she felt a rush of power as the demon channelled the raw energy of chaos radiating from the Nidhogg through the pattern. The fire that burst forth was white hot, rivalling that which came from the wyrm's maw, and it enveloped Hrym's fist. He cried out in shock and pain, pulling back his scorched and blackened hand.

Hrym cradled the injured arm and glanced back again at the Nidhogg. Its reptilian head was now fully within the chamber and its eyes were focused on him. The giant was taller, looking down on the wyrm as a man might on a dog, but the Nidhogg radiated such power that Anike was not surprised to see fear on Hrym's face.

A clawed foot dug a molten furrow in the stone floor as the wyrm pulled itself into the chamber, hissing like a thousand swords being quenched in water at a forge. Liquid fire dripped from its jaws and where each drop landed, the rock smoked and evaporated.

Hrym turned away and started to run towards the far end of the hall, stepping over the fleeing dwarves. Anike wondered where he was going to go as he was far too big to use the doors she had entered by.

Hrym gestured behind him as he hurried forward and shouted *"Ranak!"* A wall of ice appeared between him and the Nidhogg. The wyrm's view of him was momentarily blocked by the ice but fire blossomed from its jaws and the wall vanished. Its head swivelled as it focused on the giant once more and it dragged more of its body into the hall. It completely ignored Anike and breathed a sheet of fire at the retreating giant.

Hearing the roar of the flames, Hrym raised his arm to shield himself. The flesh of his hand, already blackened from Anike's spell, melted away and she could see the white bone beneath. He cried out *"Kappa!"* at the closest wall. His voice echoed with agony, but at his command the stone parted before him to create a passage. He all but fell into the dark tunnel he had opened but before disappearing from sight, he paused for an instant to look directly back at her. Then the stone closed up behind him, just in time to take the full force of the next blast of fiery breath. The wall melted away, but Hrym had already passed deeper into the rock.

The Nidhogg hissed again and followed. Its head was nearly across the vast chamber before its tail eventually cleared the wall. The creature was immense in its power and glory and its scales blazed in a rainbow of scintillating colours. Awe and terror filled Anike and she doubted she could have moved if her life had depended on it.

The wyrm paid her no mind at all as it slithered through the chamber, heading for the wall through which Hrym had escaped. Its body melted the floor beneath it, and once again the fire burst forth from its jaws to liquify and evaporate the stone. The creature dragged itself into the hole it was melting to pursue the giant.

The brilliant cascade of light faded. Anike let out her breath and felt the demon's energy drop to its more usual level.

She might have survived Hrym and the Nidhogg, but Enya was still in peril. The giant was no longer there to stop her following Karak and there would be time to consider the implications of all he had told her once Enya was safe. Drawing herself up, Anike laid her hand on the ice wall next to her and shattered it.

She ran up the corridor, ignoring a side room which seemed to be a store for glowstones, but any hope that she could simply follow a straight course to Enya quickly vanished when she reached a junction with large passages leading both left and right. There was no dust on these floors and nothing to indicate which way she should go.

Karak surely would not have gone far before stopping to examine the spell Hrym had given him, and understanding it could take him minutes or even hours.

She stopped, turned up the page in her spellbook and spoke, "*Izik.*" Enya was still within the range of the spell, perhaps a hundred paces ahead of her, slightly to the left and no doubt Karak would be with her. While holding Enya as a hostage against her might not have been his main purpose, he could still use her that way.

Turning to another page, she cast the flight spell on herself and took the left way, moving silently onwards and hoping not to alert Karak to her approach. This passage was very well-lit, much more so than the long corridors on the other side of Hrym's Hall. Her own glowstone was in her bag and she relied on the light from the walls as she flew.

She came to another side corridor, but it looked as if it led back towards Hrym's Hall so she ignored it. Ahead of her, the passage turned right quite sharply. Wary in case Karak was lurking just out of sight, she re-cast the flight spell, rose to the ceiling and drifted around the corner. He was not waiting to ambush her, and she breathed a quiet sigh of relief. Perhaps he had not thought she would pass Hrym.

The passageway went about another twenty paces then opened out into a wider area, and she had the impression of another vast cavern filled with many hues of light. Beyond the opening, something lay on the floor. Cautiously, Anike flew closer and saw it was Enya, lying gagged and bound. A trickle of blood ran from her temple but her chest was rising and falling slowly.

Anike resisted the temptation to dash forward to make sure she was alive. Karak could have set her there as bait so while it tore at her to do so, Anike cautiously approached until she saw why they had gone no further. The passage emerged onto a semicircular balcony, perhaps ten paces long and twice that wide, with the curved edge ringed by a parapet, looking over a cavern that disappeared into the distance. Columns of crystal shot through with glowstones shining with many colours bathed the area she was in an interplay of light. She had seen nothing like it, a vista of beauty in the depths of darkness.

There was no time to appreciate the view as Karak was also on the balcony area, sitting on the floor about five feet from Enya with his back resting against the stone parapet and his sword propped up unsheathed beside him. He was studying the stone slab Hrym had given him and gave no sign that he had seen her.

Enya's life did not appear to be under immediate threat so Anike withdrew to the corner and landed. She quietly hunted through her bag and found two elixirs. She drank the first, a potion to heal injuries and felt the wounds that the dwarves had inflicted on her close. The second potion made her immune to pain. She doubted that she would get Enya away without a fight, and she had to do what she could to mitigate Karak's superior battle skills. This time, she would face him alone and he would be trying to kill her.

She had to do more than just get Enya away, too. She could not leave Karak in possession of the binding spell. If he mastered it, he would come after another witch, most likely Enya.

Hrym had created a spell using law, but had said she could adapt it to bind her own demon. She would never have to fear it taking control again, but only if she could bring herself to cast a spell that involved sacrificing a witch. The thought was abhorrent when expressed that way. She could not bear to think of murdering even an enemy like Karak, but Hrym had told her that law demons came to Midgard in falling stars and if she could find one, she might be able to use that instead of a witch. He had also said that there were those who had been overwhelmed by their demons and lost their humanity, and she might be able to kill a creature like that, even in cold blood.

Regardless of whether she could even cast such as spell herself, she had to seize the stone tablet from Karak, as well as rescue Enya. The reality was that she would probably have to kill him, but she had never set out to take another human life and there might still be a way to avoid it.

She cast the flight spell again to give herself an advantage in mobility. With her spear, she had the reach on him and her witchcraft was more versatile. While it would be simplest for him to try to kill her, he would still be reluctant to release his demon in case it turned on Enya. Karak knew all of this too and since a fight would be a risk for them both he might talk, but Anike did not fool herself that he had sufficient honour for her to trust him.

She flew a couple of inches above the ground until she neared the balcony area then landed to walk the few remaining paces. At the sound of her approach, Karak looked up and rose swiftly to his feet, picking up his sword as he did so. He laid the blade against Enya's throat.

"Stop, Anike. Leave me be and I will let her live."

"A poor way to start, Karak," Anike told him. "You need to kill Enya to complete the spell. She is only alive because you do not understand it yet. I have a counter-offer – give me the tablet and let Enya go, and I will let you leave Svartalfheim."

"You are in no position to make demands," Karak told her. "I have the girl already. However, I will give you a choice. Take her place as a sacrifice. Your death will serve just as well as hers and I will have no need to kill her then."

Anike had not expected that and stopped. Karak had correctly understood that she would not have undertaken this monumental journey unless she wanted to save Enya. There was no guarantee that she could beat Karak and if she failed, he would kill them both, but surely he did not think she cared enough about Enya to lay down her life for her? In truth, she hardly knew the girl, however responsible she felt for her plight.

Beyond that, there was no guarantee that Enya was actually safe. Karak would have little reason to escort her home and her demon would likely attack him any chance it got. Alone, she would struggle to make the journey back and there were far too many turnings for her to find her way. If she could not locate Lalfar... Anike's thought trailed off. That had reminded her of something.

"Did you kill Lalfar and Gunnar?" she asked.

"No. They should both live." Karak said. "I knocked the skald unconscious and cut the legs out from under the boy when he tried to stop me taking the witch. Hrost may need help to get out of Svartalfheim. I would not harm him and while he is not happy with my choice, I will still be an ally to his father, even after I use my power to take over another arldom."

"Your ambition has grown, it seems," Anike noted.

He looked at her appraisingly. "How did you get past Hrym?"

"The Nidhogg came," Anike told him shortly. Let him wonder if Hrym were dead while she considered her words. If Lalfar and Gunnar were seriously injured and unable to look for Enya, she would be unlikely to find them and was probably doomed anyway.

Karak was watching her. "If you do not agree, I will hurt the girl," he said. "It would be a setback to kill her too soon, but I can inflict a lot of pain."

The threat decided her against his proposal. "I will take my chances in battle," she said, and read the spell on her spear. "*Agni.*"

A blast of fire flashed through the space between the two witches. No doubt expecting to fight, Karak countered quickly and smoothly. His fist came away from the hilt of his sword to make a shielding gesture as he spoke, "*Ranak.*" Ice crystals enclosed the fire, sending it cascading between them to disperse harmlessly.

He charged. Anike met his first cut with her spear and dived low beneath the second, then darted sideways and ascended out of his reach. Hovering well above his head she pulled out her book, on the alert for any spell he might unleash. As she did so, he was reading the runes on his blade. "*Ert,*" he said, and she saw the crystalline shimmer form around him. Ignoring it, she found the pattern she had been looking for. "*Agni,*" she intoned, directing the spell of destruction at his sword.

"*Ranak,*" he said again, disrupting her pattern then raised his left arm and intoned "*Ilun.*" A rune pattern shimmered into visibility on his left sleeve, silver thread woven into the black cloth. Anike realised that he had been using a seeming to hide the patterns, an illusion that had given the impression that there was nothing there.

Karak looked at the pattern and Anike felt the touch of runes around her, a stasis spell to drain her life away. "*Prana,*" she said as she placed the movement rune into his pattern just before he intoned, "*Ert.*" A haze wavered for an instant between them as the two forms clashed in near-invisible conflict before she sundered the spell. Her forehead creased into a frown. The direct strike at her with witchcraft changed the character of the battle.

She turned to another page. "*Prana,*" she said as she read the rune pattern, casting a new spell on herself. Karak had enhanced his strength with witchcraft. She could not use the law form of strength but had instead devised a spell to increase her speed using the movement form. She descended and struck at him with her spear.

It was an entirely new fighting experience for Karak and many of his usual moves were no use at all against an enemy hovering directly above him. It was hard for him to meet the thrusts raining down at his head, and her position limited his ability to counterattack.

Anike managed to slip the point of her spear past his guard but the stasis armour was just as strong above his head as it was from the side. Her thrust was slowed enough that instead of cutting his face, the spear point glanced off the armour covering his shoulder.

Wary now of the speed of her movements and the advantage that flight gave her, he fell back two paces and narrowed his eyes. "*Barak*," he said, reading the other spell on his blade.

Anike felt nothing and realised he had used his spell of strength. His speed now matched hers. She pursued her attack but his defences became surer as he began to adapt to the dynamics of the fight. His sword was only a little shorter than her spear and when she pressed her attack, she nearly flew straight into a stop thrust when he shifted his grip and stabbed at her one-handed. Unenhanced by witchcraft, no man would have been able to move a five-foot blade like that. Caught by surprise, she had not been able to block and only a last-second shift let her avoid taking the point in the face. Blood began to well from the cut on her shoulder.

Anike pulled back and upwards and Karak moved into a guard position. He was too skilled to fall to her attacks, which were as unfamiliar to her as they were to him. She was not by inclination or training a warrior, but he was. She had manoeuvrability but he was more dangerous at close quarters.

But she was not ready to accept a stalemate. She read the other spell on her spear and Karak, no doubt expecting another blast of fire, raised his hand in a shielding gesture. But this time she cast the dislocation spell.

In an instant, she vanished from where she had hung in the air and reappeared about four feet behind him, then reversed the spear and thrust it behind her. She did not look but trusted her instincts, knowing that if she took the time to turn, he would realise what she had done and be ready.

She felt the spear point meet resistance and an instant later there was solid impact, followed by a cry of pain. She still did not look back but leapt forward and flew up again, and only then did she turn to see what she had accomplished.

Karak had his hand on his back, and when he brought it away there was blood on it. He looked at it, then at her, and nodded in respect. "Clever," he conceded. "Would you like to try that again?"

He raised his sword into a defensive stance, both hands above his head.

Despite her success in inflicting a wound, Anike did not rush to repeat the attack. Dislocation had made her a little nauseous and she knew he would be ready for her. She shook her head. "I have other tricks yet, Karak."

"And I am getting the measure of you," he said, "In the end, my greater skill will wear you down, but it would be a shame to kill you. I will make you a different offer." He stepped back and put the sword point to Enya's throat.

Insulated from pain by her potion, Anike doubted that the wound she had taken from Karak would slow her as much as the more serious one she had inflicted on him, but she could still see merit in talking.

"Go on," she said, hovering well out of reach.

"I know you have thought about bringing your familiar completely under your control," Karak said. "You are no fool, and you can see the potential as clearly as I can. Imagine being able to use your witchcraft at will, without being tied to these written patterns."

The last few days had emphasised the limitations of having to take hours to prepare a spell when the need was urgent. Karak was right but she did not want to admit how tempted she was by that possibility, either to him or to herself.

Karak watched her face, then continued. "I see that you have." He gave the stone slab a poke with his booted foot. "This rune pattern does do what Hrym said, and though I do not understand every part of it yet, I think you could adapt it to chaos easily enough."

This was not news to her, but it showed that Karak had given the matter some thought.

"My offer," he continued, "is to share the spell with you."

"And Enya?" she asked, though she knew the answer.

"I need her."

"You need to kill her, you mean."

"It's a small price to pay, isn't it? Think of all the good you can do, everyone you can help. I will let you copy the spell and leave before

I use it myself, so you will know there is no trick, or that I will turn on you without completing my end of the bargain."

Full access to the power of a bound demon was something Anike had always intended to deny Karak if she could not match him. She had been less sure about what to do if she could have it too. Her demon was at least as strong as his and they would remain equals. With Hrym abroad in the world again, she could see why Karak might think that the mutual increase in their power was worth more than a single life. No doubt he believed this was a real dilemma for her.

But as she had told Hrym, the desire for power was not the core of her being. She could not willingly trade Enya's life for an unknown future. The outcome of a final battle between herself and Karak was yet to be decided. He might beat her and Enya would be lost, but that would not be by her choice.

She looked at Enya, knowing that she could not abandon her. To her surprise, she saw that Enya's eyes were open, perhaps brought back to consciousness by the cold touch of steel against her throat. Anike rose higher into the air, bringing her spear around to ensure Karak kept his attention on her. Enya was looking at her, but then she closed her eyes and for a moment her features clenched. When they opened again, the demon stared out.

The balance had swung. "I do not accept your terms," she said bringing her spear to bear and swooping at him. His sword came up but her attack was a feint. She visualised a simple pattern and as Karak started to strike, she dropped beneath the blade, stretched out a hand and touched Enya. As she spoke, "*Agni*," Enya's bonds burned away and her gag flamed and charred.

Karak shifted his stance and brought her sword down towards Anike as she passed by his feet. Her one-handed block slowed the blow but his blade cut through her armour and an inch or so into her side before stopping against her ribs — a serious wound but a long way from being quickly fatal.

Beneath him, Enya spoke, "*Prana*." Having concentrated on Anike, Karak did not have time to disrupt the spell from Enya's demon and was flung away by the force it conjured. He struck the parapet, then steadied himself and began to stalk towards Enya. "I only need her to survive until I can work the spell, and I am nearly there," he told Anike and raised his blade again.

- 26 -

CHOICES

Anike dropped into Karak's path. Enya's demon would be an ally against him, forcing him to face two foes and both physical assaults and witchcraft but Enya was vulnerable without a weapon and Anike would have to defend her.

Karak would not seek to kill Enya yet but it was soon clear that he did not feel the same reluctance with Anike. He launched a dazzling flurry of blows which she was only able to avoid with her enhanced speed.

"*Agni!*" shouted Enya's demon. Concentrating on Anike, Karak was an instant slow in his response and was briefly caught within a column of fire. The flames blistered the skin on his face and he grimaced in pain. Anike felt a surge of hope. Together, they could wear him down.

Enya's demon clearly did not want to wait for victory. Without warning, it charged at the warrior barehanded. Karak was surprised by the reckless move and in an instant Enya was past his guard with her fingers clawing at his face. Only the shimmering stasis field saved him from losing an eye as he jerked his head out of the way.

There was no time to open her spellbook if she were to take advantage of the opportunity. Anike read the runes on her spear. "*Agni,*" she shouted, sending a blast of fire at Karak. She could not aim at his head or body for fear of hitting Enya but she could see his right leg clearly and struck at that. Distracted by the demon girl, he failed to counter it and hissed in pain as the flames scorched him.

With a curse, he flung Enya away with one hand and she landed on her side six feet away. Anike stepped in to press the attack but, grimacing against the pain, Karak swept her thrust aside and swung a roundhouse blow at her. She blocked it, but Anike felt her heart pound as the spear cracked under the force of the strike, the last slivers of wood barely holding it together.

Instinctively, she flew back and out of his reach, but he was not pursuing her. Instead, he turned and brought the blade down hard on Enya's shoulder as she started to rise. She fell back with blood streaming down her arm but her demon shouted, "*Prana!*" again and Karak was flung away. His injured leg gave way and he staggered backwards to lean against the wall, breathing hard.

Anike judged that he would be unable to attack for a moment and flew to Enya's side. Enya opened her eyes, and it was the human looking out through them again, not the demon.

"Run," Anike said to her. "I will hold Karak while you escape."

Enya smiled weakly through the tears running down her face. "Where can I run to? Even if I get away from this man now, I will never be free. I am not as strong as you are, Anike."

"That is your wound talking," Anike said, glancing at Karak. He was breathing hard and leaning on the rail, so she pulled her last potion out of her bag. "Drink this," she said, thrusting it at Enya.

"No. You will need it yourself," Enya said, pushing the flask away.

"You are bleeding badly. Take it."

Enya shook her head.

"Karak will be up in a moment," Anike said. "You only have a little time if you are going to get away. You must drink or you will never have enough strength to run."

"No, Anike," Enya sobbed. "I will never be able to escape."

"You can if you hurry!"

Out of the corner of her eye, she saw Karak drop an empty elixir flask and put some weight on his leg to test it. She turned and stood to put herself between him and Enya, keeping the spear pointed at Karak with one hand on each side of the fracture. His last blow had rendered it almost useless as a weapon and disrupted the pattern of runes on it too. Once Enya ran, she could fly up out of sword reach, but until the younger woman fled, they were both vulnerable.

There was a flicker of movement to her right and then Enya came into view, heading for the parapet at a run. Anike gasped – there was no escape that way. "No!" she shouted.

Enya reached the balustrade, climbed over it and looked back, holding on with her good hand.

Anike dropped the remnants of the spear and pulled out her book, feeling for the well-thumbed page that contained the spell to lift someone into the air.

Enya looked back at her. "I am so sorry, Anike," she said. "I meant it – I am not strong enough for this and I will not be the cause of your death. Even if you beat Karak, I will still be just me. You can't know what it is to be weak and frightened."

She sobbed, leaning further out over the drop. "The demon inside me takes over so often and I am barely holding it back now. One of the first things you told me is that it is with me until I die. If I come with you and we ever get out, someday it will make me kill someone, perhaps Lalfar or you." She looked down, then back at Anike's face. "Tell Lalfar I am sorry."

Anike briefly considered looking for page containing the levitation spell but knew that if she broke eye contact Enya would be gone. Fear and urgency tinged her voice. "You can learn to control the demon, Enya. You don't have to give up."

"I can't. I won't take anyone's life, Anike. I am sorry to have let you down."

"You can't kill yourself," Karak said, one hand outstretched. Anike and Enya ignored him.

"There is hope while you live, Enya. Life is about trying, about meeting challenges and overcoming them." With tears running down her cheeks, Anike took a step forward, reaching one hand out towards the golden-haired girl. "I am here for you Enya. We can do this together."

"You have tried so hard to rescue me," Enya said in a voice full of pain and regret, "but it isn't possible. I know that now. This is my chance, my choice. I will never be able to live without fear of what I can do, what I will do. This is the only way out before I kill an innocent."

Enya gave one last faded smile. "Goodbye, Anike."

She let go of the railing and fell.

Anike started forward, but as she took a third step there was a crunch from below and a cry of pain, swiftly cut off.

Grief and horror at her failure filled Anike. She had allowed Enya to be possessed by the demon, failed to give her the strength to withstand it and had not been able to save her. Anger and frustration rose to drown her grief and a howl escaped her lips.

The demon struck in her vulnerability and overwhelmed her. "*Prana*," her body said. Caught by surprise, Karak was thrown across the room to crash against the wall.

Anike rallied, forced the demon back into its prison again, and turned from him and back to the railing. She went to the edge and looked down. Forty feet below, she could see Enya's broken body lying between scintillating crystals, blood flowing in a pool around her. Her own heart was in her mouth.

The flicker of shadow on the railing warned her. She flung herself sideways just as Karak's sword passed through where she had been standing, but he brought the blade back in a flowing loop and the point cut into her arm. The strength drained out of it, and she dropped her spell book.

Anike dodged away. Karak did not follow but instead placed one hand on the parapet to support himself. Blood flowed from cuts on his head, and more from the wound in his back soaked his legs.

She measured the distance to her spellbook with her eyes, but Karak pushed himself away from the railing and limped towards her. She tried to lift away but her flight spell had expired, and she felt her stomach tense in fear.

Seeing her grounded, he lunged. She shifted sideways to avoid the blow but he had not been aiming at her body. The sword caught in her cloak and he lifted his blade, drawing her towards him.

Anike knew how strong he was and that if he got his hands on her, she was finished. She ducked out of the cloak and spun away towards the railing, putting some distance between them.

Rather than follow her, Karak went for the spellbook. He picked it up and threw it into the air towards the edge and his sword sliced. The book parted and Anike saw the pages fluttering apart as they dropped out of sight to join Enya's body below.

Karak was in a poor state, limping and bleeding, but he still had his sword and his eyes shone with determination. Her flight pattern was on her cloak and her other spells lay scattered in the cavern below. The spear lay on the ground roughly halfway between them, but it was broken and she doubted she had the strength to wield it effectively with her wound. She took an involuntary step backwards, unable to see how she could best him now.

The pulse from the demon beat within her. Its urge to strike out at Karak filled her, the hunger to kill him meshing with her own desire to punish him for dragging Enya to this place where she had lost all hope. Anike could let it attack, and it would serve her own ends, using it as Karak had used his own demon. There was a certain justice in that.

But she had vowed to herself not to do that again. Rocked by Enya's death and wounded, even if the demon did kill Karak, she might never regain control and then she would die here. If this was to be her end, she wanted to remain true to herself.

And even now, she was not helpless. Her arms were weak from the injuries he had inflicted, but her potion insulated her from pain and her legs were sound, at least until her body weakened from blood loss. She had one potion left. If she wanted to, she could run, leaving him behind. He might not even make it back to the surface. Her spellbook could be replaced.

But if she fled now, she would leave him alive and in possession of the binding spell, and he was tough and resourceful. He might still make it back to the surface despite his wounds, and she had seen the lengths he would go to for power.

Her gaze fell on the rune-covered slab. It was lying near the parapet where Karak had left it before they started their fight, and she was closer to it than he was. If she could escape with it, she could deny him the power he craved.

She ran forward and dived, and her hands closed around the tablet. Her left arm was weak, but the slab was thin for its size, and she was able to lift it easily. Karak's uneven step closed on her and she rolled, coming to her feet and she used the stone to parry his blade. A chip of it fell away, and Karak hissed. He did not want to damage the tablet, and she took advantage of his momentary hesitation to retreat from him.

Despite the threat he posed, Anike glanced at the slab in her hands and the runes Hrym had warped into the stone, unable to help herself. The pattern was very complicated, but she instantly recognised the preponderance of law-aligned runes. One look was not enough to understand the spell but given time she should be able to comprehend it. It offered power, control and freedom from fear, if she survived.

At the sound of a footfall, she raised her eyes. Karak limped towards her, looking for the best opening. Without weapons or spells, she could not defeat him, but she could run now she had the tablet. She started edging around him towards the exit.

Karak read her move and hobbled sideways to put himself between her and the passage. The hall was wide but his blade had a very long reach.

She might be able to get past, but Karak half turned and raised his right arm to read the pattern on his sleeve. "*Ranak*," he said, conjuring a wall of ice to cover the entrance and cutting off her escape.

She was trapped. While she could dispel the barrier if she could touch it, she would be vulnerable in the few seconds she would need.

Karak turned back towards her and lifted his sword. She raised the stone tablet like a shield, and he hesitated. He had to be wary of breaking the stone or giving her no choice but to release her demon as he would have done.

"A truce," Karak said, eyes fixed on her. "Copy the spell and leave. Then we are even."

With Enya's death fresh in her mind, Anike did not see that as close to even, but it was a way out. She still had her slate and chalk, and this would preserve her life and parity between them.

Once again, she contemplated having mastery over her demon, a prize beyond price. No more reliance on spell books. She could go anywhere, do anything, even save other witches and teach them to control their power, then use the spell to bind their own demons to them. She doubted any witch since Ragnarok had commanded such power.

The thought was a siren call but sharp warnings sounded inside her mind, and she caught her breath. Even with such power, she could not bring Enya back from the dead and her witchcraft would only be able to destroy. Her old master, Olaf, had tried to have her killed because he feared she would do terrible things in pursuit of what she thought was right and it would be so much easier to travel down that path if she had only to wish for destruction for it to happen. It would be too simple to use her power to solve problems and once she showed what she could do, people would fear her. Some would oppose her, and she would be forced to destroy them or abandon her plans. It would become easier and easier to justify the former to herself.

Olaf had very nearly been right. She was on the point of taking a step into the dark future he had wanted to prevent with her death. With the power of a god, she could not stay human. Such might was too much for a mortal.

She looked into Karak's eyes. "No," she said. "No one should have this power. Not me, and certainly not you." She turned to face the parapet and raised the tablet.

Karak cried out, "No!" and lunged towards her.

Anike threw the stone slab with all her strength.

Karak dropped his sword and dived after it as it sailed into the void. He went over the rail, arm outstretched, and his hand closed on the tablet. He shouted wordlessly in triumph and reached back to grab the rail with his other hand, but his leap had carried him too far. His fingers brushed the stone of the balustrade, but only for an instant before he fell towards the rocks below, the tablet still held in one hand. A moment later, there was a final crunch. The tablet fell from his limp hand and shattered on the rocks.

RESTING PLACE

In the sea of crystalline light, Anike looked over the parapet at the two figures lying on the sharp rocks below. Karak's head was in the centre of a pool of blood and his body was still. Shards of the tablet still lay beside his hand.

Enya lay a few feet away from him and as Anike watched, her arm moved. Hope rose within her and Anike visualised her simple levitation spell. It lasted long enough for her to reach the ground fifteen paces below. She looked down and froze at what she saw.

Enya lay on her back, with a crystal spike piercing through her body. Blood stained the pale blue rock on which she lay. Her eyes were closed but her right arm still twitched.

Anike knelt beside her and took her hand. It was still warm. "I am here for you, Enya," she said. Even though it was clear that Enya's wounds were far too serious for it to work, she unstopped the last potion.

Enya opened her eyes. "In a moment, I will be free," she said.

Anike shook her head, trying to hold back the tears. "You will be fine," she said, but she knew that nothing she could do would save Enya now.

A smile touched the girl's lips. "I am dying. It is what I want. I can feel the demon inside me but knowing the end is so close is giving me the strength to hold it. I will die as myself and I will take it with me." Her eyes found Anike's. "Did you win?"

"I did, Enya. Karak is dead."

"I am glad you survived. I wish I had time to get to know you better but that won't happen now." Enya's voice was growing weaker. "I want to ask you to do one thing for me, in my memory. Will you?"

"Of course I will, Enya. Anything." Tears filled her eyes.

"Save my sister, Auda. She has been taken to Lartenland as a slave."

Anike nodded and clasped her hand harder. "I will. I swear it."

"Thank you." Enya squeezed Anike's fingers, then her hand went limp. Anike barely noticed Enya's demon surge towards her and then vanish.

She did not know how long she sat there with Enya's hand growing cold in hers but eventually, her tears dried and she looked around. The crystal cave, spectacular with its myriad of reflected colours, seemed lifeless and bare.

Pain was beginning to intrude into her consciousness as her elixir began to wear off. She had been more badly hurt than she realised, and she drank the potion she had hoped to give to Enya.

Pulling herself together, she stood up. She needed to take Enya's body back to Lalfar and then out of Svartalfheim but first she went to search Karak. There was no unnatural sense of hostility – his demon had disappeared when he had died. Hrym had not said if the demon perished with its host or if it returned to beyond the sky, unable to remain within the World Tree, but it was gone.

Karak had left his sword on the balcony above when he had jumped for the tablet but he had a money pouch with both silver and gems inside. She had no qualms over taking it.

She considered the armour. It was well-made leather with metal inlays, but it was heavy. She decided to leave it.

Standing again, she started to look around for the pages of her spellbook. She located the one she was looking for and returned to the stone tablet by Karak's hand. Picking up the largest fragment which still held a good number of runes, she blew it to dust. She did not ever want to feel tempted to return to seek it.

She gathered the remaining pages of her book. Some she did not find, but there were a couple of blank pages she could use to recreate them.

Finally, she went back to Enya and with two spells lifted herself and Enya's body back to the balcony above, then covered the dead woman with her cloak. She took Karak's sword too. While it was too heavy for her, one of the men might be able to use it and she laid it on top of Enya's body, along with her broken spear, then flew towards Hrym's Hall. Along the way, she stopped to pick up half a dozen glowstones from the room she had passed. Some were in the shape of figures or intricate designs, exquisitely carved or perhaps warped by dwarven power. They might have held some significance in the reverence of Hrym and deserved study.

She soon reached the hall, Enya's body floating behind her. Before she had pursued Karak, she had not appreciated the ruin that the Nidhogg had wrought, but what must have been years of work for the dwarves in honour of Hrym was now little but fused and twisted stone. There was no sign of the Nidhogg and she could feel neither it nor Hrym, so it had probably pursued him far away. She wondered if it would catch him or whether it would give up but was not tempted to follow the tunnel it had made to find out.

There was no sign of the dwarves who had fled before the wyrm, and no sense from the demon to suggest that they were close by, and as she crossed into the silent dwarven passages, she began to wonder if she would need to use the runes to find Lalfar and Gunnar. The thought of telling Lalfar about Enya's death made her stop. Guilt ran through her again. She had failed Enya time and again, before finally letting her die. Anike knew she could have kept her away from Cairn so his demon would never have had the chance to pass into her. Her ignorance and choice to be with Enya that day meant she had taken risks.

Perhaps she was being too hard on herself, but Lalfar would blame her. She could not help that. She could not spare him his grief and anger unless she left Enya's body behind and lied to him, but even if she could do that, he would wonder what had happened and would never know how brave his sister had been.

Anike looked at that thought. She had not seen it that way before, but Enya had been brave. She had sacrificed herself rather than risk hurting people she loved, accepting her own weakness and making the best choice she could. Sometimes it required the greatest courage to accept the truth.

Lalfar deserved to know everything, and that included Enya's last request. He had described how their sister Auda had been taken by Larten raiders. When he had first told her the story, Anike had not used the runes to find out what had befallen Auda, but her promise to Enya made it vital to know. If Auda lived, Anike was now oath-bound to find her.

She got out the hide map and cast the runes, wincing against the pain as she drew the knife over her arm. She closed her eyes for a moment, suddenly fearful of what she might learn, but then opened them to read the answer.

Auda was alive, in western Lartenland, but in the house of a cruel master. The response was vague, but Anike now knew she had a long journey ahead of her and there would be time to get better answers. She doubted that even the news that Auda was alive would console Lalfar. It certainly did not change how she herself felt about Enya's death.

She picked up the runes and set off again. It was not long before she heard voices ahead of her, talking in Norse. She hurried forward, rounded a curve in the passage and came upon three men.

Gunnar was lying on the ground with Hrost and Lalfar standing nearby, deep in an animated discussion. Gunnar was the first to notice her, and Anike was relieved to see him sit up and point. "Anike!" he called out, and Lalfar and Hrost looked around.

Anike watched Lalfar's face light up. Then he saw the body floating next to her and the light died in his eyes.

"I am so sorry, Lalfar. I tried to save her, but..." Her voice trailed off.

Lalfar ran forward and she let Enya's body onto the ground, so very gently. Lalfar pulled the cloak off so he could see his sister. He squeezed his eyes shut and let out a howl, before burying his face in her hair. No one else moved. Eventually, he looked up at Anike. "What happened?"

"Karak was going to sacrifice her. I got there in time to prevent that, but she chose to throw herself over a cliff rather than live in thrall to her demon. It was a brave thing that she did." Anike choked for a moment, then continued. "I tried to stop her, Lalfar, I really did, but she had made up her mind."

"But why?"

"She was terrified of letting her demon hurt people, especially you."

Lalfar stood, his face cold. "You did this. You told her about the demon. In fact, you were the one who let it take her in the first place."

Hearing the truth in his words and knowing that nothing she could say would comfort him, Anike could not meet his gaze.

He looked as if he would strike her and Anike almost wished he would, but he bent down to take Enya's body in his arms and held her close. "I am so sorry, Enya," he whispered. "I swore I would protect you and I failed."

"Before she died," Anike whispered, "she asked me to save Auda, and I agreed."

"You think that makes it better?" Lalfar almost spat.

"I thought you should know."

"Auda is dead, or might as well be," Lalfar said. "I couldn't save her either."

"She is still alive," Anike said. "But she is a slave in Lartenland. I will go there and free her."

"It won't bring Enya back."

"I know that."

"You killed her," Lalfar said. "If you go after Auda, you will destroy her too. Stay away from her."

"I made a vow."

"I hope you fail then," Lalfar said bitterly.

There was a silence, then Hrost said. "What of Karak? You have his sword. Did you kill him?"

"No." Anike shook her head. "He is dead though. His own ambition killed him. He died trying to save a thing, a stone with a spell he coveted on it. He intended to forswear service to your father."

"I think he did that when he took your friend and left me here."
He paused. "What happened to the giant? How did you get through
the sea?"

"The sea wasn't real, only Hrym's dream made solid. He woke just
before the Nidhogg came, and fled. The Nidhogg pursued him, but
I imagine he escaped."

"So you failed to stop him waking too, Anike?" Lalfar said
scathingly. "Who will pay the price for that?"

"I suspect I will," Anike said, shuddering at the memory of Hrym's
gaze falling on her in the last instant before he disappeared.

She pulled herself together and turned to Gunnar. "How do you
fare?"

"I am pleased to see you, Anike," he said.

Anike managed a smile. Gunnar's youthful enthusiasm remained,
and perhaps his faith in her too. "I meant, are you injured?"

"Yes, but it is not too bad. Karak dealt me a serious wound, but I
still had one of my father's potions and I had to drink it. I can't really
stand and I certainly can't fight, but I am not getting any worse."

"I reached an accord with the dwarves. They should leave us alone
now," Anike said and bent down. "Let me take a look at that wound."
She ignored the slight prickle between her shoulder blades when she
turned her back on Lalfar and examined what had been a deep cut
on Gunnar's calf. It was mostly healed, though he was no doubt very
weak. "I can splint that so you can walk," she told him.

"Can I come with you? I have no idea where to go," Hrost said.

"Of course," she told him. "I would not leave anyone alone here."

Anike broke her spear down into shorter lengths and tied them to
Gunnar's leg. "On the way, I will harvest some healing plants and
brew a curing elixir, but this will have to do for now."

She turned back to Enya's body, but before she could use the spell
to raise her again, Lalfar spoke. "I will carry her." He laid Karak's
sword on the ground and lifted his sister's body over his shoulder.

Anike gave the long blade to Gunnar for a crutch and they
limped slowly back through Svartalfheim. She did not want to risk
the guardians at Ivaldi's archive – for all she knew the doors would

shut by themselves if left alone and reactivate the stone figures — so she used the runes to find a way around. They saw no dwarves, though Anike sometimes felt eyes upon them.

Even after she had found enough bread fungus for elixirs to heal Gunnar, they still moved slowly as Lalfar carried Enya. The journey to the surface lasted three days, and the skald did not speak to Anike at all during the entire time.

Gunnar and Hrost seemed to be getting along, and both tried to draw Anike out, but she was lost in her own thoughts. She grieved over Enya and regretted how Lalfar had taken his sister's death even though she understood his feelings about her mistakes. Although Lalfar would not talk to her, the numbness she had felt faded on the journey back as she allowed herself to feel again and accept the pain of her failure and loss.

Lalfar was right that finding Auda would not bring Enya back, but Anike knew she had to make the attempt to fulfil her vow, and not everything she tried had failed. Karak had not bound his demon. Hrost was free and that might be a good thing in the future, a tie to another kingdom. She could not give in to despair just because everything had not gone well. As she had told Enya, life was about trying.

Beyond their personal loss, Anike could not but worry that Hrym was free. Without the gods in physical form to oppose him, he might be a terror to the people of Gotlund and perhaps beyond. While he had run from the Nidhogg in apparent fear, the wyrm was more like a storm than a thinking being, dangerous if you were too close to it but elemental and without plans. Hrym, on the other hand, was cruel and cunning and in the long term could be a much greater threat. She had freed him, then hurt him and his final look at her suggested that he would remember the latter.

Despite that, it still stung that she had allowed Hrym to trick her into completing his awakening, even though she had gained knowledge about demons that she had been seeking for years.

She had felt echoes of truth in his words as if they resonated with her demon's own understanding. After the demon had bonded with her, when she had encountered runes, it was as if its knowledge of them had become hers too, and once she had been told their names, she had recalled their meanings as if she only needed a gentle reminder. The story of the demon's origin had felt similar, and within her she now recognised fragmentary memories of the void which would have been meaningless without Hrym's tale to give them context. The giant was certainly not above lying to her, but he had not expected her to survive and it would have been more difficult for him to make up a lie than tell her the truth, particularly as he needed to keep her attention and would not have risked telling her something she might know to be false.

At the final junction, Anike was relieved to see that someone had removed the dwarf that her demon had killed by smothering him in lava.

Rek would not welcome her return so they did not take the route to the arlberg but instead went to the one the dwarves had used with Enya. As Anike had suspected, it led to an exit in the hills. She had to disintegrate the final part of the passage as the dwarves had collapsed it behind them but eventually they emerged into the cold night air. Torches in the distance marked the town of Kindiski in the valley below them.

It was amazing how sweet the night air was, despite the chill. Anike had almost forgotten the smells and the sensation of wind on her face, and she breathed in deeply.

The others were doing the same and even Lalfar's mood seemed to lighten. He turned to Anike.

"I know that you did not mean to hurt Enya," he said, his first words to her in days, "but you did cause her death. You should have saved her."

"I tried."

"You failed. If you had let her be, none of this would have happened. I should have kept her away from you from the start."

He looked over the valley for a moment then said. "We will bury her here." He indicated where the small ravine opened out into the wider valley. "I want her to have a good view."

They dug a grave for Enya beneath the stars on the last day of autumn.

When they finished, Lalfar spoke again, "I meant what I said about Auda though. You carry disaster with you. If I could keep you from trying to find her, I would. And I swear that if you hurt her too, I will find you and kill you."

Lalfar shouldered his shield. "Goodbye Gunnar, fare well, and you too, Hrost."

They watched him start down the slope, heading west and away from the town.

"He is wrong about you," Gunnar said.

"He is in pain," Anike replied, "and he is not wholly wrong. I failed Enya."

"You did more than anyone else could have," Gunnar told her.

"It was not enough." She looked down at the grave.

Hrost coughed. "I suppose I am your prisoner," he said to Gunnar.

"I think that is right," Gunnar said. "Isn't it, Anike?"

"I believe so." Anike smiled at the mundane concern.

"I could try to escape," Hrost said, "but that would not be honourable. And winter will be with us soon and I have no idea where I am."

"We treat hostages well," Gunnar told him.

Hrost nodded. "It will probably be warmer here over the winter anyway."

There was no hostility between them at all, and it was not unheard of for hostages to form friendships with their captors which eventually led to alliances. Anike smiled to herself, glad at that one small piece of good fortune.

Anike turned to Gunnar. "Come on, let us get you back to your father."

They walked down the hill. Gunnar said "It is over, isn't it? We completed the quest, and you are leaving."

"I have to, Gunnar. Not only have I sworn an oath which will take me to Lartenland, but your father would have no choice but to put me on trial, and would probably execute me."

"I know," Gunnar said sadly, then he smiled. "But it was a great adventure."

They came to the edge of the fields near the town. "Here we must part. I want to collect a few things from my house," Anike said. "Can you walk the last part slowly, please? I will need a little time, and things will get very busy as soon as someone recognises you."

Gunnar nodded.

Anike bent slightly and kissed him on the cheek. "Thank you, Gunnar. You saved my life in Svartalfheim, and I will never forget that."

Gunnar smiled, and Anike took a step back. "*Prana,*" she said, reading the spell from her cloak, and rose into the air. She looked down at the boy, now a young man, watching her then she disappeared into the night.

Having checked from the air that no one was guarding her house on the outside, Anike landed. She had half expected Arl Rek to have left a warrior there in case she returned, but her home was empty. After over a week, Rek must have decided that other things needed his attention.

Anike held a glowstone in her hand and looked around the single room in its pale light. Most of her possessions had been removed. The shelves that had held her potions were bare and the chest had been smashed. The furs on her bed had been tossed aside. Some of her clothes lay on the floor, though no longer stored neatly beneath it but her cooking utensils and larger cauldrons were gone. Empty earthenware flasks remained but anything with obvious value or utility had been taken. She had hoped for more but it was no real surprise.

She shifted her work table and dug into the earth beneath. The small bag of silver was still there and she slipped it and the flasks into her satchel.

It was hard to say farewell to the place. She had been happy living there, but it seemed she was no more destined to have a stable home than someone to share her life with. Hers was a different path.

She closed the door behind her and rose into the night air.

THE END

GLOSSARY

Runes

Chaos Forms
Agni – Fire
Eneki – Lightning
Folor – Luck
Izik – Chaos
Prana – Movement
Vata – Wind
Osc – Veil

Law Forms
Ranak – Frost/Ice
Unda – Water
Barak – Strength
Log – Law
Ert – Stasis
Kappa – Earth
Ilun – Seeming

Other Forms
Vit – Life

Rune – a symbol representing an aspect of reality
Form Rune – a rune symbolising an elemental part of reality, such as fire
Aspect – a more complex concept based on modification of a form, such as light or smoke
Effect Rune – a description of how a Form acts, such as flight

Mythology

Demon – a spirit seeking death or destruction. When bonded with a human, it makes them a **witch**

Draugr – a mythical creature, a dead lord or warrior who rises from the grave to seek vengeance

Eitri and **Brokkr** – the dwarves that made **Thor's** hammer **Mjonlir**

Fenris – a giant wolf, one of the sons of the god **Loki**, reputed to have killed **Odin** at **Ragnarok**

Frey – god of peace, good weather and fertility

Freya – goddess of love and war

Frigga – goddess of motherhood and women, wife of **Odin**

Giants – enemies of the **gods**, who fought them at **Ragnarok**

Gods – most of the gods died during **Ragnarok**, but they are believed to live on as spirits

Gungir – **Odin's** spear

Heimdall – a god, who once travelled through **Midgard** and ordained the three castes of humanity, **jarls**, **karls** and **thralls**. **Loki** and **Heimdall** killed each other at **Ragnarok**

Hel – goddess of the dead

Hrym – a frost giant king, who fought the gods at **Ragnarok**

Idun – a goddess, guardian of the apples that gave the **gods** youth

Ivaldi – an ancient dwarf crafter

Jormungang – the Midgard Serpent, a child of **Loki** so vast that it could encircle the whole of the world

Jotunheim – the traditional home of the **giants**

Kvasir – god of knowledge and wisdom

Loki – a god, who turned against the other gods and fought against them at **Ragnarok. Loki** and **Heimdall** killed each other at **Ragnarok**

Midgard – the human world

Mimir's Well – a legendary well whose waters gave mystical knowledge

Mjonlir – **Thor's** hammer

Muspelheim – the fire world ruled by **Surtur**

Niflheim – realm of the dead who did not die in battle, ruled by **Hel**

Nokken – a mythical creature that takes the form of a beautiful man, woman or horse to lure the unwary into the water to drown them

Odin – ruler of the gods, reputedly died at **Ragnarok**, killed by **Fenris**

Ragnarok – a climactic battle just over a thousand years ago, in which almost all the **gods** and **giants** were killed fighting each other. The gods that died are believed to live on as spirits.

Sif – a goddess, wife of **Thor,** known for her golden hair

Skilbladmir – a ship made by dwarves for the god **Frey**

Surtur – the chief fire giant, ruler of **Muspelheim**

Svartalfheim – the realm of the **dwarves**, beneath the surface

Thor – god of thunder; died at **Ragnarok**

Tyr – god of battle and honour; died at **Ragnarok**

Utgard-Haloki – once king of the **giants**

Valhalla – the afterlife for heroes who die in battle

Vali - a god, known as The Avenger

Vanir – godlike beings, allies of the gods

Yggdrasil – the World Tree, which holds all the worlds in its branches

Culture

Archipelago – islands that make up the known world
Arl – the ruler of a town and the surrounding area
Arlberg – a walled compound containing the arl's hall and supporting buildings
Dazarak – a dwarven herb that enhances the effect of elixirs on dwarves
Dwarves – a non-human race, who lived in Svartalfheim. They call themselves the **svart alfar**
Darkstone Occupation – the time when the dwarves ruled the surface, around twelve hundred to four hundred years ago, often referred to as the **Occupation**
Elixir – a potion, salve or oil made from herbs with very potent properties
Elves – A rare non-human race that lives on the surface. They call themselves the **lios alfar**
Got – a resident of **Gotlund**
Gotlund – island and kingdom in the southeast of the archipelago
Huppik the Clever – the first High King who led the humans against the dwarves to end the **Darkstone Occupation**
Jarl – highest status caste, made up of warriors and rulers
Karl – middle caste of craftsmen, farmers and traders
Kindiski – a town in mid **Gotlund**
Larten – a resident of **Lartenland**
Lartenland – island and kingdom north of **Gotlund**
Lios Alfar – the elvish name for their race
Seer – a wise man or woman who casts runes to reveal information
Svart Alfar – the dwarven name for their race
Thrall – lowest caste of bonded servants and slaves
Trollgard – a town on the north coast of Gotlund
Ulsvater – a town on the north coast of Gotlund, west of Trollgard
Witch – a human who has joined with a **demon** and uses supernatural powers to bring death and destruction
Witch weather – a sudden storm, usually appearing out of a clear sky, considered to be an omen of disaster

ACKNOWLEDGEMENTS

Thank you to everyone who contributed to this book, both consciously and in less direct ways.

My parents, both published authors, gave their constant support and much-needed criticism throughout. My writing group have given constant help, suggestions and encouragement and made the whole process much more enjoyable.

My gratitude goes out to all of my beta readers whose comments helped develop the characters and their relationships, and made the story a great deal better, and to the very dear friend who gave me the name of my protagonist, albeit unwittingly.

A special mention to the one who sat through the iterations of the cover, giving support and suggestions.

Finally, I must thank my child for being my inspiration.

ABOUT THE AUTHOR

Rohan Davies lives in Norfolk, in the United Kingdom, near the sea.
He has read and enjoyed fantasy books his entire life, and has spent most of it designing and playing role-playing games. The world for the Saga of the Witch was originally created for a role-playing game.
In recent years, Rohan started to write and design games full-time.

Look out for

THE HUNTER
AND
THE WITCH

Book Three of the Saga of the Witch

www.ingramcontent.com/pod-product-compliance
Lightning Source LLC
Chambersburg PA
CBHW030532190726
48283CB00006B/1879